MERLINE LOVELACE
The Right Stuff

Harlequin
Mills & Boon

Intimate

First Published 2004
First Australian Paperback Edition 2004
ISBN 0 733 55126 2

Published by
Harlequin Mills & Boon
3 Gibbes Street
CHATSWOOD NSW 2067
AUSTRALIA

Printed and bound in Australia by
McPherson's Printing Group

MERLINE LOVELACE

spent twenty-three years in the air force, pulling tours in Vietnam, at the Pentagon and at bases all over the world. When she hung up her uniform, she decided to try her hand at writing. She's since had more than fifty novels published, with over seven million copies of her work in print.

To Maggie Price—friend, partner in crime and
the world's greatest writer of romantic suspense.
Thanks for all the quick reads and the great adventures!

Chapter 1

"Pegasus Control, this is Pegasus One."

"Go ahead, Pegasus One."

U.S. Coast Guard Lieutenant Caroline Dunn tore her gaze from the green, silent ocean flowing past the bubble cockpit of her craft. Her heart hammering against her ribs, she reported the statistics displayed on the brightly lit digital screens of the console.

"The Marine Imaging System reports a depth of eighty feet, with the ocean floor shelving upward at thirty degrees."

"That checks with our reading, Pegasus One. Switch to track mode at fifty feet."

"Aye, aye, Control."

Cari whipped her glance from the marine-data display to a screen showing a digital outline of her craft. There it was, the supersecret, all-weather, all-terrain, attack/assault vehicle code named *Pegasus*. It was in sea mode, a long, sleek tube with its wings swept back and tucked close to the hull. Those delta-shaped wings and their tilted rear engines would generate a crazy sonar signature, Cari thought with grim satisfaction. The enemy wouldn't know *what* the hell was coming at him.

Once *Pegasus* completed testing and was accepted for actual combat operations, that is. After months of successful—if often nerve-racking—land and air trials, *Pegasus* had taken his first swim at a fresh-water lake in New Mexico, close to its secret base.

Now the entire operation had moved to the south Texas coast and plunged the craft into deep water for the first time. It was Cari's job to take him down. And bring him back up!

Her palms tight on the wheel, she brought her glance back to the depth finder. "Seventy feet," she reported, her voice deliberately calm and measured.

"We copy that, Pegasus One."

Her steady tone betrayed none of the nervous excitement pinging around inside her like supercharged electrons. *Pegasus* had proved he could run like the wind and soar through the skies. In a few minutes, Cari would find out if the multi-purpose vehicle would perform as its designers claimed or sink like a stone to the ocean floor with her inside.

"Sixty," she announced.

"Confirming sixty feet."

The green ocean swirled by outside the pressurized canopy. A coast guard officer with more than a dozen years at sea under her belt, Cari had commanded a variety of surface craft. Her last command before joining the Pegasus test cadre was a heavily armed coastal patrol boat. This was the first time, though, she'd stood at the wheel of a vessel that operated equally well above *and* below the surface. *Pegasus* wouldn't dive as deep as a sub or skim across the waves as fast as a high-powered cutter, but it was the first military vehicle to effectively operate on land, in the air and at sea.

So far, anyway.

The big test was just moments away, when Cari cut the engines propelling *Pegasus* through the water and switched to track mode. In preliminary sea trials at New Mexico's Elephant Butte, the craft's wide-tracked wheels had dug into the lake bed, churned up mud and crawled right out of the water.

Of course, Elephant Butte was a relatively shallow lake. This was the ocean. The Gulf of Mexico, to be exact. With Corpus Christi Naval Air Station just a few nautical miles away, Cari reminded herself. The station's highly trained deep-water recovery team was standing by. Just in case.

Her gaze zeroed in on the depth finder. Silently she counted off the clicks. Fifty-five feet. Fifty-four. Three. Two...

"Pegasus One, shutting down external engines."

Dragging in a deep breath, Cari flicked the external power switch to Off. The engines mounted on the swept-back wings were almost soundless. Even at top speed they caused only a small, humming vibration. Yet with the absence of that tiny reverberation, the sudden, absolute silence now thundered in Cari's ears.

Momentum continued to propel *Pegasus* forward. Silent and stealthy as a shark after its prey, the craft cut through the green water. The depth finder clicked off another five meters. Ten. The sonar screen showed sloping ocean floor rising up to meet them dead ahead.

"Pegasus One switching to track mode."

With a small whir, the craft's belly opened. Its wide-track wheels descended. A few seconds later, the hard polymer rubber treads made contact with the ocean floor.

"Okay, baby," Cari murmured, half cajoling, half praying. "Do your thing."

A flick of another switch powered the internal engine. Biting down on her lower lip, Cari eased the throttle forward. *Pegasus* balked. Like a fractious stallion not yet broken to the bit, the craft seemed to dig in its heels. Then, after what seemed like two lifetimes, it responded to the firm hands on the reins.

The wheels grabbed hold. The vehicle began to climb. Fathom by fathom. Foot by foot. The water around Cari grew lighter, grayer, until she could see shafts of sunlight spearing through its surface.

A few moments later *Pegasus* gave a throaty growl of engines and broke through to the light. Waves slapped at the canopy and washed over the hull as Cari guided her craft toward a silver van positioned almost at water's edge. The mobile test control center had been flown in from New Mexico along with most of the personnel now manning it. They'd staked a claim to this isolated stretch of south Texas beach to conduct their deep-water sea trials. Heavily armed marines from the nearby naval air station patrolled the perimeter of the test site. The coast guard had added its small Padre Island fleet to the navy ships that kept fishing trawlers and pleasure craft away from the test sector.

By the time *Pegasus* roared out of the rolling surf, a small crowd of uniformed officers had spilled out of the van. They hurried across the hard-packed sand as Cari killed the engines. Blowing out a long breath, she patted the console with a hand that shook more than she wanted to admit.

"Way to go, *Pegasus.*"

Her craft settled on the sand with a little hum, as if every bit as satisfied with its performance as she was. Smiling, Cari climbed out of the cockpit and made her way to the rear hatch. When she stepped into the bright sunlight, a tall blond god in an air force flight suit broke ranks with the rest of the uniformed officers. Ignoring the surf swirling around his black boots, he strode forward, wrapped his hands around Cari's waist and swung her to the sand.

"You took *Pegasus* for a helluva swim, Dunn!"

She grinned up at the sun-bronzed pilot. "Thanks, Dave. I think so, too."

The rest of the officers crowded around her. Army Major Jill Bradshaw shed her habitual reserve long enough to thump Cari on the back.

"Good job, roomie."

Lieutenant Commander Kate Hargrave, a senior weather scientist with the National Oceanographic and Atmospheric Service, hooked an arm around Cari's shoulders and gave her a fierce hug.

"I just about choked when the weather-service satellites picked up that squall developing out over the Gulf," the leggy redhead admitted. "What a relief it blew south, not north."

"No kidding!"

Doc Cody Richardson, the U.S. Public Health Service representative to the task force, ran an assessing glance over her face. In addition to providing expertise on the chemical, biological and nuclear defenses aboard the craft, the doc also acted as the cadre's chief medical officer.

"Did you experience any dizziness or nausea?"

"None," Cari replied, wiping out the memory of those few seconds of belly-clenching fear before *Pegasus* began his climb up the ocean floor.

Doc nodded, but she knew he'd be poring over the data with the bioengineers later to study her body's most minute reactions during various stages of the mission.

"Nice going, Dunn."

The gruff words swung her around. Major Russ McIver stood behind her, a solid six-two of buzz-cut marine. She and the major had locked horns more than once in the past few months. Mac's by-the-book, black-or-white view of the world allowed for no compromises and tended to ruffle even Cari's calm, usually un-rufflable temper.

This time, though, Mac was smiling at her in a way that made her breath catch. For a crazy moment, it might have been just the two of them standing on the beach with the surf lapping at their heels and the south Texas sky a bright, aching blue overhead.

Mac broke the spell. "Think you can get *Pegasus* to swim like that with a full squad of marines aboard?"

The crazy moment gone, Cari tugged off her ball

cap and raked back a few loose strands of her mink-brown hair. "No problem, Major. We'll add some ballast and take him out again tomorrow. Not much difference between a squad of marines and a boatload of rocks."

Mac started to respond to the good-natured gibe. The appearance of the navy officer in overall charge of the Pegasus project had him swallowing his retort.

Cari whipped up a smart salute, which Captain Westfall returned. His weathered cheeks creased into a broad grin. "Good run, Lieutenant."

"Thank you, sir."

"I could feel the salt water coursing through my veins the whole time you had *Pegasus* out there, testing his sea legs."

With the closest thing to a smirk the others had yet seen on the naval officer's face, Westfall reached out and patted the vehicle's steel hide. Cari hid a smile at his air of ownership and glanced around the circle of officers.

They represented all seven branches of uniformed services. Army. Navy. Air force. Marines. Coast guard. Public Heath Service. The National Oceanic and Atmospheric Administration.

Months ago they'd assembled in southeastern New Mexico. Since then they'd worked night and day alongside a similarly dedicated group of top-level civilians to see *Pegasus* through its operational test phase. Now, with the deep-water tests underway, the end of their assignment loomed on the not-too-distant horizon.

Regret knifed through Cari at the thought. She'd grown so close to these people. She admired their dedication, cherished their friendship. The knowledge that their tight-knit group would soon break up was hard to take, even for an officer used to frequent rotations and new assignments.

Without thinking, she shifted her glance back to Russ McIver. Her stomach muscles gave a funny quiver as she took in the strong line of his jaw. The square, straight way he held himself. The bulge of muscles under the rolled-up sleeves of his camouflage fatigues, known for unfathomable reason as Battle Dress Uniform or BDUs.

Her regret dug deeper, twisted harder.

Frowning, Cari tried to shrug off the strange sensation. She had to get a grip here. This was just an assignment, one of many she'd held and would hold during her years in the U.S. Coast Guard. And Mac…

Mac was a colleague, she told herself firmly. A comrade in arms. Sometimes bullheaded. Often obnoxious, as those who see no shades of gray can be. But totally dedicated to the mission and the corps.

"It'll take an hour to download the data and run the post-test analyses." Captain Westfall checked his watch. "We'll conduct the debrief at thirteen-thirty."

"Aye, aye, sir."

An hour would give Cari plenty of time to draft her own post-test report. Still exhilarated by the success of her run, she headed for the silver van and its climate-controlled comfort. Early October in south Texas had proved far steamier than the high, dry desert of New Mexico.

Racks of test equipment, communications consoles and wide screens filled the front half of the van. The rear half served as a work and mini-conference area. Captain Westfall went forward to talk to the test engineers while the others filed into the back room. Eager to record her evaluation of the run, Cari settled at her workstation and flipped up the lid of her laptop. A blinking icon in the upper right corner drew her gaze.

She had e-mail.

None of the officers working on *Pegasus* could reveal their location or their activities. The techno-wizards assigned to the Pegasus project routed all communications with families, friends and colleagues through a series of secure channels that completely obscured their origin. For months, Cari's only link with the outside had been by phone or by e-mail.

She didn't have time to communicate with her large, widely dispersed circle of friends and family now, but she'd do a quick read to make sure no one was hurt or in trouble. A click of her mouse brought up a one-line e-mail.

Marry me, beautiful.

"Oh, hell."

She didn't realize she'd muttered the words out loud until Kate Hargrave glanced up from the workstation next to hers.

"Are you having trouble bringing up the post-run analysis screen? That last program mod is a bitch, in my humble opinion."

When Cari hesitated, reluctant to discuss personal matters in such a cramped setting, the weather officer scooted her chair over.

"Oh." Understanding flooded Kate's green eyes. "I see the problem. How are you going to answer him?"

Cari frowned at the screen. How the heck *was* she going to answer Jerry? She'd been dating the handsome navy JAG off and on for almost a year. He was fun, sexy, and up for an appointment as a military judge. He was also the divorced father of three children. He'd learned the hard way how tough it was to sustain a two-career marriage. A bitter divorce had convinced him two careers, marriage *and* kids made the situation impossible.

Cari didn't want to admit he was right, but the figures spoke for themselves. The divorce rate among the seagoing branches of the military was astronom-

ical, almost twice the national norm. Long sea tours
and frequent short notice deployments put severe
strains on a marriage. If she wanted kids, which she
most certainly did, something would have to give.
Jerry and her parents—not to mention her own nagging conscience—suggested it should probably be her
career in the coast guard.

Sighing, Cari fingered the mouse. ''I don't know
what I'm going to tell him,'' she murmured to Kate.
''I have to think about it.''

''What's to think?'' Russ McIver put in sardoni-
cally from her other side. With a silent groan, Cari
saw that he, too, had scooted his chair over, no doubt
to check out the glitch with the troublesome new
modification.

''The choice looks pretty clear to me,'' he drawled.
''It's either yes or no.''

Irritated that her private communication had become a matter of public discussion, she returned fire.
''Why am I not surprised to hear that coming from
you?''

Mac's hazel eyes hardened. Although Cari hadn't
discussed her relationship with Jerry with anyone
other than her roommates, there were few secrets in
a group as small and tight as this one had become.
Mac in particular had expressed little sympathy for
Cari's personal dilemma. She might have guessed he
wouldn't do so now.

''It's your decision,'' he said with a shrug. ''Never mind that the coast guard selected you for promotion well ahead of your peers. It doesn't matter that you were chosen for a prestigious exchange tour with the British Coastal Defense Force. Or that you've racked up years in command of a ship and a crew. If pregnant, barefoot and permanent kitchen duty is what you want, Lieutenant, you should go for it.''

Cari's brown eyes lasered into the marine's. ''Last I heard, Major, it wasn't a court-martial offense to want to get married and have children. Nor is every woman who chooses to leave the service a traitor to her country.''

The two other women officers present instantly closed ranks behind her.

''Lots of *men* leave the service,'' Jill Bradshaw pointed out acidly. A career army cop, she took few prisoners. ''In fact, the first-term reenlistment rate for women is higher than it is for men.''

''And in case you've forgotten,'' Kate Hargrave snapped, ''the military is like any other organization. It's a pyramidal structure that requires a large base of Indians, with increasingly fewer chiefs at the more senior ranks. The services don't *want* everyone to stay in uniform.''

Doc Richardson arched a brow and exchanged glances with USAF Captain Dave Scott. They were too wise—and had each grown too involved with one of the women now confronting McIver—to jump into this fray. Russ, however, appeared undaunted by the female forces arrayed against him.

"You're right," he agreed, refusing to retreat. "The military doesn't want everyone to stay in uniform. Only those who are good at what they do. So damned good they're hand-picked to field test a highly classified new attack/assault vehicle that could prove critical to future battlefield operations."

Cari clamped her mouth shut. She had no comeback for that. Neither did Kate or Jill. Like the male officers assigned to the Pegasus project, they'd been chosen based on their experience, expertise and ability to get things done. They *were* among the best their services had to offer and darn well knew it.

Still, she wasn't about to let the marine who alternately irritated, annoyed and attracted her have the last word.

"If *any* of us want to stay in uniform," she said tartly, "we'd better get off the subject of my personal life and onto the task at hand."

Swirling her chair around, she clicked the mouse to save Jerry's e-mail. She'd answer him later, when she figured out what the heck her answer would be. Another click brought up the analysis program. Wiping her mind clear of everything but the task at hand, she began drafting her preliminary post-mission report.

She was still hard at work when Captain Westfall wove his way through the racks of equipment to join his crew some time later. His expression was unexpectedly somber for a man who'd watched his baby perform flawlessly.

"Let me have your attention, people." His steel-gray eyes swept the crowded area, dwelling on each of his officers. "I've just received a coded communiqué from the Joint Chiefs of Staff. The Pegasus test cadre is being disbanded effective immediately."

Shock rippled through the group, along with a chorus of muttered exclamations.

"What the hell?"

"You're kidding!"

"Why?"

Captain Westfall stilled the clamor with an upraised hand.

"Our cadre has been redesignated. We're now the Pegasus Joint Task Force. Our mission is to extract two United States citizens trapped in the interior of Caribe."

The announcement burst like a cluster bomb among the stunned officers. Cari's mouth dropped open, snapped shut again, as her mind scrambled to switch from test to operational mode.

A map of Caribe flashed into her head. It was a small island nation, about sixty nautical miles off the coast of Nicaragua. Its internal political situation had been steadily worsening for months. The island's president for life was battling ferociously to hold on to his sinecure. In response to his repressive tactics, rebels had stepped up their action and the fight had turned bloody.

The Joint Chiefs of Staff had alerted Captain Westfall weeks ago about the possibility of using *Pegasus* to extract U.S. personnel, if necessary. As a result, he'd compressed the test schedule until it was so tight it squeaked. Evidently the deep-water sea trial Cari had just completed would be the final test. From now on, it was for real.

But two hours! That was short notice, even for a military deployment. Westfall made it clear they were to use that time to draw up an op plan.

"The U.S. began evacuation of its personnel this morning," he advised. "All are accounted for and are in various stages of departure except two missionaries. A squad of marines has gone into the interior after the missionaries and will escort them to a designated extraction site."

"I've flown over Caribe," Dave Scott commented grimly. "The jungle canopy is two or three hundred feet thick in places. Too thick to permit an extraction by air."

"And rebel forces now hold the one road in and out of the area," Captain Westfall confirmed. "The only egress is by river."

"Pegasus!" Cari breathed. "Now that he's demonstrated his sea legs, he's the perfect vehicle to use for an operation like this."

"Correct. Captain Scott, you'll fly *Pegasus* on the over-water leg from Corpus Christi to Nicaragua. Their government is maintaining a strict neutral position with regard to the political situation on Caribe but has given us permission to land at an unimproved airstrip just across the straits from the island."

Dave gave a quick nod. "I'll start working the flight plan."

"Once in Nicaragua, Lieutenant Dunn will pilot *Pegasus* to Caribe and navigate up the Rio Verde to a designated rendezvous point. Major McIver, your mission is to make contact with the marines and bring out the two stranded missionaries."

"Yes, sir."

"You'll be operating under strict rules of engagement," Westfall warned. "To avoid entangling the U.S. in the internal political struggle, you're not to fire lethal weapons unless under fire yourself. Questions?"

Her blood humming at the anticipation of action, Caroline joined the chorus of "No, sir!"

The steel-eyed navy officer turned away, swung back. His glance skimmed from Mac to Cari and back again.

"Things could turn ugly down there. Real ugly.

Make sure your next-of-kin notification data is up-to-date. You might also zap off a quick e-mail to your families,'' he added after a slight hesitation.

He didn't need to explain. Since 9/11, Cari had participated in enough short-notice deployments to know this might be her last communication with her folks for a while. Or her last, period.

Cari followed the captain's orders and zapped off one quick e-mail. Pumping pure adrenaline, she swung back around to find Mac contemplating her with a tight, closed expression.

''You didn't bat an eye at the prospect of going into Caribe.''

''Neither did you,'' she pointed out.

He hooked a thumb toward the now blank screen. ''What about Jerry-boy?''

Her shrug made the question irrelevant. This was what she'd trained for. This was what wearing a uniform entailed.

''Jerry isn't your concern. We've got work to do.''

Chapter 2

Mac couldn't believe it. Here he was, stuffing spare ammo clips into the pockets on his webbed utility belt, less than twenty minutes away from departing on a mission to extract U.S. citizens from a potentially explosive situation.

Yet for the first time in his life Mac couldn't force his mind to focus solely and exclusively on the task ahead. Every time he thought he'd crowded everything else out, the damned e-mail Cari had received a while ago would pop back into his head.

Marry me, beautiful.

What kind of a jerk proposed to a woman via e-mail? Particularly a woman like Caroline Dunn.

Mac had worked alongside a lot of professionals in the corps, male and female. The small, compact brunette currently frowning over a set of coastal navigational charts left most of them in the dust.

Hell, who was he kidding? Cari left *all* of them in the dust. He'd never met any woman with her combination of beauty and brains, and he'd tangled with more than his share. Particularly in his wilder days before the United States Marine Corps started him down a different path thirteen...no, fourteen years ago.

Fourteen years! Shaking his head, Mac shoved another spare clip into his belt. Hard to remember now how close he'd come to ending up on the wrong side of anyone in uniform. Harder still to remember the woman who'd almost put him there. He'd had no idea the thrill-seeking blonde who'd climbed on the back of his beat-up Harley was married to a California state senator. And he sure as hell hadn't known the woman was carrying a stash of Colombian prime in her fanny pack.

When the cops hauled the still underage Mac into her husband's office, the wealthy politician had given him a choice. A trumped-up possession charge and jail time or the United States Marines. It wasn't much of a choice. Mac had been staying just one step ahead of the law since flatly refusing to let the state put him in yet another foster home. He figured the marines would kick him out fast enough, just as his series of foster parents had.

Instead, the corps had molded a smart-mouthed punk into a single-minded, razor-edged fighting machine. In the often painful process, Mac found the home he'd never had. He'd also finished high school, earned a college degree, learned to lead as well as follow, and been chosen for Officers' Candidate School.

He'd never forget that crystal bright April morning at Quantico, when he'd raised his gloved hand to be sworn in as a commissioned officer. He took his oath to protect and defend the United States against all enemies *very* seriously. So, apparently, did Lieutenant Dunn. She'd served for more than ten years, had several command tours under her belt, and had played a key role in the war against terrorism during the coast guard's transition from the Treasury Department to the new Department of Homeland Security.

Yet here she was, actually debating whether to give up her career and her uniform to marry a smooth-talking JAG who'd probably never seen the business end of an assault rifle. The idea torqued Mac's jaws so tight he wasn't sure he'd ever get them unscrewed. They stayed locked the whole time Kate Hargrave and Cari pored over the charts.

''I've updated *Pegasus*'s onboard computers with Caribe's tidal patterns, riverine data and predicted climatic and atmospheric conditions,'' the weather officer was saying. ''You might see some swells from that squall on the way in, but rough weather shouldn't hit until you're on your way out.''

''How rough?''

''Better pack some extra barf bags for you and your passengers.''

''Oh, great!''

Shaking her head, Cari bent to stuff the charts in her gear bag. Her green-and-black jungle BDUs stretched taut over a trim, rounded rear. The enticing view had Mac grinding his teeth. Wrenching his glance away, he jammed another clip into his belt.

Okay. All right. He could admit it. The idea of Lieutenant Caroline Dunn marrying *anyone,* including a pansy-assed JAG, rubbed him exactly the wrong way. The woman had tied him up in knots more than once in the past few months. If he hadn't learned the hard way to avoid poaching on another man's territory—or if Cari had given the least hint she was interested in being poached on—he might have made a move on her himself.

But he had, and she hadn't.

With a little grunt, Mac reached for his assault rifle. He was checking the working parts when a low whine brought his head around.

Pegasus was spreading his wings. Like the mythical beast he'd been named for, the craft fanned out its delta-shaped fins. When they locked in place, the engines slowly tilted upright. Another whine, and the propellers unfolded like petals. In this configuration, *Pegasus* would lift straight up like a chopper. Once airborne, Dave would tilt the engines to horizontal and fly it like a fixed-wing aircraft.

The air force pilot was in the cockpit, clearly visible through the bubble canopy. Hooking a glance over his shoulder, he gave Captain Westfall a thumbs-up. The captain nodded and turned to Mac.

''Ready, Major?''

''Yes, sir.''

''Lieutenant?''

''All set, sir.''

Cari's calm reply did nothing to loosen the knots in Mac's chest. He'd been air-dropped into Afghanistan by a female USAF C-17 pilot. Had a bullet hole patched up by a particularly sexy navy nurse. Had relied on enlisted female marines to provide ground support and combat communications. He valued and respected the vital role women played in the military.

But this was the first time he was going into harm's way with a woman at his side. If she'd been anyone other than Caroline Dunn, the prospect might not have put such a kink in his gut.

Shouldering his assault rifle, he followed her through the open hatch.

*   *   *

Four hours later *Pegasus* was once again in sea mode—wings swept back, engines tilted rearward, propellers churning water like a ship's screws. Nicaragua lay well behind. Caribe was a gray smudge on the horizon. In between was a big stretch of open sea.

An increasingly turbulent sea, Cari noted.

"Kate was right on target," she commented, pitching her voice to be heard above the engines as she steered her craft through rolling green troughs. "Looks like we're starting to pick up some of the swells from that squall."

Mac responded with a grunt that earned him a quick glance. He didn't appear to appreciate the craft's agility to cut through the deepening troughs. In fact, he was looking distinctly green around the gills.

"The seas will probably get higher and rougher when we hit the barrier reef around the island," Cari advised. "You'd better pop a couple of those Dramamine pills Doc put in the medical kit."

"I'll make it."

"That wasn't a suggestion, Major."

The deceptively mild comment slewed Mac's head around. Cari could feel his gray-green eyes slice into her, but didn't bother to return the stare. He might outrank her on land. Aboard this craft, she was in command.

She kept her gaze on the gray smudge ahead as

Mac dragged out the medical kit. Only after he'd downed the pills as ordered did she slant him another glance. Like her, he was dressed for the jungle—web-sided boots, black T-shirt, black-and-green camouflage pants and shirt. Instead of a ball cap, though, a floppy-brimmed "boonie" hat covered his buzz-cut brown hair.

He looked leather tough and coldy lethal. *Not* someone you wanted to suddenly come nose to nose with in the jungle. Cari had to admit she was glad they were on the same side for this operation.

"Is this freshening sea going to slow us down?" he asked with an eye to the digital map displayed on the instrument panel.

Their course was highlighted in glowing red. It took them straight across the fifty-mile stretch of open water, through the outer reef encircling Caribe and into a small bay on the southern tip of the palm-shaped island. Once inside the bay, they'd aim for the mouth of the Rio Verde and head some twenty-six miles upriver.

"*Pegasus* can handle these swells," Cari said in answer to his question. "We should arrive right on target."

"Good enough. I'll confirm with Second Recon."

He'd already established contact with the six-man reconnaissance team that had been sent into the jungle to retrieve the American missionaries. Luckily, they were equipped with CSEL—the new Combat Survivor/Evader Locator. Not much larger than an ordinary cell phone, the handheld radio provided over-the-horizon data communications, light-of-sight voice modes, and precise GPS positioning and land navigation. The handy-dandy new device was state-of-the-art and just off the assembly line. Neither the rebel nor government forces in Caribe could intercept or interpret its secure, scrambled transmissions.

"Second Recon, this is Pegasus One."

"This is Second Recon. Go ahead, Pegasus."

The marine in charge of the reconnaissance team sounded so young, Cari thought. And so grimly determined.

"Be advised we're twenty nautical miles off the coast of Caribe and closing fast," Mac informed him. "We're holding to our ETA."

"We copy, Pegasus. We're about five klicks from the target."

Five kilometers from the mission put them about eight from the river, Cari saw in another quick glance at the digital display. The marines still had some jungle to hack through.

"We'll bundle up our charges as soon as we reach the target and proceed immediately to the designated rendezvous point," the team leader promised.

"Roger, Second. We'll be waiting for you."

Frowning, Mac took a GPS reading on the team's

signal and entered its position with a few clicks of the keyboard built into the instrument console. His frown deepened as *Pegasus* plowed into another trough. The hull hit with a smack that sent spray washing over the canopy.

"The swells are getting heavier."

"They are," Cari agreed.

He shot her a hard look. "Can't we put on a little more speed? I don't want to leave those marines sitting around, twiddling their thumbs with the rebel forces combing the jungle for them."

"We won't."

The calm reply brought his brows snapping together under the brim of his hat. "Are you that sure of yourself or is this the face you put on when you're in command?"

"Yes, I'm sure," she answered, "and what you see is what you get."

For the first time since they'd departed Corpus Christi, Mac relaxed into a grin. "From where I'm sitting," he drawled, "what I see looks pretty good."

Her hands almost slid off the throttle. "Good grief! Is that a compliment?"

"It is."

A tiny dart of pleasure made it past the butterflies beating against Cari's ribs. After all these weeks of butting heads with the stubborn marine, she hadn't expected any warm fuzzies just moments away from

entering a potential hostile fire zone. Her brief pleasure took a back seat to business when she checked
the displays and saw they'd entered Caribe's territo-
rial waters.

"We're within twelve miles of the island. We'll hit
the coral reef in a few minutes. You'd better get ready
for a bumpy ride."

Bumpy didn't begin to describe it.

Waves pounded the sunken coral reef. The swells
that had kept Mac's stomach churning became monster waves. The huge walls of green curled and
crashed and roared like the hounds of hell. He
clamped his jaw shut and tried not to wince at the
vicious battering *Pegasus* took.

Cari, he noted, didn't so much as break a sweat as
she worked the throttle and wheel. Somehow she
managed to dodge the worst of the monsters while
keeping her craft aimed straight for the calmer waters
inside the reef.

Finally, *Pegasus* broke through the pounding surf.
Mac mouthed a silent prayer of relief and swiped the
sweat off his forehead with a forearm. Squinting
through the canopy, he searched the vegetation front-
ing the beach for some sign of an opening.

"We're right on track according to the GPS coor-
dinates," Cari confirmed after another read of the instruments. "The river mouth should lie dead ahead."

"Bring us in closer."

Keeping a wary eye on the depth finder, she took *Pegasus* into the bay. "The ocean floor's shelving fast. If we don't find the mouth soon, I'll have to switch to track mode and take us…"

"There it is."

The narrow gap in the tangled vegetation was almost invisible. Mac would have missed it if not for the rippling water surface where the river eddied into the bay.

Getting a lock on the ripples, Cari swung the wheel. Moments later, *Pegasus* was fighting his way against the powerful current. Before the green gloom of the river swallowed them, Mac needed to advise the recon team they were on their way up the Verde.

"Second Recon, this is Pegasus One."

He waited for a reply. None came. Frowning, he keyed his mike again.

"Second Recon, this is Pegasus One. Acknowledge please."

Long, tense seconds of silence passed. Cari pulled her gaze from the instruments. Mac saw his own mounting worry mirrored in her brown eyes. His jaw tightening, he was about to try again when the unmistakable rattle of gunfire came bursting through the radio. The patrol leader came on a second later, his voice sharp-edged but remarkably calm given the stutter of small arms fire in the background.

"Pegasus One, this is Second Recon. Be advised we've run smack into a heavily armed rebel patrol."

"Do you have them in your sights?"

"We do, but our orders are to avoid returning fire unless under extreme duress."

The sergeant broke off, cursing as another loud burst made extreme duress sound a whole lot closer than it had a few seconds ago. Mac's fists went white at the knuckles. Those were marines taking fire. He didn't breathe until the team leader came back on the horn.

"We can give these bastards the slip, but we'll have to fall back. We'll try to lead them as far as possible away from the target. Sorry, One. Looks like you're on your own from here on out."

"Roger that."

"Good luck, sir."

"You, too."

The transmission cut off. The sudden silence drowned out even the muted whine of *Pegasus*'s engines. His jaw locked tight, Mac took another GPS reading from the radio signal and noted the team's position on his map. They were still a good four klicks away from the mission.

"We've entered the river channel. I'm going to take us under, then power up to full speed."

The calm announcement brought Mac's head snapping around. Cari's profile was outlined against the dark vegetation lining the riverbank. She kept her attention divided between the instrument panel and the view outside the bubble canopy, now narrowed to a fast-flowing river crowded above and on both sides by jungle.

She had every intention of pushing ahead, with or without fire support from the squad of marines they'd planned to rendezvous with. Evidently, it hadn't occurred to her to abandon their mission. It hadn't occurred to Mac, either, until this moment.

"Listen up, Lieutenant. We need to take another look at our operations plan. I…"

"Don't even think it."

The flat comeback snapped his brows together, but she didn't give him time to respond. Slewing around, she raked him with a wire-brush look.

"This is a two-person operation, McIver. If you go in, I go in."

He bit back the reminder that he was in command of the land phase of this mission. He knew damn well she'd remind *him* he hadn't yet set foot on dry land.

Satisfied she'd made her point, Cari prepared to take *Pegasus* under the river's green surface.

Twenty-six torturous miles later, she brought her craft up from the murky depths. Cari had seen more than her fill of submerged tree stump, twisting roots, slime-covered boulders and darting water snakes.

Once above the surface, the jungle reached out to envelop them. When the water sluiced off the canopy, Cari got the eerie feeling she and Mac were alone in a dark, still universe. Only an occasional stray sunbeam penetrated the dense overgrowth hundreds of feet above. Strangler vines drooped down like ropes from entwined branches. Giant ferns fanned out to cover the riverbanks.

Carefully, Cari navigated the last few yards to their designated rendezvous point. No one was waiting on the riverbank. No marines. No missionaries. No rebels or government troops.

Mac swept both banks with high-powered Night Vision goggles. The goggles could penetrate the gloom beyond the banks far better than the human eye.

"It looks clear," he said tersely.

Cari nodded. "Hold tight."

Repeating the process she'd tested only this morning in the Gulf waters just off Corpus Christi, she switched *Pegasus* from sea to land mode. The outer engines shut down and tucked against the hull. The propellers folded. The belly doors opened and the wide-track wheels descended.

Like some primeval beast crawling up out of the swamp, *Pegasus* clawed his way up the riverbank. The wheel tread ate up the giant ferns and spit them out. But even a high-tech, all-terrain, all-weather assault vehicle was no match for the impenetrable jungle.

Mac would have to hoof it from here. Killing the engines, Cari hit the switch to open the rear hatch. Smothering tropical heat instantly rushed in. So did an astonishing variety of flying insects. Swatting at a winged critter in a particularly virulent shade of orange, Cari climbed out of her seat and followed Mac to the hatch.

"I'll bring out the two Americans," he told her. "You stay with *Pegasus*."

She swallowed her instinctive protest. With her craft secured and on dry land, the baton had passed. She was no longer in command. From now until Mac returned with the missionaries, this was his show.

Feeling a little deflated, she watched as he hunkered down on his heels and dug through his pack. A few, quick smears decorated his face in shades of green and black. Thin black gloves covered his hands. He performed a radio check, chambered a round in his assault rifle, and slung the weapon over his shoulder. His gray-green eyes lasered into her as he confirmed their communications pattern.

"I'll signal you at half-hour intervals. If I miss one signal, wait another half hour. If I miss two, get the hell out of Dodge. Understand?"

"Yes."

His gaze speared into her. ''I mean it, Dunn. No stupid heroics. They could get us both killed.''

He was right. She knew he was right. Yet her throat closed at the thought of leaving him in this smothering heat and darkness.

''Two missed signals and you're gone. Got that, Lieutenant?''

She gave a tight nod. He returned it with a jerk of his chin and started off. He took two steps, only two, and swung back.

''What the hell.''

The muttered oath had Cari blinking in surprise. She blinked again when he strode back to her and caught her chin in his hand.

''Mac, what are—?''

His mouth came down on hers, hard and hot and hungry. Stunned, she stood stiff as an engine blade while his lips moved over hers. A moment later, he faded into the jungle. She was left with the tang of camouflage face paint in her nostrils and the taste of Mac on her lips.

Chapter 3

"That was smart, McIver. Really smart."

Thoroughly disgusted with himself, Mac moved through the dense undergrowth. He'd made some questionable moves in his life. Tangling with the senator's wife had been one of them. Laying that kiss on Caroline Dunn was another. What was this thing he had for married—or almost married—women?

Calling himself an idiot one more time, Mac forced his thoughts away from the woman, the kiss and the heat that brief contact had sent spearing right through his belly.

The mission lay some three kilometers from the river. Five or six kilometers beyond that Second Recon had run smack into a heavily armed rebel force. The marines had said they'd fall back and draw the rebels away from the mission, but Mac wasn't taking any chances. He kept his tread light on the damp, spongy earth and his assault weapon at the ready as he pushed through the giant ferns.

Once away from the river, the ferns thinned and the going got easier. The overhead canopy was so thick only the occasional stray sunbeam could penetrate. It was like moving through a dim, cavernous cathedral with tall columns of trees spearing straight up to support the vaulted ceiling. The deep shadows provided excellent concealment for him and, unfortunately, for potential enemies.

He pushed on, using the GPS built into his handheld digital radio to check his position and send Cari a silent signal at the prearranged times. With each step, his jumpy nerves steadied and his concentration narrowed until there was only Mac, his weapon and the gloom ahead.

As swift and stealthy as a panther, he cut through the jungle. Every sense had moved to full alert, every flutter of an orange-winged butterfly and slither of a spotted lizard sent a message. So did the sudden, raucous screech of a parrot.

Mac spun to his right, dropped into a crouch, and caught a flash of scarlet as the bird took wing. Peering into the gloom, Mac tried to see what had spooked it. Nothing else moved. No leafy ferns swayed.

Forcing the knotted muscles at the base of his skull to relax, Mac came out of the crouch. Without warning, something hard and sharp smacked into his forehead just above his right eyebrow.

Cursing, he ignored the blood pouring into his eye and aimed his assault rifle at the base of a hollow-trunked strangler fig. When the shadows moved, his finger went tight on the trigger.

"Whoever's in there better show yourself. Now!"

He repeated the warning in Spanish and was searching for the few words of Caribe he'd memorized when another missile came zinging at him. This one he managed to dodge. It ricocheted off the tree behind him and landed at his feet.

A rock! Mac saw in disgust. Damned if he'd hadn't taken a direct hit from a rock.

"You've got five seconds to show yourself," he shouted, blinking away the blood. "Four, three, two…"

The shadow burst out of the tree trunk. With a frightened look at the gun aimed at his chest, the attacker whirled and ran.

With another muttered curse, Mac eased the pressure on the trigger. His assailant was a kid. A scrawny, barefooted kid in a Spider-Man T-shirt, of all things. Judging by his size, the runt couldn't be more than six or seven.

"Hey! Hold on! I won't hurt you!"

Fumbling for the Spanish phrases, he hotfooted it after the kid. He couldn't have him spreading the word that there was an armed *Americano* roaming loose in the neighborhood. Not until after Mac had departed the scene with the two missionaries, anyway.

His longer legs ate up the ground. He caught the kid by the back of his ragged shirt and swung him around. The little stinker put up a heck of a fight, grunting and kicking and jabbing with his bony elbows. Keeping well clear of those sharp elbows, Mac held him at arm's length.

"I'm a friend. Amigo."

The kid twisted frantically. He wasn't buying the friend bit. Considering the violence now ripping his country apart, Mac couldn't exactly blame him. He gave the boy a quick little shake.

"Where's your village? *¿Dónde está su,* uh, *casa?*"

Still the youngster wouldn't answer. His lower lip jutted out and his black eyes shot daggers at the marine, but he refused to speak so much as a word. Instead, he made some motion with his hand that Mac strongly suspected was the Caribe version of buzz off, pal.

"Stubborn little devil, aren't you?"

Well, no matter. He had to be from the village where the Americans had set up their mission. It was the only settlement in this vicinity.

Bunching his fist, Mac kept a firm grip on the boy's shirt with one hand while he slung his weapon over his shoulder and probed the cut above his eye with the other. The skin was tender and already rising to a good-sized lump, but the blood had slowed to a trickle. He'd clean the cut when he got to the village. Unless the navigational finder in his radio was sending faulty signals, it couldn't be much farther.

It wasn't.

Another ten minutes brought Mac and his sullen, squirming captive to the edge of a clearing. Although the boy hadn't as yet uttered a single sound, Mac clamped a hand over his mouth. Eyes narrowed, he surveyed the scene.

It didn't take him long to determine the village was deserted. No dogs yapped. No pigs snuffled in the dirt. No goats were tethered to stakes beside the huts. Nor could Mac discern any sign of human habitation…until an unmistakably female figure in a sleeveless white blouse and baggy tan slacks emerged from the clapboard building at the far end of the dirt track that served as the village's main thoroughfare. Obviously agitated, the woman thrust a hand through her cropped blond hair.

''Paulo! Where are you?''

The woman repeated the shout in Spanish, then Caribe. Mac was congratulating himself on having located at least one of the missionaries when his attacker gave a strangled grunt and renewed his frenzied attempts to escape.

This time, Mac let him go. The little squirt shot off, his skinny legs pumping.

"Paulo! There you are!"

Her shoulders sagging in relief, the woman dropped to her knees and opened her arms. The boy charged straight into them. The woman hugged him fiercely, rocking back and forth.

Mac decided he'd better make his presence known before the kid painted him as an enemy. But when he stepped out from behind the tree, the woman's horrified glance whipped from his black-painted, blood-streaked face to his assault rifle. Before Mac could identify himself and assure her he meant no harm, she let loose with a piercing yell.

"*¡Los soldados!*"

"Lady, it's okay. I'm…"

He started toward her, then stopped dead as the shutters covering the windows of one of the huts banged open. In the ominous silence that followed, he heard the snick of a weapon being cocked.

Impatiently, Cari swatted at a persistent mosquito and searched the towering ferns lining the river.

Where the heck was Mac?

Why hadn't he contacted her in… She drew another bead on the functional black watch strapped to her wrist. In fifty-two minutes?

After he'd missed his last signal, she'd waited ten endless minutes before trying to raise him on his radio. When another ten had crawled by, she'd tried again. Each time she'd received nothing. Nada. Zilch.

Now she was eight minutes away from the point where he'd insisted she get out of Dodge.

Could she abandon him?

She was no closer to an answer now than she'd been for the past fifty-three minutes. She glowered at the leafy ferns, willing them to part.

Dammit, where was he?

And what the heck had that kiss been all about?

She didn't have an answer for either question.

Grinding her back teeth in frustration, Cari pulled out her sidearm and released the magazine. A quick check verified the clip was full. She snapped it back in, holstered the Beretta, and swiped her damp, sweaty palms down the side of her BDU shirt.

She could still taste him on her lips. Still feel the scrape of his bristly chin on hers. With all her years in uniform, she would never have imagined she'd be feeling this kind of prickly, itchy, physical awareness smack in the middle of a mission!

Or at all, for that matter.

She was no nun. She'd dated her share of smart, sexy men. Had drifted in and out of several heavy relationships before meeting Jerry. And he was certainly no slouch when it came to stirring her senses. Yet Cari was darned if she could remember ever experiencing such a severe reaction to a single kiss.

She'd be a fool to attach too much significance to it, though. It could only have sprung from tension, that peculiar combination of nerves and adrenaline that came at times like this. Mac had no interest in her outside the professional. None he'd demonstrated during their months in the New Mexico desert, anyway. And she found him almost as irritating as she did attractive.

So why the heck couldn't she lick his taste from her lips? Scowling, she slapped a palm against the side of the hatch.

Where *was* he!

"Pegasus One, this is Two."

The sharp, clear communication almost had Cari jumping out of her skin. Gulping down her relief, she keyed her radio.

"Go ahead, Two."

"Be advised that I'm en route back to your position, approximately fifty meters out. Prepare to cast off as soon as we get our passengers on board."

"Roger."

He'd done it! He'd located the missionaries and

brought them out. Cari would have a word with him later about the grief his missed signal had put her through. Right now, she had to power up her craft.

The engines were humming and she was back at the open hatch when the ferns began to shake. Seconds later, Mac popped through the leafy wall. He was carrying something on his back. Not something, Cari saw in surprise when he turned to hold aside the ferns. Someone. A child.

A woman pushed through the greenery after Mac. She was followed by a boy in sneakers and scruffy, white cotton pants. Another child poked through a second later, this one a scrawny girl in pigtails and tattered, pink sneakers.

Her jaw dropping, Cari watched as several more children emerged. A tall, lanky man with a wide-eyed little girl on his shoulders brought up the rear of the column. Mac hustled them all toward the waiting craft.

The woman reached the vehicle first. Cari stretched down a hand, grasped her wrist, and helped her up the steps.

''Thanks.'' She raked a hand through short, sweat-spiked blond bangs. ''I'm Dr. White. Janice White.''

''Glad you made it, Doc.''

Nodding, the missionary stood back as Cari reached for the child Mac lifted up. He was a tousled-haired boy of three or four. He was also blind, Cari

realized when his groping hands failed to connect
with hers. Gulping, she took a better stance and
stretched out her arms. His chubby fingers found her
sleeves and dug in.

"Okay, I've got him."

To her consternation, she soon discovered each of
the children possessed some form of physical disability. One dragged his right leg. Another had a cleft
palate that left his young face tragically disfigured.
The merry gap-toothed girl had a spine so twisted she
couldn't stand upright. Dismayed, Cari waited for
Mac to climb aboard.

"I had to bring them," he said in response to her
silent query. "The Whites wouldn't leave them."

Dragging off his boonie hat, he swiped an arm
across his sweat-drenched face. Only then did Cari
see the vicious-looking cut on his forehead. Someone—Dr. White, she guessed—had added a few neat
stitches. Before Cari could ask Mac what he'd run
into, the tall, lanky missionary grabbed her hand and
pumped it.

"I'm Reverend Harry White. I can't tell you how
grateful we are to you for coming after us. The fighting in the area drove off the villagers weeks ago. We
had no one to help us bring the children through the
jungle."

"Yes, well..."

"Our church has arranged adoptions for them, you

see. My sister and I have been trying to get them to the States for almost two years.''

''Sister?''

Cari's glance cut to the doctor. She'd assumed—they'd all assumed—the Whites were husband and wife. Obviously the intelligence supplied for this hastily mounted operation had missed a few minor details.

''We've paid a fortune in bribes,'' Janice White put in, picking up on her brother's comment. ''Obviously not to the right people.''

''No matter,'' the reverend said with a smile. ''We're on our way now.''

''Hang on a minute!''

Cari shot a quick glance at Mac. His shrug indicated he'd already covered this ground once with the Whites. Biting her lip, she faced the minister.

''Are you suggesting we smuggle these kids out of Caribe?''

''Yes,'' the man of God replied simply.

Cari pursed her lips. She was an officer in the United States Coast Guard. A major portion of her job was to prevent the kind of illegal emigration the missionary was suggesting. She'd lost count of the number of vessels crammed with refugees she and other coast guard crews had been forced to turn back. Small boats carrying whole families across miles of open sea. Fishing trawlers trying to slip fifty or so desperate souls past coastal patrols. Container ships with hidden compartments stuffed with starving, suf-focating cargo.

"Smuggling them out is our only recourse at this point," Reverend White said earnestly. "As Janice said, we've been working on their papers for more than two years. Finding a responsible official to deal with was difficult enough before the fighting erupted. Now, it's well nigh…"

"Harry!"

His sister's frantic cry jerked the missionary around.

"Where's Paulo?"

"Isn't he with you?"

"No."

"Dear Lord above!" The reverend spun back to Mac, his face contorted with panic. "He was right ahead of me. I can't imagine how… When…"

"I'll find him," Mac said grimly. His glance cut to Cari. "You'd better get *Pegasus* ready to swim. I picked up some radio chatter a while back. It sounded close. So close I didn't want to risk using my own radio until I knew I could get the kids safely aboard."

Well, that explained why he'd skipped an interim signal. Unfortunately, the explanation didn't particu-larly sit well with Cari. The idea that the bad guys were poking around nearby upped her pucker factor considerably. Climbing over kids and backpacks, she made her way to the cockpit.

Scant minutes later she had *Pegasus* ready to plunge back into the river. He sat nosed half on, half off the bank. Cari kept the engines churning gently in reverse, with just enough power to keep her craft from being dragged along with the current. The rear hatch remained open. All the while her heart pounded out the seconds until Mac returned.

She hated this business of being left behind. She was used to sailing her ship, her crew and herself into action, not sitting at the controls while someone else took the lead. She wanted in on the action.

Mac had been right, she thought grimly. She wasn't the barefoot, pregnant and in the kitchen type. As much as she ached for a child of her own, she knew she belonged right here, right now. No one else could have maneuvered *Pegasus* up this narrow, twisting river. No one else could get it back down.

Which she hoped to do.

Like, *soon!*

They only had a few hours of daylight left. She didn't relish navigating the Rio Verde in the dark, even with all the sophisticated instrumentation crammed into *Pegasus*. It was time to make tracks.

Where the heck was Mac?

He came crashing through the ferns several heart-pounding minutes later. He had a scruffy little boy tucked under one elbow and his assault rifle tight in the crook of the other. Cari's breath wheezed out on a small sigh of relief.

The next instant, she sucked it back in again. Right before her eyes, the fronds above Mac's head began to dance wildly. A heartbeat later, she heard the deadly splat, splat, splat of bullets tearing through the leaves.

He was taking fire!

Twisting in her seat, Cari shouted a terse order. "Dr. White! Reverend! Get the children down flat on the deck! Now!"

She waited only long enough to see Mac and the kid come diving through the rear opening. Slewing back around, she hit the switch to close the hatch, wrapped her fist around the throttles and thrust the engines to full forward.

Pegasus sailed off the bank. His belly hit the river's surface with a smack that would have rattled Cari's teeth if she hadn't already clenched them tight. Her jaw locked, she aimed her craft for the dark, rushing channel in the middle of the river.

She expected to hear bullets pinging off the canopy at any second. The bubble was made of some new composite that was supposed to be able to withstand a direct hit from a mortar, but she wasn't particularly anxious to test the shield's survivability.

She made it to midstream without any bullets cracking against the canopy. As soon as the depth finder registered enough clearance, she took *Pegasus* under.

The water closed around them. The view ahead became one of swirling currents, darting fish and dark, fuzzy shapes. As she had during the torturous journey upriver, Cari kept her gaze locked on the sonar screen. All she needed to do now was ram a jagged stump or slimy green bolder.

She didn't relax her vigil until Mac slid into the seat beside her and assumed duties as navigator. Blowing out a ragged breath, Cari slanted him glance.

"Is the kid okay?"

"Yeah. He's a tough little runt." A rueful smile flitted across Mac's face. "He's the one who put this crease in my forehead."

"How'd he do that?"

"He beaned me with a rock."

Despite the tension still stringing her as tight as an anchor cable, Cari had to laugh. "That's going to make a great story at the bar when we get back to base. So what happened? How did you lose him?"

"My guess is he fell back and couldn't call out to us to wait for him."

"Couldn't?"

Mac's smile faded. "When I first collared the kid, I tried to get him to tell me his name and where he'd sprung from. He got stubborn and clammed up. Or so I thought. It wasn't until Doc White was stitching me up that I found out he can't talk. He was born without a larynx.''

''Oh, no!''

''The most he can manage is an occasional grunt.''

Cari slumped back against her seat. Her stab of pity for the little boy battled with practical reality.

''You know the crap is going to hit the fan big-time if we take these kids out of Caribe without authorization from their government.''

''Maybe.''

''There's no maybe about it. Remember the international furor over the Cuban kid, Elian Gonzales?''

''There's a difference here. Elian Gonzales had a father who wanted him back. These kids are orphans. Throwaways, as Janice White described them, probably because of their disabilities. If their government had bothered with them at all, they would have been shuffled into some institution or foster home.''

A muscle ticked in the side of his jaw. For a moment his expression was remote, closed, unreadable. Then he tore his gaze away from the screen. The hard edges to his face softened and he gave Cari a quick, slashing grin.

''I say we take them out with us.''

She fell a little in love with him at that moment. Here he was, the all-or-nothing, you're-in-or-you're out, gung ho marine, putting his military career on the line for a boatload of kids.

Only belatedly did she remember she'd be putting her career on the line, too.

Oh, well. If she'd learned nothing else during her years of service, she'd discovered it was a whole lot easier to ask for forgiveness after the fact than obtain permission beforehand.

"Seeing as they're already on board," she replied with an answering grin, "I say we take them with us, too. But I'll let you advise Captain Westfall of our additional passengers," she tacked on hastily.

Chapter 4

Cari was actually starting to believe she'd get her craft and its passengers safely away from Caribe when disaster struck. Unfortunately, she didn't realize that hazy blur dead ahead represented disaster until it was too late.

"What the heck…?"

That was all she got out before *Pegasus* plowed into what looked very much like a net. It *was* a net, she discovered as the prow pushed hard against the barrier. Made of thin, loosely woven vines. No wonder it hadn't returned any kind of a sonar signature.

The vines snared *Pegasus* like a giant fish, held him for a moment, then yielded to his powerful forward momentum. The net ripped apart. The vessel's prow poked through. A long length of the hull followed. The swept-back wings and rear-tilted engines, however, snagged on the tangled remnants of the netting.

"Hell!"

Cari yanked the throttle back and reversed thrust, but it was too late. Dangling vines had wrapped tight around the propeller shafts. The twin engines gave a little sputter and died.

For a moment there was only silence.

Dead silence.

Cari felt a bubble of panic rise in her throat. Sailors the world over had nightmares about just this kind of a situation. She was trapped underwater. With her boat experiencing total engine failure.

As quickly as it rose, her panic evaporated. She shot a glance at the depth finder and confirmed they were less than ten feet below the river's surface. Even without engines, she could float *Pegasus* up enough to pop the canopy and check out the situation.

"We'll have to surface," she told Mac.

"Not until we figure out what the heck snared us," he returned, craning his neck to peer through the gloom at the entangling vines.

"My guess is it's a fishing net."

"Why didn't we hit it coming upriver?"

"Could be the locals only string it in the afternoon, when the river's running with the tide."

"Or it could be a trap set specifically for us."

The same possibility had occurred to Cari. "I don't think so," she said, chewing on the inside of her lip. "We swam upriver underwater. As far as we know, no one observed us going in."

"Someone sure as hell observed us coming out. Those weren't bees buzzing around my head back there."

"They saw *you,* but I don't think they saw *Pegasus.* We got you aboard and went under before whoever was taking potshots at you charged through the ferns."

Mac's eyes narrowed. "All anyone needed was a glimpse. Just a glimpse. They could have radioed to their buddies downriver, had them string a net."

The terse exchange helped resolve some of the awful doubts gnawing at Cari. "Their buddies couldn't have chopped down vines and strung something this elaborate in an hour. My guess…my considered opinion," she amended; "is that we'll soon come face-to-face with some local fishermen who are going to be very surprised at what they've netted."

By now the questions were coming at her from the Whites as well. "What's happened?" the reverend called anxiously from the back.

"Why are we stopped?" his sister wanted to know.

"We hit a net," Cari called back. "A fisherman's

net I think, and fouled the engines. We'll have to surface and try to clear them.''

Slowly, foot by foot, Cari floated *Pegasus* up from the murky depths.

The canopy broke the surface first. Eyes narrowed, shoulders tense, Mac twisted around and did a swift three-sixty. The only signs of life he spotted were two red-furred monkeys hanging from a branch extending over the river. The creatures ceased their antics and gaped at the monster rising from the depths before emitting high-pitched shrieks of alarm and scrambling away.

Pegasus pawed his way up inch by inch. Still tethered by the net, the craft remained caught in midcurrent. The swift moving river flowed past, rushing over the wings, swirling just a few inches below the canopy.

Cari assessed the situation once again and saw only one option. ''I'm going to pop the canopy and try to cut through the vines.''

Mac shot her a swift look. ''You sure opening the canopy won't flood us?''

''Pretty sure.''

The possibility she might be putting the children at grave risk generated a sick feeling in the pit of her stomach. She saw no other way to free her craft, however. It was either pop the canopy and cut the vines or drift at the end of this tether indefinitely.

"Go back and tell the Whites what we're doing," she instructed Mac. "Stay with them and be prepared to pass the children up through the cockpit if we start to take on water. Worst-case scenario, we swim them to shore."

He nodded, not questioning her decision or authority, and climbed out of his seat. When he signaled that they were ready in the rear compartment, Cari hit the button to raise the canopy.

The hydraulic lift pushed the nose down a few inches. River water rushed in, soaking her from the waist down. After a heart-stopping second or two, the nose bobbed upward again and the flood ceased.

"All right," she breathed. "Okay."

She unhooked her seat harness, her fingers shaking a little. Nothing like almost sinking a ship and its passengers to take the starch out of a girl.

"I'll crawl out onto the wings and assess the damage," she told Mac when he climbed back in the cockpit. "You'd better get on the radio and advise base we've, ah, hit a slight snag."

Her feeble attempt at a pun fell flat. Mac didn't crack so much as a shadow of a smile. Shrugging, Cari unbuckled her harness and hooked a leg over the side of the cockpit. Once on the swept-back wing, she dropped to all fours.

The swirling river water turned the wing slick and the going tricky, but she made it to the half-submerged engine without too much difficulty. A single glance at the vines wrapped tight around the propeller shaft had her muttering a smothered curse.

The vines were as thick as her wrist. She'd need a chain saw to hack through them. Unfortunately, the emergency equipment aboard *Pegasus* didn't include a chain saw. A fire axe, yes. An acetylene torch. An assortment of other tools, hoses and spare electronic parts. But no chain saw.

Balancing carefully on all fours, Cari traced the path of the twisted vine cable that formed the spine of the net. It was anchored to trees on either side of the river. Maybe she could use the axe to chop through one end. The other end would then act as an anchor chain and swing *Pegasus* in a wide arc toward the opposite bank. Once in shallow water, she could try to unfoul the engines.

It might work. It had to work. She wasn't going to abandon a multimillion-dollar prototype vehicle to the river gods unless she had no other choice.

Before she tried to salvage her craft, though, she wanted the Whites and the children ashore.

Mac went first to reconnoiter.

Using the vine cable to pull himself through the water, he swam to the left bank and clambered up.

Once again, he disappeared into the thick greenery lining the river's edge. The seconds crawled by. Stretched into minutes. Cari was sweating profusely from the oppressive jungle heat and stomach-twisting tension when he reappeared.

Gulping, she saw he prodded three wide-eyed, disbelieving fishermen ahead of him at gunpoint. Mouths agape, they stared at the monster they'd snared in their net.

"Their village is about fifty yards in from the river," Mac shouted to Cari. "Get Reverend White up to the cockpit so we can communicate with these guys and determine whether they're friend or foe."

Harry White soon ascertained they were friends. Or at least they claimed no recent contact with either government forces or the rebels waging vicious guerilla warfare in the area. The reverend also extracted an offer of food and shelter for the night that would soon drop over the island like a blanket. Still wary but trusting to instincts that said the villagers represented no immediate threat, Mac holstered his sidearm and organized the process of ferrying the children to shore.

Cari was the last to leave her craft. Plunging into the river, she used the net to pull herself hand over hand to dry land. Once there, she stayed to keep a watchful eye on the vehicle while Mac, Harry and Janice White shepherded the children to the village.

Mac returned with what had to be most, if not all, of the local population. Agog, they gaped at the long, sleek craft trapped in what remained of the net. Several villagers jumped into the river and paddled out for a closer look.

Using Harry White as an interpreter, Cari explained her idea of hacking through the far side of the thick vine cable and swinging *Pegasus* toward the near bank.

"I want to anchor it here," she said, jabbing a finger at the river's edge, "out of the current, so I can get to the vines fouling the engines."

The plan elicited a lively discussion among the men. Like most natives of this part of the Caribbean, they were a handsome people. Their rapid speech rose and fell in a musical rhythm that bespoke their mixture of island and Spanish heritage. After some debate, they agreed Cari's plan would work.

Before any work was done, however, Mac requested two men head back upriver to act as sentries. Just in case someone should come looking for an unidentified river craft. The headman agreed and dispatched two sturdy young villagers in a dugout canoe.

Then it was a matter of waiting while another crew paddled across the river to hack at the far end of the cable. While they paddled, Cari swam back to *Pegasus* and crawled into the cockpit. Mac stayed on shore with a troop of men armed with poles to keep the craft from plowing too hard and too fast into the bank.

Despite her swim, Cari was once again drenched in nervous sweat by the time *Pegasus* was tethered to the shore. She was also squinting to see through the fast-gathering shadows.

"Night drops like a stone this deep in the interior," Harry White warned. "Unless you rig some lights, you'll be working blind in a few minutes."

As little as she liked berthing overnight alongside the river, Cari had to nix the idea of using shipboard batteries to power external lights. "We'll need every ounce of juice to restart the engines. We'll have to wait until morning to unfoul the propellers."

Assuming she *could* unfoul them, that is.

Mac concurred. "It's best not to fumble around underwater in the dark. Lieutenant, why don't you accompany the reverend back to the village, grab some chow and snatch a few hours sleep? I'll use what's left of the netting to camouflage *Pegasus* and take first watch."

He made the suggestion so naturally Cari suspected he didn't even realize he'd assumed command. Since they were once again ashore, she yielded to his authority.

This passing the baton back and forth was becoming a habit with them, she thought wryly. What's more, they were getting pretty good at it, each allowing the other to exercise their unique skills and expertise.

That thought was still in her mind when she made her way back to the river four hours later.

She'd downed a fantastic meal of roast fish, black beans and plantains. She'd also scrubbed away her dirt and sweat, and curled up on a straw mat for three hours of total unconsciousness. Now it was McIver's turn.

She found him stretched out on the bank, back propped against a tree, boots crossed at the ankles, sharing a fire with two of the men from the village. The fire was carefully banked, a mere red glow in the darkness, but it emitted enough smoke to keep the worst of the mosquitoes at bay. Either that, or they shied away from the awful stink put out by the thin, long stemmed pipes clamped between the men's teeth.

"Banana leaves," Mac explained when she dropped down beside him and wrinkled her nose. "Flavored with what I'm guessing is some sort of guano."

"Guano? Like in bird poop?"

"I'm thinking it's more likely bat droppings."

"You're smoking bat droppings?"

His shoulders lifted. "When in Rome…"

This was a whole new side of the man, one Cari

was seeing for the first time. In their months together at the New Mexico test site, she'd pretty well decided his personality and general attitude were every bit as starched as his BDUs. Yet here she was, sitting cross-legged on a riverbank beside him while he smoked bat dung and carried on a lively conversation with two grinning Caribes via grunts and hand signals.

Then there was that kiss.

Now that the tension of the afternoon had eased some of its brutal grip on her mind—and on her neck muscles!—the memory of Mac's mouth coming down hard and hungry on hers kept sneaking into Cari's thoughts. She still couldn't figure out where that kiss had come from, and the fact that she couldn't was driving her nuts.

Unfortunately, she found no opportunity to slip the topic into the conversation. A ferocious rumble from the vicinity of Mac's stomach reminded her he had yet to chow down or get some rest.

"It's my watch," she reminded him. "You'd better go feed that growling beast something other than banana leaves and bat dung."

Mac didn't argue. Like Cari, he'd spent enough years in the field to know the importance of snatching food and rest whenever the situation permitted.

"I'll be back in four hours." Gesturing to his companions to stay and keep her company, he pushed to his feet. "You've got your radio?"

She tapped her shirt pocket. "Right here."

"Contact me if you see anything—anything—that makes you nervous."

"The only thing that worries me at the moment is the possibility these guys might press me to take a turn on your pipe."

In the dim glow from the fire she saw his teeth flash in a quick grin. "You should try a puff or two. It's really not all that bad."

"No, thanks."

He stood for a moment, a dark shadow against the even deeper black of the jungle. "It's been a helluva a day."

"That it has."

Cari couldn't believe she'd jumped out of bed at 5:00 a.m. this morning convinced the most momentous challenge she'd face was taking *Pegasus* into the Gulf of Mexico for his first deep-water swim. Eighteen hours later, she was stranded on a Caribbean island with a boatload of kids, two missionaries and one U.S. Marine.

"You did good today, Lieutenant."

Good grief! Two compliments in one day! Coming from Russ McIver, she was sure that constituted some kind of a world record.

"We both did good," she returned. "Although some people might say I fell a little short of excellence when I hung my boat up on a fishing net."

"Yeah, well, there is that minor problem to rectify. Still…" He hesitated a moment before moving into dangerous territory. "Your friend Jerry might have had his eyes opened if he'd seen you in action today."

She was still formulating her answer to that when another loud rumble cut through the buzz and whir of night insects.

"Go eat something," she insisted.

"Aye, aye, skipper. I'll back in four hours."

He started off, his boots squishing on the spongy vegetation lining the riverbank. Cari debated for all of four or five seconds before unfolding her legs and following after him.

"Hey, McIver!"

"What?"

"You remember that e-mail Captain Westfall suggested we send before departing for Caribe?"

"That isn't something I'm likely to forget in the space of one day."

"I e-mailed Jerry."

She sensed rather than saw his shrug.

"Understandable."

Moving toward him, she wondered why the heck it was suddenly so important to clarify the matter of Commander Jerry Wharton. "Not that it's any of your business, but I turned down his proposal."

Surprise colored his voice. "You did?"

"I did. I also ended things between us."

"Why? Not that it's any of my business."

She hated to surrender ground to a marine, but saw no other choice in this instance. "You were right back in Corpus. I'm good at what I do. Damned good. What's more, I love being part of something important. I ought to be able to find a way to combine a career *and* a family. Other women have certainly managed it."

"You're not other women, Dunn."

The flat assertion left her almost as confused as his kiss had earlier that afternoon. And more than a little irritated. She wasn't sure what kind of reaction she'd been expecting to the news she'd ended things with Jerry, but this certainly wasn't it.

"See you in four hours," she said, turning to make her way back to the two fishermen.

Mac let her go.

He wasn't about to admit her cool announcement had rocked him right back on his boot heels. Nor would he give in to the suddenly fierce urge to grab her wrist, spin her around, and feed the beast inside him that hungered for something other than smoked fish and black beans.

They were on a mission, for God's sake! Responsible for the safety of two Americans and a passel of kids. But when they got the Whites and their charges out of Caribe…

A vivid image leaped into his head. Cari sprawled on a bed. Her hair tangled and dark against white sheets. Her lips swollen. Her brown eyes languorous. Mac went so hard he almost doubled over.

Gritting his teeth, he forced the image out of his head. The vivid detail blurred, but the ache stayed. All these weeks they'd worked together, Mac had refused to let himself think of Caroline Dunn that way, had done his damndest to keep her out of his head. Now he wanted her in his bed so badly he ached with it.

Somehow he suspected he wasn't going to drop off to sleep any time soon.

He had that right.

Stretched out on a raised sleeping platform in the hut given over for the visitors' use, he caught only fitful snatches of sleep. Finally, he dozed off—only to jerk awake again sometime later.

A slow, stealthy rustling in the darkness had him grabbing his assault rifle.

Chapter 5

Rifle to his shoulder, Mac picked out a glowing green figure in the weapon's Night Vision scope.

"Hold it right there!"

His snarled command froze the ghoulish shape in a half crouch. A head whipped around. Eyes surrounded by iridescent green shadows stared at Mac.

Disgusted, he lowered his weapon. "Didn't anyone ever tell you sneaking into a room in the dark of night is a good way to get hurt, kid?"

Evidently not. Paulo scrunched his face into a scowl and looked distinctly unintimidated.

"What are you doing here?" Mac growled. "Why aren't you bedded down with the others?"

As soon as the words were out, he gave himself a mental kick. Oh, that was smart. Why not ask the kid a couple more questions he couldn't respond to? Besides, the answer was obvious now that Mac had shaken the sleep out of his head. The boy was crouched over the webbed utility belt, conducting a little midnight raid.

The possibilities of what he'd find in those pockets made Mac's stomach clench. He'd stuffed a small arsenal of spare ammo clips, grenades and other deadly items in that belt. None of which made suitable toys for children.

Rolling off the woven straw platform, he flicked a match and put it to the wick of the kerosene lamp hanging from a low rafter.

"What are you after?"

At his approach, the kid sprang up and hotfooted it for the straw mat that served as a door. Mac caught him by the collar of his shirt before he could escape.

"Oh, no you don't."

He swung the boy around and faced off with him for the second time that day.

"We need to have a little powwow here, kid. You can't... Ow!"

For a scrawny little runt, the boy sure knew how to put his boney elbows and knees to use. Mac took a sharp whack on the shin that left him feeling distinctly unfriendly.

Paulo gave no signs of feeling any friendlier. With an inarticulate little grunt he twisted around and tried to lock his teeth on a handy patch of wrist. Swearing under his breath, Mac held him at arm's length.

"Now look, pal. Let's get something straight. We're on the same side."

Maybe.

And maybe not.

Now that he thought about it, could be the kid wasn't real anxious to leave Caribe for a new home and as yet unknown adoptive parents in the States. Or could be the boy had an aversion to authority figures. The Lord knew Mac hadn't been on the best of terms with very many in his younger days.

Keeping a firm grip on the ragged Spider-Man shirt, he dragged the sullen boy back over to the belt. "What were you after here? *¿Qué usted, uh, desea?*"

Paulo made an abrupt gesture with one hand. The Whites had taught the boy to communicate via sign language. Mac had never learned signing, but this particular gesture was universally recognizable.

"*¿Que?*" he growled. "Show me."

Scowling, Paulo pointed a grubby finger at the survival knife attached to the belt. The six-inch parkarized steel blade with its serrated top edge and leather-grooved handle lay nestled inside a canvas scabbard.

Mac's eyes narrowed. What the heck did the kid want with a blade like that? The mystery was solved a moment later, when a distracted Harry White came in search of his missing charge.

"There you are! What are you doing?"

Paulo shrugged, leaving Mac to answer. "From what I can gather, he came after my knife."

"Oh, dear."

White directed a torrent of Caribe at the boy, who answered with a flurry of hand signals.

"He didn't want the knife," the minister interpreted. "Just the sheath. Show him, Paulo."

With a fierce scowl, the boy dug his hand into the pocket of his shorts. When he withdrew it, his grubby fist was clenched tight. It took a gentle prod from the missionary to get him to uncurl his fingers.

In his palm lay a small pocketknife. The handle must have been inlaid with mother-of-pearl at one time, but most of the iridescent shell had chipped away. Shooting Mac an evil look, Paulo dug out the blade. The steel was broken off at the tip and rusted in spots, but it was clear the knife was the boy's prize possession. It was also clear why he'd wanted the sheath of Mac's survival knife. Hunkering down, the boy drew the broken blade along the narrow whetstone sewn into the side seam of the canvas scabbard. For a moment the snick of steel against flint was the only sound in the hut.

"The knife was in his pocket when he showed up at the back door of the mission," White explained while Paulo methodically sharpened the blade. "He was only four or five at the time. Far too young for such an implement, of course, but every time we took the thing away and hid it, he'd ferret it out. We've since discovered he's very careful with it. And quite good at carving beads and toys for the other children from seed pods and monkey wood."

Mac would bet the little tough could probably carve his initials in a man's shinbone, too. He kept his thoughts to himself and expression neutral, though, until the boy had whetted the blade to his satisfaction. Rising, he snapped the blade shut, dropped the knife in his pocket and started to saunter off.

"Paulo!"

White said something in Caribe. The boy's lips pressed tight. His jaw jutted.

Sighing, the minister tried again. "The major let you use his whetstone. What do you say?"

At the gentle suggestion, the youngster flashed a quick hand signal. The tips of the missionary's ears turned a bright pink.

"He, er, said thank you."

Yeah, Mac just bet he did.

Quickly, White shooed the boy into the other room. His ears still glowing, he spread his hands apologetically. "Paulo has had a rough time. From the little we've been able to pry out of him, he apparently saw his mother murdered by the rebels, along with half of his village.''

So it wasn't just anyone in authority the kid reacted so strongly to. It was anyone in BDUs. Feeling a tug of pity for a child who'd taken some major hits in his six short years, Mac asked about his father.

''We don't know who he was or what happened to him. Paulo just showed up at the mission one day. No one in the government bureaucracy can produce so much as a birth certificate or baptismal record for him. It's pretty much the same story with all the kids. That's why we've had such a difficult time getting them out of Caribe. They have no papers, therefore they don't exist.''

Remembering his earlier thought, Mac posed another question. ''Are you so sure they want to leave Caribe? It's their home.''

''We're sure. They know they're going to families who've waited for years to adopt. All except Paulo. We've had some difficulty placing him, but finally found a family who's willing to take him after he completes his surgery.''

''What surgery?''

''My sister's been in contact with doctors at the M.D. Anderson Cancer Center in Houston. They've experienced considerable success implanting artificial voice boxes in patients with severe throat cancer. It would take a number of delicate operations, but we're hoping they can do the same for Paulo.''

The thought of the scruffy kid in the next room going under the knife for a series of operations left Mac feeling distinctly uncomfortable. So much so, he couldn't get back to sleep after Reverend White returned to the other room. Edgy and restless, he hooked his utility belt over one shoulder, jammed on his hat and slipped out of the hut.

He used his pencil-thin high-intensity flashlight to find his way to the river. All around him, the jungle was alive with the sights and sounds. Night-feeding creatures crunched on leaves and insects. Bats whooshed through the trees. A dozen or more red dots glowed in the inky blackness, steady, unblinking eyes that followed Mac's passage.

The carefully banked fire was little more than an orange blush in the darkness, but provided enough light for Mac to observe the trio keeping *Pegasus* company. Cari had assumed the same comfortable position Mac had earlier—her back against a peeling banyan trunk, legs crossed at the ankles. She'd evidently declined their hosts' offer of a pipe, however. The two Caribe fishermen squatted comfortably nearby, providing more than enough pungent smoke to keep the mosquitoes away without her assistance.

"It's McIver," Mac called out in a quiet voice so as not to startle them too much. "I'm coming in."

Cari sat up, chiding herself for the ridiculous way her pulse skittered at the sound of his voice. How like McIver to materialize out of the night just when her wayward thoughts had returned to him…for only the ninth or tenth time in the past few hours!

She darted a quick look at the illuminated face of her watch, confirmed it *was* only a few hours since she'd relieved him. "What are you doing back here?" Her voice sharpened. "Is there a problem?"

"No problem. I just couldn't sleep."

Nodding to the two fishermen, Mac folded his legs and made himself comfortable beside her. She scooted over a few inches to give him a share of the tree to lean against. The other men seemed to take his arrival as a signal for them to abandon their post. In a mix of Spanish, Caribe and eloquent hand gestures, they indicated it was time for them to hit the rack and melted into the jungle.

A minute ago, the muted symphony of night sounds and mostly incomprehensible murmur of her two self-appointed guardians had lulled Cari into a relaxed, sleepy state. All of a sudden she was wide-awake, her every nerve tingling. Deciding some conversation would force her mind away from Mac's close proximity, she angled her face toward his.

"Why couldn't you sleep?"

"I kept thinking about that e-mail you sent Wharton."

"What about it?" she asked, surprised and just a little wary.

He hesitated a moment or two before making a grudging admission. "Maybe I was out of line, pushing at you the way I did back in Corpus."

"Maybe?"

"Okay, I tend to come on a little strong at times. The point is, I shouldn't have ragged you. Not about something so important. And maybe you shouldn't have given Wharton his walking papers. That isn't the kind of decision a person should make right before taking off on a mission."

The comment took Cari completely aback. After the bone-rattling kiss that afternoon, she would have supposed he'd be the last one to suggest she'd made a mistake with Jerry.

Or maybe this was his way of suggesting *he'd* made a mistake, she thought with a sudden lurch in her belly. Maybe he was worried she'd read too much into a simple lip-lock.

"I knew what I was doing," she said coolly. "*Not* that it's any of your business."

"You tried that line already. It didn't work the first time."

"What is this?" she asked, confused and beginning

to feel a little annoyed. "When did my personal life become a matter of such interest to you?"

"Since the first time I laid eyes on you back in New Mexico."

He dropped that bombshell so calmly, so casually, that it took a few seconds for the full impact to hit.

"Are you saying you've…you've…"

She stumbled, not quite sure how to phrase matters at this point. Mac supplied the missing link.

"Had the hots for you since day one? As a matter of fact, I have."

Her jaw dropped. Several scenes from the past months flashed into her mind. In most of them, she and Russ McIver had been squaring off for another round.

He must have sensed her shock. She saw the ghost of a grin sketch across his face.

"I know. It's kind of knocked me off my stride, too."

"Ha!" That at least she could respond to. "If I knocked you off stride any time in the past four months, you sure as heck hid it well."

"Every time I was ready to make my move, you'd get another call from Wharton. I saw the pressure those calls put on you. I wasn't going to add to it."

Cari had no idea Mac had observed her so closely. Or pegged her uncertainty over her relationship with Jerry so accurately. More confused than ever, she pushed away from the tree trunk, sat up straight and tried to see his face in the gloom.

"You didn't hesitate to add some pressure this afternoon," she reminded him pointedly. "You didn't know I'd ended things with Jerry when you laid that kiss on me."

"No, I didn't. We can chalk that one up to galloping adrenaline."

That was pretty much what Cari had figured. Still, hearing Mac confirm it put a decided dent in her ego. Before she could formulate an appropriate response, however, he reached over and curved a palm around her nape.

"This one," he said as he tugged her closer, "is for real."

It was. Most definitely. For real.

His mouth came down on hers, not as hard as it had that afternoon, but every bit as hungry. Surprise held Cari stiff-shouldered for a moment. Only for a moment. Then his lips moved over hers and hunger spiked through her.

She wanted more than a taste this time. She wanted teeth and tongue. A little full-frontal contact would be nice, too, she decided on a rush of heat. Twisting sideways, she wrapped her arms around his neck. The move brought their upper bodies into play, but left the lower portions at an awkward angle. Mac solved the problem by snaking his other arm around her waist and hauling her across his lap.

"There," he murmured against her mouth. "That's better."

"Much better."

Her agreement began on a breathy laugh and ended on a gulp. She was still at an angle, but wouldn't complain about the amount of contact now. She could feel his thighs under hers, his ribs against her breast, the bristly hair on the back of his neck beneath her palm. His front was bristly, too, she discovered when his cheeks and chin rasped against hers.

"This isn't real smart," she gasped after she came up for air.

"Not smart at all," Mac agreed, nuzzling her throat. "Want me to stop?"

His teeth scraped a path along the tender skin, his tongue ignited a trail of fire.

"Later," she got out on a breathless gasp.

Much later.

First she wanted to feel his hands on her, wanted *her* hands on him…without several layers of chemically treated jungle BDUs between them. She fumbled with the buttons on his shirt, shoved the flaps aside, ran her palms over the planes and curves covered by a wide expanse of black cotton T-shirt.

Mac did the same, except he made shorter work of her buttons and didn't stop with her T-shirt. One swift yank pulled up the hem, exposing her sports bra. Another tug brought the springy spandex lower, baring the slopes of her breasts. They were on the small side, like the rest of her, but provided more than enough material for Mac's busy, busy hands and mouth to work with.

His breath came through the spandex, hot and wet. His teeth found the tight, eager nipple pushing against the elastic. Within moments, fire was shooting from Cari's breast straight to her belly. Moments more, and she was squirming frantically on his lap.

"Oh, babe," he half muttered, half groaned. "Another move like that and it will be *too* late."

"Huh?"

Lost to the sensations piling one on top of the other, Cari struggled to put the skids on her whirling senses. It took a hard, insistent probe at her left rear cheek to penetrate her sensual haze.

"Oh. Right."

Tugging down her bra, she wiggled off his lap. She heard a long, low hiss, followed by a sound that could only be teeth grinding.

"Wrong time, wrong place," she said with a shaky laugh. She was pushing the buttons of her shirt through their holes when Mac curled a knuckle under her chin and tipped her face to his.

"There'll be a right time," he promised gruffly. "And a right place."

''Will there?''

''Damn straight.''

Now that some semblance of sanity had returned, Cari wasn't so sure. With any luck, they'd depart Caribe and hit the open sea by noon. After that, it was only a matter of weeks—maybe days—until the Pegasus test cadre disbanded. When that happened, she'd go back to her home station in Maryland and Mac would return to the marine corps base at Cherry Point, North Carolina.

The thought depressed her. More, she realized with a small shock, than her abrupt decision to terminate her yearlong relationship with Jerry Wharton.

Whoa! How the heck had she let things get so heavy, so fast? She'd just opted out of one relationship that had presented insurmountable challenges. She had to be crazy to even *think* about jumping out of that situation into one involving a gung ho marine. Particularly a marine who held very definite opinions on just about everything and didn't hesitate to express them.

Torn between regret and relief that they'd stopped when they had, Cari shoved the last button through its hole and tucked her shirt inside her waistband to keep out the mosquitoes. A quick glance at her watch provided an excuse to put some distance between her and Mac and let the dust settle a bit.

''It's almost four. You sure you don't want to go

back to the village and grab another hour or two of sleep?''

''I'm sure.''

The dry response told Cari he was still wound as tight as she was. Neither one of them were likely to uncoil in the remaining hours before dawn.

''Then I'll head back and round up a work crew as soon as it turns light. With the help of some strong backs and sharp machetes, we'll soon have *Pegasus* back in trim.''

Or so she hoped.

Chapter 6

Seven hours later, Cari stood on the bank of the Rio Verde while Janice White doctored a deep, slicing cut in the web of skin between her thumb and forefinger. Wet hair straggled in long tangles around her face and shoulders. River water slicked down her face and plastered her pants to her body. She'd discarded her BDU shirt but a large, boisterous crowd of observers had prevented her from stripping down to her bra.

Shaking her head, she surveyed the scene of what had begun as a recovery operation and now looked more like a three-ring circus. Dugout canoes were strung across the river, filled with Caribes calling out advice and beating the surface with sticks to keep away any unwanted underwater creatures. Women squatted on the bank, laughing and chatting and offering their own opinions on the operation. Shrieking children cannonballed through the ferns into the river and sent up sparkling geysers. With the quicksilver agility of minnows, they darted around the craft Cari and Mac had yet to free from the last remnants of the fishing net.

The Whites and their charges had joined the throng who'd turned out to observe the recovery operation. Rosa, the bright-eyed little girl with the twisted spine, sat cross-legged next to the boy with the cleft palate. Together they described events for Miguel, whose sightless eyes couldn't see what was happening. Paulo stood a little apart from the others. His face was set in its habitual scowl as he glared at the marine treading water at *Pegasus*'s stern.

Like Cari, Mac had discarded his fatigue shirt. He'd also stripped off his black cotton T-shirt. Water glistened on his bare shoulders and arms as he waited for Janice White to finish treating Cari's cut.

His lip curling, Paulo looked from the marine to Cari. When he whipped up his hands and signed a message, Janice White interpreted.

"Paulo says the major has big paws."

No kidding! Having experienced the movement of those paws over strategic points of her body just last night, Cari could vouch for their size.

"*Too* big, Paulo says."

For their current task, anyway. She and Mac had already conceded that point.

After determined hacking, they'd cut through the larger vines and cleared away most of the obstruction. Now they were down to the small, fibrous tentacles caught in the threads of the engines. It was painstaking work, done under water in murky light with only the pencil-thin flashlights to guide them. Mac was now relegated to holding the light while Cari's smaller, more nimble fingers probed the sharp blades and screws. The *very* sharp blades and screws.

Another cut like this one and she'd start worrying about piranha being drawn by the blood. The hastily thrown together briefing she and Mac had received on Caribe's riverine conditions hadn't indicated any native man-eating species besides crocs, which the villagers were keeping a sharp eye out for. But then their pre-mission brief hadn't included the fact that the Whites were brother and sister, either. Cari wasn't particularly anxious to discover another gap in their intelligence.

A flash of hands to her left drew her gaze.

"Paulo says his fingers are smaller," Janice duly reported. "He wants to help."

Without waiting for a go-ahead, the boy reached into the pocket of his shorts and dug out a pocketknife. Flipping open the blade, he plunged into the river.

"No, wait!"

Cari's protest was lost in a loud splash. Paulo went under, bobbed up again a few yards away from the stern, and tossed his head to get the water out of his eyes. His mouth set, he paddled toward Mac and the half-submerged craft.

"He'll hurt himself," Cari said worriedly, trying to yank her hand free.

Dr. White kept it in a firm grasp. "The boy is remarkably handy with that knife. Perhaps he can help."

Turning a six-year-old armed with a rusty pocketknife loose on a multimillion-dollar test vehicle wasn't Cari's idea of smart. Mac obviously shared her concerns. As Paulo shot underwater, the marine kicked up his boot heels and went after him.

Her cut bandaged, Cari was at the bank ready to dive in when Mac popped back up. Paulo followed a moment later. Raising a fist, he displayed a long, stringlike trophy.

Mac acknowledged his accomplishment with a grin. Reaching over, he knuckled the boy on the head. "Good job, kid."

An answering grin split Paulo's face. It only lasted a moment or two, but for those moments a smug, happy child replaced the sullen boy.

"Want to give it another shot?"

Nodding, Paulo tossed the stringy vine into the swirling current, jackknifed, and disappeared under the surface once again. Mac up-ended, scissor-kicked and followed. Still worried that the boy would hurt himself and/or her craft, Cari dived in as well.

It took a dozen more dives before they cleared the twin propellers of all foreign objects. By then Mac's chest heaved and Cari had to pull in deep, ragged breaths each time they surfaced. Paulo, on the other hand, appeared to have a child's inexhaustible source of energy. Popping in and out of the water like a playful seal pup, he swam circles around Cari and Mac as they prepared to board *Pegasus*.

"Better wait on the bank," Mac advised his young helper. "We need you and everyone else to stay clear while we fire up the engines."

If they fired them up, Cari thought grimly. Praying she hadn't stripped the gears or bent the blades when she plowed through the net, she grabbed an edge of the open cockpit to haul herself up. Mac planted a hand on her rear and gave her an added boost.

"Thanks," she drawled, scrambling over the edge.

With a flex of water-slick muscles, he pulled himself up after her. He looked like a pirate rising out of the sea to board a captured vessel, Cari thought. Dark bristles shadowed his cheeks and chin. Water sluiced down his bare chest. His mottled green-and-black pants hung low on his hips. All he needed was a cutlass thrust through his belt to complete the image. Forcing her gaze from that expanse of naked chest, she settled into her seat.

''We'd better advise Captain Westfall that we're going to attempt to power up. Why don't you take care of that while I run the preignition checklist?''

''Will do.''

Cupping his hands, he called to Harry White to toss him his handheld radio. The instrument came sailing through the air. Moments later, Mac had a link to the navy captain.

They'd been providing Westfall periodic updates of their situation. He'd called in a Pavehawk helicopter as backup and was fully prepared to launch another expedition to extract both the Pegasus crew and their passengers. If she couldn't power up her craft, Cari thought, that's what it would come to.

Hating the thought of abandoning *Pegasus* deep in the Caribe jungle, she checked the gauge on the auxiliary power source. They had barely enough juice left for ignition. Once the engines were running, they could recharge the batteries and power up the navigational systems.

''Here goes,'' she muttered to Mac.

Her finger hovered over the auxiliary power switch for a moment before flicking it on. The gauge's needle shivered, whipped from red to green, danced back to yellow. When Cari pressed the switch to fire the starboard engine, the needle zinged into the red again.

"Come on, baby."

She lifted her thumb, pressed the switch again. The needle stayed glued to the red. Her stomach was tying itself into knots when the engine gave a low growl. Slowly, the props began to churn.

"Yes!"

The watchers on the bank sent up a round of shouts and cheers. Cari barely heard them as she quickly throttled the starboard engine to Neutral and hit the switch for the port side engine. The needle on the auxiliary power gauge jerked once, a pathetic little bob, then lay flat. But there was enough juice, *just* enough, to ignite the second engine.

The propellers began to turn, raising another chorus of whoops and cheers. This time Cari acknowledged them. Keeping a careful hand on the throttle, she waved wildly with the other. A wide grin split her face when she turned to Mac.

"Well, whaddya know! Looks like we might not have to leave *Pegasus* behind, after all."

"Looks like." His hazel eyes glinting, he keyed his radio. "Pegasus Base, this is Pegasus One. We've powered up both engines."

"That's good to hear, One."

Westfall didn't try to disguise his relief. This super-

McIver's wet, naked chest snuggled against her cheek?

"Next up are, uh, the defensive systems."

"Be good to get our eyes and ears back on line," he commented, pushing upright. "It makes me feel real goosey having only a couple sentries out there between us and the bad guys."

It made Cari feel goosey, too. Almost as goosey as the final squeeze Mac gave her shoulder before sliding open the panel to the rear compartment. The ripple effect of that casual caress went all the way down to her toes.

For Pete's sake! What the heck was going on with her? One short, hot session in Mac's arms and she approached total meltdown if he so much as looked sideways at her.

Exasperated, Cari shook her head. So much for her decision to back off and let the embers stirred by one man die before jumping into the fire with another. In two short days Major Russ McIver had crowded Commander Jerry Wharton right out of her head.

How long he would stay there after the Pegasus cadre disbanded had yet to be determined, Cari reminded herself.

Well, what would happen, would happen. Right now her focus had to be getting *Pegasus* ready to swim again.

secret vehicle was his baby, his project, but he would have ordered Cari and Mac to abandon it in a heartbeat if faced with undue risk. Thankfully, that hadn't proved to be the case. So far.

"The engineers indicate it'll take ninety minutes to fully recharge the batteries and power up all systems," the captain advised. "How's your fuel?"

Cari gave Mac a thumbs-up.

"We should have enough to bring us home," he relayed.

"We'll be standing by," Westfall replied tersely. "Just in case."

The whole Pegasus team would be standing with him, Cari knew. Jill. Doc. Kate. Dave Scott. She could count on any or all of them to charge to the rescue.

That's what separated the military from civilian institutions, she acknowledged silently. This unspoken bond, this brotherhood of arms. She'd become part of that brotherhood the first time she'd raised her hand and sworn to protect and defend. After all these years, the military was in her blood. Had she really thought she could give it up? Did she *have* to give it up to have a family?

Her heart said no, but the stubborn little voice of practicality inside her head wanted to know just how the heck she thought she could raise children and take off at a moment's notice on missions like this one.

Shoving that question aside to be addressed later, Cari concentrated on the task at hand—recharging *Pegasus*'s batteries.

"You'd better tell the Whites we'll be ready to depart in ninety minutes," she said to Mac. "I'll watch the power levels and bring up our onboard systems one by one."

Nodding, Mac made the transition from ship to shore. After a brief consultation, the Whites decided to shepherd their charges back to the village to gather their few belongings and down a quick meal. Mac lifted the bright, chattering Rosa to her customary riding place on Reverend White's shoulders. Janice White took Miguel's hand firmly in hers to lead him along the narrow jungle path. Paulo carried a younger child piggyback and got another knuckle-rub from Mac as he passed. The boy hunched his shoulders and shied away, but his scowl lacked some of its usual ferocity.

Since the show appeared to be pretty well over, the rest of the women and children trailed along after the Whites. Even the men brought their canoes to shore and made for the cluster of huts.

"We need to come up with a gift for the villagers," Mac said when he rejoined Cari in the open cockpit. "Something to thank them for their hospitality."

"I've been thinking about that, too. *Pegasus* is designed to carry troops or cargo pallets. There are sev-

eral rolls of cargo webbing stowed in the rear compartment. The webbing is super-lightweight nylon and almost indestructible. A roll of that stuff would make an excellent replacement for the fishing net we chewed up."

"So it would. Good thinking, Dunn. I'll dig a roll out of the hold." He clambered out of his seat, but paused as an amber light began to blink on the instrument panel. "Is that the Marine Navigational System?"

"It is!"

With a quick jab of relief, Cari watched the MNS display screen come to life. The dull gray of the screen faded and was replaced by a digitized map of Caribe. A long, squiggly line represented the Rio Verde. The amber dot, now a steady glow, indicated their current position.

Mac clapped a hand on her shoulder and gave it a squeeze. "Looks like we're back in business."

"Almost."

To Cari's consternation, the clean, sharp scent of river-washed male cut right through her elation at getting the navigational system up. Her concentration took another hit when Mac leaned over her shoulder to peer at the checklist in her lap.

"What's next?"

Oh, sure! Like she could read a checklist with

* * *

She had half of the systems powered up and was tapping her fingers impatiently on the checklist when Mac called from the rear compartment.

"Hey, Dunn!"

"What?"

"Thought you might want to know the environmental systems are fully operational. It's downright chilly back here."

"No kidding?"

The prospect of even a few minutes relief from the suffocating jungle heat was too tempting to resist. Cari checked the instrument panel, estimated it would take another twelve minutes for the hydraulic system to achieve maximum efficiency, and tossed the checklist onto the seat next to hers. Mere seconds later, she was leaning against the sliding door separating the cabin from the cockpit, bathed in blessedly cool air.

"Ahhhhh."

Mac flashed a grin. "Feels good, doesn't it?"

"*Good* doesn't begin to describe it."

She closed her eyes, letting the heat and suffocating humidity leach from her bones. The climate-controlled air felt so wonderful she didn't notice when her sopping BDU pants and T-shirt went from merely wet to downright clammy.

Mac did, however. "You've got goose bumps popping out up and down your arms."

She waved a careless hand. "What are a few goose bumps compared to such bliss?"

"My T-shirt's dry." Scooping up the wad of black cotton, he tossed it in her direction. "You're welcome to change into it."

It was more than just dry, Cari discovered after snagging the garment midair. It was soft and warm and carried the scent of sun. Not to mention a distinctive blend of raw masculinity that was all Mac.

Dropping it on the webbed seat, she dragged up the hem of her wet shirt. She'd bared two inches of midriff before she noticed that McIver had crossed his arms and propped his shoulders against the bulkhead.

"I take it you're just going to stand there and enjoy the show?"

His eyes glinted. "That's the plan."

"Hmm."

Pursing her lips, Cari debated whether to perform for her one-person audience. She certainly hadn't had any reservations last night. She'd come within a breath of stripping to her skin. Okay, she'd pretty well *ached* to shed every scrap of clothing she had on.

As hot and heavy as those moments had been, though, there was something infinitely more disconcerting about peeling off a wet T-shirt in the bright light of day, with Mac's very intent, very interested gaze aimed in her direction. Which was crazy, since that same wet T-shirt made it obvious she was wearing another garment under the cotton.

Crazy or not, Cari's skin prickled from more than the cool air as she raised her arms and dragged the damp, clingy cotton over her head. Common sense told her to grab Mac's shirt and pull it on. A perverse, wholly feminine instinct told her to take her time.

Casually, she tugged at the lower hem of her bra to adjust the wet spandex. The fabric stretched taut over the tips of her breasts, which had gone tight and stiff in reaction to the cool air. To Cari's intense satisfaction, Mac's breath left on a little hiss.

Shoving away from the bulkhead, he stepped over the roll of cargo netting he'd retrieved from the storage compartment. His voice held a rough edge but his touch was tender as he drew a knuckle down the slopes of her breasts.

"Do you have any idea how gorgeous you are?"

She hadn't looked into a mirror in going on thirty-six hours and would probably shriek when she did. She wasn't about to argue with the man, however.

"You aren't so bad yourself, big guy."

"You're just saying that because you've got a thing for buzz cuts and sidewalls."

Buzz cuts and sidewalls and little white squint lines at the corners of sexy hazel eyes, Cari admitted silently. Not to mention a strong, square chin and a set of pecs right out of *Bench Press Quarterly*. Tiny shivers rippled along the surface of her skin as his knuckle traced a path down the slope of her other breast.

After the frenzied urgency of last night, this slow, soft caress was incredibly arousing. She stood still under the whisper-light stroke as long as she could before giving in to the need to touch him.

Gliding her fingertips across his chest, she imprinted every sensation. The damp heat rising under her fingers. The smooth bulge of skin and muscle. The dusting of dark hair arrowing down to his waist. She kept her touch every bit as light as Mac's, yet her breath was soon coming as fast and rough as his.

She should have known touching wouldn't be enough—for either of them. Her pulse pounding, Cari tipped her head back and opened her mouth eagerly under his. One kiss and they'd picked up right where they'd left off last night. She clung to him, every nerve in her body singing.

The rush of blood was so swift and fast she almost missed the echo of a distant shout. Mac caught the sound, though. Jerking his head up, he listened intently for a moment before thrusting her away.

''Get dressed.''

She was already grabbing at the dry T-shirt. Yanking it over her head, she clambered into the open cockpit after Mac. The sight of two men paddling furiously downriver in their direction started a curl of dread in her stomach. Something had obviously alarmed the sentries.

It alarmed her, too, when they relayed their news using a mix of English, Spanish, and Caribe.

"Boat comes. Big boat. With gun."

The sentry held two fists waist high, as if gripping handles, and stuttered like a machine gun.

"Sounds like a patrol boat," Cari forced out through a suddenly dry throat.

"They come slow," the other fisherman put in. "Stop many times. Search bank."

"How far away?" Mac asked urgently.

"Three bends of river."

Cari drew a map in her head of the snaking Rio Verde and came up with a rough guesstimate.

"I make that a half hour. Maybe more if the boat is moving as slowly as they say."

Her mind racing, she weighed their options. They could abandon *Pegasus* and fade into the jungle with the Whites and the kids. Or they could make a run for it.

"How long before you can get us underway?" Mac snapped, breaking into her thoughts.

"We're barely halfway through the sequence of powering up the onboard systems."

"How long?"

Desperately, she drew on the months she'd spent

prepping for *Pegasus*'s water trials. "Ten minutes, if we stay on surface. Twenty, if we want to go below."

Mac didn't hesitate. He was as determined as Cari not to leave their craft behind.

"We'll go surface." Scooping up the roll of cargo webbing, he headed for the cockpit. "I'll get the Whites and the kids. I'll also see if I can convince our hosts to rig another fishnet, like fast. With any luck, they'll snag the patrol boat the same way they did *Pegasus* and buy us a little more time."

Chapter 7

Cari raced through the checklist and brought up only the absolute essential systems. The last to come alive was the Satellite Surveillance System, which picked up the infrared heat signature of a watercraft some miles upriver and displayed it in the form of a faint amber dot. The signal was weak due the satellite's inability to fully penetrate the dense jungle canopy, but strong enough to confirm the craft was in fact a patrol boat—heavily armed and moving slowly, but definitely heading in their direction.

Keeping one eye on that amber dot, Cari had the engines revving and *Pegasus* ready to shake free of the mooring lines when Mac came charging out of the jungle with Rosa on his shoulders. The two missionaries and the rest of the children scrambled after him. In their wake came most of the village.

While Mac handed the Whites and the kids aboard, the local men made for their canoes. Cari had time for only a few shouted words of thanks and a wild wave before Mac freed the mooring lines. As soon as he'd jumped into the cockpit, she closed the canopy, steered her craft out to midchannel and throttled up. To her infinite relief, the twin, rear-tilted engines gave a throaty roar. Their propellers cut into the water. With the delta-shaped wings acting like a hydrofoil, *Pegasus* raised his nose out of the water, sprayed a long silver arc behind him, and sped downriver.

Cari kept her eyes on the instruments and her hands fisted on the controls. "You'd better get on the horn and inform base of the situation. See if they can get the particulars on that patrol boat."

They could and did. Captain Westfall came back on the radio within moments with the information that rebels had seized the boat two days earlier from government forces, killing all aboard. He also confirmed that it was heavily armed.

"Be advised that we'll have a Pavehawk in the air within the next ten minutes," Westfall said tersely. "The chopper will be waiting for you when you exit the mouth of the river and fly cover while you cross the open sea."

That was welcome news. *Very* welcome news. A highly modified version of the army's Blackhawk helicopter, the Pavehawk had enough firepower to hold off a dozen patrol boats. Now all Cari had to do was get her craft and her passengers to the mouth of the Rio Verde.

Her heart in her throat, she put on as much speed as she dared given the river's sharp twists and turns. At the same time, she gauged the progress of the glowing amber dot trailing them.

Mac, too, kept his jaw locked and his eyes on the display screen. He gave a muttered curse when the patrol picked up speed and inched closer, an exclamation of relief when it suddenly stopped dead.

"Yes!"

Cari tore her gaze from the green river ahead to take a fix on the boat's location. "Looks like they're at about the same spot where we hit."

"Looks like."

"Think they're caught?"

"Either that or they spotted the cargo webbing and decided to stop and investigate."

"I hope the villagers don't take heat for helping us."

Mac shook his head. "They won't. The headman told me he and his people would melt into the jungle at the first sound of an engine. How far to the coast?"

Her glance dipped to the instruments. "Three miles

as the crow flies. Forever, the way the river snakes back on itself at every turn.''

''Just keep us heading in the right direction and… Hell!''

The terse expletive sent Cari's hope that they'd make a clean escape plunging straight to the river bottom. Her jaw tight, she watched the amber dot begin to move again.

''They must have cut through the webbing,'' Mac muttered. ''They're picking up speed.''

''I see.'' She dragged in a deep breath. ''Go back and make sure our passengers are strapped in. I'm going to open it up.''

The next twenty minutes were the longest of Cari's life. Her heart pounded out every second, every bend they rounded, every centimeter the patrol boat nudged closer. They were still a long, twisting half mile from the mouth of the river when Mac bit out a terse command.

''Pop the canopy.''

''What?''

''Throttle back and pop the canopy.''

She tore her gaze from the green-shrouded river and saw he'd snapped the ammo clip out of his assault rifle. He checked the rounds and shoved the clip back in before meeting her slicing frown.

"They're closing too fast," he said grimly. "I'll have to slow them down."

"Mac, no!"

"It's our only chance." He jerked his chin toward the rear compartment. "Those kids' only chance. I'll stir up a little rear-action diversion, then hotfoot it downriver. The Pavehawk can pick me up."

"I don't like this."

"Throttle back, Cari."

She shot a look at the amber dot, snarled a vicious curse, and pulled back on the controls. Mere seconds after the canopy lifted, Mac splashed into the river. She saw him go under, bob to the surface, kick for shore. Then she shoved the throttle forward and sent *Pegasus* racing around another bend.

Her chest squeezing, she divided her attention between the twisting waterway ahead and the small screen. The patrol boat was less than a hundred meters behind and coming on fast. When it took that last bend, its crew would have her in their gun sites.

"Okay, Mac. If you're gonna do it, you'll have to do it now."

She gripped the wheel, prepared to take evasive action, when the patrol boat swerved wildly, took a sharp turn, and doubled back.

The roar of her craft's engines swallowed all other sounds. Cari had no idea whether Mac had opened fire, couldn't tell if the rebels were returning it. Every instinct screamed at her to go back, to employ *Pegasus*'s not inconsiderable firepower as cover for Mac. Only the safety of the passengers she'd been sent in to rescue kept her on course.

By the time she rounded a final bend and caught a shimmer of blue far ahead, her jaw had locked tight. She'd also come to an unshakable decision. She was damned if she'd leave Mac to fight a rearguard action through a half mile of jungle.

The Pavehawk couldn't go in for him. The dense canopy was too thick for the chopper to penetrate. So Cari would transfer her passengers to the helo and go back herself. Snatching up her radio, she contacted the HH-60.

"This is Pegasus One. Be advised I'm approaching the mouth of the river. Request you set down on the beach immediately and prepare to receive passengers."

The reply was swift and unquestioning. "Roger, Pegasus One. Setting down now."

The river widened. Green water merged with indigo, eddied into sapphire. Tangled vines and giant ferns gave way to a fringe of palms and a snowy-white beach. *Pegasus* shot out of the darkness of the jungle into a light so dazzling Cari had to throw up an arm to shield her eyes.

She spotted the chopper mere yards away, its huge blades churning up a vortex of sand as it settled onto the beach. Spinning the wheel, she cut through the rolling surf, hit the switch to open the belly and lower the wide-track wheels. A moment later, *Pegasus* churned to a stop just outside the reach of the chopper's whirling blades.

The Pavehawk's side hatch opened. A half-dozen uniformed figures jumped out and ducked under the whirling blades. They included, Cari saw with a jolt of surprise, most of the Pegasus cadre.

There was no mistaking Kate Hargrave's flaming auburn hair or Jill Bradshaw's distinctive black armband with the initials ''MP'' emblazoned in big yellow letters. Doc Richardson charged across the sand behind the two women with Dave Scott at his heels. Cari caught a glimpse of Captain Westfall's tall, spare figure as she popped her seat harness and scrambled into the rear compartment.

''We've got a chopper all ready to ferry you and the children out of Caribe,'' she informed the anxious Whites. ''Let's get you transferred.''

The moment Cari opened the hatch, her friends were all there to help with the transfer. Kate took little Tomas. Doc Richardson hefted a wide-eyed Rosa in his arms. Dave Scott hustled Paulo to the Pavehawk, where the boy dug in his heels and refused to climb aboard. His chin set at a stubborn angle, he signed an urgent demand.

"He wants to know where the major is," a harried Janice White interpreted.

"Tell him the major will rejoin him at the base," Dave said.

"He's mute, not deaf," Cari explained as she passed one of the youngsters to the Pavehawk's load-master. "Dr. White, you'd better take a head count."

Nodding, the missionary poked her head inside the chopper and conducted a swift inventory. "...seven, eight, nine with Paulo here. We're all here."

"See you back at base."

Cari spun away, her mind already on the journey back up river. An insistent tug on her fatigue shirt brought her back around.

"Paulo, I've got to go!"

The boy hung on to her fiercely with one hand while he dug his other into the pocket of his shorts. When he produced his rusted pocketknife, Cari looked at him blankly.

"You want me to take your knife?"

Jerking his chin in a quick affirmative, he shoved it into her hand and signed another urgent message.

"He says you might need it," Janice White trans-lated. "To cut the major's ropes if the rebels have him."

Her throat tight, Cari closed her fingers over the small implement. If the rebels had taken Mac alive, she'd need more than a pocketknife to free him. But the fact that this child was willing to part with his only possession to aid in that effort made her throat go tight.

"Thank you," she said gruffly. "I'll return it to you when we get back to base."

Clutching the knife in a tight fist, she raced back to *Pegasus*. The rest of the cadre was already aboard. Jill. Kate. Doc. Dave. Even Sam Westfall. The captain wasn't about to leave one of his own behind. With Dave Scott strapped into the copilot's seat beside her, Cari took the multimillion-dollar craft back up the river.

The rebels hadn't captured Mac. As the tense recovery team discovered when *Pegasus* careened around the second bend in the river, he was still fighting a fierce rearguard action.

Cari's heart leaped into her throat when she spotted tracers from the patrol boat's bow-mounted machine arc from ship to shore. Vegetation flew into the air, shredded by the vicious stream of bullets.

"They're hunting someone," Dave Scott bit out as he searched the bank with high-powered goggles. "Has to be Russ."

Sure enough, an answering stream of gunfire ripped through the ferns lining the bank some distance ahead of the patrol boat. The short burst cut in front of its prow and threw up a high curtain of water. The shielding spray gave Cari the few precious seconds she needed to activate *Pegasus*'s offensive fire systems.

She ached to launch a missile. Just one! The sophisticated, laser-guided rocket would blow the patrol boat out of the water. Unfortunately, their orders were to get in and out of Caribe without engaging either government or rebel troops unless under extreme duress. The fact that Mac had directed his fire in front of the boat's prow indicated he, too, was trying to adhere to the rules of engagement by creating a diversion and not taking out the boat or its crew.

Good thing *Pegasus* came equipped with a few surprises besides precision-guided missiles. Keying her mike, Cari barked out an update for the folks in the rear compartment.

"We have the patrol boat in sight. Hang tight. I'm going to launch a smoker."

Before the words were out of her mouth, she jammed her thumb on the button. The small, cylindrical emergency position marker whizzed through the air, hit river just yards from the patrol boat and exploded in a burst of orange smoke. Thick orange smoke. Dense enough to be seen by rescue craft a mile away. On an *open* sea, that was.

But the Rio Verde flowed through a green tunnel of jungle. Branches and vines crisscrossed above it to form an arching roof. Trapped, the smoke spread across the river like a noxious cloud. Even before Cari launched the second capsule, a thick orange haze had completely enveloped the patrol boat.

"That'll have their eyes watering," Dave said with grim satisfaction. "Take us over closer to the bank and I'll…"

The pilot broke off. Reaching up to adjust his goggles, he strained against his shoulder harness.

"What?" Cari demanded. "What do you see?"

"Movement along the riverbank."

"Is it Mac?"

"Hang on. I can't… Oh, crap!"

"What?" she demanded again, her whole body twisted into a mass of tension.

"It's Mac," Dave confirmed tersely. "And he's got what looks like half the patrol boat's crew on his ass."

Cari jerked on the wheel, brought *Pegasus* around, aimed for the bank. She caught a flash of gunfire, saw the ferns part as Mac dived through them. He cut the water cleanly and went under. She didn't wait for him to surface before launching her last smoker. It went into the bank and exploded in a blossom of bright orange.

"Obstacle ahead!"

Dave's warning came at exactly the same moment the sonar gave off a loud, warning buzz. Cursing under her breath, Cari jerked the wheel again and nar-

rowly avoided a collision with a half-sunken tree
trunk. She was forced to angle away from the obstacle
and wait while Mac fought the current with a strong,
slicing stroke.

She felt a presence at her shoulder, knew Captain
Westfall had crowded into the cockpit.

"The smoke's thinning," Dave advised grimly, his
hand hovering over the missile system activation.
"Do you want me to arm and lock?"

As captain of the vessel, Cari had the conn, the
stick, the overall responsibility for the operation.
She'd followed the rules of engagement to this point,
had avoided inflicting casualties on either the government forces or the rebels. If the patrol boat started
shooting, however, she'd damn well shoot back.

"Arm and lock," she ordered crisply. "Don't fire
until I give the word."

Behind her, Westfall was silent. Cari gave no
thought to the fact that he outranked her, that a bun-
gled operation could mean the end of his career as
well as her own. Another swift check of the instruments confirmed *Pegasus* rode high enough in the
water to open the side hatch without flooding the rear
compartment.

"Stand by!" she instructed those in the back via
the intercom. "I'm opening the hatch."

"It's up," Kate confirmed at moment later. "I'm
ready with the Survivor Retrieval System."

"Deploy SRS," Cari instructed tersely.

The SRS could shoot a lifesaving line across a mile of open sea. In this case, though, a mile of tough nylon rope presented almost as much of a problem as a solution. Kate could overshoot, tangle the rope in the trees, force them to hack free again.

She should have known Kate could handle it. All those years aboard the National Oceanic and Atmospheric Administration's hurricane hunter aircraft had taught her a thing or two about retrieval systems. She aimed for a skinny patch of sky and sent the weighted lead in a high, smooth arc. It shot up, came down again, and landed just a few feet behind Mac. The coils of lightweight rope trailing after the lead plopped down into the water all around him.

He cut his stroke, snatched at the rope, and gave a thumbs-up. Before they could reel him in, little waterspouts began to rise all around him. Cari whipped her glance to the bank, saw a figure in ragged BDUs with an automatic rifle to his shoulder stagger out of the orange pall.

"Mac's taking fire." Jill Bradshaw's voice came over the intercom, cold and deadly. "I'm in position to return it."

"Go!"

Jill let loose with a short, vicious barrage. A military cop and an expert marksman, she sent the scruffy rebel scrambling back into the orange cloud. But not before he got off a final burst.

Cari saw Mac jerk, rise out of the water a few inches, sink back under the surface.

No!

The silent scream ripped through her. Dying inside, she waited one heartbeat. Two.

Mac didn't reappear. But the nylon rope he'd been grasping did. The line curled on the river's surface, writhing like a thin, tensile snake. She keyed her mike, had opened her mouth to order Dave to take the throttles, when someone dived through the open hatch.

Sam Westfall, she saw when he broke surface and began cutting toward the spot where Mac had disappeared. The navy officer went under, came back up after long, heart-shattering moments dragging a limp form. Hooking an elbow under Mac's chin, he swam him back to *Pegasus*.

To Cari's horror, Westfall's boots churned up a sickening wake. Mac's blood was tinting the Verde from green to red. Praying as she'd never prayed before, she gripped the wheel so hard her short, trimmed nails splintered on the hard composite.

"They're aboard!" Kate relayed mere seconds later. "Get us out of here."

Slamming a fist down to close the hatch, Cari whipped the wheel around with one hand and shoved the throttle forward with the other. *Pegasus* leaped forward.

Doc Richardson was back there, she reminded herself fiercely as she steered her craft downriver. He'd stop the bleeding. Keep Mac alive. He would. He *would!*

She repeated the mantra over and over, aching to go to Mac, chained to her seat by her responsibilities as commander. Only after she'd rounded the last bend and spotted a patch of blue did she prepare to pass the baton.

"Open sky ahead, Dave."

The pilot nodded. "I'm ready. As soon as we clear these trees, I'll take us airborne."

Chapter 8

The next twenty minutes would remain forever seared in Cari's mind.

When she turned the controls over to Dave and ducked back into the rear compartment, she found Mac lying facedown on the deck in a pool of bright red blood. Cody Richardson was bent over him. He'd started an IV and had cut away Mac's shirt to expose the bullet hole in his right shoulder. Kate held the IV pack aloft, while a drenched Captain Westfall steadied himself with a hand against the bulkhead and watched every move through narrowed, steel-gray eyes.

Jill knelt on Mac's other side. As a cop, she'd seen

her share of gunshot wounds. She'd also received training in emergency medical procedures for first responders. The grim cast to her face told Cari this particular gunshot wound was bad. Very bad.

Captain Westfall confirmed that when Cari moved to his side. "Doc Richardson thinks the bullet nicked Mac's subclavian artery," he told her. "It's the main artery from the heart to the upper extremities. Doc's got to repair it fast, before Mac bleeds out."

A hard, bruising knot formed in Cari's throat. She couldn't swallow, couldn't breathe as Cody ripped open a small kit containing surgical instruments wrapped in sterile plastic. The doc was just reaching out a hand covered in a blood-drenched rubber glove when the deck shuddered under them and the kit danced out of his reach.

Swiftly, Cari retrieved it and went down on one knee beside him. "Dave's switching us to airborne mode. The next few minutes could get bumpy. Can you wait until he has us in the air?"

"No."

The terse reply stabbed into her with the vicious thrust of a bayonet. Cody didn't so much as spare her a glance.

"Every second counts right now. Get back in the cockpit and hold us as steady as you can."

Spurred by the order and a slicing fear that cut right through her, Cari sprang to her feet. She dropped into

her seat and cut Dave off just as he was about to tilt
the engines upward.

"Delay that. We're holding in this position until
Doc gives us the green light. He's…" She forced
herself to speak around that aching knot in her throat.
"He's got to repair one of Mac's arteries or he might
bleed to death."

"Hell!"

Dave's strong, tanned face set into rock-hard lines.
He'd come late to the Pegasus cadre, brought in on
short notice after the original air force representative
had suffered a heart attack. As a result, he'd been
forced to muscle his way inside the tight clique the
other officers had already formed. In the process, he'd
also bowled the vivacious Kate Hargrave right off her
feet. He was part of the team now—heart and soul.
The possibility they might lose one of their own hit
him almost as hard as it did Cari.

He recovered swiftly. He had no choice. He'd faced
that grim possibility before, as had every other member of the Pegasus cadre. It came with wearing the
uniform of their country.

Mouth tight, Cari eyed the swirling currents ahead.
They were drifting fast toward the point where the
river emptied into the lagoon. To keep the craft
steady, they'd have to fight both the drag of the sea
and the force of the waves rolling in from the outer
reef. The maneuver would require every bit of Cari's

seamanship and then some. Setting her jaw, she forced herself to concentrate on the task at hand.

"I'll take the controls. You keep an eye on the radar screen. If those bastards in the patrol boat come within range," she promised savagely, "they're gonna suck in something other than orange smoke this time."

Cari forgot all about the patrol boat when Captain Westfall came forward long, agonizing moments later.

"Doc's stopped the hemorrhaging."

She slumped back against her seat. Closing her eyes, she sent a silent prayer of thanks winging upward. Westfall's next words brought her jerking upright again.

"Mac's not out of the woods yet. He's lost a lot of blood and the bullet did some serious damage to tissue and bone. We need to get him to a first-class medical facility, fast."

That let out the forward operating base in Nicaragua, Cari realized with a sick feeling in her stomach. Their medical facility consisted of two tents.

"We'll have to head back to Corpus," she said tightly.

"Have you got enough fuel to take us in?"

"No," Dave answered after a quick check of the

gauges, ''but we can request a tanker to pass us some gas enroute.''

''Do it.''

The terse command underscored the continuing urgency of the situation. Cari didn't need a second order.

''Tell everyone in the back to buckle up,'' she bit out, then tacked on a belated, ''sir.''

Since Dave had piloted *Pegasus* on its first flight, she acted as copilot while he raced through the procedures to compete the transition from sea to air mode. Mere minutes later, he tilted the engines upright. Moments more, and *Pegasus* lifted straight up into a hover. The steamy green of the jungle was below, an endless marriage of turquoise sea and azure sky ahead. Then Dave brought the craft's nose down, angled the engines again and applied full power. Caribe fell away behind them.

Cari got on the mike before they'd cleared the reef ringing the island. The USAF Coordination Center agreed to scramble a KC-135 out of Barksdale AFB, Louisiana. The tanker would hook up with them over the Gulf and supply both *Pegasus* and the Pavehawk helicopter with fuel, which indicated it would tail them back to Corpus Christi.

Her next hook-up was to the Operations Center at

the Corpus Christi Naval Air Station. The controller promised to have an ambulance waiting when *Pegasus* touched down.

With its faster speed, *Pegasus* beat the Pavehawk back to Corpus by several hours.

The promised ambulance was waiting to whisk Doc and Mac to the Naval Hospital. With the wail of the siren knifing into her heart, Cari helped Dave shut down *Pegasus*. Once the multimillion-dollar vehicle was secure, Captain Westfall disappeared into the Mobile Control Center to make a report of the mission to his superiors via secure comm. Cari didn't stick around to provide additional input. She and Dave and the rest of the team raced to the hospital.

Mac had already been wheeled into the operating room. He was still there when the Whites and their charges arrived at the surgical waiting room where the Pegasus crew was camped out. The missionaries looked harried, the children a little frightened, and the U.S. Customs Agent accompanying them distinctly disapproving.

While Dave, Jill and Kate helped settle the kids in front of the TV with soft drinks and candy bars from a nearby vending machine, the customs agent confronted Cari.

"I understand you made the decision to bring these children out of Caribe."

"That's correct."

"I also understand they have no papers or emigration documents of any sort."

"We left Caribe in something of a hurry," she replied with considerable understatement.

The agent pursed his lips. He was a short, pudgy man with damp stains ringing the armpits of his white uniform shirt and a plastic nameplate that gave his name as Scroggins.

"I'll have to notify the Immigration and Naturalization Service," he said with a shake of his head. "INS is responsible for minors arriving in the States unaccompanied by relatives or legal guardians."

"I've told you," Janice White snapped. "Reverend White and I are their ex officio guardians. At least until we can contact the families who've agreed to take them in."

"But you have no papers granting you that authority."

"We have copies of our applications," Harry White put in earnestly. "To the Caribe authorities, the U.S. government, and our church sponsors."

"Applications aren't good enough. Sorry, folks. My hands are tied. I have to notify the INS. They'll take the kids into administrative custody and hold them until their status is resolved."

Cari's lips curled back. She leaned forward, got two inches from the man's nose. "The hell they will!"

Startled, Scroggins took an involuntary step back. "Hey, Lieutenant, I'm just doing my job."

She'd seen this coming, had witnessed too many heartbroken refugees being taken into custody for deportation back to the very country they'd risked their lives to escape. She'd also had a good idea of the bureaucratic battle the Whites would face once they landed in the States. But that was before Mac had taken a bullet trying to get these kids to safety. Before Doc had worked feverishly to keep the marine from bleeding to death. Before the aching fear that he wouldn't make it had carved a permanent hole in Cari's gut.

Captain Westfall must have sensed she was about to tell the customs rep what he could do with his job. He cut in smoothly, wielding his authority like a blade.

"We appreciate that you have certain responsibilities, Agent Scroggins. For your information, I concurred with Lieutenant Dunn's decision to transport these children out of Caribe. Please inform the INS representative to contact me personally on this matter."

The customs official wilted under the captain's cool stare. "Yes, sir. I'll do that."

Cari bit her lip. Westfall *had* concurred with her decision—but only after the fact. And after some rather choice words on the subject of sidestepping in-

ternational law. She didn't want him to take the heat
for her actions, but training and respect for rank went
bone deep. Junior officers didn't contradict their superiors in public. Particularly when said superior sent
her a look that suggested she'd be smart at this point
to keep her mouth shut.

"Thanks," Janice White said when Scroggins had
scurried off to make his call to the INS. Shagging a
hand through her short, blond crop, she gave the captain a thorough once-over. They'd met only briefly
during the transfer from *Pegasus* to the Pavehawk.
Evidently the captain passed inspection.

"Harry and I better get busy and make some calls.
Hopefully, we can reach each of the families who've
applied to adopt the children before the INS shows
up."

"Why don't I line you up with some temporary
quarters here on base?" Westfall suggested. "You
can get the kids fed and cleaned up, then make your
calls."

"Fed and cleaned up would be wonderful."

"Give me a list of what you need for them in the
way of clothes, food and games or books. I'll see it's
taken care of."

"It could be a long list."

The captain gave her one of his rare, flinty smiles.
"I can handle it."

She tipped her head and measured him with those cool green eyes. "Yes, I imagine you can."

His gaze followed her as she moved to the small group clustered around the Reverend White.

"They make quite a pair."

"Yes, they do. Harry told me she gave up a very lucrative private practice to assist him in Caribe. He thinks the world of his sister."

"Sister?"

The captain's glance lasered back to Cari. Despite the weight of her worry over Mac, she formed the distinct impression that she'd snared Westfall's full attention with that bit of information.

"Sister," she confirmed. "Our intel on the Whites was a little incomplete."

"Hmm."

With that noncommittal reply, the captain walked to the wall phone and requested a connection to the naval air station C.O. He was back a few minutes later with word that the Whites and their charges could stay at the Transient Lodging Facility until they'd squared matters with the INS.

"I've got a car outside," he told the missionaries. "I'll drive you over."

The arrangements suited everyone but Paulo. For a child with no larynx, he'd developed rather expressive means of communicating. In this instance, it was by crossing his arms, pushing out his lower lip and refusing to vacate the chair he was occupying.

"It could be several hours yet," Janice White told him patiently.

The lip stayed pushed.

"Lieutenant Dunn will let us know the moment Major McIver is out of surgery," Reverend White chimed in, throwing Cari a look of silent appeal. "Won't you?"

"Yes, of course."

Obviously unconvinced, Paulo uncrossed his thin arms and signed an urgent message. Janice White interpreted.

"He says he wants to stay here. Harry, can you manage the others? I'll wait with Paulo."

"There's no need for that," Kate Hargrave countered. Smiling, she hooked a stray tendril of gleaming auburn behind her left ear. "There are enough of us here to keep an eye on him."

Janice eyed the weather scientist with a combination of relief and doubt. "Are you sure? It's difficult to understand him if you don't sign."

"One of my nephews is deaf. I'm not real fast at speaking, but I can read the basics like French fries, cheeseburgers and the latest X Box video game titles."

"All right then."

Turning to the boy, Janice issued some instructions

in Caribe. He signaled his agreement with a quick nod. Satisfied, Janice started to push to her feet. A tug on her baggy tan slacks stopped her in half crouch. Paulo looked from her to Cari and flashed a series of hand signals.

"He wants to know if you still have his knife," the missionary related.

"What? Oh, yes. I do."

It took some digging, but she found it in one of the side pockets of her BDU pants. She held it out, palm up, and the boy snatched it up.

In the midst of her misery over Mac, Cari had room for a new ache. That rusted bit of steel was the kid's most precious possession. He'd offered it to her back in Caribe to aid Mac. Now, he clutched it in a tight, grubby fist while he kept vigil with her.

Their wait lasted another agonizing forty minutes.

The INS agent came, took statements and left again to find the Whites. She was a calm, precise type who came across as considerably more sympathetic to the children's plight than Agent Scroggins had. Her wry admission that the Immigration and Naturalization Service had recently been slapped with a class-action suit on behalf of the more than eight thousand children they held in detention, most of whom couldn't speak English and had no inkling of their rights, might have had something to do with her promise to grease the skids if possible.

After that there was nothing to do but pace the hall. Cari did take one side trip to the ladies' room, only to stare blankly at the straggle-haired harridan in the mirror. Her BDUs showed the effects of a night spent stretched out on a straw mat and repeated dunkings in the Rio Verde. Her eyes looked haunted. Makeup was only a distant memory.

Impatiently, she splashed cold water on her cheeks and tugged a comb borrowed from Kate through her tangles. A quick twist and a plastic clip anchored the dark brown mass on top of her head. She was back, wearing a path in tile so bright and clean it still stank of pine-scented antiseptic, when Doc Richardson pushed through the double doors leading from the surgical unit.

He caught the instant attention of everyone in the waiting room, and the look on his face started Cari's heart pumping pure terror. She froze, unable to move, to think, to breathe, while he walked the length of the corridor.

Paulo, too, saw the physician's approach. Wiggling out of his chair, he moved to Cari's side and slid his hand into hers. They stood side by side, their fingers locked in a bone-crunching grip, until Doc sliced through their paralyzing tension.

"He's going to make it."

Cari's breath left on a long whoosh. The small hand gripping hers squeezed tighter in a reflex of silent, heartfelt relief. Cody gave the group a few moments to savor the good news before delivering the rest of his report.

"The bullet tore through Mac's muscle and pulverized his right shoulder. The surgeons here patched him up as best they could, but he's looking at eventual replacement of the entire joint."

Cari swallowed hard. "Can they do that? Replace an entire shoulder?"

"The procedure isn't as simple or as common as a hip or knee replacement, but it's doable."

Doc scraped a palm across his jaw. Like the rest of the Pegasus team, he was showing the effects of the past few days. Dark bristles shadowed his cheeks and chin. His eyes were rimmed with red.

"I'm not real up on the stats for that particular orthopedic procedure," he said quietly. "I do know patients have a fairly high chance of recovering at least partial use of their arms."

Cari was so relieved it took a moment or two for the full import of that "partial" to sink in. They were talking about all-or-nothing, you're-in-or-you're-out Russ McIver here. The man who'd found not only a profession, but a home in the United States Marine Corps.

Something perilously close to pity fluttered deep in

the pit of her stomach. She'd just begun to discover the man behind the marine. Had shared only a few shattering kisses. Yet she knew with gut-wrenching certainty Mac wouldn't settle for "partial" use of anything. He'd go for one hundred percent no matter how long it took or how much pain he endured in the process.

"Is he conscious?" she asked Doc. "Can we see him?"

"They're moving him out of Recovery into a room as we speak. I'll take you to him."

Chapter 9

The room was typical of military hospitals. Walls painted in what was probably meant as a soothing cream and tan color scheme. Two beds, only one of them occupied. Floors so clean Cari's boot-soles squeaked when she entered.

Paulo still gripped her hand. The boy's face settled into its habitual scowl as he viewed the figure stretched out in the bed. Mac lay propped over toward his good side, with mounds of pillows at his back. The bandages swathing his injured shoulder showed snowy-white against his tan.

Doc Richardson ran an assessing eye over the patient before dragging him from his drugged stupor.

"Wake up, McIver. You've got people here who want to say hello."

Mac's right eyebrow inched up. Slowly, one lid lifted. The dilated pupil indicated anesthetic was still swimming through his veins, but he seemed to recognize at least one face in the crowd.

"Ca...ri."

She loosened her death grip on the boy's fingers. Dropping into the chair beside the bed, she snaked a wrist through the bed rails and found Mac's good hand. A smile trembled on her lips.

"You gave us a helluva scare, big guy."

"Did...I?" He blinked a few times, obviously struggling to focus. "What...happened?"

"You took a bullet in your right shoulder."

He scrunched his forehead. "The...kids?"

"They're okay. The Pavehawk brought them into Corpus a few hours behind us. In fact..."

Without letting go of Mac, she hooked her elbow in the air and motioned for Paulo to duck under it. He came up inside the circle of her arm, mere inches from Mac's face. Somehow the wounded marine summoned enough strength to arrange his still-slack features into a lopsided grin.

"Hey, pal. You...made...it."

Paulo responded with a series of quick, flashing hand signals, which Kate took a stab at interpreting. "He says we should have taken him with us when we went back for you. He wouldn't have let you get shot.''

"Next...time, kid."

The haze in Mac's eyes was slowly dissipating. Pain slipped in to take its place. Cari noted the crease that formed between his brows, the pinched look at the corners of his mouth. Doc Richardson picked up on the same signs.

"Feeling that shoulder, are you?"

Mac responded with a grunt.

"I'll get the nurse to administer your pain medication."

Doc made for the exit just as Captain Westfall returned from seeing the Whites and the other children settled in temporary quarters. The captain's BDUs showed the aftereffects of his dive into the Rio Verde and dark bristles shadowed his cheeks and chin. Yet when he entered, he carried with him the charged atmosphere and aura of command Cari had come to associate with the man. The usual flint was gone from his eyes when he stood beside Mac's bed, though.

"Good to see you awake, McIver."

"Good to...*be* awake, sir."

"You and Lieutenant Dunn did one fine job getting the Whites and those kids out of Caribe."

"Let's hope the INS agrees," Cari muttered.

"Prob...lem?"

She lifted her shoulders. "Pretty much the bureau-cratic B.S. we expected. Nothing we can't handle."

She could tell from his expression he didn't quite buy the breezy explanation but was too weak to de-mand details. What he needed at this point, Cody Richardson suggested when the nurse arrived with his pain medication, was rest. Lots of it.

Cari hated leaving Mac like this, weak and hurting. Fact of the matter was, she hated leaving him at all.

"He'll be okay."

At Cody's quiet assurance, Cari untangled her fin-gers from Mac's grip and eased her hand between the bed-rail bars. "I'll come back later," she told him. "After I've washed off the stink from the Rio Verde."

He managed a nod that led to a wince, followed by a fierce scowl reminiscent of Paulo at his most belligerent. Cari didn't envy the nurse waiting to dope him up. Something told her Mac wasn't going to make the best patient. She started to push out of the chair, was startled when he brought his good arm over the rail and snagged the lapels of her shirt.

"Good...job, Dunn."

"Back at you, McIver."

Pain carved a deep furrow between his brows, but he flexed his bicep and tugged her down.

"Mac, what...?"

That's all she got out before he dragged her down

the last inch or so and covered her mouth with his. The kiss didn't compare to his previous efforts in either skill or duration, but it was enough to stop Cari's breath in her throat.

"La...ter," Mac muttered, releasing her shirt.

"Later," she agreed softly.

Levering upward, she turned to face a solid wall of spectators. Kate wore a gleeful expression. Jill looked smug. Cody and Dave were grinning. Captain Westfall maintained a noncommittal air, but Cari noted he didn't look at all surprised by the fact that two of his subordinates seemed to have developed a close sense of teamwork on this mission. A *very* close sense of teamwork.

Cari knew she was in for a grilling later, after they'd finished the post-mission debrief. Hopefully she'd have an answer ready by then that would satisfy the lively curiosity dancing in her friends' eyes.

Thankfully, Kate and Jill waited until the team had cleaned up and finished the grueling four-hour debrief to demand an explanation. The two women rapped on the door to Cari's room in the naval air station's visiting officers' quarters just as she was getting ready to head back to the hospital. After months of sharing a cramped modular unit in New Mexico, all three were enjoying the privacy and space afforded by their separate quarters. Privacy only went so far, though, as Kate proved when she aimed a finger square at Cari's chest and marched her back into the sitting room.

"Okay, girl. We want details."

Like Cari, Kate had changed out of her uniform. The weather officer's jeans and fuzzy red knit tank top clung to her lush curves. Jill, too, wore jeans. Hers were paired with a crisp white blouse and black leather belt that cinched her slim waist. Mirroring Kate's avid curiosity, the cop plopped down in the sitting room's only comfortable chair.

"What the heck happened down there in the jungle between you and Mac?"

"We took *Pegasus* in," Cari replied with deliberately provocative brevity. "Brought the Whites and the kids out. Ironed out a few of our, ah, differences."

Kate gave a huff of derision. "Nice try, Dunn. Back up and expand on the ironing part."

Shoving her hands in the front pockets of her jeans, Cari hunched her shoulders. "I thought it was just the adrenaline," she admitted. "The first time Mac kissed me, we were both strung tight as anchor cables."

"The *first* time," Kate echoed. Waggling her brows, she shot Jill a knowing look. "Ha! I told you."

"Okay, okay." The blonde threw up her hands in good-natured defeat. "You win."

"I bet her a dinner of char-grilled red snapper that

hospital smooch wasn't the first time you'd locked lips with our resident leatherneck,'' Kate explained with smug satisfaction.

"Jill should have known better than to bet with you," Cari said, laughing.

Kate possessed unerring instincts, a nose for fine nuances and an intelligence network that rivaled the CIA's. She'd picked up on Jill's attraction to Cody long before the rest of the team had a clue about it. The scientist had also ignited a blaze of her own with tall, tanned Dave Scott, but she made it clear she hadn't come to talk about anyone but Cari and Mac.

"The first time you kissed you were both strung tight," she prompted, hitching a hip on the arm of the sofa. "And the second time?"

"I was strung pretty tight then, too," Cari confessed. "So tight I came close to forgetting that I was under orders and on a mission."

Kate sobered instantly. Fooling around was one thing. Fooling around to the point where it jeopardized a crew or an operation was an entirely different matter.

"But you didn't forget."

"No, I didn't. It was touch and go there for a while, though."

Looking back, Cari couldn't believe how ferociously she'd ached to drag Mac down to the spongy earth. Even now her nipples tightened at the memory of his hands and teeth and tongue working their magic on her body.

"What about Jerry?"

Jill's question sliced through the haze of sensual memories. Wrenched back to the present, Cari grimaced.

"I ended things with Jerry before I left for Caribe. By e-mail, I'm embarrassed to admit."

"Why are you embarrassed? Didn't he propose electronically?"

"Yes, but…"

"Hey, it wasn't like you had time for anything else," Kate pointed out. Curiosity brimmed in her green eyes. "How did Commander Wharton take his marching orders?"

"I don't know. I haven't checked my e-mail since I got back."

She didn't intend to, either, until she got back from the hospital. There wasn't room in her head for anyone else but Mac right now.

Kate was like a dog with a juicy bone. She wouldn't let go. "Okay, so you dumped Jerry and almost got it on with Mac. Where do you and our macho marine go from here?"

Cari had already asked herself that question. Several times. She still hadn't come up with an answer. Snagging her purse, she hooked the strap over her shoulder.

"*I'm* going back to the hospital."

Her two friends scrambled to their feet. "We'll go with you."

The entire test cadre popped into Mac's room at various times that evening, but the pain medication had knocked him out. He slept through their visits and straight through the night, the charge nurse reported to Cari the next afternoon. She also confirmed Cari's suspicion that Mac would make a less than optimal patient.

"He insisted on going to the head under his own steam this morning," the navy nurse drawled. "Would have fallen flat on his face if we hadn't rushed in and caught him."

Her glance went to her patient, now attempting one-handed spins in his wheelchair. He was surrounded by the giggling swarm of youngsters who'd come to visit him.

"Typical marine," the nurse murmured with a mixture of exasperation, affection and admiration. "I expect we'll have to tie him down to get him to rest."

"I expect you will."

She moved off, and Cari joined Janice White at the edge of the small crowd surrounding Mac.

"Good morning, Doc."

"'Morning, Caroline." Smiling, she took in Cari's freshly shampooed hair, dusting of makeup and sharply pressed khakis. "I see you washed away the Rio Verde."

"So did you."

The missionary had shed her jungle grunginess and taken on a whole new aura. In a slim black skirt, strappy sandals and sleeveless pink top that brought out the strawberry highlights in her blond hair, she looked cool and competent and years younger than Cari had thought her.

The kids had undergone the same transformation, she saw. Gone were the ragged shorts and hand-me-down shirts. Rosa beamed amid the ruffles and frills of a Barbie-doll blue dress. Little Tomas couldn't see his spiffy high-top sneakers but obviously delighted in the tinkling tune they emitted. He stood with legs widespread, lifting first one foot, then the other, and added a musical beat to the proceedings. Paulo, Cari saw with a smile, sported a brand-new Spider-Man T-shirt. This one was done in Day-Glo colors that lit up the hospital corridor in electric red and blue.

"When did you find time to take the kids shopping?"

"Sam came by last night and hauled us all to the local mall."

Sam, was it? Cari swallowed a grin. Captain Westfall certainly hadn't wasted any time making good on his offer of aid and assistance.

Her inclination to smile fled as little Rosa clambered into Mac's lap, however. The girl's malformed spine made the maneuver difficult and she accidentally knocked against the arm strapped tight against Mac's chest. His jaw went rigid, but he waved Janice back when she would have retrieved the girl.

"She's okay."

He relaxed enough to give Cari a crooked grin. "Hi, Lieutenant."

"Hi yourself."

"Want a ride after I wheel Rosa down the corridor a few times?"

"I'll think about it."

"Don't trust my driving, huh? And here I trusted you to steer me across an open ocean."

"*Pegasus* comes better equipped. With navigational aids," she added hastily when he sent her a wicked look.

Beside her, Janice White choked back a laugh. The two women watched him sail down the corridor with Rosa planted firmly in his lap.

"How are you doing with INS?" Cari asked over Rosa's high-pitched squeals.

"Harry's still battling with them. We spent an hour on the phone last night contacting the families who've applied to adopt the children. We explained that they'll have to stand as sponsors to the children until the INS works out their legal status. Most of the couples are flying into Corpus Christi today."

Cari shot her a quick look. "Most of them?"

The missionary blew out a breath. "Turns out the folks who applied to adopt Paulo are in the middle of rather nasty divorce proceedings."

"Oh, no!"

"Unfortunately, they didn't bother to notify our church adoption agency that their marriage had fallen apart. The agency is scrambling now to find another home for Paulo. It might take a while, though, given the expensive surgery he's facing."

Cari's glance went back to the boy. The Whites must have told him the news. He stood a little apart from the others, observing but not participating. The sparkle had gone out of his brown eyes and his face was once again a sullen mask.

"INS is insisting they have to take him into protective custody pending deportation," Janice said quietly. "He's not particularly happy about the prospect."

Neither was Mac, Cari discovered when he wheeled back down the corridor with Rosa still perched in his lap. Tomas followed the squeak of the chair, his sneakers beeping out a merry rhythm. The other kids tagged along, as well. All except Paulo, who maintained his distance.

Mac's gaze lingered on the boy for a moment before meeting Cari's. "Janice tell you about Paulo?"

"Yes. What a bummer."

"Did she also tell you about the INS detention centers?"

"They're supposed to be administrative holding centers," the missionary said when Cari shook her head. "The kids put into these centers don't know that, though. Most of them think they're being punished. They don't speak English, don't understand their rights and, unlike adults detained by the INS, aren't eligible for release after posting bond. They spend weeks or months until deportation in bare cells, sometimes with local youths accused of violent crimes."

The thought of Paulo locked in with young toughs spawned a sick feeling in Cari's stomach. The boy had endured so much in his own country. Now, just when he thought he'd found a safe haven in the United States, he'd be thrown to the sharks again.

"The Berks County Youth Center in Pennsylvania serves as the INS detention center for the East Coast," Janice continued, her voice grim. "They had the kids doing push-ups for every infraction of the rules. It took a class-action suit to make them admit most of the children couldn't *understand* these so-called rules."

Mac's jaw set. His eyes went flat for a moment, as though he was seeing things he'd rather forget.

"It's not going to happen," he said flatly. "I want to talk to this INS official."

"She wants to talk to you, too," Cari told him. "She took statements from the rest of us yesterday afternoon and said she'd come by for yours today."

"Fine. I'll have a thing or two to say to her."

Cari didn't doubt it, but she knew as well as Mac that talking wouldn't hack it with the INS. She was turning over possible options in her mind when the charge nurse swooped down on the small group.

"Your surgeon will be making rounds soon, Major. I refuse to let him find you in the hall doing wheelies. You need to be in bed."

"We'll leave," Janice said, lifting Rosa into her arms. "The kids just wanted to see for their own eyes that Major Mac was all right."

Cari stayed her with a quick request. "Can you hang loose a few minutes?"

"Sure."

"I'll be right back. I just need to make a phone call."

She was back some moments later and relayed the gist of her conversation to Janice, who hustled the kids out of the ward so she could in turn relay the news to her brother.

Cari waited until the nurse and an aide had Mac settled before entering his room. He was stretched out on the smoothed white sheets, his face turned to the dazzling October sunlight streaming in through wide windows. They gave a sweeping view of the naval base and the aquamarine waters of the Gulf of Mexico beyond.

She guessed from Mac's fierce frown that he wasn't concentrating on the view. He confirmed as much when he turned at the sound of her footsteps on the tiled floor.

"Paulo's not going into a detention center, Cari. Not if I can help it. I know the kind of scars they can leave on a boy like him."

The kind that faded, but never quite went away, she guessed.

Mac had never talked about himself in the months they'd spent together in New Mexico, had never mentioned his family that she could recall. Cari had picked up only bits and pieces of his background.

As chief of security for the Pegasus project, Jill Bradshaw had access to the complete security dossiers on all assigned personnel. Jill took her responsibilities too seriously to ever divulge details from those dossiers. Kate, on the other hand, had experienced no qualms about activating her informal intelligence network to come up with tidbits of essential information. Like the fact that Mac had joined the marines before finishing high school. That he'd never married. That he'd been wounded twice, once in Afghanistan, once in the Iraqi War.

This was Cari's first hint that he'd been wounded well before he joined the corps. She wanted to probe, to learn more about the man who'd bulldozed his way into her heart, but the closed, tight expression on Mac's face didn't invite questions. Saving them for later, she perched on the edge of his bed.

"I think I might have won Paulo a reprieve."

"How?"

"I called my sister, Deborah. She and her husband are currently raising two dogs, two cats and four kids, with another about to make an appearance. Their house has all the calm of Grand Central Station during peak rush hour, but Deb insists there's room for Paulo until the Whites' church locates another family for him."

The grim expression on Mac's face eased into one of relief tinged with only a shade of doubt. "Sounds like the perfect place for the kid. Think he'll be able to make himself understood in that crowd?"

Cari laughed. "Paulo doesn't seem to have much difficulty making himself understood in *any* crowd. Deb said she and Jack will drive down from Shreveport as soon as he can get someone to fill in for him at work. We'll have to hold off INS until they get here."

Mac's eyes glinted. "I think we can manage that. In the meantime…"

"Yes?"

He reached up with his good hand, snagged the lapel of her khaki uniform shirt. "I have this hazy recollection of talking to you last night. And a promise of later."

"Remember that, do you?"

"Oh, yeah."

Bracing her hands on either side of the bed to make sure she didn't jar his injured shoulder, she leaned over him.

Chapter 10

Cari spent the next few days in a whirl of worry and frenetic activity.

The Pegasus team holed up in their mobile command center to evaluate their craft's performance in actual operations and prepare a detailed report for the Joint Chiefs of Staff. Captain Westfall was scheduled to deliver the report in person the following week.

Mac drafted his input in his hospital room and gradually began to make brief forays to join the rest of the team at the command center. He regained strength daily, if not the use of his right arm. Fretting at his impaired movement, he was forced to await an evaluation from orthopedic surgeons as to when they could replace his shattered shoulder joint before being discharged from the hospital.

"It's more a question of *if* they can replace the joint, not *when*," Doc Richardson confided to Cari after escorting the increasingly restless patient back to the hospital. "The procedure requires sufficient bone to anchor the replacement joint. Given the damage that bullet did to Mac's shoulder, he may not be a candidate for the surgery."

Side by side, they walked out of the hospital into the bright October sunlight. The stiff breeze blowing in off the Gulf carried a salty tang, but Cari paid no attention to the scent that usually stirred her senses.

"Will he regain use of his arm without the surgery?"

"Some use, certainly."

For anyone else, "some" might be enough. But not for her all-or-nothing, one hundred percent, gung ho marine. Concern over how Mac would adjust to a future that might include limited capabilities to perform his duties nibbled away at the edges of Cari's overwhelming relief that he'd beat the odds and survived the bullet.

She knew the choices that lay ahead of him. If surgery to reconstruct his shoulder wasn't an option, Mac would go before a military medical evaluation board to determine his suitability for continued service. The

eval board could decide to retain him on restricted
duty or recommend him for a disability retirement.

A tight knot formed smack in the middle of her
chest at the thought. The Pegasus team had already
lost one of their own to medical retirement. Lieutenant Colonel Bill Thompson, the original air force rep
to the cadre, had suffered a heart attack after contract-
ing the virus that had swept through the isolated site.
As a result, he'd been yanked off the team and replaced by Dave Scott.

"How long before Mac learns whether he's a candidate for the surgery?" she asked Cody.

"The surgeons here sent his X rays and records to
two of the country's top orthopedic surgeons who
specialize in shoulder replacements. Hopefully, we'll
hear something back within a few days."

In the midst of Cari's worries over Mac and her
work on the report detailing *Pegasus*'s seaworthiness,
officials from the adoption agency run by the Whites'
church flew in to iron matters out with the INS. They
also expedited legal proceedings and helped with the
first meetings between the children and their prospective parents. The couples themselves flew in from all
parts of the country, some nervous, all excited. One
by one, the children departed with their new families.
The departures were a wrenching mixture of joy and

wariness as the kids exchanged the familiar if bleak past for an unknown future.

Paulo remained with the Whites, who delayed their departure from Corpus until his situation was resolved. Faced with the combined resistance of the missionaries, the Pegasus team and one very determined marine, INS held off taking the boy into custody pending evaluation of Cari's sister and brother-in-law as temporary guardians.

Deborah and Jack drove down from Shreveport late Friday afternoon. They arrived with all four kids and, thankfully, only one household pet in tow. Trading her uniform for a pair of floppy sandals, comfortable slacks and a red-checkered blouse, Cari met them at the beachside condo on Padre Island she'd rented for them. It sat near the northern tip of the island, close enough to watch the fishing fleet putting out from Aransas Pass but far enough away from the docks to avoid the fish aroma that permeated the air when the fleet returned.

When the Hamilton family piled out of their SUV, laughter bubbled up in Cari's throat at the chaos that ensued. Her two nieces and two nephews whooped with delight at being released from their seat belts and car seats. They treated their aunt to bear hugs and wet, sloppy kisses before making a beeline for the sandy beach. The chocolate-colored, full-sized poodle Deb had tried to pawn off on every one of her relatives lumbered alongside the kids, emitting earsplitting woofs of joy.

"No going in the water without one of us there to supervise!" their father shouted. The kids swerved in time to avoid the surf. Pierre the Poodle plowed right in.

Undaunted by the prospect of coping with a wet animal the size of a small horse, Deb levered her very pregnant self out of the car and enveloped her sister in a fierce hug. She and Cari were about the same height, with the cinnamon dark eyes and glossy mink-brown hair that ran in their family, but the similarities ended there. Deb dabbled in watercolors, loved any and all sweets and had married her first and only love right out of high school. She took vicarious delight in her sister's adventures in uniform, but shuddered at the thought of being subjected to anything resembling military discipline herself.

Cari returned her hug and that of her big, ham-fisted brother-in-law. It had always amazed her how perfectly her petite sister and this high-school-football-star-turned-math-teacher fit together.

"Thanks for coming to the rescue like this. I owe you, Jack."

"Don't think I won't collect, too." His blue eyes laughed down at her. "Deb and I plan to dump kids, dogs, cats, parakeets and gerbils on Aunt Cari one of these days and take off for a blissful week of solitude.''

"Any time. Just give me a little advance notice.''

"Advance *warning,* you mean. You'll need at least twenty-four hours to batten down the hatches and do whatever else you coast guard types do before a hurricane hits.'' Waving aside her offer of assistance, he shooed the two women toward the condo. "You girls go on inside. I'll bring the bags and the rest of the tribe.''

Hooking her arm in her sister's, Cari escorted her to the beachside cottage. It was an airy, four-bedroom unit with additional sleep sofas in the living room, a fully equipped kitchen and a breathtaking view of the Gulf. It was also, Cari had been assured by the rental agent, kid- and dog-proof. Evidently this particular condo catered to families on vacation as well as the sun-seeking and often rowdy college-age hoards that descended on Padre Island every spring break.

"Oh, man,'' Deb breathed when she viewed the dunes rolling right to the sliding glass doors. "The kids are going to love this place. They'll also bury this carpet in about six inches of sand.''

"Not to worry. I suspect that's why the rental agency put in sisal carpets. It's tough enough to withstand sand and wet feet. I stocked the fridge for you. Want some Triple Fudge Ripple?''

"You sweetheart!'' Keeping one eye on her kids

through the sliding glass doors, she sank into one of the chairs grouped around a glass-topped table. "Pile a bowl full for both of us and tell me more about Paulo."

"We don't know much about his background," Cari said as she heaped ice cream into two bowls. "Janice White—one of the missionaries who brought him out of Caribe—says he just showed up at their mission a year or so ago, half starved and sporting a set of vicious bruises. From what they can gather, the rebels killed his mother. There's no record of his father. There's no record of Paulo, either, which adds to the complications of his, uh, precipitous departure from Caribe."

"A departure you had something to do with, I take it."

"Right. I can't go into details, just that Mac and I were sent in to extract the Whites. The kids came with them."

"Who's Mac?"

"A marine I've been working with for the past few months."

She didn't use any particular inflection, but Deb's spoon paused halfway between bowl and mouth.

"A few months, huh?"

"We've been assigned to a special project."

"Is he cute?"

''Cute, no. Rugged and compelling, most definitely.''

''I see.'' Catlike, Deb swiped her tongue along the back of her spoon. ''Just out of curiosity, where does your lawyer friend fit into this equation?''

''He doesn't,'' Cari admitted. ''I broke things off with Jerry.''

''Thank goodness!''

Startled by her sister's emphatic response, Cari blinked.

''None of us in the family thought he was right for you,'' her sister confided. ''We also thought you were crazy to give up a career you love to become a stay-at-home mom.''

''That's interesting, coming from a woman who takes such joy in doing just that.''

''Isn't it?'' Complacently, Deb downed another spoonful of ice cream. ''But then I never wanted anything else. You, on the other hand, decided to join the coast guard almost the first week the family moved to Maryland.''

That was true. After investing in a home on a spit of the Chesapeake's eastern shore, their parents had purchased a sailboat. Before they'd let any of their lively brood set so much as a toe aboard the sleek twenty-four-footer, however, they'd enrolled them in a water-safety course conducted by the local coast guard auxiliary. The tanned, curly-haired sailor who'd conducted the course had fascinated the thirteen-year-old Cari. The bits and pieces she'd learned about the coast guard's mission had come to fascinate her even more. She'd applied to the U.S. Coast Guard Academy, had been accepted right out of college, and never looked back.

Until the urge to nest had started to ping at her, that is. Now she wanted it all. Her career. A family. Mac.

Almost the instant the thought formed, Cari rejected it. Sometime in the past few weeks, her priorities had inexorably altered. The order of importance was now Mac first, a family and her career second.

The realization hit her with gale force impact. She wanted Mac. Period. In any way, shape or form she could get him. Everything else would have to fall in after him.

Now, she thought wryly, all she had to do was determine what Mac's priorities were.

She got her first inkling later that afternoon, when she escorted her sister to her first meeting with Paulo. Jack stayed with the kids, having decided it was best not to bombard the boy with their whole tribe right away. Instead, Deb brought pictures of the family and their home in Shreveport to show Paulo.

They arranged to meet the Whites and their charge

at the hospital. Harry and Janice were in the waiting room when the two sisters arrived. With the Whites was one of the counselors from their church's adoption agency.

"Paulo's down the hall with Major Mac," Janice explained. "We wanted a chance to talk with you first, Mrs. Hamilton, and answer any questions you might have about the boy."

Nodding, Deb lowered herself into one of the waiting room's armchairs. The missionaries took seats facing her, the official from their church just behind them. He was a slight, scholarly looking gentleman in neatly pressed tan Dockers, a blue oxford shirt, and a red polka-dot bow tie. Introducing himself to Cari and Deb, Henry Easton explained a little about his mission and the difficulties of placing children with disabilities such as Paulo.

"You understand he was born without a larynx."

"Cari told me. She also said an artificial voice box could be implanted."

"That's correct," Easton confirmed. "Our church had arranged to share the costs with the couple who'd applied to adopt Paulo, as their insurance wouldn't cover preexisting conditions. Now, of course, we'll have to put the operation on hold until we screen other prospective parents for the boy."

"Or our bishop convinces the doctors involved to

donate their time and skills," Harry White put in. "He's pretty good at arm-twisting."

"Which is why Harry and I will be on another plane less than a week after hotfooting it out of Caribe," Janice said dryly. "But only after we get Paulo settled. He carries some psychological scars in addition to his physical disability," she warned. "He wouldn't tell us much about what happened before he came to us, but from what we could gather he saw his mother raped and shot by the rebels."

"Dear Lord!" Pity flooded Deb's brown eyes. "What about his father?"

"He doesn't know who his father is, or was. Nor does the Caribe government." She hesitated, let her glance linger on Deb's rounded belly. "You have four children of your own and another on the way. Are you sure you want to take on one more, even temporarily?"

Cari smiled as her sister's chin lifted to a determined angle. Anyone in Deb's rambunctious family would have recognized the warning signals and immediately ceased doing whatever had generated that look.

"I'm sure," she said firmly. "So is my husband. We wouldn't have driven down from Shreveport otherwise."

Satisfied, Janice nodded and sat back. Deb wasn't quite finished yet. Turning to the church officials, she demonstrated the shrewd mind behind her small, heart-shaped face.

"To avoid any potential difficulties, we'll want to meet with the INS. We also want to have our attorney look over the temporary guardianship papers."

"Yes, of course."

"And I'll need a crash course in sign language, so I can understand Paulo's needs."

"We can arrange that, as well."

"This is all dependent on Paulo wanting to stay with us," Deb conceded, recognizing that the issue of temporary custody was far from decided. "He might not take to a family as noisy and lively as ours."

"I don't think that will be a problem," Janice said, truly relaxing for the first time since she'd learned the couple who'd applied to adopt Paulo had hit the divorce courts. "He was a godsend at the mission, helping us with the other kids."

"Then I guess the next step is for me to meet him."

When she planted both hands on the arms of her chair and would have levered herself up, Cari waved her back. "Stay put. I'll go get him."

She made her way down the hall, both relieved and regretful that Paulo would have to make yet another wrenching transition before he gained a sense of permanence and stability.

The door to Mac's room stood partway open. She heard the unmistakable sound of canned laughter coming from the TV and rapped twice before poking her head inside.

"Mac?"

He was stretched out on the bed, sound asleep despite the raucous cartoon on the TV. His blue hospital pajamas were gone, traded for cutoffs and a gray USMC sweatshirt with the arms ripped out. The sickly pallor that had tinged his face after the loss of so much blood had disappeared as well. Cari's glance lingered on the sling and bandages strapping his right arm to his chest before drifting to the boy curled up at his good side.

Paulo was zonked out, too. His dark head lay tucked right next to Mac's chin. He wore his favorite Spider-Man T-shirt, of course. Janice had confessed that she washed it out for him every evening.

A little ache started in Cari's chest and spread to her throat. The thought flashed into her head that here was her family, ready-made and waiting. Just as quickly, she pushed it out again. She couldn't let herself start weaving fantasies like that. Not yet, anyway. They all faced too many uncertainties at this point, not the least of which was whether Mac reciprocated this confused feeling Cari was becoming more convinced by the moment was love.

Extracting the TV remote from Mac's slack grip, she clicked off the cartoons. "Hey, you two," she said in the blessed quiet that followed. "Wake up."

Mac pried up one eyelid, then the other. "Aren't you supposed to wake your sleeping prince with a kiss?"

"You're not real up on your fairy tales, are you? The prince is the one who wakes up Sleeping Beauty."

"Hey, I'm easy. Either way works for me."

Cari grinned, but the realization that Paulo had blinked awake and was listening to the silly exchange kept her from accommodating Mac's wishes right then and there.

"No time for fairy tales right now. You two need to haul your buns out of bed and come meet my sister."

"She's here?"

"Yep. With a promise to take Paulo to the fast-food joint of his choice while they get to know one another."

"Hear that, kid? You can have your pick. Pizza, tacos or hamburgers."

His brow knitting, the boy eased upright, but the magic last word killed his scowl before it could fully form. He signed something neither Mac nor Cari could interpret. Impatient, he shaped a high arch with his hands.

''That didn't take long,'' Mac said, laughing. ''One trip to McDonald's and you're already hooked. Come on, kid, let's go meet Lieutenant Dunn's sister.''

Mac swung his feet off the bed. The rest of him followed without so much as a wince, Cari noted. The man was leather tough, she thought with a stab of admiration that got all mixed up with greedy hunger when he maneuvered into a pair of black rubber flip-flops. His cutoffs ended about midway down hard, muscled thighs. The ragged armhole his gray sweat-shirt afforded a tantalizing glimpse of more male flesh.

As they exited the room and started down the hall, Paulo's hand slipped into Mac's. The boy would never admit it, Cari was sure, but he had to be scared. Once again his world was about to shift around him.

Deb, bless her, knew exactly how to ease his fears. She sent Mac a curious glance, but focused her warm smile on the boy. ''Hello, Paulo. I'm Deb. I'm hoping you'll come and stay with me and my family for a while. I should warn you, though, we have two dogs. Big dogs. And two cats. Here, I'll show you a pic-ture.''

Janice said something quietly in Caribe. The boy edged closer to Deb's chair. His expression remained wary as she pulled out the photos she'd brought.

"The one with the curly hair is Pierre the Poodle. The one with the dirty face is my son Ben. He's about your age and heavy into action figures. He sent one for you, as a welcome gift."

She delved into her tote again and produced a plastic, lizard-headed toy.

"This is Darcon. Or Dracon. I'm not sure which. He's for you," she prompted, holding out the figure.

Paulo glanced at Janice, who signaled he should accept the gift. He played with the movable arms and legs for a moment, then tucked the figure against his side and flashed a quick sign.

"He says thank you."

"You're welcome," Deb returned. "I'm sorry I can't understand sign language. I'm going to learn, though. Will you help me?"

Paulo's quick nod led to another warm smile and more photos. Fifteen minutes later the boy left with Deb, Janice and the dapper church official to find the closest hamburger joint. Harry White departed for another session with the attorney the church had flown in, leaving Mac and Cari alone for the first time since those quiet hours just before dawn in Caribe.

The memory of how they'd killed those hours started a tight curl of desire deep in her belly. Mac's edgy restlessness when faced with the prospect of going back to his room had her suggesting an alternative.

"If Nurse Ratchet gets an okay from your docs, are you ready to blow this joint for a few hours?"

"More than ready."

"Let me go talk to her."

Nurse Ratchet, otherwise known as Lieutenant Commander Smallwood, got the okay.

"Dr. Atwater agrees it'll do the major good to get away from here for a while," she related, her glance on the tall, tanned marine at the far end of the hall. "He wants to talk to him in the morning, though."

The guarded note in her voice brought Cari's head around. "Has he heard from the orthopedic surgeons about Mac's shoulder replacement?"

The lieutenant commander hesitated. "From one of them."

She wouldn't say more. She didn't have to. Cari walked back down the hall praying that the second specialist would offer a different assessment of Mac's candidacy for replacement surgery.

Twenty minutes later, she parked her rental car outside a waterfront restaurant that advertised the meanest crabs in south Texas.

Chapter 11

"I like your sister," Mac confided over a late lunch of steamed crab and fried clams.

"You'll like her even more after you see her in action." Smiling, Cari dunked a clam in creamy tartar sauce. "Deb swears she could never take the discipline of military life, yet somehow manages to get her kids off to school, the dogs and cats to the vet and her husband on his way to work each morning wearing a silly grin."

"A four-star general in the making," Mac agreed.

"My whole family is like that. I don't ever remember my mom raising her voice to us kids—and I know we gave her plenty of opportunity—but she kept the troops in line."

"Must be where you inherited it," he commented. "You've got a core of solid steel inside that pint-sized package."

"That's a compliment, right?"

She was never quite sure with Mac.

"That's most definitely a compliment." Smiling, he wrapped his fist around a giant-sized mug of iced tea. "If your sister has half your bullheaded determination to see things through, she's a remarkable woman."

Her skin warmed with pleasure. The flush added to the heat generated by the sight of Mac downing a long swallow of his tea. She found her glance riveted to the strong column of his throat, the smooth play of muscle and tendon, the beginnings of a five o'clock shadow darkening the underside of his chin. Suddenly, she ached to rub her cheek against his, to enjoy the scratchy contact.

One lascivious thought led instantly to another. In the blink on an eye, she was imagining how it would feel to rub areas other than his cheek. Heat speared through her, and the muscles low in her belly spasmed.

"What about you?" she asked, as much to recover from the sudden wallop as to keep the conversation rolling. "Any brothers or sisters?"

"None that I know of, although…"

"Although?"

"My mother departed the scene when I was about ten. For all I know, she could have produced a whole passel of additional offspring."

"What about your dad?"

"He departed shortly after that."

His tone was easy, but Cari sensed the walls going up. This time, she decided to go around them.

"So who raised you?"

"A series of foster families."

He deflected her rush of pity with a wry smile.

"I wasn't the easiest kid to take in. Like your sister, I had a distinct aversion to discipline."

"Uh-huh. That's why you chose the U.S. Marine Corps."

The smile deepened. "It was either the marines or jail. For once, I made the right choice. Looks like you need a refill on your iced tea."

With that neat change of subject, he turned and signaled the waiter. The windows behind him were hooked up to allow the breeze from the Gulf to skip through the restaurant, fluttering the paper napkins. The late-afternoon sun bounced off the water in a thousand sparkling pinpricks and framed Mac in a nimbus of light. Another wave of heat washed over Cari again as she took in the rugged masculinity of his profile.

Her glance slid down to the bandages encasing his shoulder. She had no idea how much pain he was experiencing, if any. The nurses had told her he'd stopped taking the pain medication two days ago and refused so much as an aspirin to get him through the past few nights.

It was the night ahead that occupied her thoughts.

"How's your shoulder?" she asked when they departed the Crab Shack and made for her rented vehicle.

"It's there."

"Are you in a hurry to get back to the hospital?"

"What do you think?"

"What I think," she said, sliding into the driver's seat, "is that it's still early. Why don't we detour by the visiting officers' quarters? You can take a look at the final draft of the report," she added conversationally. "I have it on my laptop."

Cari let him go on thinking she had work on her mind until the door snicked shut behind them. She leaned against it, intending to inform him her intentions were somewhat less than honorable.

She never got the chance.

Mac's intentions evidently ran along the same lines as hers. He propped his good arm against the door, leaned his body into hers and swooped in for a kiss that knocked the breath back down her throat.

"So I guess you're not interested in the draft report," she teased when they both came up for air.

''Not as interested as I am in the buttons on this shirt,'' he replied, zeroing in on her red-checkered blouse.

One by one, the buttons gave under his fingers. Shivers danced just under Cari's skin as his knuckles traced a path from her neckline to her waist. One-handed, he shoved the material aside. When his breath left on a long hiss, she gave silent thanks that she'd opted for a lacy bra and high-on-the-thigh bikini briefs this morning instead of her usual cotton and spandex.

''If you hadn't suggested coming back to your quarters,'' he growled, his palm hot on the soft mound of her flesh, ''I was going to prop a chair under the door handle of my hospital room and ravage you.''

''You've been wounded in the line of duty. How about I do the ravishing this time around?''

His hand stilled. Eyes glinting, he gave her a wolf-ish grin. ''Works for me.''

''Okay, Major. The first step is to get you semi-horizontal.''

Hooking two fingers in the waistband of his cut-offs, she tugged him to the sofa.

''Sit!''

''Yes, ma'am.''

He lowered himself to the sofa and watched with interest as she unzipped her slacks. They slithered down her hips, landed in a heap on the carpet. She stepped out of them and undid the last few buttons on her blouse. It followed her slacks to the floor. Yanking at the clip that held her hair up in a loose twist, she shook the thick brown strands free. A moment later she'd kicked off her sandals, planted a knee on either side of Mac's hips and straddled him.

"This is nice," she observed, brushing his lips with hers. "We're eye to eye and mouth to mouth."

"*Very* nice."

She dropped a string of kisses that trailed from his lips to his chin to the taut cords at the side of his neck. He took advantage of her crouched position to find the curve of her bottom with his good hand.

As he fondled her through the silky fabric of her briefs, fiery hunger ignited in Cari's veins. She wanted to crawl all over him, chew him up and swallow him whole. Nipping at his warm flesh, she issued a husky demand.

"Promise me you'll tell me if I hurt your shoulder."

Mac couldn't help himself. Laughing, he squeezed her butt. "Oh, babe, you've already got me hurting so bad you could sit on my shoulder and I wouldn't feel it."

He slouched against the sofa back, taking her with him. Her tight, trim behind filled his hand. Her breasts brushed his chest. All inclination to laughter fled as

Mac met the thrust of her hot, wet tongue with his own.

He hadn't lied to her. He was hurting from his neck to his knees. Had been, one way or another, since the first time he'd laid eyes on this stubborn, seductive, incredible woman. He'd buried his hunger for her all those weeks in New Mexico. He'd had a job to do. So had she. She'd also been on the phone to that wuss up in Washington almost every night.

That was then, he thought on a surge of desire so hot and raw it seared his entire body. Now…

Now, she was his.

The primitive male urge to possess her, to leave his scent on her, slammed into him. It took him a moment to remember he was a United States Marine, not some Roman mercenary or robber baron who could cart a woman off as plunder. Another moment to admit Cari wasn't the carting-off type. She'd probably deck him if he tried any Neanderthal tactics on her.

Besides, he didn't have a single damned condom anywhere on him!

Cursing his lack of foresight, Mac slid his hand between her thighs. His thumb rubbed back and forth, generating a friction that soon had her gasping and Mac sweating. Gritting his teeth to keep from hooking his arm around her waist and dragging her under him, he found the leg opening of her briefs.

Her inner flesh was smooth and hot. Mac slipped

a finger inside her, then two. With slow, sure thrusts, he stoked the fires that flushed her skin and left it slick and damp. Fierce satisfaction gripped him as Cari's head went back. Writhing, she rode the waves of wild sensation.

Suddenly, she went stiff. Her eyes flew open. "Mac, I'm too... I can't..."

"So don't."

She tried to wiggle away. "I'm supposed to be...doing the rav...aging here."

"We'll take turns."

Ruthlessly suppressing his own raging need, he exerted just enough pressure with his thumb to produce a long, ragged groan. Once more Cari's head went back. Her eyes squeezed shut. Violent shudders racked her small, perfect body.

Mac almost lost it himself right then and there. She was his most erotic fantasy come to life. Slender curves. Hot flesh. Her back arched. Her hair was a spill of dark, tangled silk.

Slowly, her thighs relaxed and she sank down onto his. Mac ground his back teeth together until the last throes of her climax passed and she opened her eyes.

"Wow!" She essayed a wobbly smile. "Give me a minute and I'll take my turn."

Still in the grip of his own aching desire and the primal need to possess this woman, Mac started to tell her he intended to give her a whole lifetime of minutes. Just in time, he bit back the words. He wasn't in any shape to stake that kind of a claim on her. Not yet.

Once the docs fit him with a new shoulder, though, she couldn't run far or fast enough to get away from him. Forcing himself to bide his time—mentally and physically—he stayed perfectly still until Cari had regained enough strength to slide off his lap onto her knees.

With a small, wicked smile, she popped the snap on his cut-offs. The zipper came down. Her hands found him, freed him, gripped him. She trailed the tip of a finger down the rigid shaft. Drew it back up again. Wet her lips.

Then it was Mac's turn to throw his head back and let out a long, low groan.

The rap on the door came while Mac's heart was still trying to pump blood back to his outer extremities. He dragged his head up and rasped out a hoarse query.

"Expecting company?"

"No." She dropped her voice to a husky whisper. "Maybe if we keep real quiet, whoever it is will go away."

The ploy didn't work. Another rap rattled the door, harder this time.

"Hey, Cari!" Dave Scott's deep voice boomed

from the hallway. "I spotted your car in the parking lot. Haul your buns over to the door and open up. I need your chop on the sequence we used to take *Pegasus* from sea to air mode down in Caribe to finalize this report."

Muttering an oath worthy of a true salt, Cari snatched up her blouse and fumbled with the buttons. "Hang on a sec! I'll be right there."

Mac got himself together well before she did. Not surprising, since she'd stripped down to her skivvies and he was still more in than out of his clothes. He pushed off the sofa, then waited until she'd scrambled into her slacks and shoved the shirttails inside the waistband before strolling across the room.

When he opened the door, surprise sent the pilot's sun-bleached blond brows soaring. "McIver! What the heck are you doing out of the hospital?"

Dave's glance winged to Cari, cut back. A delighted grin split his face. "Never mind. I'm a little slow on the uptake sometimes, but this one's a no-brainer."

With a flash of her bright copper hair, Kate poked her head out of the open doorway of the room across the hall. "What's a no-brainer?"

Her green eyes brightened when she saw who Dave was talking to. "Hey, gang, Mac's here."

She came across the hallway, followed in short order by Jill Bradshaw and Doc Richardson. When Captain Westfall appeared at the threshold of the room across the hall, Mac's easy smile slid off his face. Instinctively, he straightened and squared his shoulders. Or tried to. The knifing pain had him biting back a curse and brought Cari instantly to his side.

"At ease, man."

Westfall issued the gruff order, then shifted his gaze to Cari. Despite the calm smile she plastered on her face, he couldn't fail to note the whisker burn reddening her cheeks and chin. Nor could any of the others. Kate shared a look with Jill, while Doc Richardson manfully tried to smother a grin. Captain Westfall, thankfully, ignored the red flags.

"Did they discharge you or did you just decide to go AWOL?" he asked Mac.

"Neither. The doc gave me a few hours' shore leave."

"Good. How about you use what remains of it to go over the final report I'm delivering to the Joint Chiefs of Staff tomorrow?"

"Yes, sir."

"Lieutenant Dunn, we'll need your input as well."

"Of course. I'll be right there."

He turned and retreated into the suite across the hall. The others straggled after him, leaving a rueful Cari to shag a hand through her tangled hair.

"We need to work on our timing," she muttered to Mac. "Seems like every time we get hot and bothered, we wind up with someone shooting at us or the entire test cadre gathered around as interested observers. How's your shoulder?''

He should have known she wouldn't miss his involuntary wince when he tried to go into a brace.

''It's fine,'' he lied, toeing a bit of plastic out from under the couch. ''Is this yours?''

''Yes. Thanks.''

While she twisted up her hair and anchored it to the back of her head, Mac slid his feet into his flip-flops. Marginally presentable, they joined the group crowded around a small table in the suite across the hall. Chairs bumped and elbows jostled as the others made room for two more.

''Here you go,'' Kate said, passing them copies of the report. '';The latest version, hot off the press. We've made some changes to the draft you need to take a look at.''

The printed pages immediately absorbed Cari. They should have absorbed Mac, too. The report represented the culmination of long months of tests, trials and evaluations. The fact that it might also represent the culmination of his military career carved a small hole in his gut.

He'd demanded and received brutal honesty from the surgeons who'd tried—and failed—to patch together the shattered remnants of his shoulder. The damage to both tissue and bone went beyond their capacity to repair it. In their considered opinion, it went beyond being able to support even an artificial joint. His only hope was that one of the specialists they'd sent his case file to would accept him as a candidate for replacement surgery despite the odds.

The tension Cari had drained from him with her hands and her mouth and her supple, incredible body crept back. The muscles in the back of his neck knotted. His fist tightened on the report. With a silent curse, Mac eased his grip and forced himself to focus on the lines of print.

Forty minutes later, Mac realized this meeting presaged the end of something else, something that seemed to hit each of the officers present when Captain Westfall gave his nod to the last page of the revised report.

"Well, that's it." With careful precision, he aligned the pages. "The analyses we've provided here should give the Joint Chiefs sufficient information to make a go or no-go decision on *Pegasus*."

He slid the thick report into a folder stamped with the appropriate classified markings.

"Jill, I'll leave the draft copies with you to shred and dispose of."

"Yes, sir."

"Dave, I'm relying on you to make sure every system aboard *Pegasus* is thoroughly shaken down before you fly back to New Mexico on Monday.''

"Roger that, sir. Neither *Pegasus* nor I will lift off unless I'm confident we can come down again soft and easy.''

"Good.''

The captain speared a glance at each of his officers.

''Whatever the Joint Chiefs decide, I want you to know I was proud to have you on my team.''

This was it. Possibly the last time the Pegasus cadre would work together. The captain and the other five would return to New Mexico to close down test operations. Mac would remain here in Texas until the docs rendered their verdict. The realization that their urgent mission and tight-knit team had both come to an end punched into each of them.

Silence gripped the room. Every officer present knew the usual hearty handshakes and promises to grab a beer the next time their paths crossed wouldn't hack it. But that was the standard formula, one they'd all relied on when readying for the next move to a new duty station. The only one they had to rely on now.

The handshakes were hard. The smiles were warm and genuine. They dispersed with a chorus of promises to gather for the official ceremony marking *Pegasus*'s acceptance as an operational vehicle—whenever and wherever that might occur.

* * *

A pensive silence filled the rental car as Cari drove Mac back to the hospital. After the searing intimacy of their stolen hours together, they now had to factor a pending separation and Mac's uncertain future into their still tenuous relationship.

At Mac's insistence, Cari pulled up to the front of the hospital. "We have the rest of the weekend," she reminded him when he reached across his strapped arm to open the passenger door. "All day tomorrow and Sunday. I want you to meet Jack, Deb's husband, and their kids. Maybe we could spring you loose again tomorrow morning. We'll have a picnic on the beach with Paulo and the whole gang."

"Sounds good."

He made an effort to sound enthusiastic. She knew how much he must hate the thought of being left to twiddle his thumbs when the rest of the cadre dispersed. She also noted the white lines that bracketed his mouth. He'd need more than an aspirin to get through tonight, she guessed.

Her rush of guilt at pushing him to his physical limits got all mixed up with an urge to cradle him in her arms and soothe away his pain.

She lifted a hand to stroke his cheek. Mac caught it in his and tugged her close. Forcing a smile, he dropped a hard kiss on her mouth.

"See you tomorrow, beautiful."

Chapter 12

Cari arrived at the hospital just past ten the following morning. The dazzling sunshine of the previous
day had given way to gray, sullen skies and a stiff
breeze off the Gulf that carried a definite nip to it.
Shivering in her lightweight chinos and daffodil-
yellow cotton drifter, she hurried across the parking
lot.

They'd have to revise their plans for a picnic on
the beach with Deb and Jack and the kids, she
thought. Go for some kind of indoor activity instead.

Instantly, her thoughts zipped back to the indoor
activity she and Mac had indulged in the evening before. A rush of heat warmed her skin, countering the

goose bumps raised by the breeze. She still couldn't quite believe she'd jumped Mac's bones the way she had. Or that he'd turned the tables on her so skillfully. Using only one arm, he'd managed to dissolve her into a shivering puddle of ecstasy. She could just imagine the magic he would work on her eager body when he regained full use of his other arm.

If he regained full use of that arm.

The distinct possibility he might not took some of the spring from her step. The little he'd told her about himself yesterday confirmed her suspicion the corps was more than just Russ McIver's career. It was his life.

Well, if the worst happened, they'd just have to come up with a strategy to deal with it. Mac wasn't the kind to sit around and feel sorry for himself. Nor would Cari let him. They'd get through this together.

It wasn't until she was in the elevator, stabbing the button for the fourth floor, that Cari realized she was now thinking in plurals. *They* would have to come up with a strategy. *They* would get through this.

Sometime during the night she'd taken that next step. From wondering if she and Mac could carve a future out of the uncertainties facing them, she was now determined to make it happen.

Impatient now, she waited for the elevator doors to whir open and hurried down the hall. When she reached Mac's room, the door was open. The bed was neatly made, sheets turned down and tucked in at sharp angles. Its occupant stood at the window. He was in uniform—green gabardine trousers, precisely aligned brass belt buckle, tailored khaki shirt with gleaming insignia and rows of bright, colorful ribbons. Even the blue sling strapping his arm tight against his chest was perfectly squared.

Her heart skipped happily at seeing him standing tall even as a tiny thread of worry snaked along her veins. She could think of only one reason for him to be in uniform.

"Hello, Mac."

Her suspicion was confirmed when he turned his head. He arranged his expression into a welcoming smile, but Cari could see he had to work at it.

"What's with the khakis?" she asked, although she could pretty well guess the answer.

"The docs made their rounds earlier. They're discharging me."

Skirting the bed, she joined him at the wide window. The storm clouds piling up over the Gulf seemed an appropriate background for the news Mac delivered in a carefully neutral tone.

"The surgeon says he can't do anything more for me. Nor can either of the civilian specialists he consulted, it turns out."

"Well, hell!"

His smile almost reached his eyes. "That pretty well sums up my sentiments, too."

She ached for him, for the hope that was now smashed along with tendon and bone and muscle.

"Your arm's a long way from healed. Surely the doc's not sending you back to duty?"

"He's putting me on restricted duty until the bones knit as best they can and I complete a regimen of physical therapy."

"Then you'll meet a medical evaluation board."

It wasn't a question. Cari understood the process as well as Mac did. Nodding, he sidestepped the unsure future to focus on the immediate.

"I called Captain Westfall this morning and caught him as he was leaving for D.C. He agrees with the docs that I should ship back to my home station at Cherry Point to begin the physical therapy."

That made sense. The dispensary at the Pegasus site wasn't equipped for the kind of therapy Mac would require. Still, the knowledge that a half a continent would soon separate them carved a little hole in Cari's heart.

She'd known it was coming. With the Pegasus project winding down, the entire team would soon disperse to their various home stations. They'd pretty well said their unofficial farewells after the meeting last night. She wasn't ready to let go yet, though. Not of this particular member of the team, anyway.

"You don't have to leave today, do you?"

Mac hesitated. The docs had urged him to take some time off and fully regain his strength before going back to his duty station. Captain Westfall had echoed the recommendation, but understood Mac's need to focus on something, *anything,* other than the black hole that used to be his career.

It yawned under his feet now, threatening to sink more than his military career. If he wasn't damned careful, it would swallow Cari, too.

"Stay the weekend," she urged softly. "With me."

He wanted to. God knew, he wanted to! He'd spent most of last night alternating between the grinding ache in his shoulder and the far fiercer ache stirred by the mere thought of this woman. Every time he'd closed his eyes, he'd see her. Her head thrown back, her hair a tangled tumble, her sleek, supple body shuddering in glorious release.

Along with that erotic vision came vivid reminders of how she'd used her hands and her mouth and her teeth to bring him to the same shattering state. Just the memory was enough to put Mac into a sweat.

It also made him crave more than her hands and her mouth and her teeth. He wanted all of her. Under him. Around him. All over him. But not for a hurried few hours. In the dark moments just before dawn, he'd realized he wanted to wake up to Cari's hair spread across his pillow. To share the first cup of coffee with her in the morning and drift off to sleep with her body tucked tight against his at night.

He'd believed he had a shot at fulfilling one or all of those cravings until the surgeon delivered his news this morning.

"I'm not sure spending the weekend together is such a good idea," he said quietly. "Maybe it's better to make the break now, before either of us gets in too deep."

He expected the words to produce an argument, maybe anger. Quite possibly an aching sense of loss that mirrored his own. What he didn't expect was her snort of laughter. Taken completely aback, he stared down at the amusement dancing in her eyes.

"Nice try, McIver. We both know it's too late for a clean break. We're already in too deep. The question now is what the dickens we're going to do about it."

"Cari…"

She cut him off with an airy wave of one hand. "This isn't the time or the place to decide that question. You're coming with me, mister."

Mac thought about reminding her that he outranked her and should be the one issuing the orders. That he needed to confirm his travel arrangements back to Cherry Point. That a few more hours wouldn't change the situation. With a spurt of greedy selfishness, he kept his jaw clamped shut while Cari dumped his few personal items into the plastic tote bag the nursing aide had provided for that purpose.

Almost shaking with a combination of bravado and relief, Cari kept her back to him as she scooped up razor, shaving cream, soap, deodorant, toothbrush and toothpaste. Her laughing comeback had thrown him completely off balance, but he wouldn't remain off balance for long. He'd challenge her blithe assertion they were both already in too deep. Do his best to convince her they should back off. Probably suggest they wait until time and distance and the results of the medical board had added perspective to their situation.

Well, she wasn't backing off. Not now, and not any time in the foreseeable future. What's more, she fully intended to use the next forty-eight hours to storm the citadel of Mac's heart in pretty much the same manner the marines had once stormed the halls of Montezuma.

Her resolve firming with every second, she tossed in his shorts, sweatshirt and skivvies, along with his rubber flip-flops. The neatly folded hospital pajamas she ignored. If matters progressed as she intended them to, Mac wouldn't need them.

The plastic bag bulged at the sides by the time she'd finished. She swept a last look around. "Do I have all the essentials?"

When he hesitated for several long moments, Cari drew in a deep breath. She didn't want to discuss their future in the hospital. She'd prefer to have him away from the scent of antiseptic and shiny, squeaky tiled floors when they talked about what came next. She'd lay her feelings out here if she had to, though.

Before she could fully marshal her arguments, Mac spiked them by moving to the wood-grained metal cabinet beside the bed and extracting a small paper sack. With a wry grin, he tossed it her way.

"*Now* you have all the essentials."

Curious, she snuck a peek at the box inside the sack. The box of condoms kicked her pulse into immediate overdrive, and laughter once again danced in her eyes.

"Think we'll need an entire dozen?"

Mac's answering smile melted her insides. "A man can only hope. I was caught unprepared last time. This time, we'll do things right."

She led the way out of his room, fervently wishing she hadn't committed to spending a portion of their precious remaining hours with Deb and her noisy, lively brood.

When Cari called ahead to advise her sister they were on the way, Deb suggested an indoor pizza and game fest as an alternative to their planned picnic.

Evidently the rented condo came equipped with a large selection of board games.

Rain had begun to lash the Gulf by the time Cari and Mac pulled up at the beachside condo. Spray flew up from the gray sea in lacy spumes. Waves rolled and crashed on the beach. Thinking Mac might want to change out of his uniform, Cari grabbed the plastic sack and made a dash for the condo. Mac followed hard on her heels.

Her brother-in-law answered the door and attempted to make himself heard over the shrieks of laughter and rafter-rattling barks emanating from the living room.

"Jack Hamilton, Major." Out of consideration for Mac's injured right arm he didn't offer to shake hands. "Glad I finally get to meet you. From the way Paulo perks up whenever your name is mentioned, it's obvious you're his hero."

"I don't know about the hero part, but we have become pals. He's a good kid."

When he wasn't beaning marines in the head with rocks, Cari thought wryly.

"Sorry 'bout the noise," Jack apologized as he led the way inside. "Deb's doing her best to keep the kids entertained until the storm passes."

"It might not blow over until tomorrow," Cari warned as he led the way into the living room. "Kate—our associate from the National Oceanic and

Atmospheric Administration—says the front has settled over this corner of the Gulf.''

Jack didn't seem to find the prospect of being cooped up in a small condo with a pregnant wife, five children and an eighty-pound poodle the least daunting. That was only one of the reasons Cari loved him. The goofy smile that came over his face when his glance rested on Deb was another.

Her sister sat at the table set strategically near the sliding glass with their panoramic view of the Gulf. Her youngest was nestled against her distended belly. The rest of her brood were in chairs crowded around the table.

''Thank goodness!'' Deb exclaimed when she spotted the newcomers. ''Reinforcements! Grab a chair and help me fight off this hoard of warlocks.''

''Not warlocks, Mom.'' His eyes serious behind his round, Harry Potter-style glasses, her eight-year-old corrected her. ''Wizards.''

''Right. Wizards. Major, this is our eldest, Ben.'' She gave each of the kids crowded around the table a quick nod. ''In order of age but not importance, these are Julie, Logan and Pitty-Pat, also known as Patricia. Paulo you already know, of course.''

From her precarious perch on her mother's almost nonexistent lap, two-year-old Pitty-Pat thrust her thumb in her mouth and regarded Mac with wide brown eyes. He returned her solemn look before knuckling Paulo's dark head.

"Hiya, kid."

The boy tried for one of his scowls at this rough and ready treatment, but couldn't quite disguise his relief at seeing a familiar face. He settled back in his chair, making no effort to shrug off the hand Mac rested on his shoulder while the older kids peppered the newcomer with questions about the badges and ribbons adorning his uniform shirt.

"Are you in the coast guard like Aunt Cari?"

"What's that shiny metal thing?"

"Do you know how to navigate by the stars?"

The last came from Ben, who, his father explained, was working on a merit badge for scouts on celestial navigation.

"I'm in the United States Marine Corps," he answered with an easy smile, "not the coast guard. This is an expert marksmanship badge. And yes, I can find my way using celestial navigation but prefer to use GPS."

"Then you should be really good at hunting down witches and wizards," Deb said cheerfully. "Here, take my place. I need to make a potty run."

"Again?"

"Mo...om!"

From the groans that rose from the group at the table, this wasn't her first potty run of the game. Nor,

Cari suspected, would it be her last. Unperturbed, Deb shifted Pitty-Pat off her lap onto the one next to hers, which happened to be Paulo's. The toddler went willingly, and the boy caged his arms around her with the same casually protective air he'd used with little Rosa.

Jack dragged a chair in from the living room for Cari and wedged it in next to the one Deb had turned over to Mac. She took it willingly, but wouldn't let them abandon the game in progress to start over and include her.

"I'll just watch while you finish this game."

Jack and Ben did their best to explain the complex and apparently fluid rules of engagement to Mac, Deb's stand-in. To Cari's amusement, the marine was soon racing for his life through nests of giant spiders and smacking into castle walls that inexplicably moved when he did. After his third encounter with one of these board-jumping walls, even Paulo was chuffing with laughter.

"Think that's funny, do you?" Mac rattled the dice. "Better watch it, kid. I'm hot on your tail and coming after you."

The noise levels rose with each roll of the dice. Squeals of delight, shrieks of dismay, exclamations of triumph all reverberated through the condo. Pierre the Poodle added to the pandemonium by dashing back and forth. Torn between the action at the table and his self-appointed duty of warning off the pesky sea-gulls swooping down outside, he emitted nonstop growls, yips and woofs.

Despite the pandemonium, Cari found herself wishing the game would go on forever. This was what she wanted. For herself *and* for Mac. A noisy room filled with love and laughter and children. All happy, all giggling. Swallowing the lump in her throat, she took in the sight of Mac and Paulo trading mock scowls while engaged in seemingly mortal combat.

Deb returned from the bathroom, but waved Mac back when he would have relinquished her place at the board. "You're doing great. Keep rolling those dice and I'll order the pizza. Who wants what on theirs?"

She noted the long list of particulars with the mental agility of a waitress and ambled into the kitchen. Cari abandoned her observation post to join her. Thankfully, the swinging door to the kitchen cut the noise level from ultra high frequency decibel level to almost bearable.

"I don't know how you maintain your calm in the midst of all that chaos," Cari commented with a wry smile.

Laughing, Deb dragged the fat local phone book out of the drawer under the wall-mounted phone. "The same way you maintain yours when you take your coast guard cutter out in near gale-force winds to chase down some dope smuggler.''

Pizza ordered, the two sisters set out soft drinks and plastic cups, then claimed the rattan bar stools set at the kitchen counter. With their backs to the swinging door and a view through the windows over the sink of the storm-tossed Gulf before them, they stole a few moments of relative calm and comfort.

''I like your major,'' Deb commented while waiting for the fizz in her soft drink to subside.

''Funny, he said exactly the same thing about you.''

''What's funny about that? He's obviously a man of discerning taste and unerring judgment. But then we already knew that. He hooked you, didn't he?''

''Yeah,'' Cari admitted softly. ''He did.''

''So what's the deal with you two? When are you going to take him home to meet the folks?''

She answered the easier question first. ''Not any time soon. The docs are sending him back to his duty station on restricted duty while he completes a regimen of physical therapy.''

Deb's brow knit. ''They're not going to do that shoulder replacement you told me about?''

''Apparently he's not a viable candidate.''

''Bummer!'' She digested that for a few moments. ''Back to the first part of my question. What's the deal with you two?''

"There is no deal. Yet. The surgeons just delivered the bad news this morning. Mac and I haven't had a chance to talk about where we go from here."

"What's to talk about? It's obvious you're crazy about him. If the feeling's mutual, why don't you just go for it?"

"That's pretty much my plan, but it's not as simple as it sounds. Mac has to return to the marine corps base at Cherry Point, North Carolina, for one thing. I'm heading off in a different direction. For another, he won't know whether he'll remain on active duty until after he meets a medical evaluation board."

"I don't see the problem. You love him. You think he loves you. You should do what comes naturally and work through the problems as they come."

Leave it to Deb to strip matters down to basics. Her husband and her family came first. Everything else came a distant second.

"Besides which," she added, "that boy needs a home. A permanent home."

"Paulo?"

"Yes, Paulo. Don't tell me you haven't thought about adopting him. I saw the way you watched him and Mac together. You want the whole package, sister mine. I could read it in your face."

"Yes, I do. But it can't happen, Deb. Not any time in the foreseeable future, anyway. My duties take me away for long stretches at a time. Mac is facing months of painful therapy before he meets that eval board. The therapy could take months, even years. No court is going to grant us custody of a child under those conditions. Particularly when the child himself may have to undergo a series of operations.''

Deb's jaw locked in stubborn lines. She wasn't about to concede the point, but had trouble coming up with cogent counterarguments. Absorbed in the discussion, neither sister noticed the boy who'd nudged the swinging door open a few inches, an empty glass in his hand.

His young face twisted into an expression too old for his age. As silent as a shadow, he backed out of the kitchen.

Chapter 13

The battle of the boards carried over until the doorbell buzzed. Instantly, the kids lost all interest in witches and wizards.

"Pizza!" five-year-old Logan shouted.

"Peasa!" Pitty-Pat echoed joyfully.

"Okay, kids." Their father shoved back his chair. "You know the drill."

Mac watched the resulting scramble with an appreciative eye. The Hamilton clan could have shown a platoon of new recruits a thing or two. With a furious burst of energy, Ben and Julie cleared the table and put away the board game. Logan dashed into the kitchen to help his mom and aunt Cari bring in plastic plates and drinking glasses. Pitty-Pat's chubby fingers curled around Paulo's to draw him into the whirlwind of activity.

"I show you."

His mouth set, Paulo jerked his hand free. The toddler's face screwed up for a moment but she was too well used to the vagaries of older siblings to make a fuss. Curling her rosebud lips around her thumb, she trotted off.

Mac noted the exchange. He also noted that Jack was reaching for his wallet. "Lunch is on me," he said easily, dropping a hand on Paulo's shoulder. "Come on, squirt. Help me carry in the pizza."

The deliveryman was huddled under the skimpy front overhang. Rain splashed off his red carrying case onto the cardboard boxes Mac piled in Paulo's outstretched arms. He gave the man a generous tip for braving the weather and closed the door on the storm.

When Paulo started for the living room, Mac stayed him with a gentle hand. "You okay, kid?"

The boy's eyes lifted. Mac caught a flash of something he couldn't interpret in their dark depths. Frowning, he eased the boxes out of Paulo's hands onto a handy hall table and dropped down on one knee.

"What is it? Why did you suddenly get so quiet in the middle of the game?"

Paulo hesitated, then used his hands in an attempt to communicate. Frustrated by his inability to understand, Mac shook his head. "Sorry, I don't get what you're saying."

Scowling, the kid reached out and lightly touched his sling.

"Are you worried about my shoulder?"

Paulo answered with a quick jerk of his chin.

"I won't lie to you. It hurts like hell, but it'll get better. Eventually."

The boy's fingers fluttered upward, dusted over the gold oak leaf on the collar of Mac's khaki shirt.

"What?"

Small white teeth bit down on a lower lip. Once more Paulo fingered the oak leaf, this time with an urgent question in his eyes.

Hell! The kid had picked up more than Mac had realized during his visits to the hospital.

"Did you hear I might get booted out of the marines?"

The nod was slower this time.

"Well, I might. But not for a long time yet. They're going to make me do some exercises for a while, see how the shoulder works before they make any decisions."

The urgency faded from the black eyes. It was replaced by something that hovered between resignation and despair. His thin shoulders sagging under the Spider-Man T-shirt, he reached for the pizza boxes.

"Listen to me, kid." Curling his good hand under Paulo's chin, he tipped the small face to his. "I know you've got some tough times ahead, too."

Tough didn't begin to describe it. Mac knew all too well what it was like to move into a strange house and try to fit in with a new family, all the while knowing both were only temporary.

Added to that, the kid faced the possibility of a series of operations followed by the excruciating experience of learning to speak through an artificial voice box. Mac decided right then and there that wherever he was, whatever private hell he might be going through himself, he'd be there when the kid went under the knife.

"I'm going to talk to the Hamiltons. Ask them to keep me posted on how you're doing. I'll talk to you, too. Regularly. And if you decide to have the operation Dr. White told you about, I'll fly in to be with you. I promise."

Paulo didn't believe him. Mac could see it in the kid's expression. He'd been abandoned too many times to pin his hopes on anyone but himself.

Not for the first time Mac cursed the bullet that had landed him in this frigging state of limbo. He couldn't plan, couldn't act, couldn't direct the course of his own life much less affect anyone else's. Savagely, he shoved aside his crazy, half-baked idea of standing sponsor to the kid and sharing a hospital room while the docs gave Paulo an artificial voice and Mac a new shoulder. The shoulder wasn't going to happen, but he'd damned well go AWOL if necessary to hear the kid speak his first words.

"I'll be there," he promised again. "When you go into the hospital or any other time you need me. You just have the Hamiltons call, okay? One call and I'll hotfoot it down to Shreveport. Got that?"

Paulo nodded but wouldn't meet Mac's eyes. Retrieving the pizzas, he carted them into the other room.

Coming on top of the grim verdict on his shoulder, Mac's inability to offer the boy more than promises frayed the edges of his temper. The easy smile stayed on his face. He downed his share of pizza. He even managed to hold his own against Pitty-Pat and Logan in a rowdy game of Mr. Potato Head. But he was coiled as tight as a cocked pistol by the time Cari told her sister they had to leave. Although the kids raised an instant chorus of protests, Deb didn't try to strong-arm them into staying. Mac got the distinct impression Cari had indicated the two of them needed to talk.

Talking wasn't the only item on his agenda. Nor was it the first. The need to tumble this woman into his arms and into bed grew with each whishing roll of the car's tires on the rain-soaked pavement.

His rational mind said he should put the skids on. Now. Despite Cari's assertion that they were already in too deep, he knew he could slice through the web of desire they'd woven around themselves. One swift cut, that's all it would take to sever the silken ties. Then all he'd have to do was get through the months and years ahead knowing he'd shoved the one woman he'd ever wanted in his life right out of it.

Not that Cari was the type to let a man shove her in *or* out of anything. She had her own agenda, Mac discovered when they dashed through the rain and gained the dry warmth of her rooms at the visiting officers' quarters. An agenda that didn't rank discussing their future within the top two must-do's.

Her first priority, she informed him on a husky note that put an instant kink in his gut, was to get them both naked. Her second, using up the contents of that box of condoms.

She set about the first task almost as soon as the door thudded shut behind them. Her hands eager, she tugged his shirt free of his pants and worked the buttons. As each button slipped through the hole she treated him to nipping little kisses.

Mac held back, reminding himself of all the reasons they should talk before making use of his emergency supplies. Cari's tongue and busy little hands torpedoed the last of his rapidly disintegrating restraint. She got his shirt down his good arm, but the sling stymied her.

"How the heck do you get your clothes on and off over this thing?"

His mouth curved. "Very carefully."

Unbuckling the sling, he eased down the straps. He ignored his shoulder's instant scream of protest and kept his arm bent. Frowning in concentration, Cari carefully removed his uniform blouse and undershirt. They hit the floor while Mac rebuckled the sling.

"You're pretty good with that left hand," she observed, trailing her fingertips down his sternum. As light as it was, her touch set every one of his nerves jumping like sailors on a hot steel deck. And when her fingers slid inside his belt, he gave up any thought of postponing the inevitable.

He wanted this woman with a hunger that gored a hole right through his middle. The flush of desire staining her cheeks told him she wanted him with the same vicious need.

"Come into the bedroom with me," he said on a low growl, "and I'll show you just how good I am with my left hand."

He was better than good, Cari thought on a rush of heat some moments later. He gave a whole new meaning to the term *ambidextrous.*

Wedging pillows under his injured shoulder, he propped himself up enough to explore her sprawled body. He took his time about it. Skimming his left hand from her neck to her knees, he traced every curve, every valley. The calluses on his palm raised little pinpricks of sensation everywhere they brushed. The lazy circle his thumb rasped over her nipple drew it into a tight, tingling bud.

Within moments he'd progressed from her breast to the curve of her belly. When he slid his hand between her thighs and pressed the heel against her mound, Cari shot straight from tiny pinpricks to giant waves of pleasure. Her belly clenched. The sensations piled up, receded, came crashing in again like the surf pounding the south Texas coast. She arched up, careful not to jar his shoulder, and locked her mouth on his.

His hand pressed harder, his fingers probed deeper. Cari teetered on the edge and pulled back only by a sheer effort of will.

"We took turns last time," she panted. "Let's do this together this time."

More than willing, he rolled onto his back and fumbled for his stash of emergency supplies. Cari usually made it a point to take the necessary precautions herself, but the fact that Mac would put her protection before his pleasure melted her heart and left her swimming in a puddle of want.

This task he couldn't manage one-handed, though. Grinning at his muttered curse, she leaned across him and made short work of the foil wrapper. Her hands slow, her smile wicked, she rolled the thin sheath down his rigid, straining length.

Her smile stayed in place until she'd straddled him. It slipped a little as he positioned himself, and disappeared completely when he flexed his thighs and drove upward. Gasping, Cari fell forward and planted her hands on either side of his head.

Her climax came too fast, too hard, too damned soon! Groaning against Mac's mouth, she clenched her muscles and rode the wild, tossing waves. He tangled his hand in her hair, kept her mouth hard on his and flexed his thighs again. A moment later, he followed her over the edge.

If the first time was hard and fast, the second was slow and sweet.

They more or less drifted into it. She was sprawled facedown on the tangled covers, still lazy with pleasure, when he padded in from the bathroom. She watched him with the one eye she didn't have buried in the pillow.

Russ McIver in uniform epitomized today's modern, highly skilled warrior. Out of it, he was all sleek muscle and satisfied male. His weight set the mattress springs creaking as he settled beside her and nuzzled her neck.

"Mmm. That's nice."

"We need to talk, Cari."

"I know. Could you do that a little lower?"

Nuzzling soon gave way to nipping. The bristly rasp of his five o'clock shadow added to the scrape of his teeth. Cari had come fully alive again when she felt a suspicious prod at her backside. Twisting, she aimed a laughing look over her shoulder.

"You certainly recharge your batteries faster than *Pegasus* does."

Grinning at the compliment, he proceeded to demonstrate several other areas in which his performance exceeded that of an all-weather, all-terrain attack/assault vehicle.

By the time they finished, late afternoon had darkened into stormy night and Cari was limp with pleasure. Mac, on the other hand, appeared remarkably together for a man who'd already made a serious dent in his emergency supplies. Hooking his left elbow under his head, he smiled across the pillow at her.

"Have I told you what a remarkable woman you are, Lieutenant Dunn?"

"Not lately." She thought about it for a moment. "Not ever, as a matter of fact. Nor, I would like to point out, have you told me you love me."

He blinked in surprise. "Sure I have."

"Is that right?" Dragging the sheet up, she tucked it under her arms. "When?"

"What, you want the exact time and place?" He searched his memory. "That night in Caribe, after you told me you'd called things off with Jerry-boy. I told you then I had it bad for you."

"Actually, your exact phrasing was that you had the hots for me."

One corner of his mouth tipped up. "That's pretty much the equivalent of saying I love you in marine-speak."

"Not in coast guard lingo. Say it, Mac. I want to hear the words."

His smile took on a curve that was tender and tough and rueful all at the same time. "I love you, Cari. I have from the first time you squared up to me and suggested I get my head out of my butt, or words to that effect."

Snuggling closer, she bent an elbow on his chest and propped her chin in the crook. Her heart was in her eyes as she answered the question in his.

"I love you, too, big guy. So much I was prepared to use your sling to tie you to this bed until you admitted the feeling was mutual."

"Well, damn! I didn't know you were into kinky stuff. It's still not too late for ropes and chains."

Grinning, she ignored his exaggerated leer. "The

question now is whether we take the next step slow, or jump on a plane and zip out to Vegas before returning to our separate duty stations. Personally, I vote for Vegas.''

Just like that, Mac felt the worry and frustration and disgust at his lack of control over his life slide out of him. She was so sure, so certain. Her brown eyes held not the faintest trace of doubt.

He knew then that it didn't matter what the medical evaluation board decided. The corps had filled his mind and his heart all these years. He suspected both would be now fully occupied by Lieutenant Caroline Dunn.

Before he could tell her so, a ferocious pounding rattled the door in the other room.

''Oh, no!'' Cari groaned. ''Why does this always happen when we get naked?''

''You stay naked. I'll get it this time.''

Shaking his uniform pants, he stepped into them and dragged them on. Cari reached across the bed to keep them up around his hips while he worked the zipper.

''Thanks.'' His flashed her a quick grin. ''We make a heck of a team, Dunn.''

''So we do,'' she returned smugly.

Still grinning, Mac left her amid the tumbled covers and closed the bedroom doors. He opened the one in the living room to find Jill Bradshaw in the hall, her fist raised to pound again. The cop's startled glance zeroed in on his bare chest, dropped to his shoeless feet and whipped up to his amused face.

"Sorry to interrupt," she said got out after a moment. "If Cari's in there with you, she might want to turn on the television."

The sound of her former roommate's voice brought Cari's head popping through the crack in the bedroom door.

"Why? What's up?"

"A news flash just came on. Evidently a cruise ship out of Galveston lost one of its stabilizers. The storm's tossing the liner around like a toy boat."

"Oh, Lord!" Dragging the sheet she'd wrapped around her, Cari made for the TV. "Anyone want to bet two thousand passengers are upchucking all over that ship right now?"

Neither Mac nor Jill took her up on the bet, which was smart, as the news chopper's aerial shot of the floundering ship made even Cari's stomach turn queasy. The helicopter's high-powered spots barely cut through the sheets of rain and winds that sent walls of angry water smashing across the vessel's bow.

"She's floundering," Cari muttered, her gaze narrowed on the screen. "They'd better start taking off her passengers, like fast."

As if to confirm her assessment of the situation, the

newscaster pitched his voice over the howling winds to advise that the coast guard had ordered them to vacate the area immediately so as not to interfere with rescue operations. White knuckled, Cari clutched the sheet.

"The coast guard units here and at Kingsville will respond," she told the others. "Navy rescue craft, as well. They'll have to shuttle the passengers in by shifts. The operation will take all night."

Dropping into the chair at the desk, she reached for the phone and asked the operator to connect her to the coast guard operations center. She wasn't surprised when the on-duty controller ascertained she wasn't reporting an emergency then put her on hold for a good five minutes. When he came back on, Cari cut right to the purpose of her call.

"This is Lieutenant Caroline Dunn, United States Coast Guard. I'm on detached duty here at Corpus Christi. Tell your C.O. I'm available if he needs more hands to assist in the rescue operation."

"Will do, ma'am. Give me your number and I'll pass it to the skipper."

After that, there was nothing to do but watch as the local rescue units battled nature's fury. Cari and Mac retreated to the bedroom only long enough to dress. Two hours crawled by, long stretches filled with tossing seas and a steady progression of rescue craft pinned in the unrelenting glare of the aircraft circling overhead. Jill rapped on the door again, this time with Cody, Kate and Dave in tow.

Her face grim, Kate delivered more bad news. "I just checked the weather service computers. We've got another front moving down from the north. The two are going to collide right over this corner of the Gulf. The situation is going to get a whole lot worse before it gets better."

Her prediction was right on target. Where the seas were angry before, they soon turned vicious. The news agencies reported forty- and fifty-foot swells. Shots of the cruise ship showed the liner battered by white-capped swells that leaped and crashed around it like furies.

Cari was huddled in front of the TV with the rest of the Pegasus team when the phone rang. Thinking it was the coast guard controller, she snatched up the receiver.

"Lieutenant Dunn."

"Cari!" Her sister's frantic voice jumped across the line. "Is Paulo there with you?"

Her fist went tight on the phone. "No, he's not."

"We can't find him. We think he's run away."

"Why, for God's sake?"

"Jack found him playing with a rusty old pocket-knife. He was afraid one of the other kids might cut themselves and tried to take it away."

"Oh, no!"

She'd forgotten all about the boy's prize possession! She should have warned Deb he had it, explained how much it meant to him.

"How long has he been missing?"

Mac pushed out of his chair and came across the room. "How long has who been missing?"

"Paulo."

She angled the receiver so he could listen to Deb's rushed account.

"Paulo agreed to give Jack the knife. I thought he understood we were only holding it for safekeeping, but when we went up to check on the kids, he was gone. So was the knife."

"Have you called the Whites?"

"I checked with them first."

Mac snatched the phone out of Cari's hand. "What about the hospital? He might have gone there looking for me."

"I already called there. No one's seen him. Jack went out to search up and down the beach." Her voice wavered, cracked. "Oh, Mac, I hate to think Paulo might be wandering around in this storm."

Chapter 14

After instructing Deb to notify the police about Paulo's disappearance, Cari, Mac and the rest of the Pegasus cadre raced through the sheeting rain to the Hamiltons' beachside condo. The Whites arrived mere minutes later, as did a team of police officers and a hastily assembled group of local volunteers.

While Deb manned a mini-command post set up in the kitchen, searchers combed an area stretching from the populated sectors in the north to the Padre Island national seashore farther south. The searchers stayed out until well past midnight. Buffeted by wind, lashed by rain, they went door to door in the developed areas and used ATVs to comb the dunes.

The police called a halt to the official search just after 1:00 a.m. and asked the volunteers to reassemble come daylight. Mac, Cari, Jack, the Whites and the rest of the Pegasus crew gathered at the condo to re-group. Downing mugs of steaming coffee, they pre-pared to go back out again. A thoroughly miserable Jack shoved back the hood of his canary-yellow rain jacket and dragged a hand over his face.

"I feel lousy about that business with the knife. I didn't have any idea it meant so much to Paulo."

"That was our fault," Janice White said wearily. She was as soaked as the rest of them. Water dripped from her lashes and her strawberry-blond hair stood up in wet spikes. "We should have explained how careful Paulo always was with it around the other children. I'm surprised he ran away because you took it, though. The first few times Harry confiscated it, Paulo just rooted around the mission until he found it again."

Jack took small comfort from her words. Mac un-derstood how he felt. He'd sensed something was troubling the kid, had tried to ferret it out of him. The best he'd been able to do was offer hearty assurances he'd be there when and if Paulo went into surgery.

A kid needed more than assurances. From bitter experience, Mac knew they needed a hand to hang on to. One that wouldn't let go through the rough times or the good.

"I'm going back out," he said abruptly.

He returned his mug to the kitchen counter with a thud, slopping hot coffee onto the back of his hand. He ignored the sting and dragged up the hood of his borrowed squall jacket. His uniform pants were drenched from the knees down and his shoes would never take another shine, but a lack of military precision didn't concern him at the moment.

Cari edged around the counter. Her hand caught his and made soothing little circles on the still-stinging skin.

"We'll find him," she said softly.

She'd guessed his guilt, his gut-wrenching sense of having failed Paulo as so many adults had failed Mac during his younger, wilder years. Despite the worry darkening her eyes, she was taking time to let him know she understood.

Funny, he'd never talked about his past. Had never needed to talk about it. Cari was the only one he could remember opening up to, and then with little more than the sketchiest details. Yet the bits he'd shared with her had given her a clearer insight into his thinking than he'd realized. For the first time, Mac had an inkling of what it would be like to share his life, his bed, even his thoughts with someone.

No, not *someone*.

With Cari.

Turning his palm up, he gave her fingers a tight, reassuring squeeze. "Damn straight, we'll find him."

He was halfway to the door when the shrill of the phone froze him in his tracks. Everyone in the kitchen jerked toward the wall-mounted unit. Leaping out of his seat with a look of anxious hope, Jack reached across the counter and snatched up the receiver.

"Hamilton here."

A moment later his shoulders drooped in disappointment. Turning, he held the phone out to his sister-in-law.

"It's the coast guard operations center."

"Oh, hell," Cari muttered. Her wet sneakers squishing on the tile, she crossed the kitchen. "I forgot about that cruise ship. God, I hope it hasn't gone down."

For several tense moments, it looked to the others in the kitchen that the worst had indeed happened. Cari identified herself, listened to the controller for a few seconds and suddenly stiffened.

"How far out are they?"

Her knuckles turned bone-white where she clutched the phone. Every vestige of color drained from her face. Her glance cut to Mac to her sister and back again.

His insides went cold. The call was about Paulo. He could see it in her face.

"Advise the RCC I'm on my way."

Slamming the phone into its cradle, she faced the tense, silent group.

"The coast guard Rescue Coordination Center just received a distress call from the captain of a commercial fishing boat. The *Aransas Star* put out from the docks just north of here earlier this evening, intending to edge around the worst of the storm so its crew could set their tuna lines come dawn. The boat had almost cleared the storm area when the second front hit. Its engine took a horrific beating fighting those swells and seized."

"Seized?" Deb gasped. "Like in *died?*"

"Like in *died.* When the crew went down to try to restart the engine they discovered a stowaway. He won't tell them his name..."

"Because he can't," Mac guessed grimly.

White-lipped, Cari nodded. "Their description of the boy tallies. It's Paulo."

The questions flew at her then, fast and furious.

"Did they get the engine restarted?"

"Are they bringing Paulo in?"

"Is the coast guard going after them?"

She shook her head. "No to the first two. As for the third, the Rescue Coordination Center is looking to see what assets they can redirect from the crippled cruise ship. Hopefully, they'll have a chopper or a cutter on the way by the time we get there."

''We're wasting time here,'' Mac snapped. ''Let's go.''

Deb and Jack stayed with their kids. The Whites remained at the condo as well, since their civilian status wouldn't allow them access to the restricted RCC. The six Pegasus team members piled into their vehicles and tailed Cari back to the naval air station.

The Rescue Coordination Center was like a dozen others Cari had pulled duty in. A wall-sized screen displayed a huge, computerized map of the Gulf. Controllers sat at a U-shaped console that gave them an unobstructed view of the screen while they synthesized the information pouring in by phone, fax, radio and computer. Given the level of activity, the very air inside the center vibrated with tension.

Cari pinpointed the location of the cruise ship with a single glance at the screen. The flashing red icon representing the ship looked like a giant queen bee, surrounded by hoards of rescue craft that buzzed around her like drones. Several pleasure boats were in distress as well, Cari saw. And there, in the northeast corner of the operational sector, was the flashing signal marking the position of the *Aransas Star*.

The center's commanding officer dragged his attention from the screen only long enough to brief the new arrivals. Mac was the only one of the group wearing a uniform, but the C.O. recognized Cari instantly. The coast guard was a relatively small service and most of the officers had crossed paths at one time or another.

Swiftly, Cari introduced the others. The C.O. accepted Jill's army status, Doc Richardson's Public Health Service background and Dave Scott's air force experience without a blink. His interest quickened when he learned Kate Hargrave was one of the National Oceanic and Atmospheric Administration's famed hurricane hunters. The National Weather Service was one of NOAA's major sub-units and, it turned out, had accurately predicted the turbulence that would occur when the second front moved in and collided with the first.

"We managed to get a warning out to most of the ships at sea," the rescue coordinator said, brushing a hand through his short, sandy hair. "If the cruise liner hadn't lost a stabilizer, she would have made port before the second front hit."

"How's the off-load of passengers progressing?" Cari asked.

"More slowly than we'd like. We've pressed all available navy, coast guard and customs service vessels into service, along with choppers from every base along the Gulf. But with these winds and swells, it's hell trying to bring the rescue craft alongside the liner."

"What about the fishing boat? We think the stow-

craft in position over the boat. Everyone aboard held their breath until he raised the boat's captain on an emergency frequency.

"They see our lights," he informed those in the rear, shouting into his mike to be heard above the screaming winds. "The captain says we got here just in time. They're taking on water, fast."

"What about Paulo?" Mac yelled into the mike. "Is he okay?"

"Roger that. I'm going to raise the hatch. Make sure all lifelines are secure."

They took the warning seriously. Without the harnesses securing them to lines hooked into ringbolts in the bulkhead, they might well be sucked out into the maelstrom. Mac got a thumbs-up from the other three and confirmed their ready status.

"All secure!"

When the side hatch slid up, hell poured in. Rain lashed through the rear compartment. Wind ricocheted off the bulkheads and slammed into every immoveable object. *Pegasus* bucked wildly again, gyrating through the sky while Dave fought to compensate for the now gaping hole in the side of his craft.

For a few terrifying seconds, Cari's worst nightmare came back to haunt her. Only this time they weren't skimming along a green river with an enemy patrol boat on their tails. This time, they were sus-

---

away they found aboard is the same child we reported missing some hours ago."

His face etched with sharp creases, the commander eyed the flashing red icon in the northeast sector of his operations area. "They're more than a hundred nautical miles out. I'm diverting a chopper but will have to refuel it in flight. We're requesting a tanker orbit now."

Cari's stomach sank. Bellying the rescue chopper up to a tanker in these winds would eat a precious thirty minutes. Sending it across a hundred nautical miles of storm-tossed sea would eat at least another hour. The fishing boat couldn't take another hour and a half of being pounded by these murderous swells.

Mac did the math as swiftly as Cari did, but grabbed on to a different solution.

"We've got our own craft," he informed the commander brusquely. "It's got twice the air speed of a chopper. What's more, it's fueled and ready to fly."

Cari whipped around. "*Pegasus* isn't configured for deep-water rescue."

"It's equipped with a Survivor Retrieval System," Kate reminded her. "We used it to haul Mac out of the river."

"The SRS won't hack it in these kinds of seas. We'd need a harness sling or a basket."

She spun around again, an urgent question on her face. Her coast guard comrade answered with a quick nod. ''We can supply a sling, but the baskets are all in use.''

His pronouncement galvanized the entire Pegasus cadre. Dave Scott jumped in with confirmation that he'd prepped the craft for departure and had it ready to fly. Kate added that she could program in the current weather patterns en route and take them around the worst of the storm. Jill, ever conscious of her responsibilities as chief of security for *Pegasus*, issued a quick caution.

''We're talking about flying a multimillion-dollar prototype vehicle into howling, gale-force winds. We should obtain Captain Westfall's concurrence before we put the vehicle at risk.''

''Get him on a secure line,'' Mac bit out. ''Now!''

They tracked him to his hotel in Washington. Jill's call dragged Captain Westfall from a sound sleep. Succinctly, she explained the situation and requested his concurrence to include *Pegasus* as part of the multiservice rescue operation. She flipped her cell phone shut a few moments later with a tight, satisfied smile.

''He says to get our butts in gear and *Pegasus* in the air.''

Cari's admiration for the lean, taciturn naval officer kicked up another notch. He shouldered overall responsibility for the Pegasus project, had invested months of his life and countless hours of sleep attempting to shake the last of the bugs out of the pro-

totype. Yet he didn't hesitate to give them the green light and send his baby into harm's way once more.

''Okay, people,'' Mac snapped. ''Let's move it.''

After a fast detour to their on-base quarters to retrieve their gear and scramble into uniforms, the team raced to the hangar the navy had turned over to house *Pegasus* until its flight home. Dave had called ahead to the ground crew. The crew had *Pegasus* prepped and preflighted when the team arrived at the hangar. Moments later, a coast guard truck came screeching up with a harness sling.

Every member of the crew donned inflatable life vests and climbed aboard. Kate settled into the cockpit beside Dave and maintained a direct link to the National Weather Service throughout the turbulent flight. As promised, she directed the pilot around the worst of the storm, but even on the perimeter the winds were still so strong they whipped the craft around in the sky.

Forty stomach-twisting minutes later, Dave got a radar lock on the fishing boat. Struggling with the controls, he throttled back, tilted the engines and took *Pegasus* from forward flight to hover mode. Instead of flying into the winds, the craft was now at their mercy. They slammed *Pegasus* from what seemed like a dozen different directions at once. Sweating, straining, Dave fought to keep the wildly bucking

pended above a crashing sea, tossed around like a toy by nature's most malevolent forces.

The stomach-twisting fear was the same, though, as was the desperate realization that the odds were against them. She allowed herself one throat-closing glimpse through the hatch at the boat wallowing in the vicious seas below. There was one instant of liquid panic before she spotted the crew scattered across the deck, clinging desperately to lifelines.

Then her mind snapped into focus. Eyes narrowed to slits against the stinging rain, she searched the deck until she spotted a small figure huddled against the forward bulkhead. Like the others, Paulo was bundled into a bulky life jacket and tethered to a lifeline to keep from being swept overboard.

Her heart lurched, but she forced back her suffocating fear for the boy and reminded herself she was an officer in the U.S. Coast Guard. Years of command kicked in. Training and experience took over. Her gloved hand went to the lever that operated the Survivor Retrieval System.

"I'm activating the SRS," she bellowed into the mike. "Advise the crew of the *Star* to watch for the lead and try to hook it in."

While Cari extracted the firing tube and primed it, Jill and Doc checked to make sure the weighted lead was securely attached to the lightweight but almost indestructible nylon rope.

"Stand clear!"

The other two scrambled back. Cari braced herself as best she could in the open hatch. Rain slashed at her face. Wind whipped her hair into her eyes. Eyes narrowed to slits, arms extended, heart pounding, she aimed at a patch of boiling sea beyond the bow of the boat.

The weighted lead exploded out of the tube and shot through the air. For a wild, joyous moment, Cari thought she'd calculated the force and direction of the winds exactly right.

What she couldn't factor into her calculations was the capriciousness of the storm. The lead was still sailing through the swirling gray clouds when the wind suddenly shifted. A blast came out of the west, knocked *Pegasus* sideways and would have tossed everyone in the rear compartment onto their butts if not for their lifelines. When Cari got her feet under her again, she saw the lead had hit well aft of the boat.

With a vicious curse, she slammed the system into Reverse and reeled the lead back in. While she loaded another cartridge into the firing tube, Mac went down on one knee and coiled the wet, snaking rope to keep it from tangling when it shot out again.

It took four desperate tries to land the line within a few yards of the *Aransas Star*. Almost sobbing with relief, Cari watched the life-jacketed figures aboard the boat hook the line and drag it in.

It took only a few seconds to attach the rope to the flexible steel cable wound around the winch, a few more to make sure the rescue sling was securely attached to the cable. Once that was done, Cari hit the switch to deploy the hoist.

The moveable arm swung out. Another flick of the switch released the winch. Its gears sang as cable played out and the rescue sling plunged downward. Below, the crew of the *Star* frantically hauled on the nylon lead rope to guide the sling onto the deck.

As much as she wanted to take Paulo off first, Cari knew he needed to see how the hoist worked, had to understand that he should keep his arms locked to his side and the harness tight around his chest.

"Tell them to send up one of the crew first," Cari shouted to Dave via the intercom.

He didn't question her decision. The radio crackled with static as he relayed the order. Almost blinded by the sheeting rain, Cari hung on to her lifeline and leaned out of the hatch to watch while one of the crewmen scrambled into the harness.

He was still yanking on the chest straps when the *Star* plunged into a trough and the deck dropped out from under him. He dangled like a puppet above the boat, spinning in the wind.

Cari shoved the SRS into Reverse and brought him

up. When he was level with the hatch, she swung the retrieval arm in. Doc caught the man's arm, Jill one of his legs. The moment they had him free of the sling, Cari swung the arm out again.

Her heart jumped into her throat when she looked down and saw the *Aransas Star*'s decks were almost completely awash. The crashing waves had knocked the slicker-clad figures off their feet. They whipped back and forth through the frothing water at the ends of their lifelines, as helpless as the tuna they hooked on their fishing lines. Cari didn't breathe until she spotted Paulo among the frothing water. Praying the boy understood what he had to do, she shouted into her mike.

"Tell them to send Paulo up next!"

"Roger."

Mac shortened his lifeline and fought the winds at the open hatch. His jaw clenched so tight the bones ground together. He'd served two combat tours, first in Afghanistan, then in Iraq. He'd seen men go down, had heard their screams as bullets ripped into them. The icy, controlled terror of combat didn't compare to the fear that ripped into him now.

Paulo was so small, so thin. If he lifted his arms, if he wiggled or twisted too much, he could slip right out of that harness.

Mac knew Cari had already considered and discarded the only other option—having one of the other crewmen strap himself in and bring the boy up with him. The savage wind could tear the kid right out of the man's arms.

Mac's heart hammered as two crewmen staggered across the deck toward the boy. They dragged him to his feet. Buckled on the harness. Unhooked his lifeline. Waved to the wildly gyrating craft.

"Hang on, kid. Hang on. Hang on."

Mac repeated the low, fierce litany with every turn of the winch. He could see the boy rise foot by foot. His dark hair was plastered to his skull, his face chalk-white above his orange life vest.

Cari's gloved fist hovered over the switch that would swing the retrieval arm inward. Mac was just letting himself believe they'd get the boy aboard when a brutal downdraft slammed into *Pegasus.* The craft nosedived, spiraling straight down. The steep drop knocked Jill and Cari off balance. Doc threw himself over the rescued crewman to keep him from crashing into the forward bulkhead. Mac stayed upright by sheer force of will and an iron grip on his lifeline.

His heart stopping, he saw the waves reach up and swallow the small figure at the end of the cable. Paulo went under, popped up and was dragged through one crashing wall of water after another.

Dave brought the nose up mere seconds later, but before he could regain altitude another wave smashed into Paulo. When the towering wave rolled past, the harness was empty.

Mac didn't hesitate, didn't give his injured shoulder so much as a single thought. Whipping down his good arm, he unsnapped his lifeline.

A heartbeat later he plunged into the sea.

Chapter 15

Mac sank into a deep trough. He'd no sooner hit than a towering, eighty-foot wave smashed down on top of him. The brutal force drove him downward. So hard, the violence sucked a boot right off his foot. So deep, he couldn't tell top from bottom. So far, his lungs were bursting by the time the vicious wave rolled past and his life jacket brought him popping to the surface.

The massive swells batted at him, battered him, tossed him from side to side. Gritting his teeth, Mac kicked and twisted and rode the violent swells until he spotted Paulo's orange life vest not ten yards away. The steel cable dragged the water just beyond him.

Mac twisted onto his side and buried his bad shoulder in the water. Scissor-kicking, he used his good arm to battle through the swells.

"Paulo!"

The wind flung his shout back in his face. With it came a mouth full of salt water. Spitting, cursing, kicking with every ounce of strength he possessed, Mac cut through the last few yards and got a fist on the back of the boy's vest.

Frantic, Paulo squirmed around and grabbed his rescuer with both hands just above the biceps. As the force of the sea tried to separate them, he clung desperately to Mac's bad arm. Agony knifed through him. The white-capped waves and raging sea blurred. The pain paralyzed him. For an instant, maybe two, his mind and body froze. Teeth grinding, he forced back the black haze.

"Put your arms around my neck."

He had to shout the instruction in the boy's ear to be heard over the snarl of wind and sea.

"Paulo! Climb up and wrap your arms around my neck!"

His dark eyes dilated with terror, the boy crawled up Mac's chest and locked his arms.

"Now kick," Mac yelled. "Kick hard!"

Sandwiched together by the brutal force of the waves, they fought their way to the cable.

Cari watched the life-and-death struggle from

above. Every stroke was a desperate prayer, every pulverizing wave stabbed her agonizing hope in the heart. On the far side of the hatch Cody and Jill stood ready to unhook their lifelines and jump in. If Mac and Paulo went under once more, just once, one of them would hit the water. All the while, Dave sweated and strained to keep *Pegasus* in a hover.

"A few more feet," Cari muttered, her throat raw. "Just a few feet."

She had to time this exactly right. Her hand trembled over the switch while Mac rode the crest of a wave toward the cable. When he was a body length away, Cari hit Reverse. The winch whirred, the cable retracted, and the harness sling rose from the angry green depths. As soon as it broke the surface, she slammed her fist on the switch to halt the winch.

The harness sling dangled just feet from Mac's face. Calling on reserves he wasn't sure he had, he jackknifed his body and propelled forward. He thrust his good arm through the sling, wrestled it over his head, but wasn't about to let Paulo loosen his death grip so he could shimmy the rest of his body into it and attempt to buckle the harness one-handed. Locking the boy against his chest with his good arm, he jerked his head back.

"Bring us up!"

His hoarse bellow got lost in the wind, but Cari

was watching and waiting for his signal. Mac saw the cable go taut, felt the sling dig into his armpit.

When they cleared the roiling surface, the wind set them twisting and swinging like a pendulum. The sea leaped up, crashed around them, tried to devour them yet again. With a whimper of sheer terror, Paulo buried his face in Mac's neck.

The boy's weight dragged at him. The sling felt as though it was slicing him in half. His shoulder was a fireball of pain. Mac blanked his mind to everything but the need to keep his good arm locked around the kid.

Then they cleared the hatch, Cari swung the hoist arm in and anxious hands reached out.

"We've got him," Cody shouted. "Mac, we've got him. Let go!"

An exhausting hour and a half later, *Pegasus* swooped down on the naval air station's rain-drenched runway. A watery dawn was graying the sky to the east as the endless, storm-wracked night slowly gave way to day.

The ground crew was waiting to recover the craft. While Dave went through the shut-down procedures, Kate, Doc and Jill delivered the crew of the *Aransas Star* to the Rescue Coordination Center to make the necessary notifications. Cari and Mac took Paulo back to the condo where the Hamiltons and the Whites waited.

The storm had left its mark. The slowly gathering dawn revealed uprooted palm trees and scattered debris en route to the beachside vacation rentals, but the condos themselves sustained no storm damage. Light poured through the downstairs windows of the unit Cari had rented for her sister. The kids were still asleep, she guessed, but the adults had all spent a long, tension-racked night.

She pulled into the parking space and killed the vehicle's engine. A quick glimpse in the rearview mirror showed eyes hollowed by fatigue and a face framed by the wild, wind-whipped tangles that had escaped her hair clip. Her wet uniform felt clammy in the cool October dawn. Her entire body ached from the strain and tension of the long night.

Her passengers weren't in much better shape. Paulo climbed out of the vehicle and hunched his thin shoulders under the blanket they'd draped around him aboard *Pegasus*. His face was pinched and white and scared. Cari knew he expected a scolding. Or worse.

Mac looked every bit as battered by the elements as the boy. His uniform hung in wet folds. Fatigue had carved deep grooves in his face. His plunge into the sea had left him carrying his shoulder stiffly. *Very* stiffly. Still, he managed to hunker down on one knee when Paulo balked at going into the house.

"Time to face the music, kid." He softened the gruff admonishment by knuckling the boy's head. "You need to tell the Whites and the Hamiltons you're sorry for scaring them the way you did."

He also needed to explain why he'd run away. Neither Cari nor Mac had pressed the shivering, frightened boy for answers, but they both suspected something other than a hassle over his pocketknife had driven Paulo out into the storm.

The others firmly seconded their opinion that explanations could come later. After startling the boy with a fierce hug, Deb waited only until Janice White had translated Paulo's assurances that he was all right to whisk him upstairs for a hot shower and dry clothes. Jack used their absence to supply Cari and Mac with coffee and cook up a huge batch of bacon, scrambled eggs and refrigerator biscuits. All the while, he and the Whites pumped them for details about the rescue at sea.

Deb brought Paulo back downstairs twenty minutes later. After getting the nod from Reverend White, the boy attacked his plate of eggs and bacon like a starving wolf pup. While he gulped down the hot food and glass after glass of milk, Cari and Mac gave Deb an abbreviated version of the saga they'd just related to the others.

Finally it was Paulo's turn. He set down his milk glass and tried for his habitual scowl, but Mac cut him off at the pass. "What did we talk about outside, kid?"

Pushing out his lower lip, Paulo brought up his hands. Janice White interpreted.

"He says he's sorry for frightening us."

Jack leaned forward. His voice heavy with regret, he offered an apology of his own. "I'm sorry, too, Paulo. I didn't understand how important that pocketknife is to you. I wasn't going to keep it or throw it away, just put it somewhere safe."

The boy's dark eyes held only misery as he signed a response.

"It doesn't matter about the knife," Janice translated. "It's at the bottom of the ocean, anyway."

"Oh, no!" Cari clucked sympathetically. "Was it in your pocket when you went into sea?"

His nod confirmed her guess. Slowly, reluctantly, his hands shaped more phrases.

"He says he's wants to go back to Caribe. He can survive alone in the jungle. He's done it before. That way he won't be such trouble to everyone."

"You're not trouble!" Deb protested, her mother's heart shredding at the idea of a child alone in a jungle. "No trouble at all."

Paulo turned to her and Jack, pleading for understanding with his hands and his face.

"He says you have burden enough with your family. He knows you only took him in because the other family, the one who'd said they would adopt him, didn't want him. He thought maybe…"

The small hands went still.

"What?" Janice prompted after a moment. "What did you think, Paulo?"

The boy shot a look comprised of equal parts guilt and unhappiness at the two figures in uniform.

"He thought maybe Major Mac or the lieutenant would take him. He would have been a good son. Very quiet. Work very hard."

Cari's throat closed. "We would have taken you if we could, Paulo."

"He knows you could not," Janice translated. "He understands the major must go to the hospital for a long time. And he heard you explain to your sister that you go away on ships."

Oh, God! *That's* why he'd run away. He'd heard her talking to Deb yesterday afternoon. The realization settled with sickening certainty in Cari's stomach.

She tried to recall her exact words, then realized they didn't matter. What mattered was that she'd shattered his secret hope that she or Mac would give him a home.

She couldn't tell him that she'd harbored the same secret hope. Or that hard, cold reality had forced her to abandon the idea before it could even take shape. As miserable as Paulo now, she reached across the table and curled her hand around his.

"Now it's my turn to apologize. I'm sorry if it sounded as though I didn't want you. I do. I'd give you a home in a heartbeat if I could. So would Major Mac."

She looked to Mac, expecting him to jump right in with a vigorous second. His hesitation surprised her almost as much as the sudden narrowing of his eyes when they met hers. The face he turned to Paulo a moment later, though, showed only honest sincerity.

"She's telling you the truth. Either one of us would be proud to call you son."

Once more he hesitated, choosing his words carefully so as not to offer false hope.

"Stay with Mr. and Mrs. Hamilton, kid. See how things shake out. If you still want to go back to Caribe a few months or a year from now, I'll take you myself and make sure you have a home other than the jungle. Deal?"

No one at the table needed an interpretation of

Paulo's response. Cupping his hand, he moved it slowly up and down much like a head nodding a reluctant agreement.

Mac was quiet during the short drive back to the visiting officers' quarters. Cari, too, had little to say. Weariness, guilt and a sharp, stinging regret had taken the edge off her adrenaline high from plucking Paulo and the crew of the *Star* from the sea. Not until she and Mac had showered and changed into dry clothes did she add a healthy dose of anger to her mix of emotions.

Mac sparked it when she walked into the living room after her shower, still toweling her wet hair. His glance was cool as it skimmed over her cotton sweater and slacks before settling on her face.

Cari's hands stilled. She cocked her head, trying to assess his expression. "That's the second time you've looked at me like that," she commented.

"Like how?"

"Like you blame me for the fact that Paulo almost drowned."

"What?"

Draping the fluffy yellow towel around her neck, she raked a hand through her damp hair. "You can't blame me any more than I blame myself. I hate that Paulo overheard Deb and me. You have to know I never intended to…"

"Don't be stupid. No one blames you, least of all me."

His curt tone brought her chin up. "Then why the hell are you so uptight?"

Irritation pushed through her guilt and regret. After all they'd gone through together, the man could show some consideration here. Maybe even take her in his arms.

He did neither. If anything, his expression went more glacial. "You don't know?"

"Obviously not," she snapped, "or I wouldn't have asked."

Mac crossed the room in three swift strides. Even in shorts and the flip-flops he'd brought with him, the man could be intimidating. Cari stood her ground but didn't particularly care for the dangerous glint in his hazel eyes.

"Just tell me one thing," he growled. "Last night, when we were in bed, why did you toss out the idea of jumping a plane for a quick trip to Vegas?"

The abrupt change in direction confused her. Her fists tight on the ends of the towel, she fired back in the same belligerent tone.

"Because you said you love me and I said ditto. People *do* sometimes get married when they discover they're in love."

"Or when they want to adopt a kid."

Cari reared back. "You... You think I suggested Vegas because I wanted to give Paulo a home?"

Mac's face was relentless above his sling. "Isn't that why you broke things off with Jerry-boy? Because you wanted children and he didn't?"

Her mouth opened. Clamped shut. After a seething moment, she admitted the brutal truth.

"That was part of it."

Mac hooked a brow. "Only part?"

"Okay, that was the main reason. The fact that I was lusting after a certain hardheaded marine might have had something to do with it, too."

When Mac maintained his politely disbelieving expression, Cari blew out a long breath and forced herself to let go of her anger. The need to make him understand was too important, too urgent for sarcasm or sharp retorts.

"What I feel for you has nothing to do with Jerry or Paulo or my desire to have children. I love you. I want to spend the rest of my life with you." Sighing, she reached up to curve a palm over his cheek. "You'll just have to trust me on this, McIver."

To her infinite relief, he turned his head and pressed a kiss into her palm. The icy remoteness was gone when he faced her again, replaced by the first glimmer of a smile.

"You'll have to trust me, too."

"I will. I do."

"Even when I tell you I've decided to leave the corps to become a stay-at-home dad?"

Dumbstruck, Cari gaped up at him. Her hand slipped downward, hit his chest with a thump.

"What!"

His smile slipped into a rueful grin. Reaching up with his good arm, he covered her hand with his.

"I won't be much use to the corps with this shoulder, but I figure I can give Paulo adequate guidance and supervision."

She'd known it! Sensed right almost from the day her all-or-nothing, you're-in-or-you're-out marine took that bullet he would never settle for a career of restricted duty.

Part of her ached for him. The rest of her accepted that the decision was his to make—and knew without a moment's doubt he'd apply the same one hundred percent effort to loving her and Paulo.

Still, she had to ask. "Are you sure, Mac? I know how much the corps means to you."

"It'll always be part of me. You know the old saying. Once a marine, always a marine."

His palm flattened over hers. She could feel the strong, steady beat of his heart under his shirt. The smile in his eyes was just as steady and sure.

"You mean more, Cari. So much, much more. You

and Paulo and any other kids we might have if we try real hard and just happen to get lucky.''

He was handing her her dream, a family she could share the good and the bad times with. Children she could cuddle and spoil and watch grow. A man she could love with all that was in her.

Her heart singing, she went up on tiptoe and brushed his mouth with hers. ''I vote we get started on the trying real hard part right now.''

Epilogue

The ceremony kicked off with the ruffles and flourishes appropriate to a four-star general. Flanked by Captain Westfall, the vice chairman of the Joint Chiefs marched into a spotless hangar illuminated to almost painful intensity by the New Mexico sun. Although the January wind frisking through the wide-open hangar doors carried a definite nip, none of the officers who leaped to attention noticed its bite.

They stood at the head of the Pegasus cadre. Their service dress uniforms were knife-creased. Their ribbons, badges and accouterments glittered in the bright sunlight.

Jill Bradshaw in army-green with the crossed pistols of the Military Police Branch decorating her lapels.

Dave Scott wearing air force blue and rows of colorful ribbons topped by shiny silver wings.

Kate Hargrave in her navy blue skirt and jacket, with the shield of National Oceanic and Atmospheric Administration gleaming on her cap.

Cody Richardson, also in dark navy, wearing the anchor insignia of the U.S. Public Health Service.

Cari with shoulders squared and her gold wedding band gleaming in the afternoon sunlight.

Mac standing tall and proud in his dress blues for the last time.

Another ceremony would follow this one. After three months of intensive physical therapy, Major Russ McIver was being released from active duty and medically retired from the United States Marine Corps. The ceremony would be done by Captain Westfall—newly engaged to Dr. Janice White— immediately following the vice chairman's formal acceptance of the military's new attack/assault vehicle.

Pegasus gleamed white and sleek across the hangar. The vehicle would go into full production soon. Within a few short months, personnel from combat units stateside and abroad would enter training to learn how to maximize its unique abilities. Dave Scott was transferring to the designated training base in Georgia, just a few hours up the road from

Kate's base in Tampa. Cari had been selected for the training cadre, too.

She knew Captain Westfall had pulled some strings to make that assignment happen. It would give Mac time to transition to full civilian life, Paulo time to adjust to the artificial voice box doctors had implanted two weeks ago, and Cari to have three years of shore duty to enjoy motherhood.

Resisting the impulse to grin idiotically, she kept her back straight and her hand from straying to her belly in a protective gesture as old as time. The time for wonder and delight and celebration would come later, when she and Mac could share with their comrades in arms the results of the home pregnancy test she'd taken this morning.

Right now, her focus needed to remain on the ceremony marking the end of the operational test phase. *Pegasus* had proved himself—on land, air and sea. This was his moment in the sun, a moment every man and woman present took inestimable pride in.

When the general stepped to the podium to deliver the congratulations of the six service chiefs, the massed cadre went to parade rest. Legs spread. Hands whipped to the small of the back. Spines lost only a minimal degree of rigidity.

While the general adjusted his mike, a ripple of emotion passed through the officers. One by one they slipped a glance to the right, then to the left. The

small smiles they gave each other reflected pride of
accomplishment, along with the smug knowledge
they shared that indefinable mix of adventurous heart
and fearless spirit others called—for lack of a better
term—the right stuff.

*   *   *   *   *

Darkness Calls

CARIDAD PINEIRO

Harlequin
Mills & Boon

Intimate

First Published 2004
First Australian Paperback Edition 2004
ISBN 0 733 55126 2

Published by
Harlequin Mills & Boon
3 Gibbes Street
CHATSWOOD NSW 2067
AUSTRALIA

Printed and bound in Australia by
McPherson's Printing Group

CARIDAD PIÑEIRO

was born in Havana, Cuba, and settled in the New York metropolitan area. She attended Villanova University on a presidential scholarship and graduated magna cum laude in 1980. Caridad earned her Juris Doctor from St. John's University, and in 1994 she became the first female and Latino partner of Abelman, Frayne & Schwab.

Caridad is a multipublished author whose love of the written word developed when her fifth grade teacher assigned a project—to write a book that would be placed in a class lending library. She has been hooked on writing ever since.

When not writing, Caridad teaches workshops on various topics related to writing and heads a writing group. Caridad has been married for over twenty years, and is the mother of a thirteen-year-old girl.

To Samantha—

Thank you for understanding about Mum's quirks
and time away to write, for your support in everything
I do, and for all the love that you give me.
You are the best, and I am very, very proud of you!

Chapter 1

His was a life filled only with empty dreams, if one could call those fleeting thoughts in a vampire's sleepless nights dreams. His existence was without end and ruled by a loneliness that made each day harder to bear than the one before.

High above the crowd, Ryder Latimer smelled the sting of the alcohol as the humans drank and spilled it in copious amounts in their search for oblivion or nirvana. Acrid smoke from cigarettes floated high into the air, and in that hazy cloud were the underlying tones of sweat. Sweat laced with lust, he thought, sniffing the air and detecting the ripe pheromone the humans exuded as they played their pitiful mating rituals.

Scents, he had discovered, were important to a vampire. Musks and other aromas literally brought out the beast in him. He normally avoided the smells, but it was tough to do in a crowd as large as this.

This far up, the sounds of the band and the crowd were garbled. Indistinct. A low buzz, like static, and a heavy thumping vibration from the bass of the music. An insistent lub-dub lub-dub, like the beat of a heart.

Ryder closed his eyes, placed his hands on the metal railing of the catwalk and the vibrations traveled up his arms. He took a deep breath, absorbing the smells. Soaking everything up as if by doing so he could restore a small part of the life he had lost when a strange turn of events during the Civil War had condemned him to this solitary life. It was a fleeting moment, the human scents and sounds racing through him, enervating him as he stood near the ceiling of the club.

In no time, however, Ryder was back to normal, watching like a disinterested deity, bored by the repetition of the activity below. Every night the same scene was replayed. Until tonight.

He had discovered in this morning's paper that there was some killing going on in that mob of humans. The murderer had struck last week and then a few nights ago. Maybe he would hunt another soon, Ryder thought, glancing down and wondering who might be the next one to be taken. Who might become another trophy for the psycho stalking his club. The papers hadn't mentioned The Lair, but Ryder had no doubt it was here that the hunt was on.

Ryder had sensed something different in the last few weeks, that unique smell of bloodlust that had made him wonder if another of his kind had come to feed. A club like this would be an excellent place to select a victim and then cull them from the herd.

He looked down once more and he saw *her*, standing at the edge of the crowd, searching for someone.

It wasn't possible, he thought as he hurried along the catwalk, keeping the apparition in sight. For nearly a century she'd been in his dreams. Or maybe it was better to describe them as his restless nocturnal musings.

Regardless, Ryder had stopped questioning why the spirit came to him. Sometimes she arrived at times of unrest, the visions she brought portents of things to come. At other times, when the monotony and uncertainty of his existence made him question why to go on, she'd come to soothe his soul and give him the peace he was unable to find elsewhere.

But tonight, she was no longer just an apparition—or was his loneliness deluding him?

He struggled to get a glimpse of her face, but even with his vampire night sight, he still couldn't be certain his imagination wasn't getting the best of him.

After all, for more than a century, he had been virtually alone with only a human keeper and his apparition to comfort him. Maybe that was why his mind and eyes were playing games with him tonight. It was just a trick, Ryder told himself, and yet he stood, poised on the edge of the catwalk. Watching. Waiting. Hoping.

The loud, driving beat of the bass pulsed through Diana Reyes's body, the vibrations pulling at something deep inside her. On stage, a guitarist thrashed around, his arm wildly circling as he strummed chords in sync to the pounding of the band behind him. A spotlight focused on him, picking up the gleam of sweat on his lean torso and the dark, swirling artwork on his upper right arm and shoulders. With a final jump and strum, the song ended, but the band quickly launched into another, its rhythm and violence not much different from the first.

Diana withstood the assault on her eardrums, watching from the periphery of the large crowd. There was a crush of bodies trying to make their way deeper into the space. Beyond them, other patrons lounged at tables along the border of a dance floor that was so packed she wondered how anybody could move to the music.

It was dark in the club, nearly pitch-black in spots. Overhead, dangling from an irregular maze of catwalks, wires and ropes, was an assortment of lighting equipment and mirrored balls that shot off erratic spots of light to create a jarring visual display on the dance floor. The only steady sources of illumination were those directed at the stage and at the long metallic bar along the side of the building. The bar was bathed in red spotlights, making the metal of its stainless-steel surface gleam as if coated in blood.

Apropos given that two women had lost their lives here…or at least commenced their journeys to death in this place. Those deaths were the reason FBI agent Diana Reyes had offered to go undercover. Her profile of the killer indicated this was the place where he'd selected his victims. And Diana was his type.

The two victims she had seen in the morgue days earlier had been young and pretty until the killer had gotten to them. His sociopathic handiwork suggested he was someone who liked inflicting pain. Someone who knew how to make it last. The medical examiner had implied that at some point, the victims may have passed into a "no pain" zone, courtesy of the adrenaline coursing through their bodies.

Diana absentmindedly nodded and rubbed at the ridge of scar along her own rib cage. She had firsthand knowledge of just what someone could do when her body shut down from an excess of physical and mental pain. She had crawled to her father, cradled him in her arms and tried to stop the bleeding from the bullet that had ripped into his chest, courtesy of a gang's drive-by shooting. Futilely, she had pressed her hand against the wound, watching his blood leak between her fingers as he died in her arms. It wasn't until after his death that she realized she had also been hit.

Diana was certain that for these victims, the killer had made the pain a real living thing. And at the end, she thought with a shudder, the two women had likely realized death was close at hand.

She intended to put an end to the killer's spree. She

threaded her way through the crowd, in search of her partner and hoping to become visible to the murderer.

Her investigation had confirmed that both victims had planned to come to this establishment on the nights they were killed. Even before eliminating known acquaintances as suspects, Diana was certain she had a serial killer on her hands. One who would likely strike again, and soon. The second girl had been murdered only a week after the first. Tonight's surveillance should give Diana a feel for the place before she intensified the investigation with more equipment and personnel.

The mark on her hand—the red bat used as proof that IDs had been checked and the entrance fee paid—confirmed that the victims had in fact been here. She traced the edges of the design with her hand, thinking how it marked her in another way—as prey.

A touch came against the bare skin at the small of her back. She turned and faced David, her partner. Like the others in the club, he was dressed in black, from his jacket and T-shirt to his jeans, but with his blond, prep-school looks, it was hard for him to seem tough. Even the scruffy beard he'd grown did little to help. It was barely a peach fuzz on his boyish face.

He grinned and moved his hand. Her backless halter exposed her right shoulder blade, and he traced the edges of the tattoo there. "Nice touch. Both the shirt and the tattoo. Shame it'll wash off," he said, and Diana didn't correct him.

The tattoo was a very real reminder of a moment of thoughtlessness, courtesy of a night of too much drinking. She'd only been nineteen at the time and trying to recover from the heartache of a long-term relationship that had gone sour. Her younger brother had offered to help her get over it. After many a foul-tasting tequila shooter, it had seemed appropriate to commemorate her stupidity with a tattoo. She had chosen a dagger poised upright over a heart, symbolic of the pain she suffered and hoped to guard against in the future. She had been too drunk to realize the knot of pain she carried inside her had everything to do with her father and nothing to do with the cheating boyfriend.

She kept the tattoo to remind her not to act recklessly, though she battled her impulse to be rash more often than she liked.

The knife and dagger on her shoulder was just one of the thousands of designs in the sea of bodies adorned with art and swathed in leather, chains and denim. The three earrings piercing her one ear coupled with the two on the other was a minimalist statement in this rough-looking crowd.

The club appeared to be what their sources had described: a place for those who liked to play on the edge—although neither of the two victims' lifestyles hinted at anything other than flirtation with dangerous elements. She was familiar with the allure of places such as this. In the year after her father's death, she and her brother had spent many a night in bars with a hard edge. It had been her way of rebelling against a bureaucracy that had allowed her father to be killed by people who had passed through the criminal justice system only to be released onto the streets. She'd snubbed her nose at the time she had spent conforming and striving to be good when none of it really mattered. Bullets didn't differentiate between good or bad. They were equal-opportunity killers.

She had let the anger and hatred take hold of her after her father's senseless death. In that dark place of anything goes, she had given in to her pain. She had lost herself in alcohol and dances with nameless partners.

It was only after waking one morning to find herself facedown on the floor, with her eighteen-year-old brother passed out beside her from his own overindulgence, that she realized they were heading to oblivion. In her wallowing, she had dragged him down, as well. She had reached deep inside, where she still believed good could be re-warded, and she'd found the strength to take control of her life and to help her younger brother get on his feet.

She had survived, but that need for the dark side had never really left her. She had sensed it coming back to life the moment she'd walked back into this bar. It had almost felt like…home.

Maybe that was the allure for the victims and their hunter—the loss of restraint and identity that an ambience such as this provided. Perhaps the freedom of this place made the victims careless and the killer secure enough to hunt and lure his prey.

Diana inclined her head toward her partner and pointed her finger in the direction of the bar. It was time to mingle and act as if they belonged. Time for her to become bait, which might be impossible in a crowd this size, even though she fit the profile of the killer's tastes. He liked them young and flashy. Both women had been dressed provoc-atively, in clothes similar to what she now wore. The prob-lem was that many young women in the club were similarly dressed. From a talk with the victims' friends, Diana knew that both of the women had been outgoing and liked to dance, often with more than one man. She intended to do the same and hopefully set herself apart from the crowd.

With David following her, she began to thread her way through the mass of people and over to the bar, but some-thing made her stop. *A presence? Someone watching?* She paused, carefully looking around, but she saw nothing out of the ordinary.

Writing off her unease to a case of jitters, she continued onward through the crowd.

Chapter 2

As they neared the bar, Diana glanced at the menu of drinks posted along the wall. What looked like the mummified remains of bats were affixed along the top edge. The uppermost section of the wall above held hundreds of bats hanging down, their bodies huddled tight together. Beyond that, there was nothing but the vague shapes and outlines of equipment high against a dark ceiling.

Diana looked back at the menu. All of the drinks' names dealt with the imbibing of blood, the imagined traits of bats, or the ever-popular rituals for transforming into mythical demons or monsters. The Blind as a Bat offered oblivion after only one drink due to a large amount of 151 proof rum. Maiden's Gift was a creamy concoction with Cherry Heering and other liqueurs. Vamp Venom was a variation of a Bloody Mary but laced with hot sauce for that extra burn.

She chuckled. The list was quite tongue in cheek, as if the inventor had thought the patrons somewhat silly in their dark fascinations.

Above the specials, in red letters embellished with dripping blood, was the name of the club: The Lair. Unfortunately, the crimson of the letters against the white of the chalkboard and the gleaming steel of the bar's surface were too much a reminder of the victims she'd seen in the morgue—and of the fact that someone didn't think this was all in the spirit of fun.

From beside her, David raised his hand to draw the attention of the bartender, who was dressed in a white T-shirt turned pale pink by the red lights. He scurried back and forth behind the bar, pouring and blending drinks, grabbing the money waved in the air by those fortunate enough to have snagged him. The bartender came over as they sidled up to some clear spaces at the bar.

"What can I get you?" he said, eyeing her and sparing only a quick glance at David.

"A sloe slayer screw," she said, and smiled at the young man, who grinned back at her. He was cute and quite muscular, probably a wanna-be actor.

"You sure that's what you want?" he asked, reaching for a glass from the racks suspended above the bar.

Diana leaned on the metal surface and gave him her most seductive grin. "That depends," she teased. She had his complete attention.

He leaned close, the drink and the glass in his hand forgotten. "And what does it depend on, sweetheart?"

"Is it the slayer who's slow, or the screw?" she said loudly enough to make a few heads turn and look in her direction.

"Make that two diet Cokes," David said immediately, slinging an arm around her shoulder.

The bartender shot David a look of annoyance, then turned to Diana for confirmation.

Diana glanced at David and shrugged. "Two diet Cokes it is." The bartender gave them a perturbed huff, as if he didn't appreciate being pulled into whatever game they were playing.

When he returned with the drinks, he slammed them on the counter, and despite David's presence, or maybe because of it, he leaned on the counter and favored Diana with a broad grin. "It's not too late. Sloe gin is just waiting to be slayed." He dropped his voice and lowered his head until it was almost touching hers. In a voice he must have rehearsed hundreds of times in acting class and with a wink that broadcast his invitation, he said, "And who doesn't enjoy a good screw?"

David glared at him, took the two glasses and tossed a ten onto the bar. The bartender finally walked away, and Diana raised an eyebrow at her partner and the beverage he handed her. "I think I could have handled the sloe slayer screw and remembered to check out that bartender's background when we return to the office." Despite her comment about the drink, she took a quick sip and appreciated the cool of the liquid as it traveled down her throat.

"Got to keep levelheaded, Di," he said, his words tinged with both concern and reproach. It was so in keeping with his straitlaced personality that she had to bite back a laugh. He might be dressed like the rest of the crowd, down to a small silver hoop and ear cuff in one ear, but beneath the rough clothes he was still the restrained partner she had come to rely on during the last four years. David was everything she wasn't and vice versa, which balanced their partnership perfectly. Her rashness, his calm. Her mind, which bounced all over in reaching conclusions, and his step-by-step way of solving things. Go figure, she thought with a shrug, and turned her attention to the dance floor.

Having gulped down a good portion of his drink, David chewed on an ice cube and faced the crowd. He motioned to the crush of bodies with the hand that held the glass. "Wanna dance?"

She leaned close to him and whispered in the ear without

the earpiece, "Want to check out the wire so we know you can call for help?" She had on a small earpiece, the only way she could be wired, thanks to her clothes. Her low-rise black leather slacks were tight-fitting, and also precluded the use of her customary pants holster. Her gun, a small Glock 26, was strapped into place on her ankle, hidden by the slight flare of the pants leg. Not the best place for her weapon, but the only possible one.

David, luckily, had on his holster, and a traditional wire beneath the black leather jacket he wore. She was comfortable with that and wanted her partner to stay relatively near in case her equipment failed or she couldn't reach her weapon in time.

He chuckled and buried his face against her short-cropped hair. Placing a hand at her waist as he spoke in low tones into the wire, David made it seem to anyone watching that they were lovers sharing an intimate moment.

Only Diana knew better as she heard the echo in her right ear and met his blue-eyed gaze. She slowly nodded, confirming that the wire was working and that the other FBI agents and NYPD personnel in the crowd and outside in the van would be aware of what was happening.

Faking a laugh, she ran her hand along the edge of his cheek and strolled away from him. He followed for a moment, then grabbed her hard, turning her around. She resisted, yanked her arm away and launched into the fight they had rehearsed earlier, trying to draw attention. They exchanged a few heated words and a last little tug of war as she pulled free of David's grasp and headed for the mobbed dance floor.

Ryder lost sight of her and backtracked along the catwalks until he located her once more. She was pulling away from a handsome blond man, her strides angry as she moved toward the dance floor. Was she intent on losing her partner and finding another?

There was no doubt now she was the woman in his dreams. The resemblance was…eerie.

Her hair was sleek and cropped close to her head, displaying the long, elegant column of her throat and the fine lines of her collarbones. He was too far away to see the color of her eyes, but he could tell they were almond-shaped and exotic, her most compelling feature. Her nose was straight and slim. Her mouth full, with mobile lips. A defined, stubborn chin hinted at her determination. She wasn't classically pretty, but all the elements combined were intriguing. Possibly beautiful.

Even in the darkness of the club, she radiated tanned healthiness. As she danced with another young man, a flush worked over her cheeks. The enticing amount of skin displayed by the small bib halter she wore glistened with her perspiration. The halter was a deep red that served her well, accenting the color of her dark brown hair and creamy skin.

She moved fluidly, gracefully, her body lithe and full of strength—a mortal warrior. One who would age unless death claimed her before her time. His throat constricted as he thought of all the people he had lost over the length of his existence.

He drove that fear away and returned his attention to the woman on the floor below. Her body was toned, but curvy. She moved well-shaped hips, and her unbound breasts swayed against the fabric of her shirt. Desire raced along his nerve endings. He hardened as what was left of the human in him remembered all too well the sweetness of a woman and craved her the way the demon inside hungered for blood.

As she worked her way toward the stage, through the crush of bodies on the dance floor, he hurried along the network of catwalks, stepping over wires, jumping from one shaky walk to another so he would not lose sight of her. The flashing lights of the club made it difficult, hurting his sensitive eyes.

Forcing himself to concentrate, he honed in on her. She seemed to be searching for someone. Maybe the blond man she had left earlier? Maybe she was realizing the folly of trying to find him in this group of misfits.

Or maybe she was looking for someone new, excited by the prospect of danger and to what it might lead. An unfortunate end, Ryder thought, thinking of the two other girls before her and how they had misjudged someone in the crowd.

She reached the edge of the dance floor and he was nearly straight above her, behind one of the spotlights illuminating the stage. The heat from the lamp was nearly unbearable, yet he stood there, anyway, watching from behind the safety of its light. Anyone looking up would be blinded by its intensity.

She raised her arms and ran her hands through the short strands of her hair. A slight breeze plastered the halter top to her damp body, outlining every curve. Her scent teased his nostrils, the air from outside blowing up and across the length of the room. She had a clean scent. She wore no fragrance. He closed his eyes, breathed deeper, and the animal in him memorized the smell.

When he looked down once more, she was on the move, heading toward the source of that fresh air—an open door by the stage entrance that led to a long deserted alley behind the club.

While he normally didn't get involved with the patrons in the bar, tonight would be different, for he *had* to follow her. And as he did so, he called himself a fool a thousand times over. He was certain she was a woman he would come to love and, like all the others in his interminable life, come to lose.

Humans after all, were born to die.

Logic. Reason. They were the cornerstones of her profession. Diana used them every day to solve the cases she was assigned. But sometimes there was intuition and a gut instinct that ran contrary to what logic or reason told her.

Like the feeling she was having right now that had raised the hackles on the back of her neck. An almost preternatural sense of something not quite right. It was stronger than the feeling she'd had before, when she first entered the club. So strong that she knew someone was watching. She looked around and, seeing nothing, glanced upward.

Above her, the catwalks and wires swayed. The movement was too great to be caused by the breeze. Someone had been there. The killer maybe? The high tangle of metal and cables provided a perfect observation deck.

She examined the area, but the glare of the spotlights made it impossible to see much besides the barely discernible lines and curves of the infrastructure close to the ceiling. When she lowered her gaze, the brightness of the lights left spots in her eyes, making it difficult for her to pick out anyone in the crowd who might be paying a little too much interest.

She blinked a few times, closed her eyes and experienced a kaleidoscope of color behind her eyelids. When she opened her eyes again, the sensation of being watched had passed. Still, she searched the crowd, hoping to meet a gaze or see a face that would trigger the feeling again.

Across the way, David was scoping out the crowd. For a brief moment their gazes connected across the length of the club. She motioned to him, pointing to where she was headed, and spoke softly to confirm it, hoping the wire would pick up her voice over the noise of the band and the crowd. In her ear, she heard David acknowledge her words and saw him nod. He would make his way across eventually.

She pressed through the bodies, shooting a glare at one young man who groped her as she inched past. Continuing onward, she finally reached the open door and the cool current of air she had savored earlier. There was a bouncer by the exit, sitting in a chair tilted far back on two spindly legs. She was surprised the metal chair could hold his weight.

Walking to the door, she stopped and he stared up at her, his gaze sharp and questioning. "Ya leave this way, ya gotta get back in line," he said with a growl, obviously annoyed.

Diana shrugged. Getting back in the line wasn't a problem. She was here to see and be seen. While the bulk and attitude of the bouncer might put off many, it might not have been enough to discourage the two victims or the killer who had followed them.

She exited through the door into the chill of the alley. It had rained while she was inside. The dark stone walls and cobblestones glistened with wet, and water had puddled in various spots. The sky was dark with heavy clouds that obscured a half moon.

Goose bumps erupted on her skin from the sudden change in temperature. She rubbed at her arms and glanced at the back section of the blind alley. The shadows were strong, and unlike the area leading to the street, there were no lights.

With the lack of moonlight, it would be easy for someone to hide there, waiting. And yet, with no way out, they'd have to take the victims past the bouncer at the open door or the crowd at the far end of the alley. Unless the alley had a back way out.

She took a step toward the darkness, keeping the wall of the building behind her so as not to be surprised. She had gone deep into the alley, but had not yet reached the end when the eerie sensation from before returned. The hairs on the back of her neck tingled, as did those on her arms. As her eyes adjusted to the lack of light, a colder, deeper silhouette took shape a few feet in front of her.

It was a man. She squinted, but it was too dark to see his face even though he stood close. Too close for her to pull out her weapon. It was a true Mexican standoff, the two of them considering each other in the dim light, neither one speaking. In her ear, the running comments of various agents crackled and she tried not to let them distract her.

A few feet away, a small spot of moonlight appeared as the wind drove the clouds away. If the man across from her would only move that short distance, it might give her the answers she needed. "Step into the light," she said, striving for a tone of authority despite the situation, hoping David and the others would hear.

The seconds of silence stretched out after her command and then came his short bark of a laugh. "And why would I want to do that?" he asked, his low voice gravelly, as if it had been a long time since he had used it. There was a trace of an accent. Southern, she thought. Louisiana, she confirmed as he issued his own determined instructions.

"Darlin', if you have a lick of sense, you'll turn right around and head back into the club."

He surprised her with his tone of concern. She couldn't take that statement at face value as the others might have done, turning their backs on this man and then finding themselves…

It was likely David would be here within minutes. His instructions were to keep her in sight, and he had known where she was heading. But she couldn't wait for her partner. If this was the man, a delay might prove fatal and she had no intention of ending her life in an alley that stank of stale urine.

"Step into the light where I can see you and I'll go," she said calmly, not trusting that he would listen. Preparing for what she would do if he didn't.

"Do you think—"

"You're a fool?" she finished for him.

He expelled a harsh breath and challenged, "I'm not the fool who's running around with a killer loose." Despite his comment, there was resignation in his voice, as if he, too, recognized that there was little either of them could do. She wasn't surprised therefore when he said, "On three, we both move where we can see each other."

"On three." She counted down. As promised, she took the few steps to her right, mirroring his movement.

As they both reached the safety of the light, she detected a note of surprise in his features before he carefully schooled them. He had a severe yet handsome face. His eyes were a flat, unholy black against the dark of the night. They were intense, unblinking. Soulless, she thought for a moment, but then abruptly, as her gaze finally met his, there was a moment of connection. Within her, there was a sudden strange sense of…recognition. She berated herself silently for letting her imagination get the better of her.

"Satisfied?" he asked, his voice still husky. He stood mere feet away, a commanding presence. Tall and strong-bodied, he was dressed all in black, like most of the crowd inside. Only, on him, it was more than just a color. It was an aura of dangerous energy that made her take a step back.

"Who are you?" she pressed, aware that they were *still* the only ones in the alley. She listened to the chatter on the wire. Nothing to indicate help was on the way.

Before Diana could register his intentions, he closed the distance between them and grabbed hold of her wrist, yanking her to him.

Years of training took over. An elbow to his face had him rocking backward and she followed with a jab that straightened him, leaving him totally vulnerable for a full-force roundhouse kick. She connected to the side of his head with a thick thud, and he tumbled to the rough cobblestones. Before she could react, he was on his feet and moving toward her once more.

Diana struck out with a quick chopping motion. He blocked her blow forcefully and thrust her away, which sent her flying into the brick wall.

Her head hit hard and stars danced across her vision. She

fought off the dazing blow and pressed her hands against the rough surface of the wall, struggling to find purchase so she wouldn't fall to the ground. The chatter had ceased in her ear, which meant the wire had stopped working, not that it had been doing much good up to this point.

As her assailant neared again, David finally called out, "Hold your position or I'll fire."

She closed her eyes and held her breath for a moment. When there was silence, she struggled to focus her blurry gaze on her attacker, his hands on the top of his head. David stood behind him, inches shorter, his gun pointed at the base of the man's skull.

David looked at her and asked, "You okay?"

Her cheek was throbbing painfully and she realized that the man's defensive block had caught the side of her face. She raised her hand to the back of her head. There was a lump growing there beneath her hair. Even though her head was swimming and her vision was unclear, she told herself the bumps and bruises were nothing but minor discomforts. "I'm okay," she replied, and took a step toward the man.

"Who are you?" she asked, getting right next to his face, her nose nearly bumping the edge of his jaw.

He smiled tightly and was about to answer when the bouncer realized that something was going on in the alley. "Boss man, you okay? Should I call the police?" the muscular man asked her assailant.

David kept his bead on her attacker and Diana approached the bouncer. "You know this man?"

"That's Ryder Latimer. He's the owner of the club. Came out to make sure nothing funny was going on," the bouncer explained.

Diana sighed harshly and glanced at her partner, who lowered his weapon, holstered it and then spoke softly into the wire, calling off the imminent arrival of reinforcements.

She walked up to the man and noted he bore an imprint below his left eye from one of the blows she had inflicted.

Her satisfaction was tempered by guilt, the burning pain across her cheek and the pounding in her head. "I guess we all need to talk."

"I guess we do at that," he said, and turned on his heel, barking a command to the bouncer on his way to the door of the club.

David and Diana remained behind, staring after him in surprise. The bouncer moved his head in the direction of the door and held out his hand. "After you," he said facetiously.

Diana gritted her teeth to hold back her comment. A mistake. The movement sent a shaft of pain up the side of her face and into her skull. She moaned, and David reached out to steady her as she swayed.

"You need to see a doctor," he said as she closed her eyes and battled the swirling dizziness in her head. She reached for the wall and instead encountered a rock-hard body.

Opening her eyes, she met the sharp-eyed gaze of her unwitting assailant, who actually seemed concerned. It was the last thing she thought as she passed out into his arms.

Chapter 3

She tried to open her eyes, but the glare of the light forced them closed. Reaching for her forehead, she grasped both sides of her head and cradled it gingerly.

"It's about time you came to," Ryder said, and the words ricocheted around her skull, causing more pain.

Somehow she found the grit to face him. "Haven't you done enough?" she said, surprised that all she could muster was a whisper. Each movement of her jaw brought fresh waves of pain. She moaned, and a moment later she was rewarded with the chill of an ice pack against the throbbing side of her face and the gentle pass of his hand across her brow.

"Lean back and try to stay still. I called for a doctor," he said, and Diana chose not to argue with him. If she argued, the pounding punishment in her skull would outweigh any satisfaction she might get.

A footfall alerted Diana to the entry of someone else. Diana opened her eyes to mere slits. An elegantly dressed young woman came into the room, followed by David.

"Your friend is finally awake," she said, and Diana assumed this was the doctor the club owner had called. The woman's voice was soft and cultured, colored with the accents of exclusive prep schools and money. Despite her easy tone, Diana's pain increased.

"Easy," her assailant murmured, and stroked a gentling hand across Diana's forehead once more. The tips of his fingers were rough and yet somehow comforting.

"Ryder, you never cease to amaze me. Is this another lady you've charmed?" the physician teased.

Diana wished the doctor would shut up and examine her. "Please. Let's get this over with," she whispered. A second later the doctor pried open one of Diana's eyelids, flashed a light in her eye, then repeated the same with the other eye. It was a small penlight, but it had the strength of a laser, burning away what little was left of Diana's brain cells.

"Open those eyes and tell me how many fingers I have up?" the doctor asked.

Diana slowly eased her eyes open, letting them adjust to the light. It took a while, and she had to force herself to focus so she could count the fingers the physician was wiggling in her face. "Three," she growled, then closed her eyes and leaned back against the cushions of the couch.

"She'll live, Ryder, although she's got a slight concussion," the young woman proclaimed. "Next time, try to take it a little easier on the ladies. I thought you considered yourself a gentleman." The doctor stowed the penlight in her pocket and reached into her bag. She took out a small foil packet of medicine and handed it to David.

"Here are some meds for your partner. She should be watched overnight. If there's no one who can—"

"My brother can do it, David. I don't want to go to any hospital," she replied.

The young woman nodded and glanced at Ryder. "See you later, Ryder?" she asked.

"I'll be by, unless the agents need to keep me for some reason," he replied, but David shook his head.

"Great, then. Thanks for your help, Danvers," Ryder said. The doctor walked from the room, mumbling under her breath as she did so. The calming, pain-killing chill of the ice pack returned, however, and Diana wondered why this man was being so solicitous. And why she was wondering what kind of relationship he and the good doctor shared.

She opened her eyes. This time it took only a few seconds for her to focus on his too-handsome face, which was filled with concern—and a trace of guilt. "It seems as if we should know each other's names by now," she said.

It was amazing that such a small hint of a smile could transform the harsh planes of his face, brightening his dark countenance. She sensed he didn't smile often. "Ryder Latimer. Proprietor of this club. And you two would be—"

"Special Agent Harris." Her partner walked up to Ryder, who sat on the edge of a low coffee table beside Diana.

Ryder stood as the other man approached and they shook hands. He sat down once more and faced her.

"Diana Reyes," she answered, and held out her hand. He took it in his, and when he noticed the dull rose across her knuckles from their earlier fisticuffs, his lips thinned into a tight line. Smoothing a finger across the fresh marks, he gazed at her, his face hard. His touch sent a wave of heat skittering up her arm. "I'm sorry about hurting you," Ryder said softly.

"You were watching me," she pressed, disturbingly aware of him. This close, his face was striking, undeniably masculine. A sharp, straight slash of a nose. Those dark, nearly black eyes that made her feel as if she could sink into their depths to rest. And his lips—full and well-defined…

Maybe it was the blow to her head that was distorting her sense of things, but it seemed she had seen that face before. That she knew him somehow…and knew she could trust him.

"I read the papers the other morning," he started with a shrug. "I was worried the killer might be here—"

"Maybe because of your clientele and the bar's motif?" asked David, sitting on the couch by Diana's feet.

Ryder shifted to face him, his legs spread. He rested his forearms on thick-muscled thighs and steepled his hands. He had capable hands. Large, with blunt fingers. Diana had to tear her gaze away from the sight of them. She was a sucker for men with strong hands.

"There are all kinds at the club," Ryder answered. "For most, it's a way to cut loose and be a little different."

"Why did you follow me?" she asked, although she was quite certain he had been in the alley before she arrived.

"I didn't. I was already out there. Beat you down from the catwalks."

He caught her off guard with his answer. She had been expecting him to lie. Needing time to regroup and get a fresh perspective, she peered at her partner past the pack of ice she still held to her face and said, "I think I'd like to talk to Mr. Latimer in the morning. Bright and early."

"First thing in the a.m.?" Ryder questioned, dread in his voice.

"Not an early bird, I gather," Diana replied as she rose and handed him the half-melted ice pack.

"You can't even begin to imagine," he answered, and as Diana met his gaze, she sensed there was a wealth of meaning in those simple words.

"No, I don't think I can," she acknowledged, some extrasensory perception kicking in to warn her: Ryder Latimer was clearly not what he appeared to be.

Diana turned her attention to the lists of convicted sex offenders in the area, sipping an oversize cup of café latte she had picked up on her way to work. Her caffeine-and-sugar rush was humming nicely when David showed up at nine. He plopped himself on the sofa and she brought over the lists she had already reviewed. "I've flagged a couple who seem like possible suspects."

David rubbed at his eyes, where a bleary network of red obscured the normally bright blue. "Tired?" she asked, dropping onto the sofa next to him.

"Hmm," he grunted, and grabbed the lists from her. As he examined them, he asked, "How long do we give Latimer before we chase him down?"

Diana glanced at her watch. It was already nine-fifteen with no word from him. Latimer didn't strike her as the type who would be late, which could only mean that he had no intention of showing up. She fought back the sudden disappointment and mustered righteous anger. He had not kept his promise. So much for the trust she had felt last night.

Trust being a funny and fragile thing, she thought as she ran her hand along her right cheek. It was still sore, and this morning she'd woken with a pounding headache. The medication the doctor had given her had eased the pain enough for her to concentrate on her work. Still, every time she moved her jaw, a slight sting reminded her.

She glanced at her watch again even though only seconds had passed. "At nine-thirty we go after him. If he refuses to cooperate, we'll get a warrant."

It was as if Latimer had heard; a moment later her phone rang. She hurried from the couch and grabbed it. Anger blossomed inside her as the secretary said Latimer's lawyer was upstairs. "Bastard," she mumbled under her breath as she hung up the phone, all of her earlier interest in him blown away by the call.

David picked up his head from the sofa back. "Let me guess—"

"Latimer sent his lawyer down. Probably to throw up roadblocks so we couldn't question him."

"Testy this morning, aren't we?" he said, noting her irritation.

"I don't like games. He said he'd be here. If I'd thought otherwise, I would have hauled him down here last night." She walked to her desk, slipped her jacket off her chair and put it on.

"Especially after the little incident?" She shot David a glare as she headed for the door of her office. Of course she was mad about the "incident," but she also felt betrayed.

That sense of betrayal fueled her anger as she and David arrived at the anteroom to the assistant director in charge's office. His secretary nodded and gave them a tight, uncomfortable smile. "He's waiting for the two of you."

Diana took a breath and knocked on the door. After hearing the soft "Come in," she and David entered.

In a chair opposite ADIC Jesus Hernandez sat a middle-aged man. Hernandez immediately identified him as Latimer's lawyer and the man rose, offering his hand.

Diana and David shook hands with the man but continued to stand even though the lawyer motioned for them to sit. "Mr. Ruggiero. I wish I could say it was good to see you, but I would have much rather had your client come down as he promised last night," Diana said.

The man glanced up at her and then at David. "My client has every intention of presenting himself—this afternoon."

"He agreed to come down this morning. Is there some reason—"

"Mr. Latimer made that concession under duress, Special Agent Reyes. We both know that after the altercation—"

"Brought about by your client attacking—"

"My client advises that you struck first. He was only defending himself," Ruggiero shot back.

"Your client has a foot and at least one hundred pounds over my partner, Mr. Ruggiero," David said.

Hernandez finally joined the fray and brought silence to the room with a sharply barked "Enough."

Diana nodded and at Hernandez's prompting, sat in the chair next to Ryder's lawyer. David took a seat on the couch. As she sat and listened to her boss's briefing, she wondered why Latimer had sent a shark rather than come himself.

The nattily dressed lawyer sat calmly as Hernandez advised them on Latimer's concerns and his willingness to cooperate in any way he could, including presenting himself in the late afternoon for questioning. The lawyer nodded, confirming each of Hernandez's statements.

Ruggiero must have taken fashion tips from an early *Godfather* movie—his brown hair was ruthlessly slicked back with gel and his silk suit was shiny, the oily sheen in keeping with the unctuous smile he had given her when they met. He had on an overpowering cologne that made her nauseous, as did his tight, ferretlike smile.

"My client will do everything in his power to cooperate," Ruggiero replied in seemingly sincere tones, and she wondered how he could lie so easily. Latimer clearly had something to hide, and this man was here to help him do so.

"Tell me, Mr. Ruggiero. Does your client's idea of cooperation include attempting to restrain a federal officer?" Diana countered, and gave the man some credit when he had the grace to blush.

"A misunderstanding, Agent—"

"Special Agent in Charge, Mr. Ruggiero," David corrected him.

Diana shot her partner a glare, hating that he had paraded her title. In her book, titles alone didn't earn respect. She addressed the lawyer calmly, her tone brooking no disagreement. "If your client doesn't appear by this afternoon, he'll leave me no option but to issue a warrant."

"My client has rights—"

"And it's well within his rights for us to ask him to answer a few questions. If he feels uncomfortable, he has the right to counsel and to refuse to answer. In which case, we'll charge him as the suspect and hold him for additional proceedings," Hernandez answered calmly, attempting to stop further disputes. "Do you think your client can come by this afternoon, at let's say…"

Hernandez stopped and glanced at Diana to continue. "Four o'clock would be fine," she confirmed.

The attorney nodded, rose and walked out the door.

After he was gone, Diana let out a stinging Spanish expletive. Hernandez whistled beneath his breath. David coughed uncomfortably.

"Well, what does he think we're going to do? Chinese water torture or boiling in hot oil? The last thing we want is to lose a suspect due to a technicality," she said hotly.

David shrugged. "You and Latimer got off on the wrong foot last night. Maybe that worried him."

"And speaking of that, Diana, I understand from your reports that you and this suspect had a physical altercation. One in which you may have suffered a possible injury?" Hernandez glanced at a file as he spoke.

"Has anyone here checked you out?" he continued.

"I planned on going down—"

"As soon as we are done," Hernandez instructed, and then quickly launched into a discussion of the case and their plan of action for the interrogation of Latimer.

Diana took a deep breath, her headache having intensified during the interview. She hoped Latimer wouldn't mess around with them. They needed his cooperation at the club. But something told her that even though he hadn't been on the up-and-up with them, it had nothing to do with the killings. He was hiding something else. Something more…personal.

When Hernandez dismissed them, she rose and followed

David from the office, the pounding in her head intense and almost debilitating.

"Diana?" David asked as he noted her discomfort.

She nodded and forced a smile. "A bad headache. And even if Hernandez hadn't ordered it, I'd be heading to Maggie's, anyway, to have her check me out."

David smiled a broad ear-to-ear grin at the mention of the staff physician. "Mind if I tag along?"

His eagerness was a balm. She had long hoped that her friend Maggie would get together with her very nice, but slightly inept partner. "Sure."

"Great," he said, and followed her as she walked down the hall and to the elevator.

Chapter 4

Diana entered Maggie's office and found her friend at her desk, reviewing a file. Diana stopped and David nearly ran into her back. She shot him a look over her shoulder, telling him to cool it. "Hi, Maggie. Came by for a quick checkup," she said.

Maggie rose and slinked her way around her desk. She had the kind of walk women envied and men drooled over. With her five-foot-ten-inch height and slim build, she looked more like a model than a physician. "Heard you had a small altercation," she said, and then leaned forward, to take a better look. "I can see you had more than a little physical contact."

Diana shrugged it off, but David piped in from behind her, "She was out cold for about five minutes."

Diana glared at him again and he backed off, taking a seat on the sofa in Maggie's office.

"Thanks, David. At least one of you has some sense," Maggie said with a smile that had David blushing in response.

Maggie skewered Diana with her sharp gaze. "You and I obviously need to talk about what happened."

Diana didn't argue and followed Maggie into the examining room, where she jumped up onto the table and waited as Maggie slipped on a lab coat, grabbed some things and walked over.

"Were you really out for five minutes?" Maggie questioned as she plucked a penlight from her jacket pocket, flipped it on and shined it in Diana's eyes. Like last night, Diana pulled away from it.

Maggie shut it down and placed her hands on her hips. "Sensitivity, huh? Bet you have a monster of a headache, as well."

"Yeah, and a little fuzziness every now and then, but don't worry. Another doctor took a look at me last night and said it was a mild concussion," she reassured.

Maggie harrumphed, reached out and gently applied pressure to the area on Diana's cheekbone and jawline where Latimer's forearm had connected. Diana winced, but the pain was minor. "This doctor let you go home without—"

"She gave me instructions and my brother dutifully woke me every few hours. Needless to say, I'm a little wiped today," Diana complained.

Maggie said nothing else, just grabbed a pad and wrote out a prescription. She roughly tore it off and handed the slip to Diana.

Diana eyed the paper with confusion and a little trepidation. "You're not going to say anything? Not going to warn me about—"

"Doing something as stupid as taking on a man twice your size and failing to go to a hospital like any reasonable person should have? No, of course not. You're a big girl, right? You know exactly what you're doing."

"Mama Maggie, I appreciate your concern—"

"You're as pigheadedly macho as any of those men out

there, Di. And that's not a good thing," Maggie said as she began her tirade again. "And what kind of doctor—"

"Her name was Danvers. Melissa, I think," Diana said.

"I had a professor named Danvers in med school. He had a daughter," Maggie offhandedly offered.

"Think you could dig up a little more on her? Ask around?" Diana asked, and tucked the prescription paper into her jacket pocket.

Maggie sensed there was more to Diana's interest. "For personal or business reasons?"

"A little of both. For business reasons—I want to know what kind of doctor she is. Whether she's on the up-and-up."

"And for the personal?" Maggie asked, one fine auburn-colored eyebrow raised.

"She's involved with a suspect. How involved, Maggie? Would she lie to protect him?" Diana explained.

Maggie eyed her carefully and finally nodded. "The second question—the one about being involved—sounds like it's still business? Unless of course…is he handsome?"

Handsome was an understatement, Diana thought but wouldn't admit. She shrugged and said, "I guess."

Maggie chuckled and shook her head, clearly aware of Diana's subterfuge. "Must be major-league handsome, but despite that, or maybe because of it, I will ask around for you. See what I can find out."

Diana slipped off the examining table and faced her friend once more. "Think you can do me another favor?"

Maggie let out a huff, but it was more playful than anything. "What now?"

"Do you think that liberated woman inside of you could talk to my poor partner? Ask him to have lunch or dinner? Put him out of his misery?"

"What makes you think—"

"I know you too well, Mags, just like you know me. Do yourself a favor. He's a really nice guy."

"Coming from you, that's quite a compliment," Maggie noted, and slipped an arm around her shoulders as she walked Diana back to her outer office.

David was still there, waiting patiently. He jumped off the sofa and grinned at them. "Ready to go?"

"*Sí.* I just can't wait to hit that computer and start mousing through all those entries," Diana teased. "Eat lunch at my desk while I pore over a stack of details about sex offenders and murderers and, of course, review the ME's reports again."

"We could always go out for a quick bite," David said, obviously not enjoying the prospect of eating over stomach-churning crime-scene photos.

"No, not me. I'd like to get some things done before Latimer shows up this afternoon. But you two go ahead," she said, and glanced at Maggie, who grinned and piped in with "If you don't want to go alone, I'd be more than happy to join you."

David looked from one woman to the other, a little flummoxed by Maggie's offer. Then he grinned and nodded. "That would be great. We can bring Diana back a sandwich so she doesn't have to eat fossilized food from the vending machine."

"See you at twelve, then?" Maggie prompted, and after David confirmed the time, they returned to Diana's office.

They talked over how they would handle Latimer's interrogation later that afternoon, then put in a call to the local detective heading up the NYPD part of the investigation so he could join them. It was close to noon when they finished, and despite her earlier plans, Diana needed to fill the prescription Maggie had given her. "I'm going to get this," she said, waving the small slip of paper in the air, "and grab a sandwich down at the deli. Meet me back here for Latimer's interrogation."

"Will do, Special Agent in Charge." David waved as he left the room.

Diana grabbed her purse and headed out, picking up her medication at a local drugstore and buying a premade sandwich at the corner deli. Back at her desk, she popped one of the painkillers, slugged it down with a mouthful of Coke and laid out her sandwich so she could work while she ate.

She started with the crime-scene photos, reviewing those of the locations first while she ate her sandwich. Despite years of training and investigations, she hadn't grown desensitized enough to eat while examining the more grisly photos. She then turned to the remaining evidence, carefully reviewing all the details of the injuries inflicted and the places where the killer had dumped the bodies.

The toxicology reports from the medical examiner's office had revealed the presence of flunitrazepam residues, what was more commonly known on the street as a "roofie"—the date-rape drug. If the killer administered the drug in a drink at the club, he'd have had twenty or thirty minutes before it took effect. Enough time to convince his victim to leave voluntarily.

Where he took the women had to be as equally isolated as the places where he left the bodies. But the evidence pointed to a more populated location. She glanced at the comments about the sheets in which the victims had been wrapped. They were the kind that hotels used and bore the traces of commercial laundering. The ME indicated the sheets had been clean and contained no latent prints nor hair or skin samples other than those of the victims.

But they did have DNA from the killer. Body fluids had been found on the women's bodies, although he had not sexually violated them.

She closed up the files, shut her eyes and leaned back in her chair, trying to create an impression in her mind of the kind of man who would do this. There was anger there, both at the women and at himself. He probably hated that he became aroused by what he was doing. When the arousal became too intense… It likely gave him a sense of control to be able to curb his response. It gave him a high to shame his victims and degrade them with their inability to stop him from taking pleasure. When that no longer satisfied him...

Could Ryder Latimer be that kind of man? she wondered. She didn't doubt that he was capable of violence, although he had restrained himself during their altercation. But Latimer had lied and he was hiding something. Diana's gut told her that it was a *big* something. And that she could easily have her answer by forcing Ryder to submit to a DNA test, only...

She *wanted* to believe in him. She wanted to think that he would show up that afternoon and provide the answers she needed. Restore the connection she had sensed last night.

Rousing herself, she shook her head and turned to her computer to run through all the databases at her disposal.

By the time she finished, nearly three hours later, her head was swimming. None of the materials had brought her any closer to the identity of the killer. Nor had they brought her any closer to eliminating Ryder Latimer as a suspect, although...

Her intuition kicked in again, screaming not to be ignored. Telling her that she had to keep an eye on him, but not because of the murders.

Ryder took one last look in the mirror, imagining as he had for over a century that there was an image staring back at him. It made shaving a bitch, not to mention straightening one's tie.

Slapping on some Chanel aftershave, he inhaled the light, citrusy scent. It helped mask the odors of the people with whom he came into contact. Odors that sometimes caused him problems.

Diana wore no scent. Around her, all he smelled was the clean, enticing allure of a woman. Plus leather and oil, he remembered suddenly. In addition to the leather pants she'd worn last night, he'd caught the odor of a holster with a well-maintained gun.

Glancing at his watch, he noted he had to get going. Although it was a short subway ride downtown, the New York City transit system was sometimes unpredictable. The last thing he wanted was to go aboveground and grab a cab. Staying any length of time in the sun drained him of energy. After prolonged exposure, his joints and muscles grew excruciatingly painful and stiff. Leave him out in the sun way too long… He didn't want to think about it, having once seen the shriveled remains of a vampire who had dared to think himself invincible.

No, he recognized his limitations all too well. That was why he had used his lawyer to stall the meeting. Early morning and midday sun were too much for a vampire of his age to handle, even with the protection of clothing. The late afternoon was infinitely better, and so here he was, on his way to see her. He had no delusions about his reasons for heading into the sunlight. He had told himself all night long that it was lunacy. The only way this could end would be badly. He didn't want to be attracted to her. He couldn't afford to be, he reminded himself and shook his head.

The things men did for women, he thought as he pulled the lapels of his jacket until they were flat, and walked to the door of his apartment. He grabbed a fedora from the coatrack next to the door and called his goodbye to Danvers, who was heading to the hospital for her late-afternoon rounds. "If you need me—"

"I'll call you," Ryder finished, and Melissa sailed out the door, perfectly groomed.

The brilliant doctor's orderliness and control had helped him on more than one occasion. But he worried that as his companion she had no social life. He experienced a twinge of guilt; serving him kept her from enjoying a normal life.

Running out of the apartment, he grabbed an elevator

and took it down to the subbasement level, a floor normally frequented only by the maintenance men who checked the building's electrical plant. Dark, damp and almost always empty, it had a second door that led to an underground access tunnel near Lexington Avenue. The entrance was hidden in the recesses of the building, next to a bomb shelter.

Ryder had had both built during the fifties, at the height of the Cold War. The mason who had done the work had seemed to understand why Ryder wanted another avenue of escape in the event of a nuclear attack. The man had been paid well to do the work and keep the secret of the tunnel's location and the fact that Ryder had a hand in the corporation that owned the building.

The building was just one of the many properties in which Ryder's company had an interest. After his "death" he'd recovered some of the funds he'd hidden before the Civil War, leaving the bulk of the money for his wife. With his funds, he'd bought real estate and with the earnings from the real estate, he'd invested in other things. Little by little, his holdings had grown and now money was not a concern.

He stepped into the tunnel and secured the door behind him. The smell and heat in the tunnel was always bad and only slightly better in the winter. Thankfully, it was just a few yards to a similar entrance into a maintenance tunnel for the Sixty-eighth Street subway station. The subway would deposit him at the Brooklyn Bridge/City Hall stop. From there it was a short walk to Federal Plaza. Not enough exposure to the rays to do much damage, especially since the fedora helped shade most of his head and face and the sunglasses in his pocket protected his acute eyesight from the worst of the sun.

Once out of the tunnel, he was in a little-used passage to the main subway entrance. He walked to the turnstile, pulled out his Metrocard and swiped it through the reader.

Walking to the edge of the platform, he looked uptown into the tunnel, but there was no sign of a downtown train. Despite that, his body registered the subtle vibrations and sounds of something approaching. A few moments later, the rush of air from the tunnel confirmed the imminent arrival of the number six.

With the hiss and squeal of brakes that grated on his sensitive hearing, the train lurched to a halt. Except for a number of younger people, clearly students on their way to Hunter College, few passengers got off. Most were headed to the main commuter stations like Grand Central and Times Square, where they would make the necessary connections to other trains. Ryder packed onto the crowded car and the scents and sounds of the mass of people attacked him. He closed his eyes as he always did and began a mantra he had learned many, many years ago from a Japanese man interred at a California camp during World War II.

As always, the mantra soothed the anger of the animal within and brought him some measure of peace.

Holding on to the pole, he swayed and bounced as the train rocketed to his destination. Once there, he raced up the stairs, slid on his glasses and did what he could to avoid the direct rays of the sunlight until he was finally in the cool interior lobby of 26 Federal Plaza, home of the New York City branch of the FBI. Tranquilly, he got in the line necessary to clear the security barriers, and, after waiting almost interminably, he was allowed through and directed to someone who would take him to the interrogation room.

When he arrived, Diana was waiting by the elevator, her partner beside her. They were like the eternal yin and yang. Light and dark. Good and, well…still good but with a lot of other things thrown in that weren't necessarily so straight. Things that roused something dark within him. He nodded and acknowledged their presence.

"Latimer. Nice to see you're finally here. Where's your

Mr. Ruggiero?'' Diana said icily, and beckoned him down the hall.

"I didn't think his presence was demanded," Ryder answered, sensing that her anger was simmering beneath the calm she was trying to present. "I have nothing to hide." Well, at least, nothing pertinent to the investigation.

Diana shot him a glance that clearly said she thought otherwise and then opened the door to one of the rooms. Inside, two other men waited.

He walked in, and she quickly introduced Jesus Hernandez, the assistant director in charge, and a tall, very Irish-looking man by the name of Peter Daly, who was the lead detective from the NYPD homicide squad that was assisting with the case.

A moment later he was invited to sit and the interrogation began.

Chapter 5

Ryder answered questions about his background—a fictional account of his life in New Orleans and elsewhere before he moved to New York. It was well rehearsed after years of practice. The narrative was one that had enough detail to satisfy but nothing that could be tangibly verified. No colleges attended or professional degrees earned despite the fact that at one time he had been a physician. Those details would only force him to create a tangle of lies that would trip him up and have the authorities wondering why he was being evasive.

Detective Daly seemed to notice the lack of detail, for on more than one occasion he jumped in to ask a question that might lead Ryder on a path to that tangle. Ryder deftly avoided those inquiries, but it was clear the detective was not happy.

Like Diana, this NYPD cop was not all that he seemed. Beneath the calm and observant exterior, there was a determined mind that would not be satisfied until he had the answers he wanted. Answers Ryder was not giving him.

As the three FBI representatives moved on with the questioning, the detective said nothing more. He just sat back and whittled away at the explanations Ryder gave. When talking about the club it was easier for Ryder to go with the full truth, for it was a real establishment with real people. Plus, he ran a clean business and no investigation, no matter how deep or invasive, would find otherwise.

His willingness to elaborate and cooperate seemed to mollify the investigators, although Diana and Detective Daly were not totally convinced of Ryder's intentions. It made sense. His intentions had only a little something to do with finding the killer and a lot more to do with protecting himself and his way of life.

He was smooth, Diana thought, observing Ryder as he answered another question about his past even though a moment before they had been discussing the club's bouncers and any possible altercations they might have had with the patrons.

Ryder leaned back in the chair and adopted a very casual, laid-back stance. If he was nervous, there wasn't a thing to give it away. His pupils were wide and open. His facial muscles relaxed. "As I said before, Detective, my mama home-schooled me—"

"In your place in the bayou?" Daly finished, but Ryder just shook his head.

"You Northerners don't seem to understand, we don't all grow up in the swamps, Detective. As I said before, my family lived in a small place on the outskirts of the French Quarter. That's in New Orleans, if you didn't know," he chastised, adding a slow drawl to his voice that made the city's name sound like Nawlins. Again, she had to admire him. He was either telling the truth or he was an exceptionally good liar. And his drawl...it made her think of sultry Southern nights and... She stopped herself from going there and concentrated again on the interrogation.

"And your mother—" Daly began, but Ryder cut him off.

"My mother was a waitress in various establishments, but died when I had just turned thirteen. I ended up on the streets, living however I could. Moving around a bit until I decided to leave for other opportunities," he replied, his voice hardening as if it was painful to recollect that part of his life.

She couldn't picture him as a street urchin. He was polished in a way that came from breeding and not from trying to prove he had made it in the world. The clothing he wore spoke of a man with innate taste, from the soles of his Gucci-clad feet to the Jhane Barnes suit and what she was certain was a hand-tailored Egyptian cotton shirt. This was a man used to elegant things and yet... There was a hardness under that graceful facade that only came with seeing too much of life. She had that same harsh aspect deep inside herself and recognized a kindred spirit. Maybe that was why she was drawn to him.

As he finished his explanation and met her gaze, he gave her a chagrined look as if he realized that she saw through all the polish and shine. She started to smile back, then reined it in. She was supposed to be investigating, not commiserating.

After a few more questions, the ADIC took charge. "Mr. Latimer, we thank you for your cooperation and hope you will have time to assist Special Agent in Charge Reyes and her colleagues with whatever they may need at your club or—"

"I'd be delighted to show Ms. Reyes around tonight, if she wishes. We're closed, and it would be the perfect opportunity for her to get a feel for the place. Plus, we can discuss how I can assist with the investigation." He gave her a devastating smile that warmed her with its intensity.

It was that response that had her hesitating to go anywhere alone with him, but she nodded at her ADIC and colleagues. "That would be acceptable, although Special Agent Harris and Detective Daly have other plans for tonight."

"I'm sorry to hear that," Ryder replied, although she sensed he was pleased. Did he think that by cutting her away from the others he might be able to gain some advantage? Maybe even charm his way out of any further role in the investigations? He'd be unpleasantly surprised to find otherwise. She intended to stick close...for business reasons only, she clarified to herself.

"Well, I think it's time we all got moving," she said, and rose.

She bid everyone in the room goodbye, and Ryder followed her out of the interrogation room and down to a smaller office at the end of the hall. Once inside, Diana slipped off her jacket and tossed it on the sofa near the door. She held out her hand, offering him the chair in front of her desk, and he sat, crossing one leg over the other and slouching down slightly.

He glanced around her office, his gaze sharp as if taking inventory and sizing her up. Diana wished her space was a trifle neater rather than boasting its usual clutter of files and papers. She refused to apologize for it, even though she detected condemnation.

"Comfortable?" she asked instead, slipping into her own chair, removing her holstered gun and locking it into her top desk drawer.

"No, but this will have to do, won't it?" he challenged, finally vocalizing some of his displeasure over his involvement in the case.

Diana held back her comment, dug a fat manila file from a small pile on the side of her desk, and plopped it onto the desktop between them. Opening the folder, she rotated it so he could examine the contents as she began to fill him in on the background of the case. Of course, the folder was missing what few key pieces of information they had. Call it a test, she thought, wondering whether he would slip up and give away anything that might implicate him.

He didn't. On the contrary, as they discussed the case his intelligence and observations impressed her as did his willingness to offer information on his various employees and, at times, himself. She stored away each nugget of information, using them to construct a better picture of the man sitting before her.

He was a loner. A man who had experienced great loss and still bore the weight of it in a heart that sought respite. She understood such loss. She had experienced it herself and, like Ryder, still carried scars within her that hadn't healed. And, like Ryder, a part of her hoped someone would help ease the burden and heal the wounds. But two injured people…it didn't bode well for a happy ending, she thought.

"Any ex-employees who might harbor a grudge? Maybe want to hurt you and the club by choosing its patrons as targets?" she asked, trying to pull away from what she was feeling and return to her role as investigator.

Ryder shrugged. To have enemies one had to have friends. Ryder had neither, only his companion Melissa Danvers. His employees were just that and nothing more, as were his lawyer and other business associates. "No one. I try to be fair, Ms. Reyes."

Tired of her questioning, he asked, "What do you think this killer is like? What makes him tick?"

Diana leaned back in her chair, considering him as if she wasn't quite sure if she could trust him. But he also sensed something else…interest. Unwanted attraction on her part. Her eyes narrowed and then she began her explanation. "He obviously has a lot of anger toward women. He acts out that anger by ritualistically torturing his victims."

Ryder nodded. "I noticed the cuts from the pictures," he said.

"Mmm. He likes hurting them," she continued. "I think

he makes sure that they are aware of what he plans to do. That gives him power. That gives him the ability to... He probably can't function sexually without that.''

''Not much of a man,'' Ryder intoned, and stood, stretching out the kinks in his back from the hours of sitting. ''Please continue,'' he said. She described the motivating force for the killer, the likely age of the suspect and how she believed he spent time choosing his victims before he finally took them away to be tortured and killed. As she spoke, he walked away from her and paced the small open space to the right of her desk. His movement took him past the window, which faced the water and provided a view of the East River and the Narrows. At night, it would give her a glimpse of the Statue of Liberty and the ferries going to and from Staten Island. He suspected she had been there more than one night to see those sights.

On the ledge of the window there was an assortment of orchids, some in full exotic bloom. Fussy, fragile flowers. Not at all like their owner. She was strong and capable. Resilient and yet...wounded, he thought. He wanted to understand those hurts. Help heal them, he thought as he continued to listen to her report.

''Mr. Latimer?'' she questioned. He realized she had asked him a question that he had obviously missed during his musings.

''First of all, let's make it Ryder if we're going to be working together,'' he said, wanting to break down some of the barriers between them.

She hesitated but finally relented. ''Ryder it is then, as long as you call me Diana.''

''I'm sorry, Diana, for ignoring you, but I think I need a break.''

''I asked if you wanted to get some dinner. There's a little Italian place two blocks away where we can grab a bite and then head to your club.'' She rattled off the name of the restaurant.

Ryder nodded, although the bite he intended to grab was way different than what Diana had just proposed. "I just need to make a call first," he said, and she offered the use of her phone. He declined. "It's personal."

Her expressive gold-green eyes widened, and she surprised him by giving him an amused grin. "Sorry to make you cancel a hot date. I need to freshen up, anyway, so I'll be back in a few minutes." She rose and left the room, leaving Ryder in privacy, but not to cancel a hot date. On the contrary, he needed to make plans for an ice-cold bag of blood.

He reached to his side, removed his cell phone from the clip on his belt and picked up the framed snapshot of her family. Her mother, father and brother stood close to a younger Diana. All were smiling. He replaced the frame on her desk, depressed the number one on his phone and held it until Danvers answered with a soft, almost annoyed "Yes, Ryder."

"I need you to bring a snack." He gave Melissa the name and address of the restaurant. "I'll try to stall for about half an hour or so to give you time to get there. Beep me when you're ready, and I'll meet you inside the men's room."

"Oh, come on. Not the men's room again," Melissa complained, but Ryder just laughed and reiterated his request.

"Yeah, although I think I should get paid extra for the men's room," she joked. Over the years of servitude Ryder had not provided visible remuneration to the various Danvers who had assisted him. They served Ryder as a family tradition and out of friendship. Occasionally Ryder provided funds for things like Melissa's schooling.

"I'll put something extra in this week's envelope," he answered, and heard her laugh before her tone turned serious.

"So how was she—" A knock at the door precluded any

additional discussion. "Gotta run," Ryder said, and pushed the end button on the cellular, cutting Melissa off midsentence. Diana waited hesitantly by the door until he motioned her in.

She entered, went immediately to her desk, unlocked her drawer, removed her holster and gun, and slipped them onto the back waistband of her pants. As she reached behind her, the fabric of her shirt pulled against her breasts, and Ryder couldn't help but appreciate that though she was slender and petite, she managed to have curves in all the right places.

As her gaze met his, she colored a becoming shade of pink and quickly dropped her hands to work at tucking in the hem of the soft cotton top. Without saying a word, she stalked to the door and grabbed her coat, leaving Ryder to follow her hurried flight down the hall and toward the elevator.

She angrily punched the down button and waited, her foot tapping the floor in irritation. Her arms were crossed against those very enticing breasts, and Ryder couldn't resist baiting her, intrigued by her passion. "Angry at something?"

"Mr. Latimer—"

"It was Ryder a few minutes ago, Diana." She shot him a glare over her shoulder.

"Ryder," she started, her tone brusque, "I don't appreciate you ogling me, especially if we're going to be working together."

"Darlin'—" he began, but she cut him off by raising her hand.

"I am not your darlin', or sweetheart, or whatever else it is that you good ol' Southern boys call your lady folk."

He laughed.

"Well, okay then, Ms. Reyes," he said, putting undue emphasis on the Ms. "As a man, it is, unfortunately, an inherent part of my nature to notice a very attractive woman when I see one. So, my apologies for noticing you.''

Diana turned and faced him, searching for a way to counter his last statement without sounding like a total bitch, but he had effectively trapped her. ''Touché, Ryder. I can see that I am going to have to watch myself around you.''

Ryder smiled, broadly and unrepentantly. There was something about his smile that tempered her anger and started a slow curl of warmth in parts she'd rather not have warmed.

''Darlin', that is a shame,'' he said, and again she found herself jumping as he pulled imaginary strings.

''And why is that, Ryder?''

''Because I was hoping you'd be busy watching me,'' he replied without shame, leaving her standing there in openmouthed surprise as he stepped into the elevator. ''Coming?'' he queried, one dark eyebrow raised in challenge.

Chapter 6

Luigi's was a local hangout for many of the agents and other employees of Federal Plaza. A medium-size, family-run Italian restaurant, it had been there for as long as anyone could remember. It was generally busy, even during the later hours when most regular workers had gone home.

The interior was dimly lit and cozy, with an assortment of tables and booths. The tabletops boasted paper placemats with maps of Italy and tidbits about Roman history. Small votive candles glimmered at each table in an attempt to create a more intimate mood, though they were wasted on the suits who made up the majority of the diners.

As Diana entered, the older woman at the hostess's table threw open her ample arms, embraced Diana and let out a stream of Italian that could have been expletives or endearments for all Ryder knew.

Diana smiled and hugged the woman. When there was a break in the effusive monologue, Diana responded in a halting mix of Spanish and Italian, ending with "We'd like a table'' in English. She glanced at Ryder as she spoke and shot him an awkward smile.

The hostess raised one pudgy, but well-manicured, finger and pointed it at Ryder. ''A *friend,* yes. *Il suo amico?*'' she questioned, putting undue emphasis on the word, which Diana was quick to clarify. Too quick, Ryder thought with amusement, secretly pleased that Diana was affected by him.

''Just a business acquaintance, Mama Isabel. We need to get some food. Good food,'' she emphasized, and as she finished, Ryder's beeper went off, alerting him to Danvers's presence in the men's room.

He silenced the beeper and glanced around. The men's room was down a small hall to the right of where they were standing. ''If you'll excuse me, I need to make a call,'' he said, and took a step toward the hall.

Diana looked at him oddly and pointed in the direction of the bar. ''The pay phone is in there,'' she replied, and then motioned to his belt where his cell phone was visible. ''Or you can use that.''

Ryder glanced at his phone. ''Oh, no. The beeper can wait. It was nothing important. I need to call on the facilities,'' he explained. Diana mumbled an ''oh'' and nodded. ''Get a table, and I'll find you,'' he instructed, fearing that if she waited by the entrance, she'd run into Danvers. If Diana recognized her, it might lead to a lot of unnecessary questions.

He didn't wait for Diana's reply. He knew Danvers was waiting in the bathroom, impatient and ill at ease.

''Hey, Ryder,'' she greeted in an artificially low voice. The wealth of her blond hair had been tucked under a baseball cap that was pulled low over her forehead. An oversized jacket, one of his old ones, swam on her slim physique. Loose jeans hid her shape, making it possible for her to pass as a small man, but not if anyone made a point of looking at her. Melissa's face was too feminine to allow her disguise to survive a more thorough examination.

Ryder motioned for her to wait while he checked each stall of the room. They were the only ones in the facilities. He held his hand out to his companion, wiggling his fingers with anticipation.

"Not even a thanks," Melissa mumbled. She rolled her eyes and unzipped her nylon windbreaker, extracting a plastic bag of blood. "Even got it warm for you," she groused as she slapped the bag into Ryder's hand and leaned back against a sink as Ryder stepped into one of the stalls and closed the door.

The life energy of the liquid burned the palm of his hand, starting the unwelcome change. His heartbeat accelerated as his fangs elongated in expectation of puncturing the thick skin of the bag. Hands shaking, a fine sweat breaking out over his body from the heat of his bloodlust, he brought the bag to his mouth and closed his eyes, still disgusted by his need after more than a century. As he bit down, the plastic resisted at first, and then the sharp points of his teeth found entry and the warm earthiness of the blood spiced his mouth as some of it escaped the hollows of his fangs and spilled onto his lips. He greedily sucked down the liquid, draining the bag dry in a little over a minute.

When he was done, he was breathing heavily and was light-headed with the strength that flowed into him, enervating every cell in his body. Leaning his head against the metal of the stall, he sought to control his thirst for even more blood. In the beginning, the first Danvers had had to restrain Ryder until he had been able to restore his human self. But after many, many years, he had learned to garner his control.

His restraint had slipped slightly tonight, and he wondered if it was because of Diana. Maybe the hedonistic animal in him recognized the sweetness, the pleasure to be had, in taking a woman.

A very beautiful, very alive young woman. Being with Diana… He didn't want to harbor any long-lasting thoughts of what being with Diana would be like. He couldn't deal with that.

Ryder closed his eyes and took a deep breath to quell any other unwelcome ideas. With his reenergized senses, the heavy lub-dub of Melissa's heart reached his ears. His hackles rose in recognition of her as prey.

He wrapped his arms around himself, his body not his own as he struggled against his violent urges. Against the creature that emerged whenever he fed. Slowly, through the force of his will, the animal in his body quieted, but it was a battle he always feared he might not win. Especially when temptation waited outside in the restaurant.

He unrolled a piece of toilet paper and wiped at his mouth, grimacing as the paper came away with streaks of red. He rubbed vigorously until there were no remnants of his meal and then flushed the evidence. Exiting the stall, he handed Melissa the empty bag. "You okay?" she asked, lifting the brim of her cap so she could get a better look at him.

Nodding, Ryder stepped to the sink, turned on the cold water and bent, splashing his face repeatedly. He cupped his hands and used the water to flush the last of the metallic taste of blood from his mouth. When he stood once more, he met Danvers's worried gaze in the mirror. "I'm okay. Really."

Melissa hesitated, and in his energized state, Ryder detected the slightly faster beat of her heart. The smell of fear coming off her skin. "Something wrong?" he asked.

"Are you sure about this, Ryder?" Melissa queried, and inclined her head toward the door leading to the restaurant. Had Melissa noticed his attraction to Diana Reyes?

Ryder shrugged. "I need to have some control over where this investigation is going. I have to befriend this woman."

"You're interested in her?" Melissa asked in surprise.

So she *hadn't* noticed. And he'd almost given it away. He tried to cover it up by saying, "No. I'm not. But…what were you worried about?"

"Not the investigation or the woman, that's for sure," she corrected quickly, and Ryder couldn't hide his own confusion.

"Really?" he asked.

"No way. It's the restaurant. There's enough garlic here to kill an army of you," Melissa replied, clapping Ryder on the back in a forced attempt at camaraderie.

Ryder shook his head. She was trying to bring him back to a more human level with her humor. Danvers had learned of his secret only a few years ago, and she was still a novice at dealing with his unusual condition and its demands.

"I'll make sure to watch out for it," he answered. Taking a step toward the door, he turned, wanting her to be aware of how much he appreciated the risks she took. "Thanks, Danvers."

Melissa smiled and waved him off. "No problem, but you'd better get going. The fettuccine isn't going to wait for you all night."

Ryder forced his own smile and stepped back into the restaurant. When the hostess noticed him, she took his arm and guided him to a booth only a few steps away from the main entrance. They approached the table where Diana waited with her back to the entrance, allowing Melissa to leave without notice.

"Sorry I took so long," he apologized as he slipped into the bench across from her.

"No problem," she replied. A waiter approached and slid a small, napkin-covered basket onto the table. Diana flipped open one side of the napkin and held out the basket to him. "I took the liberty of ordering some garlic bread to get us started."

The scent assailed him, and Ryder barely controlled the

urge to rear back from the table. He managed to shift away only slightly and hold up his hand in refusal. "I think I'll pass."

"Gives you *agita,* huh?" she replied, then set the basket in the middle of the table and grabbed a piece of garlicky, cheesy bread.

Ryder watched her take a bite and winced. "If *agi*-whatever means it's time for Pepto-Bismol, the answer is 'yes,'" he lied.

Diana glanced at him as she quickly devoured the first piece of the bread and reached for another. "No self-respecting New Yorker, even a transplanted one such as yourself, doesn't know what *agita* means, Ryder. So I guess you haven't been here long."

He shrugged, picked up the menu sitting on the table and answered her from behind the protection of the paper. "I've been here awhile. I just don't get out much."

"Mmm," she murmured, sensing evasion in his voice. "Too much work and not enough play has made Ryder a dull boy?" she teased, and wondered where the playfulness had come from. She should not come on to a possible suspect.

He put down the menu and faced her straight on, a challenging grin on his face. "If anyone would know, it would be you, Diana. I suspect you spend more than your share of time at work."

She shrugged, thinking it was because she had yet to meet someone who interested her as much as work did…until now. Shaking off the thought, she snagged another piece of the bread and took a bite, hesitating before answering. "I work hard, that's true. But I have my group of friends and my family," she evaded. "How about you?"

"Is your family in the area? I thought I detected a slight accent," he said, ducking her question, as the waiter stepped up to them, his pad and pen in hand.

"The usual, *bella?*" the handsome teenager said with a wink.

She nodded and returned her menu. "The usual, Rocco."

When the waiter turned to Ryder, he ordered the fettuccine alfredo. He pressed Diana again once the young man was gone. "So, family in the area?"

"A brother who moved up to New York a few months ago. He's a computer whiz who was working for a new Latino Web site down in Silicon Beach—"

"Where's that?" he jumped in.

"Miami. That's where we grew up," she answered quickly.

Ryder nodded. "Explains that slight singsong I hear in your voice. English wasn't your first language," he stated matter-of-factly.

"No, it wasn't. I'm Cuban-American."

He nodded again and motioned for her to continue with her story. "So why do they call it Silicon Beach?"

"Lots of new dot-coms down in Miami are geared for Latinos, so they've dubbed part of the area Silicon Beach." She stopped only long enough to take a sip of water and finish her piece of garlic bread. "Anyway, he got lured away by more money and a better title. Some new Latino Web site that started up in New York."

"It's nice that he's close to you."

Diana nodded. "He lives with me," she clarified, and hated how easily that statement had come. Ryder's grin made it clear that he had taken it to mean she was available. She quickly tried to deflect any further queries into her personal life. Or rather, her lack of one.

"Your mom is gone, but how about other family? Are they nearby?" she asked, and regretted it as a fleeting glimpse of sadness washed over his features.

"I was an only child. My father never acknowledged me, so I had no other relatives to speak of," he lied, feeding her the story that, after so many repetitions, had almost become truth. In reality, he'd had a loving wife and family, but they were long gone. It had been too painful to keep track of his descendants only to watch them die.

"That's a shame," Diana said, and motioned in the direction of the hostess at the front door. "You see Isabel over there? She and Luigi have three daughters and three sons, one of whom was our waiter. They all work here and, eventually, their kids will work here, as well."

Ryder laughed in disbelief. "You mean there really is a Luigi?"

Diana chuckled and leaned closer to him over the width of the booth. "Yes. His great-granddad, Luigi number one, came from Italy with his wife and opened this place. His only son, Luigi number two, couldn't cook to save his life, but married a nice Italian girl who could. That son made sure there would be another generation to keep it going by having Luigi the third and five daughters."

"These people are your friends."

Diana smiled and nodded eagerly. "When you're new in town, you try to make friends. Especially ones who cook this well. How about you?"

"I have some friends," he replied, and again she noted his hesitation. Contrary to his statements, she got the impression that he was a man with few emotional attachments. But she couldn't press the issue; Luigi's middle son, Rocco, brought their meals on a large tray.

Rocco deposited the steaming dish of creamy fettuccine in front of Ryder and a large platter of shrimp scampi before Diana. She inhaled the earthy smell of roasted garlic that Luigi used in his recipe. When she glanced up, she met Ryder's gaze and noted the look of horror on his face. "Something wrong?"

Ryder gaped at her plate of pasta, swimming in olive oil and garlic, with large prawn-size shrimps on top. "Are you a garlic-aholic or something?" he asked.

"It's good for you. Keeps your blood pressure down.

Good source of selenium and, not to mention, the absolute best trick for keeping away—''

''Vampires?'' he asked, trying to instill some humor in his voice. Had she noticed something that would tip her off to the fact that he was not what he seemed?

''Hell no,'' she replied as she began to twirl a long string of pasta onto her fork. ''There's no such thing as vampires. Unwanted suitors, however, are a dime a dozen. Keeps those pesky critters away.''

He could imagine that she might have her share of men wanting to get close. After all, she was a beautiful woman, with a confident air that increased her attractiveness. Still... He didn't want to be one of those critters she chased away. ''Darlin', if a little garlic keeps them away, they're fools.'' He was rewarded with a quick grin that displayed a dimple he hadn't noticed before.

''And you, Ryder? Are you a fool?'' she challenged, the fork filled with garlic-tainted pasta just inches from her luscious mouth. A mouth smiling at him sexily and in obvious recognition of his fascination.

Either way he answered, Ryder was damned. He reached for the basket of garlic bread, grabbed a slice and bit into it. His mouth burned, but he battled the pain. As he swallowed, the heat of the garlic continued down his throat. He would suffer for hours from its effects. Grinning at her, he reached for a glass of water and calmly took a sip, despite his very real discomfort, worse than any *agita* she could imagine. It was worth the pain to prove he wouldn't be chased off so easily. ''What do you think, darlin'?'' he finally choked out.

Diana stared at him, narrowing her eyes. Handsome. Charming. And obviously not afraid to make a play for her. Little by little, her grin broadened, and her eyes opened wide in pleasure as her rebellious side rose in answer to his attention. A soft chuckle escaped her and grew stronger until it became a full, hearty laugh. She shook her head from side to side. "Ryder, darlin'," she teased, mimicking him. "You are one heck of a fool."

It was his time of day. His senses became unusually alert to nocturnal sights and sounds.

In the country, the activity of the night was tame, natural. The hoot of a screech owl or the rustle of the underbrush as some small rodent sought out its meal. The soft whisper of wind passing through the branches of a pine, bringing with it a clean, tangy scent.

Night in the city, especially New York City, was a radically different experience. In a metropolis that was always active, the night sounds were busy. The rumble and rattle of subway cars moving underfoot. The harsh, strident screech of distant police cars or ambulances. Here, the rustle of rodents meant rats in the small alleys and breaks between buildings, rooting through garbage cans and the trash on the streets.

And the smells, he thought, were harsh and pungent. The diesel tang of truck exhaust. The stench of a particularly ripe homeless person.

Somehow, tonight, those citified attacks on his faculties were lessened as he strolled with Diana along the two short blocks back to Federal Plaza. No perfume still, just her womanly scent, leather and metal. This time from the holster with the gun he had watched her tuck against the small of her back. The combination of femininity and lethal power pulled at his insides and made him want things that were best left alone. He was an animal, after all, and could never have a life with her.

As they walked, there were only a few people on the street. The lack of activity created an artificial intimacy. Ryder leaned close to Diana, inclining his head slightly to listen as she spoke, trying to compensate for the difference in their heights. He was also using it as an excuse to take in as much of her as he could, if only for this fleeting

moment. He enjoyed the way her short hair shifted in the
breeze and the jangle of the two gold bracelets on her wrist.

He concentrated on the melody of her voice as she explained what she hoped to have prepared in time for tomorrow night's stakeout at the club. As she spoke, he
sensed the strain creeping into her voice and the increasing
tension of her body. At the corner, as they waited for a cab
to pull down the side street, she grimaced and rubbed one
temple with her fingers.

"Headache?" he asked.

She nodded, and it seemed to him that even the slight
movement pained her. Ryder reached over, cupped her head
and brought his thumbs to her temples. He began a slow
massage while softly asking, "Melissa gave you some medicine. Isn't it working?" Her skin beneath his fingers was
soft and inviting. Warm with the heat of life.

Her eyes closed, she said, "Yes, and the staff physician
gave me more, too. It doesn't work really well. But this
definitely does." Her last words were nearly a groan, and
he imagined her response to his touch in other places.

He tempered his need and continued his tender caress,
wincing as he noted the mottle of blue and purple along
her cheekbone that, at this distance, makeup didn't quite
hide. "I'm sorry, again."

She opened her eyes and grinned. "Well, this makes up
for it a little, although I don't think I can carry you around
and pop you out like one of the pills the doctor gave me."

He chuckled, dropped his hands and smiled. "You're
right, but I can guarantee that one of those pills combined
with a big cup of coffee will do the trick."

"Coffee?" she questioned as they finally crossed the
street and neared a coffee shop. "You mean I have a real
medical excuse for my one addiction?"

"It's a great vasodilator. It should help." He shoved his
hands in his pockets because he was too tempted to reach
for her again.

"And you know this because—"

"I used to be a doctor," he answered, and she stopped short.

"I don't recollect you mentioning that before," she said, catching the inconsistency from his earlier statements.

Ryder grimaced and wished he hadn't gotten so friendly with her, so at ease. After years of being alone and keeping to himself, he hadn't always had to be on guard and censor everything he said or did. Now he'd blown it and in a big way. "It was another life. One which I try to forget."

"What happened?" The question had none of the investigator behind it. Clearly, she was interested on a more personal level. The truth, if he were to tell all of it, would be impossible for her to believe. And even by telling her a part of it, it would unravel his earlier story and start that tangle he had tried to avoid.

He now had little choice but to nurture the trust between them that had been building over the course of dinner. "I volunteered to assist in a war zone, patching up the poor boys some idiot decided were cannon fodder," he replied harshly, and then grimaced at his own vehemence. He had thought himself over such emotions.

Diana paused by the door of the coffee shop and glanced up at him. Her gaze was decidedly inquisitive. Amazingly, friendly, as well. "Ryder, you've almost, but not quite, redeemed yourself in my eyes."

"Meaning?" he pressed, wanting to prolong this moment of understanding.

"You can't be all that bad if you prescribe coffee for my headaches and if you're smart enough to know it's the idiots running the show who sacrifice us poor foot soldiers," she replied lightly.

While he liked the mood that had developed between them, familiarity bred the unwanted desire to learn more about her. To develop a real relationship with her. Something he *couldn't* risk, he reminded himself.

"Let's just fill your prescription," he replied calmly, and opened the door of the coffee shop.

Chapter 7

Ryder unlocked the front door of the club and held it open for her. She stepped inside, and it was even darker than it had been the night before. Emergency signs lit the few exits here and there, leaving large sections of black so deep she imagined she wouldn't be able to see her hand in front of her face. Ryder stepped behind her and excused himself, indicating that he would go turn on the master lights.

He walked some distance away, and she heard the scrabble of metal as he unlocked a panel box and then the thunk of a large switch. Bright lights flared to life, illuminating the interior of the club and exposing its many areas for the first time.

She took a few steps farther in and looked around. The walls of the club were done in a dark gray, almost black, but with textures and molding that made it look like the inside of a cave. In the dark, only those standing along the edges would be able to make out the details.

Walking to the wall, she ran her hand along the surface. "Very…neat," she said for lack of a better word.

"I wanted to create the right ambience. It's all fire safe and up to code, I assure you," he said.

She nodded and walked away from the wall and into the center of the club. She looked up into the tangle of cat-walks, lights and wires and for the first time noticed the glass windows perched high above one end of the club. "Your office, right? We were there the other night?" she asked, unable to recall the windows from her visit.

Ryder confirmed it and held out his hand, beckoning for her to precede him. "The windows let me see what's going on down below. There's also a door to the catwalks."

"Which is how you got down to the alley the other day?" she asked as she walked ahead of him and waited directly beneath the windows.

"Yes," he said, moving along the wall to the deepest part of the club. It was dark here, even with the lights, and she had to strain to see what he was doing. The shadows didn't seem to bother Ryder in the least for he pulled out his keys once more and unlocked another door. "This leads up to my office and into the supply areas."

When he popped the door open, a stream of light came from within. Along the length of the hall were a series of stockrooms, a few offices, a locker room for the employees and an exit. At the end of the hall a door led to a narrow staircase heading up. She remembered the tight stairwell. Its confined space and turns had made her nauseous on the way down to the exit. She vaguely recollected David guiding her out the door and to their car before driving her home.

There was something about the stairwell that bothered her, even though she wasn't normally prone to claustrophobia or anything like that. It was just…too cramped and dark. When she took the first step in it was as if she was stepping into a coffin. She clutched at the railings for stability and breathed just a little too quickly. It was just a stairwell, she chastised herself, and yet her gut said she had just made a foray into something she might not be able to control.

Ryder must have sensed her unease. He grasped her shoulder and asked, "You okay?"

Diana nodded and kept on walking, relieved when the door to his office came into sight. She strode into the dark room, and a moment later lights flashed on as Ryder hit the wall switch. She turned and faced him.

"Sit," he commanded, and walked her over to the large leather sofa she was familiar with from the other night. "You don't look well."

In truth, a cold sweat bathed her body and dotted her upper lip. She wiped at the moisture with hands that were shaky. "I'm okay," she replied, but plopped down onto the sofa.

He walked away and came back a second later with a small bottle of Pepsi and a glass filled with ice. He twisted off the top, poured and held it out to her.

She took it in clumsy fingers and quickly sipped the drink, hoping the cold and sweet would settle her. Ryder waited patiently, sitting on the coffee table in front of her until she had drained nearly half the glass and was feeling a little stronger. "Thanks," she said.

He nodded, but his concern was still apparent. "Tell me what information you'd like so we can make this an early night and get you home for some rest."

As much as she might want to deny that she needed it, she wasn't going to be pigheadedly macho and ignore what her body was telling her. She needed rest, especially in light of tomorrow night's stakeout. With that in mind, she rattled off the list of things he could give them, and when she was done, he poured the rest of the soda and instructed her to stay put while he gathered everything.

As he scrounged around in a filing cabinet for papers, she examined the office, something she had not had the opportunity to do during her last visit. The walls were pan-

eled in a deep mahogany that matched the large desk and
file cabinets. Reproductions of Impressionist paintings
graced the walls, tastefully lit by high ceiling lamps. It was
a room that bespoke class and breeding and was far removed from the almost circuslike atmosphere of the club
below. The Old World gentility of the space suited him
somehow, she thought, watching as he pulled papers out of
the cabinet and made copies at a machine tucked discreetly
into the far corner of his office.

The elegance of the space matched his practiced veneer
and was clearly the room of a man used to the finer things
in life. And used to being in charge. Which made her wonder just how much he resented her intrusion into his life.

If he did, he gave no indication of it as he walked back
with the materials. "This is the layout of the club's security
system. It has the locations of all of the cameras."

She unfolded the large sheet with the schematics of the
system. The name of the security company was at the bottom edge. "Do you keep tapes of what the video cameras
record?"

He sat down beside her on the sofa and his presence
unnerved her, but she said nothing as he replied, "Only if
we had any kind of problem those nights. Like a bouncer
mixing it up with someone. A lot of cash missing from one
of the tills. Those kinds of things," he replied.

"And I'm assuming that during the last two weeks—"

"Things have been very routine. We have the tapes for
the last few days. After what happened, I decided to keep
them. Just in case. You're welcome to them," he offered
without hesitation.

"Thanks. Do you think we can keep each night's video-
cassettes from now on?"

He nodded. "I'll pick up some more tapes tomorrow and
instruct the man who watches them."

"I'd like to question him about what he might have seen.
Will that be possible?" She glanced at him out of the cor-

ner of her eye, trying to see if his cooperation was real or
feigned.

"I'll ask the employees to cooperate, but I can't force
them. You'll have to ask each one if they have any objections."

She should have been annoyed, yet the reality was that
he couldn't force anyone to talk. "Is there a list—"

"In the second file down," he answered quickly.

She opened the folder and noted that the employees'
forms had little information. "Sparse," she said, and shot
him a glance.

"I'm not hiring rocket scientists. I try to employ hard-
working, decent people. Most of my crew has been with
me for a while."

She nodded, closed the file and rose from the sofa.
"We'll be calling them in. By tomorrow I'll have some
photos of possible suspects. Do you think you can come
down and take a look?" She walked toward the door, the
folders with the information tucked under her arm.

"Sure, as long as it's in the afternoon. On the way out,
let's stop by the security office and pick up the tapes." He
followed her from his office and down the narrow, phobia-
inducing stairway.

At the bottom, she breathed a long sigh of relief and let
him take the lead to the room a few doors away that held
half a dozen VCRs and black-and-white screens. Ryder
popped the tape from each one and put them in a plastic
bag emblazoned with the logo from a local deli.

"Thanks. Do you need a ride?" Diana asked, grabbing
the bag. She would have to head back to the office and log
these in as evidence before heading home for the night.

"I'll just flag a cab, thanks."

She nodded and exited the security room. Ryder led her
through the main club and out the door, shutting down the
lights and locking up behind him. On the steps of the build-

ing, he paused and stared up at the fanciful neon sign that glowed bright red in the dark of the night.

"I picked the name as a kind of private personal joke. It never occurred to me that The Lair might become the home of a hunter," he said with a sigh.

"There could be a million and one reasons why he chose your club, Ryder. None of them having to do with the theme."

"Mmm," he said halfheartedly. "Tomorrow then, at four. Afterward you'll come here?"

She confirmed that, and he walked her to her car. He waited until she was inside and the door was locked. Then he tapped the window with a knuckle and she opened it to hear what he had to say.

"Watch your back and don't work too hard. You need some rest," he said, and motioned to her face.

"Thanks. You, too," she replied, although he didn't bear a mark on him from their altercation the night before. She had struck him hard and had seen the imprint of her blow. He must heal fast, she thought.

With a last nod, she closed the window and pulled out. As she did so, she looked for him in the rearview mirror, but he was gone.

Ryder lounged on the terrace of his apartment, enjoying the bright lights of Manhattan in the dark night sky. They said Paris was the City of Light, but Ryder was unconvinced. There was nothing prettier and more entrancing than the transformation of Manhattan at nighttime.

He observed the change every dusk from his perch high atop the city. The lights drifted on in the nearby office buildings and down on the street below. Across the way, Queens snapped on its colors—the large red Pepsi and Silvercup Studio signs along the water and the erratic string of lamps from the bridge and the Roosevelt Island tramway. Running lights from tourist cruise ships and small party boats reflected off the dark waters of the East River. Even with daylight fading, New York was alive and thriving, like Ryder had once been so long ago.

Walking away from the edge of the terrace, he sat down at the marble-topped wrought-iron table that had, at one time, graced the patio of his Louisiana home. He salvaged it and some other things from an estate sale after the death of his wife. Thinking him a casualty of war, the army had advised his wife that he was likely one of the unidentified dead, and she had remarried. She'd had children with her second husband, who took over the running of Ryder's small rice plantation. Upon the death of his wife, her children had rid themselves of the property that had become a hindrance to their lifestyles. They preferred the hubbub of New Orleans to life on a quiet plantation.

For a time, he had considered buying back the home that had once been his and returning to his life as a physician and plantation owner. But living with those ghosts was too difficult a burden to bear. And his companion, the second Danvers to serve him, had moved his family out West, so Ryder had gone with him. And then his companion died like so many others....

Those ghosts had chased him throughout his existence as people and places changed around him. He had shut himself off as best he could, trusting only his companion. It had helped temper the pain that associations with humanity ultimately brought.

Ryder had finally settled in Manhattan, following one of his companions after he was offered a position at a prestigious hospital. The change had been good for him. Until that servant had passed away and then Melissa's father had gone, way before his time should have been up. He and his wife had perished in an automobile accident. And now Ryder had Melissa to worry about, he conceded, for despite all his efforts not to become involved, it was difficult not to care about the young woman who was the great-great-

great granddaughter of William, the lifelong friend who had become Ryder's first companion.

Like Ryder, William Danvers had been a battlefield physician in a war that, unfortunately, provided them with too many patients on which to ply their skills.

William had stumbled across Ryder and the remainder of his unit in a small copse just beyond the edge of a battlefield. Ryder and his men had been attacked by a band of marauders who had turned out to be vampires eager to take advantage of the war. Demons who were unfortunately no less brutal than their human counterparts—raiders and soldiers alike who killed without remorse under the righteous banners of both North and South.

Ryder had been the only one left alive of his entire group, and his friend had tended him, helping him battle the fevers and physical injuries inflicted during the attack. At first, neither man suspected what had happened. Then it became apparent that Ryder was no longer a normal man, especially when his thirst for blood nearly drove him to kill.

Ryder had despaired of his condition, of the thirst only one thing seemed to satisfy. If not for his steadfast friend, he might have taken his own life, but Danvers convinced him that there had to be a reason for his transformation. A greater purpose to explain what had happened.

Ryder flipped open the file obtained through some of his lawyer's less respectable connections. He stared at the glossy black-and-white photo of Diana, wondering if she—and this case—were maybe his greater purpose.

He picked up his glass of merlot, took a sip and savored the wine's hearty, earthy flavor. Contrary to vampire myth and legend, he'd found he could enjoy food and liquids other than blood, although he indulged in such things only as a way of maintaining a semblance of normalcy. They gave him no sustenance.

With a hearty earthiness of its own, blood provided him

with his life force and energy. But unlike the murderous demons who had ravaged him a hundred and thirty-six years ago, Ryder refused to feed on the living. He took his strength from the occasional helping of beef blood purchased from the local butcher and the blood-bank bags Melissa brought from the hospital.

Like each Danvers before her, Melissa was sworn to uphold a secret and bear a burden some would find frightening. Indeed, one he was certain she had found shocking.

He still remembered the dismal winter afternoon when he had stood beside Melissa as they had buried both her mother and father. He had wanted to give her time to grieve, but hadn't been able to do so. The family lawyer had arrived only moments after the graveside ceremony, bearing a letter that had been passed to every first-born Danvers since William had assumed his role more than a century before. Melissa was made of strong stuff and had shouldered her responsibilities with grace. She was a woman of honor and loyalty. She was the only one who shared his secret.

But maybe soon, Diana Reyes would be entrusted with his secret, as well.

He traced the lines of Diana's face in the photo, imagining the warmth and texture of her skin instead of the slick, cold gloss of the paper. He wondered again whether he was deluding himself into thinking that Diana bore some similarity to the woman of his dreams. Was there more to Diana than the plainly stated facts in her file?

Valedictorian of her high school class in Miami, she had attended the University of Miami on a scholarship and continued there to earn her master's in psychology. Instead of using that degree as a springboard for a career in the mental health sector, she'd joined the FBI.

A surprising decision, but as he flipped through the remaining papers in her file and psychological evaluation, the explanation came all too readily and all too sadly. At nineteen, Diana's father—a Miami-Dade police officer—had been gunned down during a drive-by shooting. Diana had been there to witness it and had herself been injured.

He recalled the picture on her desk, that of Diana with her family, all of them smiling and happy. As he continued flipping through the file, it was clear that her father's death had profoundly changed her.

The history in her psych profile went to great lengths to explain the year after her father's death. Her grades in college had slipped to abysmal levels and certain parts of her life had spun out of control. The evaluator had painstakingly detailed what had driven Diana to those depths and how she had managed to tame the demons. But the evaluator also noted that Diana was at risk of allowing those emotions to control her again.

He empathized with her. Of all people, he knew what it was like to present a human face to the world, but have a barely leashed animal inside, waiting to erupt. He wondered just what it would take to bring out that part of her. To let her give in and vent all her anger and frustration. Only by doing that would she ever truly be free.

And yet, he worried she would do so at the wrong time. Still, it seemed from her file that she might be able to take care of herself should her emotions lead her to physical confrontation. She had started martial arts training at a young age, probably because of her small size. Her last physical exam put her at five feet three inches and one hundred and ten pounds, but she seemed much more fragile to Ryder.

And her undercover work put her at risk. Was it some unfulfilled death wish maybe? he wondered, thinking this piece of the puzzle made her all the more interesting. Not that he hadn't been fascinated before opening her file, he thought, taking another long sip of his wine.

From the moment in the alley when they'd stood only feet apart, he'd been intrigued. After all, she was a beautiful young woman in a difficult and dangerous position. A fearless and determined one, he recalled. Combined with what he'd seen of her since last night, it made him want to explore and savor her, find out what drove her to do what she did. He hadn't felt that way in a long time, about anyone or anything.

But he'd almost blown his secret and now was inextricably involved in an investigation that might put him at risk. He was increasing that possibility by becoming too friendly with Diana, as he had during dinner and after, when he'd slipped about being a physician.

He reminded himself that he had to deal with her professionally, and only professionally. That he could not let his personal interest interject itself into their relationship. But even as he closed her file, he paused for another long look at her photo, and silently acknowledged how hard a task that might be.

Chapter 8

Diana didn't arrive at home until close to two in the morning. She'd logged in the tapes and made the necessary arrangements to view them in the morning. She had a slew of calls from the other agents. She made notes and set up a general meeting to go over everything old and new and refine the plans for the stakeout at the club.

Her brother was still up when she came in, busy working on another computer program. He looked up at her distractedly and gave her a smile. *"Hola, hermanita.* Catch any big, bad criminals today?"

She smiled, walked behind him and affectionately ruffled his hair. "Not a one," she said as she looked over his shoulder at the screen and saw nothing but meaningless computer code. "New program?"

He nodded, tapped out a few more words on the keyboard and then said, "Watch."

She did, and after a few more commands, the opening screen of a game came up. An FBI-agent game where the users had to work their way through a series of screens to solve a crime. Of course, along the way, there were a number of criminals to be destroyed and aptitude tests to be completed. "Pretty cool. I guess this is for you and not the company?"

Sebastian nodded and glanced over his shoulder at her. "Hence why I'm working on it now. Come the morning, it's back to the grind. What about you?"

"At seven I'm back at my desk. I have a lot to get ready," she replied, gave his shoulder a squeeze. "*Buenas noches,* Sebastian."

He reached up, grabbed her hand and gave it a squeeze. "I won't be awake so let me say it now. Be careful."

She bent and gave him a hug that he returned as best he could from his sitting position. "I will, *hermanito.* See you tomorrow night. Maybe."

She entered her bedroom and disrobed carelessly, tossing her suit onto a chair that already had a pile of clothes from the past few days. She hadn't had the energy to put anything away. Setting the alarm, she gave herself extra time to get ready in the morning. She would have to pack clothes for her undercover assignment since she might not have time to return home before heading out to Ryder's club. Things were heating up, and she needed to put in whatever time she could at her office. That might mean spending the night there while they reviewed the materials and tried to get a break in the case.

As she slipped into bed, exhaustion quickly took over, pulling her into a deep sleep that was uninterrupted until the loud electronic beeping of the alarm the next morning.

She rolled out of bed and showered, staying under the heat of the water for some time, letting it relax her. When she exited, steam lingered in the bathroom and condensation had clouded the mirror over the sink. She wiped it down with her towel and peered into it, pleased to see that the bruise along the side of her face was getting better. There was still one section that was a little more purple than the other, which was turning yellowish. She moved her jaw up and down, found there was only a little twinge and smiled at her reflection in the mirror.

Quickly finishing the rest of her morning ablutions, she turned her attentions to her closet. A dozen suits hung there in addition to the two or three piled on her chair. Toward the back of the closet was a black silk suit she rarely wore to the office. David called it her "babe suit" because there was something about the way the silk clung to her that made it very feminine and very flattering.

After a moment or so of hesitation, she grabbed the black suit. She laid it on the bed and returned to the closet to select a number of outfits for the next few days. She wasn't sure how much time she would have and wanted some clothes in her office, ready to be worn. If she needed to, she could shower at one of the locker rooms in their building.

She came across her favorite pair of leather pants, in a dark olive green that worked well with her complexion. She paired it with a black knit tank top. Then she grabbed a few other tops and another pair of leather pants, black this time, for the stakeouts.

She slipped on bikini panties and a bra in a matching leopard-skin print. They were something she only wore to the office occasionally, usually when she was feeling down about the state of her life and needed a pick-me-up.

Today she was already wired despite having only four hours of sleep. It was as if she sensed that today they might have a better idea of who was behind the murders. After Ryder came by...

She stopped there. She didn't want to go down that path. He just happened to be one item on today's agenda. An item she would deal with first thing. She had not yet stricken him from the suspect list, especially with last night's slip.

Item number one on her desk would be checking out his

story to see if he was registered anywhere as a physician. That might give her a clue as to who and what he really was.

As Diana dressed and put on the bare minimum of makeup, she mentally prepared for the briefing with the other agents and NYPD personnel working the case. She was the special agent in charge on the case and needed to instill confidence in those working with her. Create trust in her capabilities. As a woman in a very male bastion, that was sometimes difficult to do. As a Latina, subject to comments about being a "quota," it was even harder.

She grabbed her bag and her briefcase on her way out to the living room, where her brother was still busy at the computer. "At it from last night?" she asked as she walked toward the front door.

"Nah. Got up when I heard your alarm go off," he said, focused on the screen.

"I won't be home until late, if at all, so don't worry about me," she said, and, at that, he finally turned to look at her.

He gave a low whistle and motioned to her. "Dressed to kill today, are we? Is there someone we want to impress?"

She shot him an exasperated look and flipped him the finger on her way out the door.

The morning meeting went smoothly, as did most of what she had planned for the day.

Everything except Ryder. She had been unable to turn up a thing to either confirm or deny last night's statement. Her specialist had indicated there were gaps in the computerized records and so the absence of his name on the lists of registered physicians might not be irregular. Also, if he had been retired from the practice of medicine for some time, his record might have been expunged.

It didn't make her a happy camper. She preferred more information about her contacts. Ryder could be their prime suspect, although her gut told her otherwise. She could waste time trying to dig deeper and force him to submit to DNA testing, but this was one time she had to go with her instincts and hope they weren't wrong.

He arrived at four as promised, giving her some sense of relief. She walked him to an interrogation room. On a table was a pile of papers that reflected all the suspects who matched key parts of her profile and were currently free and might be in the area. She led him there and asked him if anyone looked familiar.

He glanced at the stack of papers in disbelief and placed his hand on them as if measuring the height of the pile. "Rather large, wouldn't you say?"

She shrugged. "We live in a sick world with a lot of sick people."

"A rather pessimistic view."

"I've seen too much—"

"Too soon," he finished and looked her over. "You're all of what? Thirty?"

"Why, Mr. Latimer," she said, affecting a Southern accent and laying a hand over her heart. "A gentleman shouldn't ask a lady a thing like that."

"I guess you just crossed that magic line or else—"

"I'm twenty-eight going on ninety sometimes. Life has a way of doing that," she replied more seriously, and motioned to the stack of papers. "Can I get you a coffee or anything?"

"Only if you're on your way to Starbucks," he said with a smile.

She shook her head. "Nope. Only the mud from the pantry. Still game?" When he assented, she walked out and down the hall to where someone had luckily just begun brewing a pot of coffee.

She returned to find Ryder elegantly slouched in the hard plastic chair. He had gone through very few of the photos, judging from the pile that lay by his right hand, and he appeared to be reading the mug sheets as he went along.

Diana placed the coffee in front of him, but away from the papers. "Interesting?"

"I thought I'd seen a lot, but these first few are enough to make you lose your hope in humanity," he said, and seemed surprised by the statement, as if he had thought he had lost hope a long time ago.

"Especially when you realize these guys are loose again."

Ryder grimaced. "I'd want them dead if they did this to me or mine."

"In time they'll get theirs." She firmly believed in that. It was the one belief that kept her from crossing the line. Not that she hadn't been tempted in her short career as an agent. But she wouldn't give into that desire because it meant losing the piece of herself that made her different from the criminals she chased—her humanity. Something that, as Ryder had noted, seemed to be a rare commodity.

"Try not to pay attention to that and just look at the pictures. Concentrate on them. Give them more or less hair. Beards. Maybe one will remind you of a regular, an employee or someone you had trouble with."

Ryder nodded. "Have you gone through these?"

She motioned to David, who stood in the doorway, with the hand that held her cup of coffee. "We did it this morning and now we're going to go through the tapes you gave us. Maybe something will click."

"And from here it's straight to the club? Maybe we can share a sandwich before we head there."

She looked at David but didn't wait for his agreement. "We'll order up some grub and you can sit in the dark and go through the videotapes with us."

With that, she left the room, leaving Ryder and David behind, staring after her.

Ryder glanced at the other man and caught the look in his eyes. "Is she always that—"

"Determined?"

"No. Hot."

David grunted a denial and glared at Ryder, but the menace in his gaze was not very convincing. "She's strong and in charge, Ryder—"

"And wearing silk," Ryder finished, wanting to taunt this man who worked so closely with Diana.

David said nothing and Ryder found himself searching out the other man's features. His face revealed nothing, forcing Ryder to ask, "Are you and she involved?"

"Are you kidding? Falling in love with Diana would be like stepping into a bear trap."

Ryder considered him carefully before asking, "Why?"

"Because the only way to free yourself is to leave a piece behind. Stay away," he warned, and gave Ryder no time to question him further as he walked out of the room.

Ryder stared after the other man, certain of only one thing. Her partner was her friend, but nothing more. That realization shouldn't have pleased him so much.

But somehow it did.

Chapter 9

The sand beneath her feet was soft and squishy. She dug her feet into it and let it slip between her toes. A moment later, the unhurried lap of a wave washed over her feet, wiping them clean.

She laughed and twirled, arms outstretched as she savored the warm, summer day and thought—today I'm just Diana Reyes, an overworked and overstressed FBI agent taking a much-needed vacation from her current assignment.

Slightly dizzy from whirling, she bent and took a deep breath of the salt-kissed ocean breeze. The air was pure and clean, untainted by the tropical humidity and miasma she had grown up with in Miami.

The sunlight before her was bright, exceptionally so. She squinted against the glare and her breath stopped in her chest. Ryder stood before her, several yards down the beach. He was dressed in basic black. Until now, the scene seemed so real that she hadn't realized it was a dream.

For a moment, she was tempted to turn and walk away,

but she wasn't one to run from anything, even in her dreams. She strolled toward him, and the sand beneath her feet shifted into dark, gray cobblestones. All around her, the air grew colder. The sun dimmed and the sky took on a gray pall. When she looked up once more, the sun was totally gone, replaced by dismal dusk and the golden spire of a building that looked vaguely familiar. Ryder still stood, his hand outstretched, spurring her onward.

She hastened her pace and the closer she got, the more she felt…serene and accepted. As she met his hungry gaze, she understood that something existed between them. He would continue to press until she could no longer deny him.

She stepped up to him and took hold of his hand. It was warm beneath her fingers. He murmured her name with such longing it nearly broke her heart. But it was a dream, she told herself, and in her dreams, she was in charge and free to say whatever she was feeling.

"What do you want from me?" She reached up and caressed the side of his face. The bristle of his beard tickled her palm.

He devoured her with his gaze and she swayed toward him. In response, he grasped her waist. His hand cradled the side of her and her skin heated beneath his touch.

"Do you know who you are?" he asked, his voice soft, caressing.

It was only a fantasy, she thought again, and in that wonderful state where anything was possible, she smiled and raised herself up on her tiptoes, leaning into him. "No, but I'm sure you'll tell me."

He smiled and bent his head, bringing his lips close to hers. His shaky exhalation bathed her lips with heat. "This is wrong," he murmured, even as he brought his lips to hers and she had her first taste of him.

"Ryder," she sighed against his hard, sculpted mouth.

Suddenly he wrenched away and glanced down at their

entwined hands. She looked, as well. Blood covered their hands and dripped down onto the cobblestones.

He said her name, his voice a low growl. He transformed before her eyes. Long, menacing fangs erupted from his mouth. His eyes glowed with an unusual golden light and his skin paled, becoming almost translucent. His change into a demon wrenched her out of the dream.

She sat upright in bed, breathing heavily. ''That was bad, Diana. Really, really bad.'' She dragged her hand through her short hair and found it soaked with sweat.

For too long she had suffered from night terrors. When she was a child, her mother and younger brother had been aficionados of motion pictures dealing with monsters and demons. Not wanting to be left out of their Saturday movie adventure, Diana had braved those visits to the cinema. It had inevitably resulted in nightmares that woke her in the middle of the night.

As an adult, she had learned to discount those dreams. Her best friend and college roommate, now an attorney at a Manhattan law firm, had been there more than once when Diana awoke from one of her terrors. Her friend had understood, and on her wedding day many years later, she had pressed a piece of the wedding cake into Diana's hands and told her to stick it under her pillow. With that slice of sweetness and a wish, Diana would dream of her Prince Charming.

And so, as sensible, scientific and serious as Diana normally was, that one last glass of champagne had lowered her resistance enough that she had gone home and shoved the napkin-wrapped piece of cake under her pillow and made her wish. She'd awakened, breathing heavily and shaking, fear hanging over her. No Prince Charming despite the ritual. As always, she had tried to piece together the vague, unsettling images from her subconscious and logically interpret the visions that usually became nightmares.

Tonight's fantasy had started out differently. It was rare

for her to dream of anything remotely nice and remember it. Then again, the dream had started out with Ryder in it. That should have given her a clue it wouldn't end happily.

Since their meeting a few days ago, he had plagued her waking thoughts, and now, it seemed, he would also curse her dreams. But she refused to dwell on him or the disturbing imaginings any longer.

Later today she would again be bait. The earlier stakeouts and investigations had yielded little for them to go on. They had a mile-high ream of paper listing possible suspects and they had not substantially narrowed the list. The killer was due to strike again soon, and they were running out of time.

She lay back in bed, closed her eyes and visualized all she had to get done in the morning and then at the club later that evening. As the items clicked into place, she used them like sheep, counting off each one until, little by little, her mental repetition lulled her to sleep.

This time Ryder knew the dream for what it was—a harbinger of things to come. She had somehow shared the vision with him, but he was uncertain whether or not she would recognize it for what it was.

She was in his arms, soft and warm and pliable. So slight. He had wondered more than once in the last few days how she survived as an FBI agent, as small as she was. But in that slender, petite frame was the heart and soul of a warrior.

A warrior, but a woman, as well. A woman who answered his passion with her own, her honeyed lips meeting his over and over again, opening to him so he could plunder her mouth and taste her surrender. Her spirit filled him with life, made him want more of the humanity he had avoided for so long. A humanity that could only bring pain.

"Ryder." She twined her fingers with his.

He held her tighter, wanting to go further, but there was

something invading his senses. The smell, the sensation of
something wrong.

"Diana, I—" He stopped short and pulled away, blood
staining their joined hands. He shook his head, denying
what he was seeing, and met her gaze, realizing that she
was unaware.

The sticky blood bound their hands together. She looked
down, confusion clouding the green of her eyes. Pain
erupted through him and he growled her name.

Her eyes glimmered with tears as she grabbed hold of
his shirt, her hands fisted against the fabric, trying to hold
him to her. Her perfect white teeth bit her lower lip as she
battled her emotions.

He couldn't look any longer.

Ryder forced himself from his sleep and, to his surprise,
found that he was in vamp mode, his body humming with
a need for... He wanted to feed, but he also wanted to
satisfy the human desire that had his body hard and
aroused.

In the time since he'd become a vampire, he'd had few
friends and no lovers. It hadn't been a conscious decision,
at first. In the beginning, the uncertainty of his new existence provided too many questions and too few answers.
He had preferred secreting himself in his own world rather
than dealing with the questions. By the time he had answers
to the who and what of vampire reality, the decision to
remain alone had already been unwittingly made. His sense
of loss as one human after another passed away confirmed
that his decision had been the only right one.

Until Diana. She had intrigued him, and what was left
of the human in him had responded. But now the beast in
him had emerged, as well, he thought, reaching up and
feeling the elongated fangs in his mouth.

He had no idea which would win—the human or the
demon. Maybe, he considered, as he imagined what it
would be like to bury himself in her, there wasn't much

difference between the two. He wanted to taste the honey of her mouth and the sweet tips of her breasts. Take a bite of that smooth, satiny skin.

Would she accept him or push him away?

In the short time they had been together, he had come to...care for her. She was bright, determined, beautiful. Able to take care of herself, or so she had told him on more than one occasion.

But if the dream was accurate...

Ryder wouldn't accept that. He couldn't. Fate had screwed him once.

He wasn't about to let it screw him again.

Chapter 10

The line winding away from the front door was exceptionally long. Information had been leaked, and the papers that morning had hinted that a serial killer might be picking his victims at The Lair. Diana had worried the publicity might drive the killer away. Judging from the line, caution was not the catchword of the day. As always, dozens of young women waited to enter the club, clothed to attract attention.

She walked to the front of the line and whispered something in the bouncer's ear. He let her pass, to the loud annoyance and grumblings of those waiting. As she stepped inside, she was pleased to see that everyone was in place.

Walking to the far end of the club, Diana entered the hall and strode to the security guard's office. She observed the views from the various monitors and spoke to the man responsible for watching the monitors. "You'll have those for me after you close?"

The man nodded, and satisfied with the arrangements, she told the rest of her crew, through the wire she wore, that she was heading back out into the crowd. In the hall, she ran into Ryder. His face was grim.

"Are you sure you want to do this again?"

"You sound like David. I'm sure. This guy is bound to strike soon, and we still haven't come up with anything that'll help us catch him." She walked down the hall, Ryder trailing behind her. As they neared the door to the main area, he grabbed her arm and turned her to face him.

"Be careful out there, Diana."

She got the eerie sense that he knew about her fears from the night before. Maybe he was just good at reading vibes, she told herself. She had been a little jittery all day and he must have picked up on that.

"I'll be fine, Ryder," she assured him, trying to convince herself, as well, that the blood and demon from the dream had been nothing but the workings of her tired mind and too-vivid imagination.

"I'll be watching," he said. She nodded and headed into the crowd.

Ryder kept an eye on her as she flitted from one man to another on the dance floor below.

She moved with an athletic grace, her tight body encased in snug olive green leather pants and a black tank top whose scooped neck and cropped cut showed off too much flesh for his liking. Too many men had likely envisioned how those full breasts would taste. How the muscled gap of skin visible above the waistband of the leather pants would feel.

His own body was hard with the imagining, his blood pumping thickly through him, threatening to bring out the demon. He took a deep breath, but she was too far away for him to smell her and he regretted the distance from the catwalk to the floor below.

She had chosen her position well, he thought. The wash of the lights from the stage made her act highly visible. Despite that, there had been no more than a half-dozen men who had approached. None had lingered for more than a dance or two. He wondered if they had been fellow agents or men drawn to her.

Ryder was certain that none of those who had approached had been the killer. As alluring as Diana had been, the murderer needed more to entice him into action. Ryder had no doubt about that. The darkness of the murders, the torment the killer wrung from his victims, was punishment. Payback for the sexual games the women played. Games the psychopath both enjoyed and resented.

He suspected that Diana's show on the dance floor hadn't come close to the level necessary to pique the murderer's interest, much less his anger.

Ryder intended to help her by changing that.

His strong hand slipped around her midsection, drawing her away from the agent who had been dancing with her.

She turned and met Ryder's gaze. "What are you doing?" she asked as he pulled her close, his arm encircling her waist.

"Dance," he commanded in low tones.

Because she couldn't risk making the wrong kind of scene, she did as he instructed, bringing one hand to his shoulder and moving against him to the sounds of the alternative rock band on the stage.

He could move, she thought, admiring the way his big body shifted to the beat and the natural grace of him as he pressed against her.

The hand at her back inched up slightly beneath the hem of her shirt, his rough palm flush against the damp skin at the small of her back. It sent a sensual shiver through her. One she didn't want to acknowledge.

"Ryder."

He bent his head and whispered, "He needs to see more, Diana. You know that."

To anyone watching it would look as if he was sharing

an intimate whisper and she had to keep the farce going. Pressing her cheek against his, she whispered, "Why do you think that?"

He brought his other hand to her waist and spanned its width. He slowly backed her toward the stage, his muscular body insinuating itself between her legs. His arousal pressed against the softness of her belly.

She was about to protest once more but he bent close and shifted his hands to the middle of her back. Then he turned her slightly so that virtually everyone in the club could see what he was doing.

"He likes the watching," he whispered into her ear, nuzzling his face against hers, his movements those of a lover enticing a partner. "He's done that a lot in his life. Watched...waited."

He brought one hand to the center of her back and urged her nearer while he shifted his other hand to just below her breast. With her arms around his shoulders, it wouldn't take much for him to reach up and...

Diana battled the response of her body, shuddering as he bit her earlobe and continued with his soft, sexual commentary. "You're aware of that, Diana. I'm sure it's in whatever little notes you've made that you haven't shown me."

He cupped her cheek and ran the pad of his thumb over her lower lip as she challenged, "He gets off on it. Do you?"

"I get off on you," he answered, and brought his lips down to hers, offering not a moment for her to refuse.

He moved his mouth against hers, hard and hot, stealing her breath away until she had no choice but to open to the invasion. One arm roughly encircled her waist, hauling her tight against him while with the other hand, he cupped the back of her head, making her a prisoner.

She murmured a protest, and he tempered his response, his lips and mouth becoming tender and inviting, urging her to answer him. She bit and sucked at his lower lip, then reached up with her hands and held on to his shoulders as everything around them fell away.

Finally, she shifted slightly, breathing heavily, but he didn't stop, moving his head down to the side of her neck.

Her skin was damp with arousal and Ryder couldn't resist the invitation. He buried his head against the juncture of her neck and shoulder, against the pounding pulse point that proved her need. His own pulse was jumpy, starting to grow into a steady rush that signaled his change. He battled against it, sucking the saltiness of her skin, drawing on her until she was moaning and clinging to him.

He needed more.

He drew his one hand down to her buttocks and cupped her, bringing her tight against his erection.

She didn't resist. Her body was pliant, and a soft moan escaped her as he continued with the pull of his mouth against her skin. He was near his undoing, but he held on and continued.

When she came to her senses, there'd be hell to pay.

"Holy... Reyes is gonna feed this guy his privates," David heard in his earpiece. More chatter followed, including a groan or two and assorted expletives from those close enough to see the show.

He cursed beneath his breath, angered by the liberties Ryder was taking with Diana but unable to do anything. He ripped his gaze away from the scene on the floor to discover that heads were turning to watch the spectacle. Some stole only a glimpse before shifting away. Others lingered for a little longer, then moved to their partners as if wondering, "Why not me?"

One or two showed disgust. Maybe that was what the killer was feeling, he thought, and singled out one young man at the bar who seemed a little too interested, despite the presence of a partner nearby who was making herself quite available. In a flash, disgust became lust as the young man turned his attentions to his companion.

The man was young, mid-twenties at the most. The woman seemed to have about a decade on him, if not more. She had a used look about her and her hand was busy on her partner. David had no doubt about what the woman was doing. And yet despite that, the young man's head turned to watch Diana and Ryder once or twice more before he gave his full attention to the woman with him.

David continued his surveillance and then, as the couple rose and walked toward the exit, he instructed that they be followed. There was something about the young man that struck him wrong, but he couldn't say what. Maybe it was the look of abhorrence and fascination he gave Diana and Ryder over his shoulder.

The young man nodded to himself before walking out. Almost as if he had been confirming something.

David reaffirmed his instructions for additional surveillance and headed toward the dance floor.

Chapter 11

Diana met Ryder's gaze. He had gone a little too far with his assistance. And she had responded, wanting him like she'd never wanted anything before. She didn't like that he could make her lose control. She knew where that could take her. He had almost made her forget that she was here to do a job. Almost, she reminded herself, since she had somehow managed to give some attention to the crowd. Not that it had done any good.

The killer hadn't responded to Ryder's little act.... If it even *was* an act. She wanted his hide. "We need to go. Outside."

He brushed his fingers across her cheek, and she wondered if he felt the heat bathing her body. He brought his lips to the edge of her brow and placed a kiss against her temple. "We need to make it look like—"

"I know," she said, her voice husky with both want and anger. She cleared her throat and tried to hide the obvious signs of her arousal. An arousal that came from some dark place deep inside.

She grabbed his hand and led him to the door by the back entrance, past the bouncer and out to the alley. It was empty.

She whirled on him as soon as they were outside, jabbing her index finger into his chest with each word she uttered. "If you ever, and I mean for any reason whatsoever, lay a hand on me again, you will lose it."

Ryder admired her spunk but doubted she would follow through on her threat. He grabbed the finger that had been busy poking a hole in his chest, and before he knew what had happened, she had twisted his arm and pinned him against the wall. Her hold was firm, but he knew she could have exerted more force. Clearly, she didn't want to hurt him.

She had to lean close to his body and press up on tiptoe to issue her warning. "Two strikes, Ryder. Don't push it."

"Seems to me your anger's coming from a different place," he challenged, attuned to her in a way that was hard to describe or understand.

He must have hit a nerve, for she relaxed her hold on his arm. "Don't go there and I might let you live," she replied, and shoved away from him.

Ryder turned and grabbed his shoulder, rotating it, although there was no pain. As he met her gaze, she seemed almost apologetic.

"I'm sorry. I didn't mean to hurt you."

He took a step toward her and asked, "You didn't, but... May I?"

She was clearly confused and shrugged her shoulders. He raised his hand and with one finger touched the purpling mark on her neck. "I wanted... Heck, I'd be a liar if I didn't say I used the opportunity to suit me. I wanted you," he said in low tones. "But I didn't mean to mark you. I just lost control."

His words wrapped around her, creating an alluring spell Diana wanted to avoid with every fiber of her being. "I guess that makes two of us." And before he could reply, she raced back into the club.

Ryder leaned against the wall and watched Diana flee as her partner entered the alley.

David asked, "Was it worth it?"

"Worth what?" Ryder took a step toward the entrance of the club.

"This," David said, and with all his force, punched Ryder in the jaw and sent him flying back against the rough bricks. Ryder's face collided with the wall and he fell onto the cobblestones of the alley.

Ryder reached up to wipe his face and his fingers. His skin was abraded along his cheekbone, and his fingers came away with blood. David, stood before him, his fists clenched. "I could have your badge in a second," Ryder said. "You and your partner's."

"I've already warned you to leave her alone, Ryder. She's been through too much already, and the last thing she needs is the likes of you to drag her back down—"

"To that dark place? Do you even have an idea what it's like to be like me, like her? To be able to do what you want even though it's not what's right?" Ryder taunted as he walked up to the other man.

"She's not like that," David defended.

Ryder placed his hands on his hips and laughed. "You're just afraid to face up to it. You can't handle her and it scares you. Because one day, she might get you killed."

"And you think you're different?" David challenged. "You think you can handle her? Handle death?"

Ryder backed away and stuffed his hands in his pockets.

"I've been dead for a long time, David." He turned and walked into the dark of the alley.

Ryder waited beside his security guard as the man handed over all the tapes from the machines. Diana stood by quietly while David labeled each one and wrote out a receipt for them.

"Satisfied?" Ryder asked.

Diana's brow arched upward at his choice of words. She and her partner were probably far from satisfied with his behavior.

"We're going to log these in as evidence and start reviewing them," Diana answered coldly.

"Since we lost that suspect in the crowd, what do we do in the meantime?"

"We wait. No news is good news. If there's no body by the morning, we're back. Doing what we did tonight—"

"Everything?" he challenged.

She stepped toward him and softly said, "You've had your first bite and there's no more pardons."

Like every stray dog, he thought, only no dog's first bite could ever begin to compare to the way she tasted and felt. He had been one very lucky dog indeed, Ryder thought, but didn't say. Discretion was better for the moment. "I'll be a good little doggie tomorrow and heel."

She nodded, then glanced at her partner, who eased away and allowed her to leave the room.

Ryder had been expecting David to make some comment, but her partner only glared at Ryder and said, "Be at our offices at three to go over the tapes. See if there's anyone you recognize."

Ryder grunted his assent and let the other man leave. That was when he heard the sharp exhale of his security guard, an older black man who had once been a cop himself.

"That was some show you and the lady put on tonight," he said, and leaned back in his chair, staring up at Ryder.

"It was just a show, Nate." Ryder slapped the other man on the shoulder. "Thanks for all your help tonight," he said, and then headed to his office, needing solitude. Needing to be alone to settle the errant thoughts running through his brain. Tonight's dance-floor show with Diana… Ryder blew out a disgusted breath as he entered his office and walked over to the bar. As he splashed a few fingers of whiskey into a glass, he *wished* it had all been a show.

A show he could handle. The burning ache inside of him that the liquor did nothing to appease was something new and troubling. It was the ache of his human half that had been locked away for too long. And it was better to keep it locked away, he thought as he walked to the windows of his office while sipping the fine whiskey. He stared down at the now-empty club, but it was too easy to recall the sight of her standing before him. The feel of her pressed tightly against him, her hips welcoming his erection while her pulse beat heavily beneath his lips.

At the memory of her, he hardened again and his fangs erupted in his mouth. The animal in him wanted her, too. It had taken all of his strength not to pierce the fine column of her throat and taste her life's blood. Drink of her until he was sated and then drive into the warmth of her body.

He groaned and tossed back the rest of the whiskey. It burned as it traveled down his throat. But the fire in his gut was nothing compared to that raging through his body. He had to do something to curb the needs. Heading out of his office, he called out to Nate to lock up and walked the short distance to his van, parked behind a neighboring restaurant that specialized in nouvelle Latino cuisine.

He jumped into the van, intent on getting home where he could do something to tire out the beasts raging inside him, both animal and human. With the late hour, traffic was light and he arrived at his apartment building within twenty minutes. Parking the car in the lot next to his high-rise, he rushed out of the subterranean parking facility through a back passage that opened to the service doors of his place. There was no one there at this hour, and he slipped in unseen.

Melissa was home. As he unlocked the door, in his heightened state, he could smell her perfume and hear the faint beat of her heart as he passed by her door on the first floor of the duplex. But he couldn't forget the aroma of the only woman he wanted. Of her feel next to him and the way her pulse had beat, long and heavy as she answered the call of his desire.

Ryder cursed and jogged up the staircase that took him to his space in the duplex apartment. He was stripping off his clothes as he strode through the door of his bedroom. Changing into sweats, he walked across the hall to the workout room where he had spent the wee hours of many a night when his nocturnal self assumed control and kept him awake. The physical exertion of a good workout helped him assert his human side by tiring out the vampire.

The problem was, tonight, his human side wasn't so far removed from the animal. He approached the heavy bag at one end of the room, slipped on some lightweight boxing gloves and began pounding, each blow reverberating through his hands and arms and up into his shoulders. Each blow reminding him of something vital. Diana was human. An uppercut knocked the bag upward. She was trouble. A jab made his wrist ache. Too beautiful. Stubborn. Determined. Punch after punch. And damn it, just too irresistible. A flurry of blows resounded in the emptiness of the room.

He continued, landing punch after punch until his body was aching and he was winded. Sweat dripped from his face and arms onto the mat at his feet. The animal within seemed tamed for the moment, but Ryder wasn't going to take any chances.

His arms trembled as he began yet another round of blows until, finally, he gave the heavy bag one last punch. It swung away wildly, forcing him to grab hold of it on its return. The smell of the bag's leather reached him as he grasped it—it reminded him of Diana and her damn holster. How her shirt had pulled taut against her breasts the other day as she had secured her weapon behind her back. How she'd felt tonight, pressed against him.

Ryder leaned his head against the bag and cursed as he hardened once more. Ripping off the gloves and tossing them down, he hurried to his bathroom and prepared a shower. Hot water spewed out of the various jets in the large stall and he quickly disrobed, stepped in and let the pulsating streams of water work at his body, loosening muscles and relieving tension.

He soaped up, running his hands along the muscles he had just exercised, imagining as he did so that it was her hands moving against him. Groaning, he leaned one hand on the marble of the shower stall. Closing his eyes, he imagined how she would feel, her skin slick beneath his hand. And warm, no, make it hot. Her body next to him tonight had sizzled and burned beneath his hand.

It was dangerous to do this, he told himself, but he couldn't stop thinking of how it would feel to make love to Diana. To have her surrounding him. Her warmth all around him like the heat of the water sluicing down his chest and between his legs.

He groaned, envisioning her wrapping her legs around his hips, pulling him in deeper. The soft catch of her breath and arch of her back as she neared climax. His name on her lips as she came.

Ryder sucked in a breath, wanting her as he had no one before. Wishing that it wasn't just a fantasy. That she was real and here beside him.

But he knew it wasn't possible. He was dead, he reminded himself yet again. He could never be with Diana. She was human, and he was a demon. A freak created by fate who had no place in his life for love or for want. For a human woman who would leave him.

Whatever he was feeling right now was an aberration. One he had to bring under control before someone got hurt.

The last thing Diana needed was the love of a vampire. Question was, now that he'd tasted the sweetness of her desire, did he have the strength to walk away?

Chapter 12

As Diana slipped her key into the lock of the apartment, her brother opened the door to leave for work.

"Look what the cat dragged in." He stepped aside to let her enter.

Diana dropped onto the sofa in their living room, too weary to take another step. She and David had logged all the tapes and watched them as they waited for reports from the cops staked out along the docks and piers. At seven o'clock, when there had been no word, they decided to head home for some quick shut-eye before returning to the office at midday.

Her brother sat down on the edge of the coffee table. "You look spent. Are you going to at least try to get some rest?"

Diana leaned her head back on the couch and sighed. "I'd like to sleep until tomorrow, but I need to be back at the office by lunch hour."

Sebastian glanced at his watch. "That gives you time for a long nap."

She nodded and moved her neck from side to side to ease the stiffness. That was when her brother reached out and stopped the motion of her head. She looked at him out of the corner of her eye until he pointed at her neck.

"Thought you were working last night?" His voice was almost paternal even though she was the older one.

"It's not what you think," she answered, and craned her body away from him.

"It's not?" His tone bordered on challenging. "A hickey like that usually means... Well, let's put it this way—it doesn't usually mean work."

She flinched and tried to find some explanation that would appease him. "I was undercover with someone. We got..." She stumbled over the words, still confused by her reaction to Ryder. "He got a little carried away."

"I hope you decked him." When she flushed guiltily, he smiled, knowing her all too well, and grabbed a comforter off the back of the couch. She slipped her shoes off and lay down, then he tucked the comforter around her. "Call you at eleven?" he asked.

She nodded and settled into the oversized cushions for her nap. "*Gracias,* Sebastian."

He smiled. "Take it easy, *hermanita.*" He stepped out of the apartment and locked the door behind him.

She snuggled beneath the heavy comforter, closing her eyes and trying to shut out memories of last night. Quickly, exhaustion dragged her to sleep, and to dreams that were far from calming.

His body was hard against hers as she moved to the low, insistent beat of the music. She shifted her hips slowly, dragging them across his arousal. In response, he brought his hand down to the bare skin at the small of her back, urging her to stop.

"You don't like?" She glanced up at him and met his

heavy-lidded gaze. His eyes were so dark with desire it was impossible to see his pupils.

"I like too much," he admitted in a low, sensual growl.

She laughed. A coquette's laugh, sexy and enticing, and she wondered where it had come from. She wasn't the type to tease and yet here she was, brazenly caressing him with her hips. She smiled, inviting him into another kind of dance.

He groaned, cupped her buttocks with one hand and lifted her, driving her back until the rough texture of the wall bit into her skin. She realized then that they were in his club. The lights played a game of hide-and-seek with those standing in the crowd, but here against the wall, they were hidden.

Here, it was dark enough to play, she realized as he insinuated his knee between her thighs and placed pressure on that aching spot between her legs. A little gasp left her mouth and she dragged her gaze up to his.

"Do you like?" he teased, and slipped his hand beneath the thin silk of her top. He grasped her nipple between his fingers, starting a lazy tug and pull that nearly had her coming apart in his arms.

"*Sí,*" she answered, her breath a little unsteady. "I like it very much."

"Good," he uttered sharply before bending his head and taking her lips with his. He bit and sucked as he continued to pleasure her with his hand and the insistent press of his thigh. The hard ridge of his arousal pushed into the softness of her belly and she wanted it inside her.

She was nearly panting, needing more, and he gave it to her, slipping his hand beneath her skirt and panties. He shoved the material aside roughly, parted her with his fingers and found the spot aching for his touch. He stroked her, riding his thumb across the swollen nub and slipping first one finger and then another into her.

"Ryder." She threw her head back as waves of pleasure ebbed over her body.

He brought his mouth to her neck, suckling until there was a sudden sharp pain and a rush of heat.

She pulled away and the demon of her dreams was there, wearing Ryder's face. Wearing the first taste of her blood on his lips.

But the longing in his gaze was her undoing. She knew what it was to want something that badly. To want love so intensely, that the not having made life impossible to bear.

She wanted Ryder. In that way. So she bared her neck again and held his head to her. This time the bite was rough and violent. The demand of it shimmered along her nerve endings, growing stronger the longer he suckled. She answered his call, desire snaking through every cell of her body, burning the memory of him into her.

She came in his arms, calling his name in a hoarse cry. Her body and mind were no longer her own. They were part of his darkness.

And she welcomed it.

Diana bolted upright on the sofa, her body trembling and aroused. A fine sheen of sweat covered every inch of her.

She cursed, sat up and wrapped her arms around her knees while she tried to still the aching throb between her legs. Leave it to her to finally have an erotic dream—with a demon. A demon with Ryder's face.

Dios, but it had been hard enough to think about facing him after what had happened last night. How would she ever face him now? How could she look at him and not remember the demon lover from her dreams? Not remember how he'd made her feel? Allowing herself into his darkness had brought sweet release from the pain she carried within.

She buried her head against her knees and rocked back and forth. She could handle Ryder. She would not be dragged down into the warped existence that had claimed her after the death of her father. She had struggled too hard to escape that place. A place too much like the one she had so willingly volunteered to enter by taking on this case. She had thought herself strong enough to play the role, never expecting it to call to her so potently.

And Ryder. She'd never expected him to summon her with the pain she saw within his heart. So much like her own pain that she wanted to comfort him and maybe, by doing so, find peace herself.

Working with him on this case harder than she had ever thought. Ryder intrigued her. On a personal level, she couldn't deny she was attracted to him. What woman in her right mind wouldn't be? But it wasn't just physical attraction. That she could fight. It was the emotions he roused in her that were much harder to battle.

And of course, Ryder worried her on a professional level. He seemed to know too much about the killer's tastes and yet she was certain he had nothing to do with the murders. Her instincts, however, told her that he was guilty of *something*. What, she didn't know.

The conflicts were wearing her down. The dream had just proved it. She had no control around Ryder, had not had it from the get-go. A part of her relished that loss, but the other part feared that loss with every bone in her body.

But maybe losing control was the only way to gain some perspective. Some dominion over the call of the darkness that threatened. And some peace, she acknowledged.

But she wouldn't think about it anymore. Instead she plopped back down on the sofa to try for another hour of sleep before she had to get ready for work. And Ryder.

Diana sat across from David in the small coffee shop only blocks from The Lair. The cold remains of a half-eaten burger sat on her plate, and she idly ran a French fry

through the ketchup, creating trails of red. Like blood…
She pushed the plate away.

"Not hungry?" David reached over, snagged a fry from
her plate and popped it into his mouth. His own plate was
clean of the cheeseburger deluxe he had wolfed down.

She shrugged. "Where is he? Where has he taken her?"

"What?" David asked while munching on another fry.

"The killer," she answered with a trace of exasperation.
"It's too soon for him to break the pattern. He should have
taken her by now."

David grabbed another fry, popped it into his mouth and
chewed on it thoughtfully. "We don't know that he took
the other victims on Friday."

"It was definitely Friday." She counted the facts on each
finger. "Liz Benton's roommate never saw her on Saturday. And the Mendez woman had a date on Saturday and
also never showed. He took them on Friday."

"They were found on Sunday morning," David countered. "Maybe he waited until Saturday—"

Diana shook her head and motioned for David to stop.
"I know it's possible he could take someone tonight,
but…" She sensed that it was already too late. She looked
down at the smudged and scarred tabletop and ran a finger
along its surface before facing her partner once more.
"He's already killed another woman."

David paused, French fry halfway to his mouth. "Don't
be such a—"

"Pessimist? We didn't stop him, David. I know it in
here." She placed her hand against her chest, stressing the
point.

Leaning back into the cracked red leather of the booth,
David sighed. "We're doing what we can."

Diana gripped the edges of the table. "Maybe there's
more we can—"

David lurched forward, surprising her with the intensity
in his voice. "More than what you did last night? How

much more, Di? How much harder can you press before you—''

''Cross a line?'' she blurted out, and sank against the back of the booth. ''I think it's already too late for that, David.''

Her partner looked at her, his blue eyes cold and assessing but also filled with concern. ''I clocked him last night. Warned him about coming near you again.''

Diana laughed harshly. ''Poor Ryder. Between you and me, he must have been quite sore this morning.''

''He could have us canned, you know. He could—''

''He won't,'' she said as she signaled the waitress for the check.

David said nothing as the older woman handed Diana the tab and took Diana's credit card. When the waitress walked away, he asked, ''How do you know?''

Diana couldn't say how, and that frightened her. ''I just know,'' she replied, and looked away from her partner's too-observant gaze.

He was silent for a long time, until the waitress had come back with the receipt and the busboy had cleared the table. Finally, Diana met his gaze and it was then that he said softly, ''Ryder told me that you do what you want even though you know it's not what's right. That one day, you're going to drag me down with you because I can't control you.''

There was fear in his voice. She'd never heard it before, even when they'd been in situations that warranted it. Reaching out, she grasped his hand and gave it a squeeze. ''I would never do anything to hurt you, David. You're my partner and my best friend.''

David entwined his fingers with hers. ''Stuff happens, Di. We may not want it to, but—''

''I would never—''

''You already did, Di. Last night I lost my cool over

what he was doing to you. I risked my career. Ryder was right.''

Diana sighed and dragged her free hand through her hair in exasperation. ''Ryder doesn't know me. He—''

''Knows you better than you do yourself, I think. It's what scares you. It's what attracts you to him.'' David released her hand, stood and shrugged to readjust the shoulder holster beneath his jacket. Then he held out his hand to her. She took it and rose from the booth. As David started to move away, she pulled on his hand and wrapped her arms around him. *''Gracias.''*

David returned the embrace, his solid presence reassuring and comforting. He was her stability. Her foothold on what was quickly becoming a slippery slope down to a place she didn't want to visit again.

When he finally released her and playfully chucked her under the chin, she bent and checked her ankle holster. Satisfied the gun was secure, she rose and followed her partner out of the coffee shop, intent on beginning that night's surveillance. She hoped that her feeling was wrong and that tonight the killer would make a move.

And she hoped that Ryder wouldn't.

The weather was brisk outside, with a nip of chilliness that hinted at the coming of autumn. Ryder glanced across the water and down at the trees that dotted Roosevelt Island, looking for any changes that would confirm fall was almost here. The night would soon be longer and the sun weaker, allowing him greater freedom of movement that the summer denied him.

But the trees were still a dark green in the dimming light of dusk.

''Aren't you going to be late?'' Melissa asked as she came out onto the patio.

''I'm skipping the club tonight. There's too much going on.''

"And too many unwanted people?"

He nodded and laid his hands on top of the rough brick wall that edged the patio. "Yes. Too many agents and police. Better to avoid them."

Melissa gave a thoughtful "Hmm" and faced him, leaning one arm on the wall. "Avoid them or should you say, avoid her?"

Ryder almost absentmindedly raised his hand and ran it along his cheek. It had already healed, but the memory of why he had gotten the scrape lingered in his mind. "She's an unwelcome complication, Danvers."

Reaching up, Melissa brushed away his hand and ran her thumb along his cheekbone. "She had no reason to—"

Ryder pulled away from her touch and let out a harsh laugh. "Her partner did it. But even if he hadn't, believe me, she had every reason to. What I did…" He stopped and shook his head. "In the old days, my daddy would've whupped me good for taking advantage of a woman like that."

"This isn't the good ol' days, Ryder, and modern women don't let anyone do anything they don't want done."

He whirled on her angrily. "And what the killer does? Do the women want that?"

She laid her hand on his shoulder, trying to soothe him. "This isn't about the killer. It's about you and this agent."

"This agent… Come the end of this case, she'll be gone and things will be back to normal."

Melissa slipped her hand away from him and wrapped her arms around herself. "Nothing will ever be normal about the life we lead. Nothing."

There was a harshness to her tone that drew his attention. "There's no reason why your life can't be normal, Melissa."

"Isn't there?" she challenged.

"Being my servant—"

"I hate that word," she said with a shudder. "It makes me feel like I should be a bug-eating Renfield."

Ryder smiled. "It certainly is an outdated term. You don't really serve me, but you do help keep me safe."

"Yep, that's me. I keep your blood and your health," Melissa replied, and glanced at him out of the corner of her eye. "You're wise to stay away tonight, before you risk more than you already have."

Ryder smiled tightly. "You're probably right. So what are your plans?"

"On a rare free night? Dinner with some girlfriends and then a movie. You will be here when I get home later, right?"

Ryder had planned on staying home. Staying away from the club. But then of course, God was amused by men who made plans. "Maybe" was all he committed to and she smiled tightly, shook her head and walked inside.

He returned to admiring the city below, teeming with life. With humanity. And, for a moment, he thought he could hear the deep, rumbling laughter of the God who had burdened him with this existence and who had brought Diana into his hell.

Ryder cursed under his breath and banged his fist sharply against the brick. Pain radiated through his hand, but not enough to dissuade him.

He pushed off from the wall, rubbed at his cheek and wondered what kind of wound he'd suffer tonight.

Chapter 13

The Lair was as busy as the night before. Maybe even busier.

As Diana and David had walked up to the club, early in the night, the line was already quite long. Arm in arm, they strolled to the end of the queue, just another couple anxious to get in. As they waited for admission, they leaned close to each other, looking for all the world like lovers sharing a private talk.

There was movement in the line suddenly as the doors to the club finally opened and the bouncers started taking money and stamping hands. Diana and David shuffled along in the crowd, all the time watching for anything unusual. Once inside they headed straight to the bar. The bartender from the other night was on duty once more. He sneered at them as they approached. "You two still playing games?"

Diana nodded at him as David slipped an arm around her waist. "Want to join us?"

"You know he's not my type, sweetheart," David said

pointedly, and motioned with his hand to an attractive Asian woman who was walking their way.

Diana turned and shot a smile at the other agent as she sidled up to them at the bar. "Carly," she said, and embraced the woman, then led her onto the dance floor while David hung back.

The band had just started to play, something loud with a driving bass beat. Diana released Carly's hand, but edged close to her to dance, moving suggestively to the heavy, pounding rhythm of the music.

As she gyrated, Diana glanced around. David was scrutinizing them. Behind his shoulder, the bartender had lost interest and turned his attention to the sudden rush of patrons clamoring for drinks. She continued to dance, the other agent matching her movements, until, slowly, a crowd formed around them—men hoping to be chosen to join the twosome. One of the guys was a familiar face from last night and Diana wandered toward him, thinking that his continued interest was suspicious. Perhaps the killer would establish a rapport over several nights. Create a level of trust that would make his victim share a drink. A drug-laced drink that wouldn't kick in until she had voluntarily left with him.

Diana placed herself close to the man, her back to him. A few seconds later, he moved, his front brushing her back as they shifted to the beat of the music. Looking over her shoulder, she gave him what she hoped was an enticing smile. He grinned and eased his arm around her bare midriff.

His hand was damp. The skin of his palm soft. He clearly didn't work with his hands. Unlike Ryder, she thought, whose hands were hard and rough and... She stiffened against the suspect and forced away memories of Ryder's touch.

Hard to do since he could be up there somewhere, watching. Either in his office or on the catwalks. Or down in the crowd, heading toward her... But somehow she knew that if he was at the club, she would have sensed him.

And he wasn't there.

So she forced Ryder from her mind and gave her attention to the suspect with whom she was dancing.

Ryder paced back and forth in his office, cursing his need. Cursing her for intriguing him so.

She was down there in the crowd. He hadn't seen her yet, but he had smelled her as he had slipped into the club through a back door. Her scent had made him harden, instantly.

Somehow he tamed his urges and limited himself to standing by the windows of his office. Finding her took very little time. She and another woman were surrounded by a group of men whose tongues nearly hung out of their mouths, drooling like the dogs they were. But he wasn't much better, maybe worse. After all, he'd taken his first bite. And far from being satisfied, he wanted another.

Diana was dancing with one attractive man who had his arm against the expanse of skin exposed by her cropped T-shirt. The soft cotton of the top clung to her. Tonight she wore black leather pants that lovingly hugged every inch of her shapely hips and legs.

Lord, how he ached to run his hands across her skin and all that leather. Insane, he told himself as he pushed away from the window and started pacing again. Back and forth, back and forth like a caged animal. But he couldn't be contained for long.

He stalked back to the window and stood there like a man possessed, his need for her the only thing he could think of. What normal, red-blooded man wouldn't want her? Only, he wasn't a man, he reminded himself as he stood there, waiting. Watching her like an animal watched its prey. Imagining and aching, the way a man did for the woman he wanted.

Both sides of him in a war that neither could win.

He stalked down to the main level of the club and paused by the edge of the crowd to take a deep, steadying breath. A mistake. It just intensified the smell of her, awakening all of his senses. Bringing his body to painful life. He curbed those urges as he eased through the crowd and finally reached Diana.

She stopped moving when she saw him. The man with her also stilled, glancing at Ryder. He puffed up his chest as if to warn Ryder away.

Ryder laughed harshly and kept on coming. "May I?" he asked, although it was clear from his tone that there could be only one answer.

Something inside Diana wanted to refuse his continued pursuit, only… A part of her, the one she hated to acknowledge, wanted him to touch her again. Perhaps going with him might goad the killer somehow. Might make the psychopath want to punish her and make her the next victim.

Diana turned and laid a hand on the chest of her partner. Forcing a smile, she begged his indulgence. "We have something to finish. Could I see you later?"

The man glared at Ryder but smiled at her and stepped away, brushing past Ryder with a little shove of his shoulder. In her earpiece, Diana heard David instruct another agent to follow. Out of the corner of her eye, she caught Carly's inquiring gaze. Diana signaled her colleague, and as the woman moved into the crowd to find another partner, Diana turned her attention to Ryder. "Haven't you had enough?"

He reached out and bracketed her waist with his hands. The band began to play a slow song and Diana wondered if he'd somehow arranged it. His wicked grin confirmed it. "You don't leave anything to chance, do you?"

"Shut up and dance," he replied, and eased her close, giving her no choice but to lay her hands along his shoulders as they swayed to the music. "If you try anything again—"

"Shh," he whispered into the ear without the wire, and gently stroked her waist with his hands. "I just want to hold you. Nothing else," he said, his voice low and husky.

Holding her was already too much, Diana thought, and swallowed hard. It was wrong to have it feel so good. There wasn't a part of her that wasn't touching him, warming from the contact. She tightened her hands on his shoulders, and he shifted his hands, moving one to the small of her back and the other between them. Then he eased her away slightly.

Diana gave him a puzzled look until he rested his palm on her collarbone and, with his thumb, soothed the purpling mark near her neck that was still sensitive. Especially to his touch.

She sucked in a breath, but not from pain. The sensation of his thumb sent a blast of desire racing through her. "Ryder—"

"Can I make it better?" He didn't wait for her answer. He bent his head and laid his lips against the bruise, kissed her gently.

How can this be happening? she thought as her entire body flared to life. She had to hold on to his shoulders to keep from puddling at his feet. When he opened his mouth and swiped his tongue across the love bite, she moaned and forced herself away from him. "Ryder, this is insane."

He drew in a ragged breath, nodded and in a pained whisper said, "I should go."

"You should." But somehow her hands weren't listening, nor were his. He pulled her close and they once again swayed to the music. Still, Diana managed to scan the crowd. "Do you see anyone? Anything?"

Ryder glanced around, his eyes able to explore even the darkest sections of the club. It was crowded, and as always, along the edges, people were satisfying their physical needs. He sniffed and could smell their lust, which only made his own situation worse.

"There's nothing," he said, and moved away from her slightly.

Diana examined those around them, then swung her gaze back to the bar. Her gaze collided with that of one young man, but no sooner had the connection been made than he turned away to talk to the bartender. She observed him carefully, tracking him even as her dance with Ryder forced her to swivel her head to keep the young man in sight. The bartender knew him, judging from the way the two were speaking. And if he was a regular, maybe Ryder recognized him, as well.

"Check out the bar. The sandy-haired twentysomething talking to the bartender." She took the lead, forcing Ryder to turn so that he was facing that section of the club. Unfortunately, by the time they turned the young man was gone.

"What did you see?" he asked, wondering what had caught her attention.

Diana shrugged. "Something felt a little off. I don't know why."

Ryder didn't keep her as she pulled away from him and headed toward the bar.

The Lair had emptied out. Ryder was up in his office. David and the remainder of the agents and police were finishing their assigned tasks and would shortly be headed to the next part of the investigation: waiting.

Diana despised the waiting. And she hated having no control over what the killer was doing at that very moment. Even worse, she resented having no control over what she was feeling for the man who waited for her in his office.

She shut off her earpiece and slipped it into her pocket. Heading down the hall, she paused to check on David as he collected the tapes from the night. "Ready in five?" she asked.

David looked up from his paperwork and shot her a dubious look. "Sure, but will you be?"

Diana expelled a harsh breath and dragged a hand through her hair. "If I'm not down in five, come be the cavalry."

Her partner nodded. "I'll give you ten."

She walked briskly down the hall and up the stairs to Ryder's office. The door was open, but the room was dark. She called out his name as she walked in and hit the wall switch. Nothing happened. She stepped farther into the room.

"Like the dark, do you?" she challenged as she stepped to a nearby table lamp and snapped it on.

Dim light illuminated the room, barely reaching Ryder behind his desk.

Ryder picked up the tumbler before him and took a sip. "I live in the dark, Diana, even when it's light out. You should recognize that. After all—"

"I'm not like that. Like you," she defended, both excited and afraid of the energy pouring off him.

"Aren't you?" he challenged, and shot up out of the chair. As he approached, she moved away.

He stopped and raised one dark eyebrow. "Afraid?"

Damn him, she thought, unable to refuse the inherent dare in his comment. She stepped toward him but stopped well out of his reach. "What do you want from me?"

He shrugged and relaxed his stance. "Maybe your question should be, 'What do I want from him?'" He moved a step closer, as if waiting for her to bolt. She held her ground as he said, "Maybe we both want the same thing."

"We don't—"

"Don't you?" He closed the distance between them and cradled her cheek.

"Ryder, don't—"

"Don't touch you? Don't want you?" he said, his voice low and full of need.

At this range, with his body inches from hers, she could smell him. He wore a light citrusy scent, and as he exhaled, there was the sharp bite of liquor on his breath. Power hummed around him. The energy she had sensed earlier wrapped around her, sucking her in.

Diana eased forward until barely an inch separated their bodies. Her nipples tightened, and deep between her legs, something clenched and throbbed. She drew a shaky breath and met his gaze, realizing he was as affected as she was.

The pupils of his eyes were wide, nearly black. The hand that stroked her cheek trembled, and then he shifted that hand to the back of her neck. He applied gentle pressure to close the slight distance between them.

"Diana?"

She jumped away from Ryder, startled, and turned to meet David's concerned gaze.

Her partner advanced on them, and she stepped into his path, for she had no doubt about what David intended.

"Ah, the errant knight come to save the fair damsel," Ryder taunted.

Diana turned and shot him a withering glance as David pushed against the hand she had on his chest. She tried to reassure her partner. "Stop, David. I'm okay." Although she was anything but.

David moved back a step. "We need to go." He glared over her shoulder at Ryder.

Diana nodded, patted David's chest in a friendly gesture and faced Ryder. "We'll call if we need you. Can you—"

"I can make it in the afternoon. I have a meeting—"

"On a Sunday morning?" David challenged, unwilling to cut the other man any measure of slack.

"With a young lady I can't disappoint," Ryder finished as if David hadn't interrupted.

She tried to contain the surge of jealousy that ripped

through her. After all, just because the two of them were…
What? Involved? she asked herself, and shook her head.
Looking up at Ryder, she said, "We'll let you know."

Turning, she glanced at David. He gave her a reluctant
nod and followed her out. It wasn't until they were in their
car, away from Ryder and the other agents and police, that
he finally spoke. "You need to stop what's going on with
Ryder."

He sat with his hands tight around the steering wheel.
He was as angry as she had ever seen him, and not just
about Ryder. She looked down at her feet and gripped her
thighs to still the shakiness of her hands. Her body was still
affected by her encounter, as if Ryder were a drug ener-
gizing her system. A drug that was slowly ebbing away,
leaving her shaking from its withdrawal. Making her want
to go back for more to ease her need.

Expelling a harsh breath, she finally answered him. "I
don't know if I can."

"He's nothing but trouble." He examined her in the
dark, then started the engine and pulled out.

Diana shrugged and glanced out the window as they
moved along the streets of downtown Manhattan. Pedestri-
ans strolled here and there along the main avenues and
every now and then a yellow cab blew past. There were
only a few other cars and trucks. Maybe even that of the
killer, she thought, and recalled their earlier discussion in
the diner. "Maybe he did change his pattern. Maybe he
hesitated because he knew we were watching."

David shook his head and looked at her as they came to
a stop at a red light. "Okay, this is the hopeful you talking.
The real you—"

"Thinks he grabbed her already. Right under our noses,"
she answered, meeting his gaze.

"And if he gets away with it again—"

"He'll do something bolder." She tapped one fist against
her thigh in frustration. "He'll grab someone else before

the week is up, and right now, another woman is dead because of us.''

"We're doing what we can."

His words were little consolation. "Maybe we need to
do more."

He took his eyes off the road for a moment and asked,
"Like what?"

She shrugged, "Like—"

Their cell phones went off simultaneously in a noisy
blast of sound.

Diana didn't need to answer to know the reason why.

Chapter 14

Armed with photos of the latest victim courtesy of the medical examiner, Diana, David and various other agents viewed the tapes from the last two nights at the club and began additional investigations based on amendments Diana made to her original profile of the killer.

The victim this time had been older and had been sexually assaulted. That provided Diana with a different perspective. The age of the woman and the sexual attack might have meant the woman represented an authority figure instead of a lover who had spurned the killer. Maybe an authority figure who had suffered a similar fate? And he'd tried to throw them off by removing the bat stamp from the woman's hand.

While other agents conducted investigations into decades-old crimes of passion in the Northeast, Diana and David reviewed the tapes, which yielded shots of the woman leaving the club with a sandy-haired man, obviously the killer. And he had clearly known they were watching. He had kept close to the woman and turned his face away from the camera. Add the fact that it had been dark on the street, and it was nearly impossible to get anything worthwhile from the video. Despite that, the man seemed familiar to Diana, and she suspected he was the man who had drawn her attention at the bar.

Only, the man had been there alone, which meant he took the woman on Friday as she had indicated in her earlier profile. Then he'd come back to the club last night for what? To gloat that he had pulled one over on them? Or possibly to find another victim already?

"He's broken the pattern in a lot of different ways. And I think I saw this man at the club last night. While I was dancing with Ryder."

David nodded and glanced at the notes he had taken. "Do you think Ryder saw him?"

"No, but maybe he's a regular."

Pulling her cell phone off her belt, she called Ryder and asked him to come down and look at the surveillance tapes.

Then David and she completed their review of the remaining tapes. The first tape had the only clear images, though those were of little help. And the other investigations based on Diana's new profile had yielded no leads.

By the time Ryder arrived, Diana was frustrated, on edge and waiting impatiently by the elevator. When he strode out, she tried to quell the sudden pleasure that his presence brought.

"You've been here all night?" Ryder asked. She still wore the leather pants and top from the night before. The only concession to professionalism she had made had been to toss a blazer over the revealing outfit, probably so that she wouldn't get chilled while in the air-conditioned environs of the office.

Diana nodded. "Part of the territory, you know." She didn't wait for him to answer but took off down the hallway, leaving him to follow. As he did so, he noticed the slight bulge at the small of her back and realized the blazer helped to hide her gun, as well.

She led him to a room where her partner and Detective Daly, whom Ryder had met during his initial interrogation, already sat before a television monitor. They rose and greeted him as he entered, but there was little warmth or eagerness to give him additional information on the killer. At least not right away.

He sat at the table and Diana eased into the only available seat, next to him. Her tension was palpable. He tried to ignore it by concentrating on the materials being passed to him—a series of photos of the most recent victim taken at the morgue.

"Look familiar?" Peter Daly asked, his hands folded and resting on the table.

Ryder flipped from one photo to another, but there was nothing even remotely familiar about the face of the woman in the shots. "No, sorry." He passed the pictures back across the table.

David scooped them up, shoved them into a folder and placed it to the side. "Ready to view the only tape that seems worthwhile?" he asked.

Ryder nodded and slouched in the chair to get comfortable. Diana shut off the lights in the room, and when she returned to sit beside him, he could smell her, feel the heat of her body. It was torture and distracting as hell. He forced himself to stare at the television monitor and pay attention, but it was a difficult task. The lub-dub of her heart called to him. She finally shifted away from him and he smiled in the dark, pleased that she wasn't unaffected by his presence. With that tiny tidbit of hope, he leaned forward and watched.

They were nearly at the end of the tape when he noticed the couple exiting the bar. The man with the victim was hidden behind her body and by the shadows she cast as she walked, but there was something familiar about him. "Rewind this part and slow it down,'' he instructed and shifted his chair closer to the monitor.

The couple walked out and came down the steps of The Lair. The man's arm rose, and from the edge of the shot, the fingertips of another hand were visible as they came up to acknowledge the greeting. ''Pause it.'' Ryder pointed to the screen. ''It's probably one of the bouncers sitting by the door. He knows the man.''

''Can you get us the names and addresses of whoever was working the door that night?'' Diana asked.

''Sure. Start it again.'' He watched purposefully, hoping for a glimpse of the face belonging to the killer, and for one millisecond he thought he saw something. He called for them to stop and ease back a frame or two and sure enough, there was one small section where there was a view of the man's profile, although still in shadow.

They all leaned forward at that point and examined the screen. ''Do you think you know him?'' Daly asked.

Ryder took a deep breath and shrugged. ''There's something about him. Is there any way to get this lightened or clarified?'' He turned as he asked Diana, not realizing as he did so that she was close. Very close. Their bodies nearly brushed against each other's and they were now face-to-face. With his night sight, her face was clear and engaging.

She didn't shift away. She just took a shaky breath and said, ''We can get it enhanced, but it will take some time.''

''How long do you think we have until he strikes again?''

Her gaze never leaving his, Diana swallowed hard and replied, ''This isn't a 'we,' Ryder.''

He let out a harsh laugh and eased back, stung by her comment. ''The message is loud and clear.''

''Glad you finally got it,'' David said.

Ryder shot him a hard look and rose. "I guess I'm done here, then."

He left and no one made a move to stop him.

"Congrats on royally pissing him off," Peter Daly said as he flipped on the lights.

"Ryder is a complication we don't need," Diana explained. She walked over to the television monitor. "This," she said, pointing to the frame where part of the killer's face was still visible, "is all we need to worry about."

"Trying to convince me or yourself? And how come we didn't see this or the action of the bodyguard? We looked at this over and over and didn't catch either thing."

Diana stared hard at the frozen video shot. She hadn't seen it, just as days earlier she hadn't been able to make her way in the dark of the club while Ryder walked around as if every light was on. She had ascribed it to habit and knowledge of his environment, but maybe Ryder just had excellent eyesight. Shrugging, she looked at David. "We need to get this enhanced. Can you see how long it will take? We should get photos of the victim and suspect together to show around."

David stopped the VCR, hit the eject button and grabbed the tape. "I'm on my way. I'll call you as soon as I have an ETA."

With that, he left Peter and Diana to stare at each other uneasily. "It may take some time," Diana said.

Peter jangled the change in his pockets. "Time is something we don't have a lot of." Diana's new profile pointed to the killer moving his timetable and taking another victim within a few days.

"We'll need to make the killer think that his ruse worked and we're checking out other clubs." Diana placed her arms across her chest and paced a little. "We'll get to the bouncers at The Lair as soon as we get the photos. The Lair's closed on Monday so we have a little time. But on Tuesday, we'll have to make people think the investigation has moved to another club while I hit the dance floor again.''

''What about Latimer?'' Peter asked, blocking her way as she went to walk past him.

Diana looked up and met his gaze. ''I can deal with Ryder.''

''Can you?''

''If we're lucky, we'll have the photos later tonight. I'll call and get him to take a look. Maybe he can give us a name.''

Daly gave her a dubious glance, and Diana knew it was because she was avoiding the real issue.

''What do you plan on doing now?''

Peter glanced at his watch, then faced her again. ''Hitting the bricks to check with the uniforms. I'll give you an update in an hour?''

''Sounds good.''

Diana watched Peter's departure, then plopped into the chair Ryder had occupied. It had to be her imagination that she could feel the warmth of his body on the hard plastic of the seat. And smell him—a light and clean scent. Totally at odds with his dark persona.

She sighed and the aroma teased her nostrils again. It drove her to leave the room and get to the assorted tasks she had to complete before the enhancements of the photos were ready.

Ryder was pounding away at the punching bag again, trying to work out the anger from his earlier run-in with Diana. He might have to see her later and he wanted it to go peacefully between them. Somehow he had to contain the emotions raging through him. He was, after all, an animal adopting the veneer of human civility. An animal all too eager to take her on, and in more ways than she could possibly imagine.

He drove away those thoughts and was just finishing up

his workout when Danvers came into the room. She stopped in surprise. "I thought you would be long gone. I'm headed to a lecture over at Hunter tonight and then to the hospital."

Ryder stopped and steadied the heavy bag as it swung toward him. "I'm waiting for a call from the agents on the case." Even to his own ears, the explanation sounded strained.

Danvers walked over and held the bag for him. *"She's* coming, is that it?"

"Do you have a problem with this, Danvers?"

"Melissa."

He muttered a confused "Huh?"

"Melissa. My name is Melissa. You used to call me that all the time when I was a kid, but ever since…" She didn't need to say more. From the day her mother and father had died a few years ago, she had stopped being Melissa and become the latest Danvers. He hadn't realized that she might resent that change in their relationship.

He jabbed her arm playfully with his gloved hand to try to lighten her mood. "Come on, Melissa."

She yanked away from him. "No. Things haven't been the same since…" She stepped away from him and walked out the door onto the patio. Ryder followed and stood by her until she sighed and quietly said, "I've known you all my life, Ryder. You were always there to listen to me. Hear what I had to say. But lately…"

"I'm your friend, Melissa."

Melissa glanced at him out of the corner of her eye. "You *were* my friend, Ryder. Now I'm not quite sure what we're supposed to be. Or what my life is supposed to be or if I'm even supposed to have a life of my own."

Ryder regretted that in all the time since she had become his companion he had never noticed how uneasy she was with her new role. "I'm sorry we haven't talked about this before."

She shrugged. "What's there to talk about? One Danvers dies and another is chosen."

"It's not that simple—"

"No, it isn't. Because being the next one involves not being able to have a normal life," she shot back angrily.

"There's no reason why you can't—"

"Be involved with someone? The way you're involved?"

"You know my being involved with a human—"

"Could never happen?" she parried, and faced him, her gaze penetrating and challenging. "Then why is *she* coming over?"

"She has questions to ask."

"Seems to me you're headed for trouble having her here, especially with the way you feel."

"And maybe it's time I took the chance. The same way that maybe you should think about what kind of life you want. Whether or not you want to continue to be my keeper," he said, hating that their relationship had taken this sudden turn. One which he really didn't know how to deal with. No other Danvers had ever had doubts about their role, but then again, no other Danvers had been so young, or single, or female.

"Maybe I *should* think about it. But what about Diana Reyes? If I'm any judge of women, she's attracted to you and thinking about taking it further. Will you tell her your deep, dark secret?" Melissa asked softly, obviously aware that her questions might draw blood.

Ryder took a deep breath and raked his fingers through his hair in exasperation. "I...care about Diana. In all the time I've been a vampire, I've never felt this way before. There's something driving me. Telling me I have to protect her. Be with her. It's as if it was somehow fated to be this way," he explained, wanting to restore his friendship with Melissa with that confession. "Haven't you ever felt that way?"

She looked up at him then, and her pain sliced into him. "Never, Ryder. In all my life, I have never felt that way."

Ryder drew Melissa into his arms and held her. She returned the embrace, much as she had when she was a small child and needed comfort when it was lacking from her parents.

After a minute or so, she pulled out of his arms. "I can't say that I'm not worried about this, Ryder. But as your friend, and as someone who cares about you…be careful. This is dangerous ground."

He nodded and wrapped an arm around her shoulders, strolling with her to the French doors. "Thank you, Melissa."

When she reached the doors, she turned. "If it comes time to… Check the nightstand, Ryder. We wouldn't want any messy vampire paternity suits," she teased.

He smiled, appreciating her strength and maturity. He dropped a brotherly kiss on her cheek as she entered the apartment and thought about her revelation. Maybe tonight she would meet someone interesting at her lecture, or after, at the hospital. Someone who could give her the love and happiness she deserved.

Chapter 15

Ryder's address was for a large apartment building on Sixty-sixth Street right off of Second Avenue. Upon entering the elevator, she realized Ryder was on the next-to-highest floor. Once she stepped out, it became clear he owned the whole space. She wondered how well the club did to allow for digs like these.

When he opened the door, it was apparent he had been working out. He wore sweats that rode low on his hips and a gray cotton T-shirt marked with sweat. Beads of perspiration dotted his face, and he wiped at them with the towel slung loosely around his neck. "Sorry if I'm a little messy. You caught me at a bad time."

Diana pointed to her own clothes, which were similar to his. "I was on my way to the gym, too, but this couldn't wait. Thanks for letting me come by."

"Let's get on with this then." Ryder stepped aside and motioned her into the apartment.

She was even more surprised by his wealth when she walked in. The staircase at one end of the large, spacious room meant that he had the two upper stories of the building. "Win the lottery?" she questioned, glancing around and taking note of the fine antiques and artwork she suspected weren't reproductions. The elegant Old World–style pieces managed to blend harmoniously with the very severe and modern architecture of the physical space.

Ryder appeared unruffled by her query as he answered, "Old family money. Besides, I have a roommate—Melissa Danvers, the doctor who treated you at the club the other day. She's an old family friend."

Diana experienced an unexpected surge of jealousy as she thought of Ryder sharing his apartment with another woman. She tamped it down but couldn't help wondering whether or not Ryder's roommate would mind Diana's presence. "Is she going to be around tonight?"

"She's…out and it's strictly platonic."

"Really. That's hard to believe," Diana began, a hard edge of annoyance in her voice as she walked past him and slapped the envelope with the photos against his chest. "So, here they are."

Ryder grabbed the envelope. If anyone had a right to be angry, it was he after her earlier dismissal of his involvement in the case. But despite that, he couldn't drag his gaze from the soft fleece of her sweats hugging her shapely hips, nor the cotton tank top molding itself to her breasts. What a shame tonight was going to be only about business, he thought. "Make yourself at home while I look at these," he said, and she settled herself on the couch in his living room.

He sat on the arm of a love seat while he pulled the photos out of the envelope and examined them. He had seen this man around, and often. But no name came to him. "I know him, but…I can't think of whether I've seen him at the club or elsewhere. He's really familiar. I know it'll come to me." He slipped the photos into the envelope and gave it back to her. "Did you get the bouncers to look at the photos yet?"

"David is trying to track them down now." She hesitated and juggled the envelope in her hands. "I guess I should go. If you remember anything else—"

"I'll call," he said, and rose, but she didn't move toward the door. Maybe she was as unsure of what to do as he was. "Going back to the office?"

"Yes. I'm going to try to get in that workout before David calls."

He told himself there wasn't an expectant look on her face. One that said, "Ask me to stay." He had to grab both ends of the towel to keep from touching her, to keep himself in check. It was a useless battle. "You could work out here, with me," he offered.

When she hesitated, he prompted, "Well?" trying to appear cool and calm, although he knew his uncertainty and eagerness for her company were clear.

"Yes." He unsuccessfully fought down a smile. He invited her to follow him and led her into an upper hall. In front of them, at the far end, was a set of French doors. Diana followed him onto the terrace but stopped in the center to take in the plethora of flowers, bushes and dwarf trees beautifying the space.

She recognized the oleanders in the large pots along one wall of the patio. Their branches were filled with large bunches of pink and white blossoms. At the bottom of each container, bright purple petunias cascaded downward toward the slate floor. In a larger trio of planters on the opposite wall, pines and cedars mingled harmoniously, and again, there were more blossoms, this time vivid orange and yellow marigolds. The entire patio and its flora had been carefully planned and positioned to give the illusion of a much larger space.

The views of Manhattan from the rooftop-garden paradise were just as tempting. She walked to the edge of the patio, leaned her hands on the railing and took in the panorama of the East Side of Manhattan, the Queensboro Bridge and the tip of Queens. "This is gorgeous," she told him as he joined her at the metal railing.

"Thanks. I enjoy working with my hands." Ryder sensed she was incredulous of his gardening claims, but she said nothing. "Would you like a glass of wine, or maybe something to eat before you work out?"

Facing him, she folded her arms across her chest. "Trying to delay my leaving?"

"Oh, I think I've already succeeded at that. After all, you did agree to stay and exercise."

"Maybe that was a mistake. Maybe I should go." She lifted her chin up defiantly, almost in challenge.

"Why is it that you seem to prefer to fuss and feud rather than enjoy my company?"

Diana chuckled and moved her head back and forth slowly, almost in disbelief. "Ryder, that Southern charm may work on some women—"

"But not on you. So why are you staying, then?" He cradled her cheek.

"I'm busy asking myself that same thing. Maybe I should just go and prove that I can deal with you."

"You think you can handle me? Sorry, darlin'—"

"I can handle you in every way imaginable, Ryder. What will it take to prove that to you?" she asked, and stepped away from his touch.

"Show me…if you can." He knew she couldn't resist the challenge, and he held his hand out in the direction of the French doors.

Once inside, Ryder took the lead, striding quickly to the spacious room that held various types of gym equipment, the punching bag and a large open area with a mat where he normally practiced his limited knowledge of martial arts with Melissa, who had just taken up tai chi.

Diana walked over to the universal gym and ran her hand

along the gleaming metal of the equipment. "I guess you don't get out much."

He shrugged, slipped off his sneakers and took a position in the center of the mat. "With my hours, I can't rely on the gym. It made sense to set this up so I could exercise whenever I wanted."

Diana strolled to the edge of the mat and took off her sneakers, leaving only bright white socks on her feet.

But she didn't remove the heavy gold chain around her neck. The one that draped into the valley between her ample breasts.

He took hold of the chain and met her questioning gaze. "Gold chains make excellent garrotes, I'm told."

"Really?" she challenged, seemingly aware of that fact. She brushed his hands away to undo the clasp, and as she eased the chain off, he noticed the crucifix and medallions. Reaching out, he grasped the religious medals in his hand. There was no burn. Not even the slightest hint of discomfort. It was the first time he'd gotten this close, although he'd been exposed to such religious items at the various funerals of his keepers. He'd been a God-fearing man as a human and hadn't changed his beliefs upon being turned, although he was bothered by the role God had chosen for him. He assumed his faith was why the crucifix didn't repel him. "Do you still believe?"

Sadness clouded her face as he continued to hold the chain and medals.

"I haven't in a while. Not since my dad. I wear them more out of habit than anything." She wasn't sure she could deal with talking about her father. Especially not with Ryder. That would mean taking their relationship to another level. A dangerous level. She rubbed at the scar on her ribs and eased the chain from Ryder's hands.

He laid his hand over hers as she rubbed at her side. She met his gaze and hated the understanding she saw there. It weakened her defenses.

"May I?" He didn't wait for her response before he eased up the edge of her shirt and exposed the ridge of scar along her lower ribs.

As he traced the shape of it with his index finger she sucked in a shaky breath. "Don't...please, don't."

It was a familiar plea and one that he clearly intended to ignore as he continued to trace the scar with his fingers. "Don't make you feel again? Your father died, but you didn't. You're alive and—"

She shoved him away. "What do you know about it, Ryder? What could you possibly know about the pain of losing someone like that?"

"Like how?" He came after her as she walked to the edge of the mat, grabbing her arm to stop her flight.

"Let go, Ryder." Diana glared at him, but he only seemed amused by her admonition. "I mean it."

He laughed harshly and dropped her arm. "You can't handle me, love, 'cause you can't even handle yourself."

"I'll show you just how easily I can, and after I kick your ass—"

"I'll leave you alone? Is that what you really want, dar-lin'?"

Diana quickly assumed a warrior's stance, legs braced slightly apart and bent to allow her to spring into action, her fists held up loosely but in a ready position. "When I win, Ryder, you will get the hell out of my life."

"If you win," he corrected her.

"You will leave me alone."

He assumed a fighting position and she started to circle, keeping an eye on him.

"We'll see" was all he said as he mirrored her movement, intent on avoiding her.

"Promise, Ryder, or we go no further and I ask that you get placed in a cell somewhere as a material witness." She dropped her fists to her hips and lifted her stubborn little chin.

The tone of her voice told him she was totally serious, but Ryder wasn't about to let her get away. "Since you are so eager to have your ass whupped…I promise that if you win, I will back off." It was a lie, and he sensed she knew it but wanted the confrontation anyway.

With that acknowledgement from him, she sprang into action. She quickly unleashed a series of jabs, but he blocked each one and then countered with a hook.

She evaded the punch, surprised him by slipping in under his swing and delivered a punishing shot to his ribs before backpedaling out of his reach. "You'll have to do better than that."

"Darlin', you're just managing to prove one thing to me." He moved toward her on the balls of his feet and shot out a fist that she blocked with her forearm before dancing out of his reach.

"What's that?" she asked as she attempted a jab but found her wrist encircled by his larger hand.

He hauled her close, her body bumping into his as he growled into her face, "That you're dangerous because you don't recognize your own weaknesses." When Ryder finished, he flung her away, dropped low and swept her legs out from under her.

She landed hard on the mat. He was about to move in, but she quickly did a flip, using the kick of her legs to create enough impetus to pull her upper body off the mat. She was immediately back on her feet and in a ready position, catching him off guard as he came at her.

Her kick landed square in the center of his chest and knocked him off balance, leaving him totally vulnerable to the roundhouse kick she delivered to his head. He dropped to one knee on the mat, but knew she could have hurt him much more seriously, for the roundhouse had lacked force. "Holding back?" He tongued the inside of his mouth to see if she had broken the skin with her blow. She hadn't.

Her breathing was just a little labored. Diana took a deep

inhalation and dropped her fists as he slowly came to his feet. "I don't want to hurt you. I just want to prove a point. Give, Ryder. Please."

When he refused and assumed a fighting stance once more, she rolled her eyes and adopted her ready position. He circled, testing her with a few assorted jabs and punches, all of which she blocked.

He wasn't exceptionally graceful, Diana thought, but he was strong and fast, and recovered quickly every time she managed to connect with a kick or a punch. Time and time again she dropped him, and after each fall, he resumed the battle.

She was becoming tired, her arms growing heavy from the constant punches and defensive blocks. Her steps had lost some of their spring, but she still had more strength and stamina in her legs than in her arms, like most women. With that in mind, she began an offense devised around her remaining strengths, coming at him with a combined flurry of kicks that once again brought him to the mat.

Ryder struggled to draw a breath, his ribs smarting from the last blow Diana had delivered. He might have superior strength and speed, maybe even more stamina, but she was certainly the better fighter. She recognized his weaknesses and played on them, forcing him to make moves that she not only easily countered, but punished him for with a fresh series of blows.

This last campaign had been all footwork, and he admitted she had him dead to rights. One kick after another had connected, and while he was reeling, she swept his feet out from under him. She now stood before him, trying to control her breathing, her fists braced for more conflict. A fine glisten of sweat covered her arms and shoulders, and the gray of her tank top was stained with perspiration along the neckline.

"Ready to concede, Ryder?" she asked softly, and there was no hint of derision or anger.

Ryder grasped his side and awkwardly lumbered to his feet, but he refused to concede defeat. "I can't leave you alone."

She dropped her fists and placed her hands on her hips. "Don't do this. I have to keep my mind on the case, and with you around..." Her voice trailed off as she backed down, clearly not wanting to take the fight any further.

Ryder gave her his answer by putting his fists up. "What are you, anyway?" he asked as he swayed a little.

"I'm your worst nightmare. A psychologist with a black belt in tae kwon do," Diana responded in jest, hoping to convince him to stop. She didn't really want to hurt him, but he didn't back down. "Come on, Ryder, give," she pleaded once more, but she had all choice taken from her as he charged, displaying a sudden burst of speed and strength that caught her off guard.

This time he landed a short jab that connected with her stomach, but had little force. Instinct was hard to combat, however, and she struck out at him, landing an elbow to his face. He straightened, a little surprised by the shot, and she swept his legs out from under him.

He landed hard on the mat, where he remained motionless, flat on his back.

Chapter 16

Diana slipped to the mat beside him, concern driving her to check him out. In a second, he grabbed both her wrists, flipped his body and nailed her to the mat. His weight, and the way he had pinned her arms and legs, made it virtually impossible for her to escape without doing him serious bodily harm. "Ryder, that was not fair. Now, give before I have to hurt you."

"Never underestimate the enemy, Diana. You're too quick to let yourself become committed."

"You're not the enemy, just annoying," she replied, wishing he would remove his body from hers. The weight and feel of it made her think of things she'd rather not be thinking. Like how nice it might be for him to take his shirt off and let her savor all that hard muscle.

She knew he had no plans to release her, and, quite frankly, she had no desire to go. His gaze, as it touched on her face, seemed to mirror her emotions. His eyes were warm and inviting. So dark and deep, it was as if she could slip inside them and lose herself.

When her bright green eyes, as alive as anything Ryder had ever seen, widened, her pupils dilating, he recognized her passion. Her fragrant breath, choppy as it was from her exertions, blew against his face as he leaned even closer to whisper, "You concede we might be...friends?"

She closed her eyes, as if to shut him out of her thoughts. She arched to try to get him off, but the movement only served to bring their bodies into closer contact. In response, he became aroused. He closed his own eyes, trying to ignore the sight of her face and all it revealed to him. As he brought his own strained breath under control, he inhaled the exciting scent of her. Fresh, living woman, skin soft and flavored with the light sheen of sweat from her earlier exertions.

Bending his head, he brought his face down to the gap between her neck and shoulder, inhaled again and wanted to growl. He opened his mouth on her skin, tasting the saltiness. She moaned, grabbed his head and held him tight.

"Ryder." Her voice was barely a whisper, and he reined in his most brutal of desires, trying not to think of the thickening pulse beating so close to his mouth. His heartbeat accelerated and brought a rush of blood and heat, signaling the coming change in his body.

He strove to control his animal urges and concentrated instead on the supple feel of her body moving beneath his, urging him on. As the beast in him was aroused, the human trapped within responded, and he hardened against her belly. Rotating his hips, he pressed into her, needing her to know how much he wanted her. Needing her to acknowledge it, yet certain this wasn't right for them.

"I don't want this," he whispered, fearful of so many things. Still, it had been so long since he had held a woman in his arms that he nuzzled the soft shell of her ear and tugged at her lobe with his lips, wanting to enjoy the fleeting moment before it had to end.

"I don't want this, either." She attempted to break free,

rocking her body beneath him and trying to loosen the hold of his fingers on her wrists. He maintained his grip on her, and she sighed. "What a time for us to finally agree."

Her humor gave his need a sharp, painful edge. It had been too long. And never since becoming a vampire. He was afraid of what would happen if he took it further, but was even more afraid of continuing his existence without exploring this very fascinating and multidimensional woman. Feeling the edges of his upper teeth with his tongue, he confirmed that he had mastered the animal. He pulled away from her to reach down and cup the side of her face. "I think it's nice we're finally agreeing on something," he said softly, his voice both teasing and serious. He trailed his thumb over the fine edge of her brow.

She brought her hand down to the nape of his neck, cradled the back of his head and drew him close as she raised her mouth to his. "Problem is, we're both wrong." She brushed her lips back and forth across his, her touch light and almost tentative.

He held her cheek, stilling her motion. His gaze locked with hers, and with that connection came the understanding that neither could pull away from the dangerous ground they were approaching. Her soft sigh signaled her consent, and he moved the short distance and tasted her lips.

They were satiny and full, as sweet as anything he had ever sampled. He plucked at her lower lip with his teeth, soothed the little nip with a swipe of his tongue. Her eyes widened further, in surprise, then she responded in kind, pulling at his lower lip with her mouth. He groaned and said huskily, "So what do we do now?"

She moved her mouth to the side of his face, dropping one kiss and then another on his skin as she worked her way up to his forehead and then back down to his mouth, her actions filled with tenderness. "I think we're already doing just what needs to be done, Ryder. So please, shut up."

He laughed and met her mouth, experiencing the texture and flavor of her. The hard, perfectly straight edge of her teeth. The slippery, satiny glide of her tongue dancing with his. The intimacy of the kiss, filled with the sweet breath of life. A breath he hadn't experienced in way too long.

She responded eagerly, meeting his demands, holding the back of his head to keep him close. Shifting her body against his, urging him to want so much more.

When they finally broke apart they were both breathing heavily, shaking with the force of their need. Meeting her gaze, Ryder had no doubt what she wanted, and despite nearly two centuries of telling himself that he was not meant to have a normal relationship, he knew he wanted to give her that and more.

He rolled, bringing her smaller body to rest upon his. She sat up, straddling his hips with her legs. She settled against him, his erection nestled at the center of her, and he placed his hands at her waist. She threw her head back and shifted her hips, drawing herself back and forth across him, creating even more heat with the friction of her movements.

"Diana." She opened her eyes, glanced down at him and stilled at the tone of command in his voice.

He reached for the hem of her sweat-dampened tank top, burrowed his hands beneath the edge and pulled the fabric up. When he reached her breasts, he stopped and cupped them, and ran his thumbs across the hardened tips hidden beneath the fabric of her sports bra.

Diana grabbed the hem of her shirt and pulled it off, exposing the black cotton bra. She cupped his hands as he pulled at her tight nipples beneath the fabric, for each tug sent a corresponding sensation to the awakened nub between her legs. She wanted him so badly it scared her. She knew so little about him, and she knew her dreams had been a warning of sorts, telling her to avoid him. Or maybe, she conceded, a vision of what was meant to happen.

He slipped his hands from under hers and insinuated his thumbs beneath the band of her bra. Her breath rasped in her chest and she had to shift her hips against his erection to satisfy the growing urges of her body. "It's not too late to stop," she managed to say between shaky breaths, even as she increased her movements.

He met her mouth with his lips and whispered, "It was too late before we even met."

She groaned then, knowing she was lost, and gave herself over to him. He made short work of taking off her bra.

Then he surprised her with the way he hesitantly nuzzled his head against her breast, brushing first the fine satin of his hair and then the rasp of his beard across her nipples. He took the sensitive tip of her breast into his mouth, sucking on it, gently teething until she shivered, cradled his head to her and reached under the hem of his shirt to stroke his back. Beneath her hand, his muscles flexed. His skin was hot, unbelievably so, and seemed to be growing warmer by the second.

Only a fine edge of control kept her from her climax as she slowly drew herself along the length of him, hating the barrier of their clothes. When he slipped his thumb downward to apply pressure to the nub between her legs, she slipped over the edge, crying out her completion. He held her close with one muscled arm and brought his mouth up to swallow her cries.

Her slender body shook in his arms, and her soft mewl of protest as he moved away made his heart ache. He had been denied this for so long, living in a world where he maintained only a semblance of humanity. But now he had her. A vibrant, loving woman who embraced him with her heart. A woman freely giving him something to be treasured above all else.

It was insanity to take it any further, he told himself, until her softly uttered "Love me, Ryder" breached all the walls he had erected so long ago.

Ryder rose with her in his arms and walked the long length of the room and hall to his bedroom. She clung to him, her head buried against the side of his neck. She kissed his skin and opened her mouth on him, tasting his flesh before playfully nuzzling his ear with her nose.

He stopped before his large sleigh bed and let her slip to the floor.

"Ryder?"

He faced her, placed his hands on either side of her waist and slowly caressed her skin. "Mmm," he replied as he bent his head, opened his mouth on the side of her neck again and sucked gently.

Ryder savored the quick little catch in her breath as she dropped her head to the side to give him greater access. Placing her hands on his shoulders, she urged him to sit on the edge of the bed. "I want to give you one last out. One last chance to say no before I ravage you," she said, her dimpled grin flashing.

She was too tempting, he thought, meeting her gaze as she ran the palms of her hands along the slope of his shoulders. He smiled and ran the backs of his hands along the defined muscles of her abdomen. Her skin was soft, and there were faint tan lines near her shoulders and breasts from an obviously small bikini. He regretted that he'd likely never see her in it, but he tried to keep up the light-hearted mood she had created by teasing her back. "Darlin', if anyone should be suggesting ravaging, it should be me."

He raised his hands and cupped her breasts, making her sigh. "No fair, Ryder. I can't think when you do that." She moaned, a low, needy sound.

"Then don't," he managed to say before he returned to her breasts.

Her body responded to his ministrations, but she wanted…no, she *needed* more. Reaching for the edge of his T-shirt, she quickly pulled it off, exposing his upper body to her gaze. He was lean, with muscles that were tight and well defined. There was little hair on his chest, just a smattering between his pectorals that arrowed down into the waistband of his sweats.

Even as his hands and mouth continued to draw her to the edge, she ran her hands along all the muscle and skin she had exposed, enjoying the sinewy grace of his body. His heat seeped into her, reaching through her, creating a desire that bordered on wild.

Stepping into the vee formed by his open legs, she cupped his head with one hand while encircling his erection with the other, needing to give him pleasure. She wanted to take him with her to the sensual, vital place where everything seemed amazingly alive, surprisingly sensitized.

The fleece beneath her palm was soft in direct contrast to his hard arousal. Slowly she moved her hand up and down, rubbing the fabric against him. He groaned and moved his head away from her breasts as his breathing grew labored.

Her gaze locked with his, and in his eyes she saw desire, need and, scarily, a want that went beyond anything she could have imagined. His eyes widened as she continued to stroke him while caressing the skin of his shoulders and slowly moving her hand to his back. Against her breasts, his breath came in soft, soughing gusts of warmth that bathed her skin with heat. Until he covered her hand with his, reluctantly stopping her.

She bent, removed his clothing and watched him ease onto the center of the bed after removing a condom from the nightstand. Peeling off her own socks, pants and panties, she knelt on the bed and inched to him slowly, feeling suddenly…adventurous.

She dropped a kiss on the inside skin of his ankle. Moving upward, she did the same on his knee, and as she neared his groin, she stroked the side of her face along the length of him. Beneath her cheek, he was hot, musky. His skin soft and inviting. She ran her tongue along the head of him before kissing him intimately.

Ryder nearly bolted off the bed, his breath trapped in his throat. It seemed all the blood in his body rushed to the place where she greedily loved him with her lips.

"Diana, please. Come here." The husky growl of his voice surprised him. He discreetly ran his tongue along his teeth and noted only a small bump. When she held out her hand for the condom he had removed from the packet, Ryder wondered if it was even necessary. After all, he wasn't really alive, was he? He hesitated but passed it to her. She eased it into place, stroking him as she slowly unrolled the latex over the long, thick shaft of his penis.

Shifting to her back, she opened her arms and he quickly joined her, sheathing himself in her warmth. He moved slowly at first, his thrusts long and unhurried as he let her accommodate to his size.

Diana gripped his shoulders and met his dark, unyielding gaze. "We will not regret this, Ryder."

He braced one hand on the sheets beneath her head and cupped her jaw tenderly with the other. It seemed as if he wanted to speak his mind, but the moment quickly passed. He shuttered his gaze as little by little he increased the intensity of his thrusts, pushing her along toward another climax as he strove for his own.

Ryder closed his eyes and buried his face against the side of her neck as he fought a battle within himself. Her body was so soft, warm and accepting. Would she accept him so willingly if he revealed his true self? He didn't know, but for now, she was here with him, loving him. He wanted to treasure the moment. It meant everything to him.

He shifted his hips, driving into her. The air was perfumed with the scents of their arousal. The musky aroma of her damp femininity and the answering pheromones of his own body.

Diana's skin was slick beneath his, sliding against him.

Her hands were fisted against his back, urging him on, her nails digging into his skin, the slight sting of them adding to the wild pleasure surging through him.

It had been too long, but even more so, it had never been like this, with so much passion. A passion that reached deep inside, stripping away any restraint. He braced one hand against the damp skin at the small of her back, lifting her tight against him. It was as if he needed to bring her into himself, to keep her with him always.

His senses became attuned and aware of every little thing about her. The heat of her skin. The wet of her. The soft, choppy cry of protest as one particularly forceful thrust pushed her upward on the bed.

"I'm sorry," he muttered, but she only grasped his shoulders tighter with her hands and raised her knees to hug his pumping hips.

It was those movements, the wildness inside of her answering his call, that drove him over the edge.

He no longer had a heartbeat, it was just a constant rush of blood accelerating through every cell of his body, bringing with it a feral lust that wouldn't be denied. That wouldn't be satisfied with the taking of her body.

His breath was heavy in his chest. Painful, as he smelled the scent of their sex. His fangs nearly exploded out of his mouth, intent on another kind of release.

Diana held him close as he groaned and arched his back, stilling for a moment before he again drove into her forcefully with a low growl. His thrusts were now more intense, less restrained and still she welcomed him, needing him as she had never needed anything else in her life.

He tightened his hold on her, almost to the point of pain, lifting her upward into him, as if trying to absorb her into himself.

She sensed the desperation in his grip and thought she could smell the edge of fear coming off his body. "Ryder, *mi amor.''* She kissed him softly, running her hands through his hair. ''Don't be afraid of this,'' she whispered.

His body shook at her words, human and demon fighting each other. The demon, unfortunately, had the upper hand. His mouth opened on the fragile skin of her neck, and her pulse point hammered an erratic beat against his lips. He pressed his teeth against her pulse, at the warm river of her blood racing past his lips driven by her desire. As he grazed the delicate border of her skin, intent on breaching that fragile barrier and letting that river of blood feed him, her climax swelled over her, drawing him deep into the center of her. To her most intimate, most secret place. A very *human* place.

''Ryder.'' She arched her back and clutched at his shoulders. ''Love me.''

She grabbed the nape of his neck and held tight as her body shook with the force of her release. Her human response, the desire that spoke to him of more than lust, somehow touched the man inside him.

Breathing heavily, he thought not of how her blood might taste in his mouth, but of the sweet kiss of her lips and the life surrounding him as he continued to drive into her, prolonging her release until the wet warmth of her tears stained the skin of his chest. She buried her head there and brushed a tender kiss above his heart.

Slowly, he eased back from the edge, curbed his blood-lust and strove for the paradise her body offered him. For the release of his mortal heart, imprisoned for so long in the body of a demon. He found the pleasure she was able to share with him, and, finally, with his own hoarse cry, he came.

The jump of his body and his rough call of completion tapped into Diana's protective side. As he collapsed on her, she cradled his head to her breasts, languidly running her hands across the broad expanse of his sweat-slick back, sensing his torment. Long moments passed before his body relaxed, and then he raised his head and gave her a sad kind of smile.

"It seems as if I've been waiting for that forever," he said, and shifted onto the pillows of his bed, dragging her with him, obviously reluctant to let her go.

He cradled her against his side, and she nestled there, bathed in the heat of his body, her mind soothed by some unseen connection between them. As she lingered in his arms, she admitted to herself that she had been waiting for him forever, as well.

Chapter 17

Ryder had little time to enjoy the feel of her lying naked in his arms. The distinctive ring of her cell phone echoed from the workout room and she groaned. "I need to get that."

He opened his arms and let her rise. Diana raced across the hall into the gym and then came back to sit on the edge of his bed. She checked the caller identification on the phone, dialed the number and waited.

Ryder shifted and sat directly behind her, his chest brushing her back. She murmured a halfhearted protest as he slipped his arm around her waist.

"What is it, David?" She covered Ryder's hand with hers, keeping him from reaching up to cradle her breast.

Ryder heard the muffled reply on the other end of the call. She half turned to face him and asked, "Neither of the bouncers is home. Do you have any idea where—"

"Their free time is their own. They're probably working at another club that's open tonight," he replied, annoyed that the investigation had somehow ended up in bed with them. He rattled off the names of two or three other clubs in the area. Diana repeated those names for her partner and then more softly whispered, "Yes, Ryder is still with me. I'll meet you at The Zone as soon as I can. Wait for me."

Ryder studied her as she ended the call and faced him. "I need to go."

But he knew her leaving was about much more than having to meet her partner. She was withdrawing from him already. Running from emotions she couldn't handle, just like she ran from the emotions involving her father.

He wasn't going to let her go so easily. Reaching up, he smoothed an errant lock of hair before cradling her cheek. "You need to get some rest eventually. Will you come back?"

He wanted her to say yes with every fiber of his being, knowing that a repeat performance of tonight didn't make any sense. Continuing this relationship would likely bring both of them a world of pain, but even as he thought that, he moved toward her, brushing his lips to hers.

Diana accepted the gentle invitation of his mouth, telling herself that this was it. She had faced her demon and was in control of it. But his touch sent her heart skittering in her chest and made her want to press him down into the dishabille of the bedcovers. Somehow she marshaled the strength to move away. "I need to focus on the case tonight, Ryder. I need—"

"Some space," he finished for her.

Reluctantly, she nodded.

He shifted away, leaned back against the headboard and slipped his arms behind his head, exposing the broad, bare expanse of his chest. "Go, then. Call me when…"

She sensed his irritation. A lesser man might have taken the opportunity to lash out at her, but Ryder bit back any kind of retort. He waited there as she dressed.

When she was almost finished, he eased out of bed and grabbed a robe. "I'll walk you out." When he realized she was seeking her shoes which were in the other room, he said, "I'll get them. Meet me downstairs."

Diana nodded, needing that small separation to garner her resolve. What was she going to do about him?

She headed to the lower level and stood by the door until he came down the stairs. He handed her the sneakers, and after she had put them on and stood once more, he reached out and eased her gold chain over her head. He held the crucifix and medallions in one fist and studied her. "Watch your back out there."

The intensity of his gaze, the heat and dark of it, snaked its way through her. "I will. Ryder, I..." She what? she asked herself, unsure of so many things.

Ryder cupped her cheek, rode his thumb over her lips as he tried to reassure her. "This isn't easy. For either of us. We're two creatures used to being alone." He needed her to know what he was feeling. "What we have together...I know it's complicated—"

"Ryder, that doesn't begin to describe it." She let out an exasperated sigh. "I need to think about this. About what just happened."

"What did just happen?" He needed, more than anything, to hear that it had meant something to her.

Diana searched his face. The strength of the emotion there both unnerved and excited her. Had anyone else ever looked at her like this? As if she was his heaven and hell, his salvation and damnation all rolled into one? And could she handle that burden? "I don't know, Ryder. All I know is what I'm feeling is intense and scary and...I need to go."

As she stepped through the door, he took hold of her arm and urged her to face him. He bent his head, brushed his lips against hers and murmured, "Please be careful and...call me."

She cradled the back of his head and deepened the kiss.

As she pulled away, she whispered, "Don't worry about me. I'll let you know what's happening as soon as I can."

Once on the other side of the door, Diana hesitated. She stared hard at the fine wood that separated her from Ryder. Just a few inches kept her from… She rested her hand on the door as if by doing so she could touch him. But beneath her hand there was only the hardness and chill of the wood.

With three older sisters and an assortment of female friends, David was probably well familiar with the look of a woman who had been thoroughly loved. And as Diana leaned down to speak to him through the open window of his car, she knew that it was impossible for him not to see the way her lips were fuller, almost bruised from Ryder's kisses. Not to mention the slight razor burn along the lower part of her jaw.

"Ready?" she asked, acting nonchalant, but as their gazes met and then skipped away, she knew that he knew.

But David said nothing about it, and she stepped aside so he could open the door and meet her on the curb. He filled her in on what had happened earlier in the night. "Quinn and Carpenter hit the two other clubs, but no one would admit to seeing either of the bouncers. I waited for you here, hoping a little feminine persuasion might be of help."

"No one wanted to squeal on a pal, I'm sure. You're right about the approach. Wait here while I try." She quickly walked away and up the long ramp leading to the entrance. This club clearly wasn't as popular as The Lair, where there had been a wait every night they had been there. Because of that lack of a crowd, the killer probably hadn't been there. It was the crowd that gave him a wider selection and the anonymity he needed.

The bouncer smiled at her as she paid the admission and got her hand stamped. Inside the club there was none of the attention to detail evident at Ryder's place. A few mirror balls were hung here and there. At the back of the club, a DJ in a glass booth spun tunes for the dancers. White Christmas lights along the edges of the booth made it look cheap and run-down. The dance floor itself was nothing more than painted cement. The dismal interior and canned music likely accounted for the lack of patrons.

Diana sauntered to the bar, where no more than a half dozen or so men and women were seated. One of the men was larger than the rest, but with his back to the bar, she couldn't tell if it was Manny, the bouncer for The Lair. She slipped into the seat beside him. He smiled and shifted on the stool to face her.

"I've seen you at The Lair, haven't I?" she asked with interest.

"I'm the head bouncer there." He held out his hand as he introduced himself. "Manny Rodriguez."

She took hold of his hand, shook it, then reached inside her leather jacket and extracted her FBI identification. Holding it up for him to see, she said, "I need to speak to you. We can do it outside or we can do it down in our offices, which will take a lot longer. Which will it be?"

He cursed under his breath and slammed his glass down on the bar. Motioning to the bartender, he said, "I'll be back in five."

Manny walked ahead of her out of the club and down to the parked car at the curb where David waited, holding the envelope with the photos. Diana explained to Manny just what they wanted.

The bouncer roughly grabbed the pictures, flipped through them quickly and shook his head. "Don't know the dude."

"Really? Aren't you at the door every night?"

Manny shook his head. "As the head guy, I make the rounds. Check to see everyone is where they're supposed to be. That the money is being collected. If there's a prob-

lem, I go out and try to keep it from getting out of control,"
he explained.

Diana glanced at the snapshots, studying the one with
the view of the bouncer's fingertips as he waved at the
suspect and victim. "Hold out your hands," she instructed,
and Manny immediately complied.

She studied his squat, thick fingers, realizing they were
quite distinct from those in the photo. "Who else is at the
front door on a regular basis?"

Manny thought about it for only a second, then provided
the name of the bouncer they had tried to locate earlier.

"Is he the only one?" David asked.

Manny shrugged and nodded. "Yeah, unless he's out or
taking a break."

David continued with the questioning. "If he's taking a
break, who replaces him?"

"Usually I do, but sometimes it's Rick Black. He's at
the rear entrance. We don't have that many people there.
Alley creeps them out, you know?" Manny actually shivered.

"Why's that?" she asked, wondering what would scare
a guy the size of Manny.

"Found a dead wino a few weeks back. He'd been there
for days before anyone noticed, since it's so dark. Ever
since then, people have been weirded out. Besides, Latimer
regularly checks it out, so…"

Diana was well aware that Ryder sometimes checked the
alley, but she was taken aback to find out he went there
often. "What does he do in the alley?"

Manny shrugged, looked around and then leaned close
to her to whisper, "He meets his lady friend—the doc. You
know who I mean. You know what they probably do…."

Pain ripped through her, but she tried to contain it.
"Yeah, you don't have to draw me a diagram." She faced
David and hated the commiseration on his face. "You need
anything else?"

David glanced at the bouncer and shrugged. "Only the address of where Rick Black might be tonight and..." He stopped, took a quick look at his notebook and continued. "If you can reach either him or Doug Baker, the other bouncer, let them know we aren't interested in them. We just need to ask a few questions, okay?"

Manny looked the two over, as if gauging their sincerity. After a moment, he nodded and said, "I'll try to track them down. Rick's probably at home. He's a family man."

He reached into a back pocket, pulled out a small black address book and read a number to them. After returning the book to his pocket, he confirmed the name of the bar where Doug Baker would be.

"Went by there already. Nobody would fess up to seeing him," David said.

"Doug's had problems before. He's a little skittish so he may be laying low."

David looked at her. "I think we're done here."

"Yes, definitely done." She headed for the car, needing a moment to deal with all the information the bouncer had provided. Trying to tell herself that whatever went on with Melissa in the alley was none of her business.

Ryder pounded the heavy bag, his blows hard and fast, and without pause. The animal in him simmered beneath the surface, waiting to erupt. The urge lay dormant under his skin, wanting to savor a human treat. He had passed up a taste of Diana earlier, but now he was close to the edge. He hadn't been that way since...

He couldn't remember. Maybe since he had first been turned. Back then, his bloodlust had barely been contained. It had taken years and years for him to learn to curb it. To feed without killing. And even then, it had been nearly a century since he had fed on a living being. Now he craved it like an addict craved a drug.

But it wasn't just any drug he craved—only Diana.

Playing in the background, as he worked out, were the sounds of a new alternative rock band who had sent him a demo CD in the hopes of being hired. The tunes were catchy, the rhythm easy to keep. He thought about moving to the beat with her, her body pressed tight to his, her hips swaying....

His fangs burst forth as his arousal grew, human battling animal. He stopped and grabbed the bag as he became dizzy from the desire sweeping across him. Taking a deep breath, he battled it, then went on with his workout. He would pound the heavy bag until he could no longer raise his arms. Until he was so weak and tired that exhaustion would claim him and keep him from satisfying any of those unwanted urges.

As the music played, another sound intruded. He stopped and tried to concentrate on it, but the music was too loud. By the time he reached for the remote control for his stereo, there was silence.

He returned to his workout, each blow on the bag bringing him closer to regaining the illusion of control.

Chapter 18

Diana stared at the cell phone in anger. Ryder was not picking up and she wondered where he had gone after... No, it would be better if she admitted that she was more concerned about *who* he had gone with and not where.

"He's not answering?" David asked, his arms folded across his chest as he leaned on his car.

"No." She dialed the number again. It rang and rang and the answering machine came on. She left Ryder a message, dialed the number for his office at The Lair and left a similar message. As she clipped the phone back onto the waistband of her sweats, she looked up at her partner. "Ready to hit the next club?"

"Are you sure that's what you want to do?"

"What do you propose I do? Chase after him?" she retorted hotly, stung by the fact that maybe Ryder had found her so lacking, he'd sought someone else out immediately after their... She couldn't even put a name to it. Tryst? Affair? Lovemaking?

"You can choose to avoid it or you can deal, Di."

She hated his ability to stay cool when she wanted to rage. "I'll deal tomorrow. Let's get going to the next club." She looked at her partner with a defiant tilt to her head, daring him to push her so she could vent some of her anger. Transference, she recognized as a psychologist, but, in some perverse way, satisfying.

David raised his hands as if in surrender, sensing she was spoiling for a fight. "Handle it when you can. For now, one car or two?"

Her own standard-issue nondescript sedan was parked around the corner. She needed to head home for sleep eventually. "Two. After this, I think we should check in with the others and call it a night."

David didn't argue with her. He looked tired and had been at it as long as she, without, of course, the interlude of incredibly mind-blowing sex.

She walked to her car while David got into his. She needed the time to think and to cool down. The drive to the next club, however short, would help her to get things in perspective.

The headache had settled in with a vengeance that not even her third cup of café latte had cured. Diana leaned back in her chair and closed her eyes, trying to take a few minutes to relax in the hopes of quelling the pain. The minutes passed, but the dull ache in her head remained, nagging and insistent.

It was the result of too little sleep and a restless night plagued by dreams of Ryder. Erotic dreams that had woken her and left her shaking with need. She rubbed at her temples, trying to massage the pain away. When that proved useless, she reached for her coffee and finished the last few dregs.

She was about to head for another cup when there was a knock at her door. "Come in."

Maggie made a face as she took in Diana's condition. "You look like death warmed over."

"Is that your expert medical opinion—"

Wagging a finger at Diana, she said, "Don't give me lip. How many hours of sleep have you had?"

"More than most of the squad, so don't lecture me, Mama Maggie. To what do I owe this pleasure?"

"You wanted info on Melissa Danvers, right?" Maggie eased into the chair in front of Diana's desk and crossed her long, elegant legs.

Diana remembered but had assumed Maggie's silence meant there wasn't anything worthwhile to report. "What gives?" she asked, trying to appear cool although she was anxious to hear what Maggie had to say.

Maggie shrugged. "Melissa *is* the daughter of my old professor. Her father and grandfather, and just about every other Danvers before her, were doctors. Like her dad, she specializes in hematology and is just finishing up that specialization."

Maggie was holding something back. She wouldn't meet Diana's gaze and her hands fluttered nervously in the air as she spoke.

"Now give me the dirt you think I don't want to know."

Maggie lifted her head and squarely faced Diana. "She lives with—"

"Ryder Latimer. Old news. He told me so himself."

Maggie's green eyes widened in surprise. "Didn't take you for the type."

Diana leaned forward in her chair and braced her elbows on her desk. "Type? What do you mean by that?"

"Someone willing to be part of a messy threesome— you, Ryder and Melissa."

"Ryder says she's an old family friend." The response sounded lame even to Diana's ears, and Maggie laughed harshly.

"None of my sources could confirm it, but she is living with him. In this day and age—"

It suddenly occurred to her that she'd seen nothing womanly in Ryder's bedroom. No makeup or perfumes on the dresser. For that matter, no second chest of drawers or pictures of him and Melissa as a couple. "They're not an item, strange as it might seem."

Maggie shook her head and her eyebrows rose in disbelief. "And you know this because—"

"I saw his bedroom and—"

"His bedroom? Tell me you didn't, Di! You slept with a suspect?" Maggie nearly screeched as she rose out of her chair and paced the small confines of Diana's office. She whirled and faced Diana after a few steps. "Do you realize how much trouble you could get into? How this could impact your career?"

Diana appreciated her friend's concern, but it was misplaced. "We ruled him out as a suspect after the last murder. There was nothing stopping us—"

"Except common sense. What were you thinking?"

Diana shook her head. "I wasn't. I was feeling. I was needy like I never have been before, Maggie."

Maggie ran a hand through her long auburn hair, took a deep breath and held it before finally saying, "Neediness makes you weak. Ever since your dad—"

"My dad has nothing to do with this." Diana did not like where this conversation was going.

Maggie reached out and laid her hand over Diana's as it rested on the desk. "It has everything to do with him. You're afraid of loving anyone else because you're afraid he'll leave you, just like your dad did."

Diana shook her head. "That's not it."

"Isn't it? Isn't it part of the reason you chose someone so unacceptable—because it gives you an immediate excuse to back out if it gets serious? To run away—"

"I'm not running away from anything, especially Ryder."

Maggie's gaze narrowed. "This is me you're talking to, Di. We've known each other for six years. We've nursed each other through a lot of things, so—"

"Now you're an expert on what makes me tick?"

"We've talked about how there's a part of you that's felt lost since your dad passed away. It's what drove you before and now—"

"It has nothing to do with *now*," Diana repeated, and pulled her hand away from Maggie's. "Ryder is attractive and intriguing."

"And wrong, isn't he? David says there's something not right about Latimer. He's afraid of what's going on with you two," Maggie confided, clearly uneasy about discussing David's concerns.

"I know David doesn't like him, which begs the question of just when the two of you discussed it. Is there something I should know?" she asked, trying to shift the conversation to a different subject.

Maggie shrugged and again crossed her legs. She tried to adopt a relaxed pose, but it was obvious she was nervous.

"Well, Maggie? Are you and David—"

"Involved?" Maggie finished, one eyebrow raised to emphasize the point. She shrugged and replied, "We've had lunch a couple of times. Just lunch."

Just lunch was the problem, Diana realized. Her friend wanted more from Diana's too-logical, too-responsible partner. But Maggie knew that right now David didn't have the time to spare for a relationship. "He's been busy with this case. I'm sure when it's over—"

"It'll be something else." Maggie sighed with disgust and pointed an almost accusatory finger at Diana. "You know there's a reason you law enforcement types have such high divorce rates."

Diana laughed at her normally unflappable friend's

pique. Mimicking her, she pointed a finger back and said, "The key word in that is *divorce,* which begs the question of how we get married in the first place."

They both laughed at that, and Maggie seemed to relax a little. "Okay, so could you maybe hint to your partner that dinner might be nice. When he's free, of course."

Diana nodded and rose. "You know I appreciate your concern, even if it's misplaced."

Maggie stood and gave Diana a hug. "Watch your back, *amiga.* And do me a favor," Maggie said as she walked to the door.

"Talk to David and—"

"Nope. Watch your heart even more closely."

The headache that had been with her since that morning grew in intensity as she, Peter Daly and David lingered in the squad room, discussing their plan of action for the next day. They were in agreement about how to run the surveillance: someone had to talk to Ryder.

"Do you want me to go see him?" David asked, sensing her unease.

Diana shook her head. "No. I've been the main contact. It's up to me to talk to him."

"I could go with you for moral support."

Diana shot him an annoyed look as Peter glanced from one to the other. "Is there something I should know about? Ryder giving you problems?"

"Nothing I can't deal with." Diana glared at her partner as if daring David to contradict her in front of the other cop.

David, it seemed, knew better than to incur her wrath. He held up his hands. "You going to see him tonight?"

"I think that would be best." They needed the info right away if their guess about when the killer would strike was right. She couldn't rest if she didn't have an answer from Ryder about the missing bouncer and any possible criminal activity at the club. And, of course, about Melissa. She needed Ryder's confirmation there was nothing going on that would keep them from sharing a bed for more than just an hour so she might get some sleep in between bouts of... Heat raced to her cheeks. She murmured a hasty good-bye to her two colleagues and headed to her office to make the call.

Ryder had instructed her to phone as soon as she arrived at The Lair and within minutes he was at the door of the club. As soon as he had closed it behind them, he wrapped his arms around her waist and pulled her to him.

She backed away. "Ryder, this is a business call."

He let out a harsh laugh and motioned for her to head into his office. The club was pitch black, and she struggled to find her way in the dim light. As a concession, she al-lowed Ryder to place his hand on the small of her back to guide her to the opposite wall. She walked with one hand outstretched to avoid bumping into anything and wondered how Ryder could make his way.

Of course, he probably had been doing this for years and was familiar with the layout. At the far wall, he reached past her and opened the door leading to the inner workings of the club. Light spilled in from the hall, and she walked to his office.

Ryder followed behind her, a grim set to his features, and, once in his office, he headed straight to his desk and offered her the guest chair. The large expanse of fine ma-hogany established a physical distance between them to match the one created by her earlier rebuke. "Special Agent in Charge Reyes, what can I help you with tonight?"

She deserved the deep freeze, but she wasn't about to let him dissuade her from the business at hand. Explaining about the two employees, she waited for Ryder to provide additional information.

"My bartender will do anything, anywhere, with anyone.

Greg takes pride in it and doesn't like to be interrupted. The fact that you can't reach him doesn't surprise me. He'll be here tomorrow." Ryder rested his elbows on the arms of his chair and adopted a slouch as he looked at her over steepled fingers.

"You sure about that?" She needed answers to all of the questions rattling around in her head.

"Greg rarely doesn't show, and when he can't make it, he calls so I can get another bartender. So far, he hasn't called."

"Your bouncer—Doug Baker. He's had problems in the past. Rumor has it he may be dealing again—"

"Rumor's wrong. Doug promised me—"

"Rumor has it you regularly meet people down in the alley. You have fancy digs that need money for upkeep. I wonder if the meetings have anything to do with that." If it was possible, his face grew even stonier. His eyes glittered with a hardness she hadn't thought possible.

"You can ask this after—"

"Maybe last night was a way to throw me. I know you didn't kill those girls, but maybe you need to keep me from learning what's going on in the alley."

"If you believe that I feel sorry for you," he replied icily.

She picked up her chin. "Why?"

Ryder laughed again, rose from his chair and stood before her. He cradled her cheek, and she flinched. His touch held none of the tenderness of the night before. "Because only a coldhearted witch could fail to see that what happened last night was magical."

She turned away from him, unable to answer. She couldn't let him know how much it had meant to her, but she was afraid that if she denied it, she would be the coldhearted witch he had accused her of being. Ryder wasn't going to let her go without an answer.

He knelt before her and applied gentle pressure to her

cheek until she faced him. "The woman I held in my arms last night was anything but cold. She had a passion and fire that touched me deep inside." With his free hand, he grasped her hand and brought it to his heart. "It made me feel again, in here, after years of thinking I didn't have anything left."

"Ryder, please. Don't make this any harder than it has to be." He was melting her will and exposing the neediness she had confided to Maggie earlier.

"Are you going to find reasons to push me away? To hide from me, Diana?" he pressed.

"This," she said, and motioned to the both of them with her hand, "is crazy. It's wrong—"

"Is it, now?" he said with a hint of teasing in his voice. He moved closer and brushed his lips against hers as he whispered, "If it feels as good as this, how could it be wrong?"

She wanted to challenge him. Deny what she was feeling, but it was impossible when the press of his lips urged her to return his kiss. When the gentle swipe of his tongue begged for entrance. He tasted so good, just Ryder and the slight bite of the whiskey he must have been drinking before her arrival.

Murmuring a protest, she pulled away slightly and tried to continue with her questioning. "What do you do in the alley, Ryder?"

Ryder shifted his lips to her jaw, dropped little kisses along the line of it. He paused by her ear to whisper, "Nothing illegal or immoral, if that's what you're worried about."

Diana sucked in a breath as he nuzzled her neck and laid kiss after kiss down the length of it. She was losing perspective and needed to regain it, and quickly. Tugging at the longish hair at the nape of his neck, she slipped out of the chair as he shifted away and stood. When he rose and took a step toward her, she raised her hand to stop him. "Business, remember. Do you meet Doug to deal drugs?"

He moved toward her, like an animal stalking its prey. "I've already told you, it's nothing you need to worry about. And as far as I know, Doug isn't dealing anymore. He probably ran because he's scared."

Diana nodded. "Does he trust you?"

Ryder came a step nearer. "Why shouldn't he?"

Diana inched back, slowly working her way to the door. "Call him and explain. Tell him we want to ask about the killings and nothing else. Tell him he's not a suspect."

"Done," he replied quickly, and advanced on her but she couldn't avoid that final question. "Why do you meet Melissa in the alley?"

"No reason that concerns you."

"You live with her."

"She shares my apartment. There's only one person I want to share my bed." He took another stride her way, forcing her against the wall by his door.

Diana had few choices: face him, face her fears, or run. She chose to run. "Don't do this, Ryder, or—"

"Or what? You'll kick my ass...again?" He tenderly ran his thumb across her lips. "Do you think that will prove you have control?"

"I have no control when it comes to you," she confessed. She could try to convince herself otherwise, but she knew she'd be lying.

Ryder laid his fingertips against her mouth and softly traced the shape of her lips as he said, "Do you think you're the only one with that problem? Don't you know that I've thought about what we did and wondered if it made sense to continue this?"

"Why wouldn't you want to?" she asked, a little confused and offended that he would hesitate, even though she was prepared to run.

Ryder noted the kaleidoscope of emotions that moved

across her face. *"Why?* Do you think I want the FBI meddling in my life, even if I am totally aboveboard? Do you think I like the power you have over me, both physically and emotionally?"

Surprise registered on her face and she shrugged. "If it balances things out, I've asked myself why I let you charm me—"

"I wouldn't use the word *charm*. Charm doesn't usually involve bruises." He rubbed at a tender spot on his ribs from the rough play of the night before.

"More reason I should leave. Before I really hurt you." She lifted her chin a notch.

"Too late, darlin'. You've wounded me to the quick." He was already damned.

"Ryder, I should—"

"Leave," he finished, but gave her no opportunity to run, moving his hand quickly to the nape of her neck to hold her in place while he took her mouth with his lips.

She murmured a halfhearted protest, but he was not dissuaded. As he continued to kiss her, she relented and gave herself over to him. He moved his mouth against hers, savoring the warmth and softness of her lips and the slight catch in her breath that let him slip inside and experience the flavors of her. He eased his arms around her waist, entrapping her as the kiss went on and on, growing deeper and more intense with each passing moment until he needed more. Until kissing wasn't enough.

He slipped one hand beneath the edge of her skirt while he pressed her tight against him with the other hand. Her stocking was slick beneath his palm. Until the edge of it gave way to the silky smoothness of her skin. He grinned. "Does every FBI agent wear these beneath her very proper suit?"

Diana retaliated with a quick bite to his lower lip that she then laved with her tongue. "What do you think?" She met his gaze and gave him a saucy grin.

He shifted his hand past the thigh-high stocking to the minuscule scrap of panties she wore, his mind working overtime as he imagined what that tiny piece of lingerie looked like. He hardened and barely stifled a groan as she cupped him through the fabric of his pants. "Someone better help me, 'cause I can't get enough of you."

Diana couldn't get enough of him, either. When he slipped his hand beneath the edge of her underwear, she opened her mouth on his, encouraging him to continue even though she should be putting a stop to this. Everything about them together was…

She groaned as he parted her, finding her center and stroking it with a finger. Her breath hitched in her chest as he eased first one finger and then a second into her and moved them, building the pressure and making her needy to have him there.

Still, she gave one last shot at preserving what little sanity she had left. "We need to stop," she said, even as she returned his kisses, unzipped his pants and freed him.

His breathing was rough against her face as he leaned his forehead against hers and glanced down to watch her surround him with her hand. "You only want to convince yourself that this is no good."

"It isn't," she replied between shaky breaths. "I can't control myself around you. That isn't good." But she helped him undo the buttons on her shirt and part the fabric, exposing the lacy bra beneath.

Ryder could barely think, his mind whirling with the feel of her beneath his fingers, warm and wet. Ready for him. And the sight of her breasts covered by the barest of taupe-colored lace, her dark coral nipples visible beneath the sheer fabric. His mouth watered, wanting to taste them. He reached up with his hand and undid the front clasp of her bra. Her breasts spilled free.

"Ryder."

He didn't know if his name was a plea for him to con-

tinue or to stop. He made a judgment call. Bringing his
hands beneath her buttocks, he applied slight pressure and
she eased up, encircled his waist with her legs and guided
him into her.

Ryder sucked in a breath as she surrounded him and he
lost the last dregs of reason.

He leaned her against the wall and slowly shifted in and
out of her. Needing to taste more, he bent his head and
suckled one nipple and then the other, thinking no fruit had
ever been as sweet.

She clasped his head tight to her chest and moved her
hips, increasing his penetration. The warmth of her began
a corresponding heat in his body. A heat that sizzled beneath his skin, awakening the barely leashed animal inside.
An animal that knew there was little tenderness in this mating. There was just raw, driving need that made him thrust
into her powerfully, seeking release. Seeking something
more.

Diana welcomed the harsh movements of his hips driving
her closer and closer to the edge. She held his head tight
to her breasts as his mouth pulled at her nipples. And when
he bit her gently, she cried out.

His head shot up, and there was something in his gaze
she had not seen before. Something hard and dark
and…exciting. Something she couldn't deny any more than
she had denied the demon in her dreams. "Come with me,
Ryder. Love me."

He closed his eyes and drove into her more forcefully.
His thrusts sent waves of pleasure rippling through her, and
she moaned, clasping him close.

Ryder was lost in the demand of their bodies. The beast
in him savored the smells and sounds and tastes of their
passion. He sniffed the air, running his hands along the
small of her back. The heat of her overwhelmed him now
as he moved within her. He struggled to rein in the animal,
but it was a losing battle.

He bent his head and licked the tender spot between her neck and shoulder as his fangs erupted from his mouth. He grazed them against her skin and she held him close, cradling the back of his head. The smell of her arousal was a powerful call, and as she neared the edge of her release, it urged him on.

He buried his face against her neck, sucking at the saltiness of her skin and sensing the pounding beat of her pulse beneath his lips.

And then he felt the power of her climax as it washed over her and dragged him downward into the depths of their darkness. Beneath his mouth, her pulse beat forcefully, the rhythm of it matching the need surging within him.

A need he couldn't deny any longer.

He bit down.

The sharp, stinging pain against her neck forced her to cry out and arch her back. She tried to pull away until the pain was replaced by a searing, pulsing fire that worked its way through her body. It spread across her, setting her nerves ablaze, bringing a strange kind of pleasure along with the pain.

Her world shimmered as the flames licked along her nerve endings. She continued to hold him tight, her body wrapped around him. Urging him on as her release continued until she was light-headed and barely able to breathe. Still, she cradled him close.

Her blood was earthy against Ryder's lips, spiced with their mutual passion. He drank and drank of her as the fire of their joining continued. The blood enervated him with a strength that he had never experienced before. And he knew she felt it, as well, from the way her body shifted against his and the soft guttural cries of pleasure that spilled from her lips.

Ryder was lost, trapped by the animal. He continued to move in her, driven by bloodlust. She answered, holding

him, calling out his name as he fed from her until her body
went limp in his arms.

It was then that some small measure of sanity told him
to stop. He would kill her if he couldn't master what they
were experiencing together.

He reared back, breathing heavily. Her blood stained his
lips as he realized she had nearly passed out. Her eyes were
wide and she struggled to focus on his face. His animal
face, he thought with a disgust that immediately tamped the
fire of their passion and brought the beast under control.

"Easy, darlin'. Easy," he crooned, stroking her face with
a shaky hand and withdrawing from her. His fangs retreated, but the taste of her lingered on his lips.

Her eyes drifted closed and she shook her head. As her
body went limp, he cursed beneath his breath and picked
her up in his arms.

Chapter 19

Diana came awake slowly, a vague disorientation making her groggy. Groaning, she clasped one hand to her head and realized that she was lying along the length of Ryder on the sofa in his office. She opened her eyes, met his concerned gaze and rose up on one elbow so she could see his face better. "What happened?"

"We got carried away and... I think the French call it 'la petite morte,'" he replied uneasily, and shifted their bodies so that she sat in his lap and he held her steady.

She examined his face, wondering. She'd never passed out during sex, but then again, she'd never experienced that kind of pleasure with anyone else. She remembered that much, but, as she met his gaze once again, she was sure there was more. Her body confirmed it as the soreness between her legs gave testament to how intensely they had loved each other. There had been something else there—lustful and dark and... She buried her face in her hands and murmured, "Tell me we didn't do it against—"

"The wall?" he finished, one dark eyebrow raised.

Diana jumped out of his arms. Assorted muscles protested and her head whirled. This was wrong, she thought as a weakness that was almost unnatural rocked her. She looked up at him again. "What happened?" she asked, accusation thick in her voice.

"It was more intense than either of us expected."

She didn't know what to believe. There was a kaleidoscope of conflicting images racing through her brain. He took her into his arms and held her tightly. "You need to rest. Come lie with me."

Diana hesitated, unsure if that was the wisest thing to do, but she was too physically and emotionally battered to do anything else. She hated this weakness, and she hated that it was a result of succumbing to her baser instincts. To the darkness she thought she had mastered long ago.

And even though she let him guide her back to the sofa and into his arms, she hated him for exposing her frailty.

Ryder stood by the railing on the patio, watching the sunrise. The rays bathed the land with brightness and light. With warmth…

The sun was low in the horizon. Still not strong enough to hurt him, but it would be soon. He could sense it. He smelled the coming of the dawn, and felt it in the muscles and sinews of his body. It was a vampire thing. Just like better hearing and sight, and extra strength, stamina and healing. Although in retrospect, the strength was not necessarily enough when one went up against a trained fighter. Diana had proved that.

Just as Diana had proved the wonders of some of his other gifts, like bites that healed within minutes and brought forgetfulness. The person bitten was slightly muzzy, as if they suffered the aftereffects of drunkenness. Unless it was the ultimate bite—the one that made someone a vampire.

Such wonderful gifts, Ryder thought with anger, and

gripped the railing of the patio tighter. The sun rose higher and his body screamed for him to get indoors. To avoid the rays of the sun that would rob him of his strength, and eventually, if he stayed there long enough, kill him.

Maybe that was what he deserved, Ryder thought, his guilt strong. Like any other victim, Diana had awoken with no idea of what had happened, but he'd sensed her unease even as she kissed him goodbye. She'd known things weren't right. It was only a matter of time until...

His cell phone rang and the caller ID showed that it was Diana. Ryder couldn't answer, unable to deal with her just yet. The ringing stopped, but started up a moment later.

He placed the phone into the cradle on his belt and gripped the railing again as the rays of the sun warmed the exposed parts of his body. The heat grew, until pain sizzled along his skin, not unlike what he felt when the change came over him.

Only, this change would be permanent—if he stayed out here long enough... By noon he'd be gone. And maybe, after nearly two centuries of a painful and lonely existence that would be for the best.

The phone rang again, its chirp like that of an artificial bird. A footfall came behind him. "What are you doing? Are you crazy?"

He turned and faced Melissa. She was still in her pajamas and was hastily tying the sash on her robe. When she reached his side, she took hold of his arm and yanked. "Ryder. Come on. You have to get inside."

"Why, Melissa? So I can live for another hundred years? Maybe even another two hundred years...alone?" he snapped, pain lacing every word.

Surprise flashed over her face. Surprise and regret. "When I mentioned the condoms..." She dropped his arm, turned and walked away from him, then slowly faced him once more. "Tell me you didn't—"

"Fall in love? Make love? Maybe even bite her?" Ryder

advanced on his companion, the pain of the sun as it touched his skin forgotten thanks to the greater ache in his heart.

"You didn't turn her, did you?" Melissa asked fearfully.

"I didn't but…" Ryder raked a hand through his hair and his joints ached as he did so. His exposure to the sun was beginning to take its toll on his body. How much longer would it take? he wondered. Would it be painful? Would it be harder than facing the pain in his heart?

Melissa laid a hand in the middle of his back. "You can do this, if you want to be a coward. If you want to leave her wondering…"

Ryder couldn't bear to hurt Diana, but that was the most likely outcome of all of this. Once she knew the truth of his existence.

Ryder turned and walked into the upper hall. Melissa closed the French doors with their special UV-blocking glass behind them.

"What will you tell her?"

Ryder had been asking himself that all night long. He had to end it. He had to make her not want to see him again.

His cell phone rang again. Melissa looked down at it, then up at him, and motioned for him to answer. He did.

"Hello, Diana. How are you feeling?" He closed his eyes, picturing her as they made love.

"I'm weird, Ryder. We need to talk about last night. About where we go from here," she said, and there was something in her voice that told him she wasn't going to run. It brought both joy and despair.

And he knew suddenly what he had to do to make the break.

"I can see you tonight. At the club… Meet me in the alley at two, after you're done with the stakeout," he said, hating what he was going to do but knowing there was no other way.

* * *

They'd tracked down a dozen possible leads that matched the pattern she and the others had worked out at the morgue. In the few short hours left to them that Tuesday afternoon, they'd managed to find all of the suspects. Four were behind bars, two were dead and the other four seemed to be leading trouble-free lives. Of the four who had the freedom to commit the acts, two were too far away—one in Los Angeles and the other in Philadelphia. The other two each had solid alibis for the nights in question.

Diana slouched down into her chair and let out a tired sigh. In less than an hour it was back to The Lair and a fresh stakeout. Maybe they'd have some luck with either Greg the bartender or Doug the bouncer.

She dragged a hand through her hair and went to stand by the window. In the late summer sun, everything was bright and golden. It would be another hour or two before dusk came and brought the darkness. The killer wouldn't come out until then. He'd wait before heading to the club to pick his next victim. He'd charm her, buy her a drink or two, make her feel comfortable. Making her feel as if she could trust him. And then he'd slip a roofie into the beverage.

He had to have a car nearby, and Diana had already had her squad check for parking violations in the area. Tonight, she had an extra contingent of police ready to scour the blocks around the scene, checking license plate numbers. Matching the registered owners with what physical evidence they had from the killer would limit the number of suspects.

And then there was that last bit of evidence—the analysis of the stuff in the last victim's hair. A strange piece of evidence Diana wasn't sure what to do with. Tests had shown the foreign matter to be olive oil, garlic, parsley and lemon. It was a mixture Diana was well familiar with—it formed the basis for many sauces in a variety of Latino recipes. How that tied the victim to the killer, if at all, was a puzzle. No food was served at Ryder's club, so The Lair was not where the sauce had gotten on the victim. Had it come from dinner or an after-dance snack with the killer? Was that where he'd slipped her the roofie instead of at the nightclub? Had the victim brushed against something during the course of the day and not noticed? Why hadn't the two other victims had something similar?

Diana took a quick look at her reflection in the mirror, satisfied with the bib halter and black leather pants she wore for tonight's surveillance. She planted her hands on her hips and sighed harshly. The killer was leading them on a merry chase and there was no certainty that he would strike again today.

"Diana?" David stood at the door of her office. "You okay?"

She nodded. "I'm sorry. I didn't hear you."

He shoved his hands in the pockets of his faded black jeans. He, too, had gotten dressed for the night and sported a black T-shirt and black leather jacket. The color enhanced his golden surfer-boy looks. "Are you ready?"

"You driving?"

David knew her too well by now not to realize she was either distracted or trying her best to hide something from him. "Don't you need your car for after or are you meeting Ryder again?"

"You don't like him, I know. But I can handle him."

He blew out a harsh laugh and shook his head. "What you need to be handling right now is this investigation."

"Are you implying I'm not? That I'm somehow not doing something I should be?"

"You know I'm not, but—"

"Then what is it? What's bugging you?"

"Don't shut me out, Di. I'm your partner. Don't make me try to guess what's going on."

"There's nothing there that concerns you."

He rolled his eyes and let out a long sigh. "This thing with you and Ryder. It's interfering with us."

"Us?" She motioned to the two of them. "You and I are only partners, David. Nothing that's going on with Ryder is—"

"Only partners?" His voice was loud and edged with exasperation. "That's harsh. I thought we were friends, too, but I guess I was wrong."

Diana closed her eyes and cursed beneath her breath at her thoughtlessness. "David, I'm sorry. You are my friend and—"

"Ryder? What is he to you, Di? What is it about—"

"He's my lover."

David stood there for a moment. His face registered the shock of her admission. Then his mouth flopped up and down, like a fish freshly pulled from the water. When he croaked, "Listen, Di," she slipped her palm over his mouth to silence him.

"This is too new, David. Too uncertain. Can you understand that?"

He nodded and she eased her hand away with a weak smile. "We will talk about it soon, but for now...I just need to think about this myself. Get a handle on what's happening." She took hold of his hand and gave it a shake. "Come on, partner. Time to hit those mean streets."

Chapter 20

Ryder stood high above the crowd in the maze of catwalks close to the ceiling. She was down there, somewhere below. He had yet to find her, but he could feel her presence. Even catch a slight trace of the scent of her. She was his mate now. Well, for the moment, until he could...

He tightened his grip on the metal railing until his hands hurt. It was difficult to think of what he had to do. The pain was intense. Bone deep. It would be a part of him for a long time.

His senses came awake suddenly, yanking him from his thoughts. She was closer. He sniffed the air, and her unique aroma teased him. Leaning over the railing, he examined the crowd below, anxious for a glimpse.

He couldn't see her. His heart sped up a beat and he closed his eyes, listening carefully. The animal in him filtered out every noise but the matching rhythm of her heart, beating below.

He moved, following the sound, to the farthest edge of the walk, just feet away from the bar. He opened his eyes, glanced down and there she was, seated with David. They were speaking with Greg, the bartender.

Ryder's heart pounded even harder and his body leapt to life. Blood screamed through his veins, bringing with it the heat that signaled his change. The animal had tasted her and now sprang to life in the hope of having more. He breathed deeply, trying to marshall the beast so he could go below and hold her one last time.

Something inside of her came to life.

She looked around, searching for him. Knowing he was there, watching her. Her skin nearly crackled from the energy of him and she shivered.

"Diana?" David laid a hand on her arm.

"I'm okay," she said, responding to his unasked question. She rose and checked out the crowd, wondering where Ryder was.

Her partner looked around. "Is he here?" David asked.

"Yes." Something pulled her attention to the ceiling. Because of the lighting, there was only the dark silhouette of a man on the walkway, but she knew it was Ryder. She would have known him anywhere.

Just as she sensed that he wanted her to go out into the crowd and meet him. To share a dance before the two o'clock meeting in the alley. "I have to go, David. It's time we tried to attract the killer."

David tracked her gaze, but by the time he glanced upward, there was only the faint movement in the catwalk. Diana moved into the center of the crowd and met one of the agents acting as a decoy. She started to dance, in a world of her own. Ryder appeared at the edge of the dance floor, but moved no farther. Even as Diana turned to face him, Ryder remained along the edge. Watching. Waiting.

He stood with the crowd along the periphery and yet apart from it. Alone. His gaze was riveted on her and she danced for him, even as she kept a part of her focused on the crowd.

It was difficult, for, even from this distance, the pull of attraction was strong. She was on the edge and ready to let herself fall. As her gaze locked with his, a frisson of desire snaked along her nerves. Her nipples tightened and a pulsing throb resonated through her body.

But Diana couldn't let it go further. A colleague who had been on the floor before came back to her, inviting her to dance with him once again. At the edge of the crowd, Ryder nodded, but stayed where he was, his attention solely on her.

She moved to the beat of the music and refocused her thoughts on the job at hand—catching the killer. A killer who might be at the club right now, selecting another woman as his prey.

A young man approached. He was fair, with dark brown hair and the beginnings of a goatee. Piercing blue eyes snared her gaze as he smiled at her.

She knew the killer was sandy-haired and clean-shaven, and she was inclined to ignore this young man. But there was something about him that made the hairs on the back of her neck stand on end. A normal woman would have run, but in her line of work, that feeling meant something was worth checking out. Diana stepped away from her colleague and accepted the outstretched hand of the young man. His grin widened. He placed her hand on his shoulder and put his hand at her waist.

Diana gave herself over to her role while taking mental notes about her dance partner. He was average height, just an inch or two below six feet. Twentyish and with a body that was fit, from health clubs and not physical work. His hand had moved beyond the low waist of her leather pants and was now on her bare skin. His palm wasn't soft, but it lacked the harder calluses of someone used to physical labor.

She examined his face as he moved his hand up her bare back, tracing the line of her spine with his fingers in a way that sent a shiver through her. He took her response as one of desire, and his eyes darkened to a shade of blue-gray.

"Do you like?" he asked.

"Very much."

He exerted pressure, bringing her snug against him. As he did, she noticed that he had recently shaved. There was a slight nick at the edge of his jaw and a spot he had missed. A spot of rough beard that was blondish.

He might be the one. As his arousal pressed into her, she attempted to fake it, closing her eyes and shifting her hips. Softly she said, "Do you like, baby?"

The young man sucked in a harsh breath and his hand at her waist tightened. "I'm no baby, sweetheart. Can't you tell?" He moved his hips against her a little more roughly, a hint of anger shimmering beneath his actions.

Diana smiled and ran her hand through his hair then down to the nape of his neck. "Oh, I know," she whispered suggestively, and pressed herself even closer.

He bent his head and she shifted to allow him access to her ear, the one without the wire. At this distance, there would be no way he could miss it.

"What else do you know?"

"I know you're a real live one," she replied, giving the line that would tip off those listening in that this was someone to watch. "What's your name?"

"Does it matter? Isn't it more fun when you don't know their names?" He gently bit the side of her neck. When she shivered, he added, "Like that, do you?"

"*Sí, mi amor.* I like that a lot."

He stroked her skin with his fingers as he spoke. "And I like that, too, *amor.* I had another little Latin girl like you before. She had fight."

Something went cold inside her. The first victim had been a Latina. She had struggled mightily and this creep…

He'd liked it. He'd liked her grit as she'd battled for life. Diana forced herself to smile and give him what she hoped was a teasing little jostle. "So you like it rough?"

He moved his forearms to bracket her neck. "Not real rough. Just edgy kind of stuff, if you know what I mean."

"Oh, I know, sweetheart," she said with a harsh chuckle.

He stiffened and stopped moving to the beat. Had she given herself away? Then she realized he was looking away, toward the far wall of the club.

"Is something wrong?" she asked, trying to appear unsuspecting by following his gaze.

"Your friend is watching," the young man said just as her gaze connected with Ryder's.

It was disconcerting to have Ryder watch her as another man had his hands on her. But she was on the job now. She smiled sexily at her dance partner and said, "Let's give him something to watch then, baby."

He gripped the back of her head tightly and nearly snarled at her. "Don't call me baby."

She wanted to push him. Wanted him to do something right then and there that would give her the probable cause necessary for her to arrest him on the spot. She nuzzled his face, gave a quick little bite to the edge of his jaw and said, "Come on, baby. I want a little more."

The man moved his hands against the middle of her back and hauled her close, his embrace punishing. "You'll have to wait for more, sweetheart. But for right now, I can give you this." He opened his mouth on hers, his kiss brutal and without any tenderness.

Diana wanted to gag as he forced her lips open and thrust his tongue inside. Still, she had to go with this. Draw him further and further in until he made a mistake. One they could use to bring him into custody.

He kept up the assault on her body, his hands shifting roughly across her, finally coming to grasp her hips and hold them in place as he pumped his hips against hers until he suddenly stopped and pulled away from her.

"Baby, are you okay?" she crooned.

There was a look of surprise on his face, as if he couldn't believe what he had been doing. He shook his head and cradled her cheek with his left hand. It was shaking, and as his cuff dropped down, she noticed the expensive gold watch on his wrist. No fake ten-dollar Rolex, but a high-end solid gold TAG Heuer. The bartender had said that the man in the photos, a regular named Rudy, had such a watch. And then again, beyond the edge of the watch, there was a hint of lighter hair.

"I need some air. Will you wait for me?" He brushed a gentler kiss across her lips.

Diana didn't want to lose him, but if she pressed too hard right now… "I'll be by the bar waiting for you, baby. Don't disappoint me." She ran her tongue along the edge of his lips, eliciting a groan from him.

He nodded and almost ran off the floor. David followed, as did another agent who had been lingering near the far wall, feet away from where Ryder stood.…

Where Ryder had once stood, she suddenly realized. He was gone.

She glanced down at her watch. It was nearly two. In the wire, she heard a sudden burst of talk. "He's heading out. We're following, Diana. Sit tight."

"I'm going into the alley," she said, alerting David to her location for the next few minutes. She needed to let Ryder know she had to postpone their little meeting.

Chapter 21

Diana threaded her way through the crowd and out into the alley. Ryder was beyond the edge of the light, in the shadows.

"Ryder?" she called out, wondering why he was hiding. "I have to go."

"Running from me again?" he asked, his voice low and rumbly. It had an edge to it that she had not heard before. An edge that was scary and enticing with its veiled hint of menace. "Afraid of finding out what I really am?"

"I know who you are, Ryder." She took a step toward him, but he growled a warning. "Stay away."

"Ryder, I don't know what's going on here. I—"

"Wanted to know what happens in the alley. You do remember that much from last night, don't you?" he taunted.

She didn't understand why he was being this way. Why everything had suddenly changed. "I remember everything, Ryder." Although there were large gaps in her memory that bothered her. "Why are you doing this?"

He stepped from the shadows and placed his hand on her waist. Just his hand. But it sent desire skittering through her body as he applied gentle pressure and urged her closer.

Diana went willingly, removing her wire as she did so. His eyes were dark, nearly black with longing. It called to her. Closing the final distance between them, she said, "I want you so badly, but I can't stay."

"You shouldn't stay. In fact, once you go, you shouldn't come back."

She stiffened in his arms and searched his dark gaze, frightened by his words and their intensity. "How can you say that after last night?"

"Last night?" he said, his voice rough with emotion. "Do you even remember what happened?"

"I remember—"

"You can't possibly remember this." And his face transformed before her eyes. Long fangs erupted from his mouth and were visible from beneath the edge of his upper lip. His eyes, those wonderful dark eyes that she had lost herself in, glowed with a bright, almost unnatural light. In the recesses of her mind, it came to her that she'd seen something like that before. Last night. And in her dreams.

"Ryder, this isn't funny." Her stomach did a funny kind of flip-flop.

Ryder laughed harshly and shook his head. "Oh, this isn't about fun, darlin'. This is about prey. And what I need to survive."

Ryder didn't wait for her reaction. He couldn't hesitate if he was going to accomplish what he wanted—to drive her away from him so that she would be safe. So that she could have a normal life with someone else.

He bent his head and ran the edges of his fangs along her neck. "Remember now, Diana? Remember the sting of it? The pleasure?"

Her pulse raced beneath the edges of his fangs. He exerted more pressure, until the sharp points of his teeth had almost breached the fragile skin of her neck.

Diana trembled and battled a multitude of emotions. Fear. Disbelief. Want. As he lingered at her neck, poised on the edge, images flashed through her mind. A reminder of what they had shared. Making love and the pleasure of it. A pleasure born in darkness.

Ryder sensed the change in her and increased the pressure on her skin, but then some last lingering trace of honor pulled him back. Once again he raised his head and let her see the animal he was. ''Are you ready to be my warm and willing snack?''

At his comment, something shattered within her. Diana jumped away, smacking into the wall behind her. Her knuckles scraped the rough brick, but she ignored the pain and removed the gun from her ankle holster. ''What are you?'' Diana held the gun before her, wavering a little as shock and disbelief finally settled in.

''I thought you knew. It's what you said before, darlin'.'' He took another step closer.

''Stop or—''

''You'll fire? Come on, now. You know the myths. Most people do. A bullet won't stop me, love.'' He walked up to the barrel of the gun, pressed his chest against it and met her stunned gaze.

''Please don't make me do this, Ryder.'' Conflicting emotions ran rampant through her. She loved this man.... Only, he wasn't a man, was he? He was a demon. A vampire like that in her dreams. ''This can't be.'' She kept the gun against his chest, her finger on the trigger, ready to fire.

''But it is, Diana.'' He reached up and eased the gun out of her hand. ''I'm glad you're being reasonable about this.''

She stared at his face—his demon face and not that of the man she cared about. ''If I'd pulled the trigger—''

''It would have been messy, but I would have healed.

Just like you healed when I bit you—within minutes, actually. The evidence of the bite disappears quickly. And when you wake, it just feels weird, like a hell of a hangover.'' He ran a finger along the side of her neck, the tender movement a total contrast to the violence of his face. ''You should know, Diana.''

Her stomach roiled as she recognized the truth of his statement. She turned from him, ready to lose it, and took several long, steadying breaths to keep her lunch down. Ryder placed a hand at her back to comfort her, but it was more than she could take. She shoved him away.

Ryder stared at the tight lines of her back and knew she was battling her emotions. He had to push her over the edge if he hoped to destroy whatever feelings she had left for him. He had to force her to release the rage within her. The rage she had tamped down since the death of her father. If he set it free, it would kill what little love she had for him.

''Come on, darlin'. You know that you like how I make you feel. We both love the darkness.''

She whirled to face him, her fists clenched at her side.

''You know we're not that much different, under our skins.'' Taking a step toward her, he reached for her again, but she batted his hand away. He tossed her gun, the one he had been holding all along, at her feet. ''You might need that,'' he continued. ''For the other bad guys. The ones you can hurt.''

''Oh, I can hurt you, Ryder. More than you can hurt me.'' She could physically make him pay for his betrayal. Make him suffer the way she was aching inside. But something kept her from doing so. Something she couldn't quite face yet.

''You betrayed me. You used me and…'' She stopped and took a deep breath. Raising her chin, she clenched her fists to keep from hitting him. ''If you ever come near me again—''

''You'll kill me? Do you think you have it in you?''

Diana stood before him, aching inside. She wanted to hate him and she sensed he wanted the same thing. But as her gaze met his, she *knew* he still cared for her. That he had done all of this to drive her away, and he had accomplished that...for the moment.

A confused part of her was uncertain she could stay away. She couldn't stop caring for him. She couldn't understand how she could feel anything other than loathing for the creature standing before her. And yet she did.

Gathering what little she had left of her dignity, she softly said, ''I don't think you want to test me like that, Ryder. Just stay away.''

She walked to the front of the alley, trusting that he wouldn't follow. Leaving a part of herself behind. A part she wasn't sure she'd ever be able to get back.

David was rounding the corner of the building at a full run as Diana stepped out of the alley. He grabbed her to keep her from hitting the ground.

''Sorry,'' he said, then noticed the blood on her hand and the paleness of her face. ''What happened?''

She shook her head. ''Nada. Just...'' She closed her eyes, rubbed a shaky hand across her face.

David laid a hand on her arm. ''Di, let's get you cleaned up, okay? Let's just go to the car and—''

''Okay.''

At the car, he helped her sit down and then went around to the trunk to get some first aid supplies. She slipped the earpiece back in and heard the chatter of the other agents asking what was going on, and as David rummaged in the trunk for the first aid kit, he filled them in.

''We lost the suspect outside the club. White male. Approximately five foot ten. Dark brown hair with a lighter goatee. Wearing black shirt and pants. I've got Reyes with me. She's all right, although a little shaken. Keep on the lookout for the suspect. I'll advise as to what we're doing shortly.''

There were answering confirmations from all of the agents, and when he returned to the front seat, he knelt beside her and said, "Let me see.''.

"I'm okay," she said, and held out one hand. Blood had dried across her knuckles and there was one rougher abrasion where fresh blood still oozed.

"You don't look okay." He shot her a quick glance as he laid the kit in her lap, opened it and took out a pre-packaged alcohol swab.

She sucked in a breath as he cleaned the cut and muttered a curse beneath her breath.

"What happened?"

She tried to pull her hand away. "It's not…I can't…"

He didn't press, just reached back into the kit to remove a bandage to place over the abrasions. "When you're ready." He tenderly brushed his hand across hers once he had finished. "Do you want to go or—"

"We need to go back in. Try to find that suspect," she said, feeling herself return to normality. She could deal with anything even when inside she was…

"Diana, if you need anything," David offered.

She surprised him—and herself—by reaching out and hugging him tightly.

He returned the embrace and held her until the trembling in her body ceased. She took a deep breath before releasing him, and, when she pulled away, she gave a brave smile.

They both knew it was a fake one, but he accepted it and ran a hand through her hair playfully. "Come on, tiger. We need to hit the streets."

Diana nodded and took his hand. Together they walked back into the club.

Chapter 22

Ryder walked along the wall of the club, staying out of sight until he reached the door to his office. Normally he would wait in there until the bar closed, but tonight he didn't think he could stay at the club any longer. He'd be too tempted to find her. To make things right with her, which he knew was impossible. He was a vampire and she was a human. Not the foundation for a long-term relationship.

He settled for slipping into the security area, where the guard sensed something was wrong. "You okay, Mr. Latimer?"

Ryder waved him off. "I'm fine, Nate. I'm just going to sit here and watch for a little while. Then head home."

Nate nodded but grumbled beneath his breath, "Boss, you look like you need... Heck, I don't know what."

What he needed was visible on the monitor from the camera trained on the front door. She was walking in with her partner and looked a little shell-shocked. David stood close beside her, his hand on her shoulder as if offering support.

Ryder tamped down his jealousy. Diana required David's assistance right now, on several levels. And as for what Ryder and Diana had together—it was over. He'd seen to that quite effectively. He rubbed at the sore spot over his heart. It would heal. After all, he had all the time in the world. Eternity was surely enough to heal a broken heart. And the first step to healing would be to leave. To acknowledge that he was done with her and had no reason to continue sitting here, watching her.

But he stayed, tracking her passage by way of the various cameras. He watched intently, ignoring the ache in his heart that he suspected not even his immortality would mend.

"How could we have lost him?" Diana asked as the reports filtered in on the wire.

David stood beside her as the club emptied after the last call. "I don't know, Di. We had a clear shot of him as he ran out, but—"

Another agent interrupted to say they had found a black shirt and pants tossed next to a Dumpster a few doors down, at another club.

Diana mumbled a curse. The killer might have gone into the other club and selected his next victim while they had been wasting time trying to find him at The Lair. "Spread out along the block. Advise everyone that he may be wearing something different," she instructed over the wire.

"Me and my people got the other locations covered, Diana," Peter Daly said.

"The darker hair was a dye job, Peter. Tell your people he may have washed it out in addition to changing his clothes." She stood with David until only a few stragglers lingered near the bar, finishing the last of their drinks. Finally, the bartenders shooed them out and she and David stepped outside to view the exodus from the establishments along the strip.

"This is impossible," she groused, and glanced at her partner, who was busy scouring the crowd.

Diana rose on her tiptoes, looking for the suspect and, she had to admit to herself, Ryder. She had no luck finding either. As the last lingering patrons sauntered away in search of other places to play, Peter Daly and a few of his uniformed officers headed her way.

"Any luck?"

When he shook his head, she blew out a harsh sigh and raised her bandaged hand to run it through her hair.

"What happened, Diana?" Peter asked, and she dropped her hand quickly. "Nothing. Just an accident."

He narrowed his eyes, seeing through her ruse, but only said, "You got a real good look at him."

"I did and maybe so did the cameras. Let's grab the tapes and go take a look."

"Are you sure you're up for it?" David asked, clearly worried about her.

"I'm okay. Let's just get going. I need to get some rest." There was no way she could make it through the whole night. She was too exhausted, both physically and emotionally, after her battle with Ryder.

Diana turned and headed back into the club.

Ryder watched her come back in. Her partner and the police detective were in tow, and he knew it was time for him to go. He clapped Nate on the back as he moved away from the bank of monitors.

"Aren't you going to wait for your lady?"

Ryder glanced at the monitors and noticed she was fast approaching. The last thing either of them needed was to run into each other again tonight. "The lady and I... You know how things go, Nate. Nothing lasts forever." He quickly strode out of the security room, leaving Nate muttering under his breath about the foolishness of the young.

The comment brought a strangled laugh to Ryder's throat. He had about a hundred years on Nate and was well aware of the stupidity of love. He'd made the biggest of mistakes after all.

When he slipped out via a side door, the street was almost empty, much as it was every night after closing. He fished his keys out of his pocket and walked halfway up the block. There he crossed over to the small driveway behind the restaurant where he parked his van every night. It was one of the conditions in the lease on the space for the eatery. A space he owned.

While he walked, he thought about the man who had danced with Diana tonight and whom she seemed to think was the suspect. He slowed and juggled the keys in his hand. Something finally clicked.

He looked at the back of the restaurant where an assortment of Dumpsters and bins waited for trash and laundry pickup in the morning. That was when it came to him—the man picked up the laundry for the restaurant. Ryder had seen him more than one morning on his way home.

He turned, intent on returning to the club to tell Diana and her colleagues, but he didn't get far. The young man in question was waiting behind him, a long length of wood in his hand. Ryder had no opportunity to block the first blow, which caught him against the side of the head, stunned him and drove his head against the window of the van. He laid his hand on the side-view mirror, struggling to stay upright.

The second blow took him down.

Ryder woke slowly, his head and body throbbing with pain. As he became totally alert, he realized he was hanging like a side of beef from a hook. He'd been stripped of all of his clothing and his body was chilled from the cold and damp. Ropes bound his wrists as did a chain that had been looped around a metal hook driven deep into a thick, hand-hewn wooden beam.

There was little light in the room, but Ryder didn't need much to make out the table a few feet away that held an assortment of instruments. And the metal shelves even farther away sporting an odd group of jars, more tools and a gas-powered lantern.

He tried to get some leverage by moving his legs, but they were bound, as well. The pressure on his arms was almost unbearable as the weight of his body dragged on them.

Taking a deep breath, he strained against the bindings until a fine layer of sweat coated his body, increasing his discomfort as the chill settled deeper. He cursed out loud and gave one last angry yank, but nothing gave.

Suddenly metal grated against metal, a door opened with a groan and he heard a loud metallic clank as it closed again. Footsteps sounded against the cement floor until Ryder made out the shadow of a man by the metal shelves. A match flared to life and the hiss of the propane feeding the lantern grew in intensity as the man increased the amount of illumination.

"How are you, Latimer?" the man said as he walked closer and placed the lantern on the table holding the instruments.

The voice was familiar, as was the face, only today the young man sported auburn-colored hair. "You're the driver for the laundry company, aren't you?"

"So glad you could recall. You've seen me many a time, not that you ever bothered to learn my name," he said with a trace of anger.

Ryder hoped to capitalize on that emotion, maybe make the man do something foolish that would allow an avenue for escape. "Why would I bother, a little nothing like you?"

The young man laughed, reached for something on the table and walked to stand before Ryder. He flipped the item in the air, and Ryder couldn't fail to see it was a long, sharp wooden stake.

"The name is Rudy." The young man placed the point of the stake on Ryder's chest, right above his heart and continued with his little talk. "Tell me, Latimer. Is the lore true?"

"What lore?" Ryder asked, wondering just how much Rudy suspected.

"Oh, you know. The kind about no reflections in the mirror. Holy water. All those kinds of things." Rudy ran the stake along Ryder's skin.

"Don't know what you're talking about."

Rudy chuckled again and put the point of the stake directly above Ryder's heart. "Give it up, Latimer. I watched you and your lady friend in the alley. Heard it all. So, tell me, if I stake you right through the heart—"

"Will I explode into a cloud of dust? You've watched *Buffy the Vampire Slayer* one too many times."

Rudy brought the stake down viciously, burying it deep into Ryder's side. Pain exploded through him and he strained against his bindings, but there was no escaping the agony. "I can make this difficult for you. So difficult you will wish you were dust. You will beg me to stop, like the women did."

Ryder struggled to breathe, his torment intense. Somehow he rasped, "Does having me chained make you feel stronger? Why not let me go and see just how strong you really are? Or are you afraid, little man?"

Rudy yanked out the stake, and Ryder nearly passed out from the pain. He closed his eyes, gritted his teeth and waited for another attack, but it didn't come. Against his chilled skin, there was the warmth of blood as it trailed down from the wound in his side.

"Beautiful, isn't it?" Rudy asked as he held a scalpel up for Ryder's inspection. "It was my father's."

"So this freakiness is genetic?"

Rudy let out a soft laugh. "You have guts, Latimer. For now, at least. We'll see how brave you are when I've got them in my hands." He stepped up to Ryder once more and laid the scalpel against his midsection.

Ryder didn't flinch, certain it would give the other man satisfaction. He goaded him instead. "You can take whatever you want, Rudy, but I'd still be a man. Which is more than I can say for someone like you who needs knives to make him feel strong."

"Aahh… My needs. They're actually quite simple compared to those of a creature like you," he said, and applied the barest of pressure. The scalpel slipped easily through Ryder's skin, but Rudy didn't stop there. He drew it down, creating a precise line that bisected Ryder's midsection.

There was little pain, Ryder thought with surprise. The blade was too sharp and the cut shallow. As a surgeon, Ryder had made more than his share of incisions such as this one. He watched, almost in fascination, as Rudy stepped away to examine his handiwork and then reached for another surgical instrument.

"Do you like punishing them?" Ryder asked, hoping to find out what made the other man tick.

"Do you like biting them?" Rudy challenged. "Do they taste the same or is each one different?"

"I'm sure a connoisseur such as yourself would know better than me." Ryder groaned as Rudy traced the earlier incision and pressed harder.

"Hurt much?"

Agony screamed through his brain, but Ryder kept his gaze locked with Rudy's until black circles danced before his eyes. When Rudy moved the knife one more inch, Ryder lost the battle for consciousness.

Chapter 23

Ryder woke to a world of hurt. The muscles in his arms ached and felt as if they had been torn from their sockets. His midsection was ablaze and as he opened his eyes and focused, he noted the blood that had drained from him. It coated the front of his body and his side. Though the wounds were already starting to heal.

"So glad you're finally with me again, Latimer. I was worried we were going to run out of time." Rudy slapped the stake against his hand. The wood was darker now, stained with Ryder's blood.

"We have all the time in the world, Rudy. I'm not going anywhere."

"Unfortunately, we don't. The sun will be up soon." He motioned with the stake to the banks of windows along one wall. A faint glimmer of light was already visible. "And tonight, I plan on taking your friend and letting you watch. If you survive the sunlight, that is."

Ryder experienced his first real moment of fear, but not from the prospect of the sun reaching through those windows and touching him. "She's an FBI agent. You won't be able to grab her." Ryder hoped to dissuade him from taking Diana. He was trying to protect her, something he was sure she wouldn't appreciate. Quite ironic, actually, given that he couldn't even help himself.

Rudy laughed and ran the point of the stake along Ryder's chest, delighting in the flinch Ryder couldn't control. "Afraid, Latimer?"

"They'll be waiting for you tonight. If you try taking her, you'll fail."

Walking away, Rudy dropped the stake onto the small table. As he stood there, considering the various instruments, he spoke over his shoulder. "Oh, I never fail, Latimer. And then I will have some fun. Maybe you'll be lucky enough to see it." He picked up a Liston knife and sauntered back to the beam.

Ryder refused to glance at the instrument. As a wartime physician, he had used a similar one many times during amputations. He knew just how sharp it was. How much damage Rudy could inflict with it, but he didn't acknowledge that. Doing so would play into Rudy's head games. "Did your victims beg when they saw the knife, Rudy? Do you like that, 'cause if you do, you'll be sadly disappointed in both me and Diana."

Annoyance flared on Rudy's face before he drove the knife through Ryder and into the wood. "I'll make you beg, and your little friend, as well. Or maybe you'll beg for her. How do you think she'd like that?"

Ryder pulled against his bindings and sucked in deep lungfuls of air as he battled for control. Of course Rudy's earlier victims had begged, he thought, nearly biting his tongue in half to keep from begging himself. He fought back the plea, not wanting to give Rudy the satisfaction. "Why do you punish them?" he rasped between pain-filled breaths.

Rudy released a harsh chuckle and picked up one of the

jars from the metal shelf. "You know what this is, don't you?"

Ryder forced himself to focus and concentrate on the item Rudy held—a jar with a trophy from one of his victims. "You're a sick animal," Ryder said, not caring about what punishment would follow.

"Funny you should call me that. You feed and kill and yet call me an animal."

Ryder heard the edge of annoyance in the other man's voice. "The animal in me wants them dead, but the human…the human understands how precious life is," Ryder said in rebuke, his voice growing weaker as the effects of the injuries drained him of strength.

"Precious?" Rudy advanced on Ryder, another knife in his hand. Barely controlled insanity was visible in the young man's eyes. "I want them dead because they're whores, each and every one."

"They hurt you?" he asked, and whatever small connection he had made with Rudy vanished.

"Do they have their own bouquet, their own essence, like a fine wine?" Rudy smacked his lips as he spoke and ran a finger across Ryder's chest. "I've never thought about it before—the life's blood you crave. So complex. I can understand your need, but can you understand mine?"

Ryder tried to lift his head, but he was too weak.

Rudy smiled. "Does her blood run in your veins, vampire?" he asked, and Ryder had no doubt he was referring to Diana. "Did you taste her?"

Ryder didn't have it in him to answer.

"I think so, Ryder. I think the beast emerged and savored her, but I think the human felt something for the little slut."

Rudy grabbed Ryder's hair and forced his head back to meet his gaze. "Shame that you will lose her so soon."

Ryder moaned and pulled at the tight ropes binding him to the beam. They held fast and his breathing increased, a fire igniting within him. He was too weak to battle the beast and the pain transformed him. His fangs emerged, and a low, angry growl erupted from him.

"Ah, that's better," Rudy said with satisfaction. "But not for long."

He laughed and motioned toward the dirty and broken windows along the upper wall of the building. "The morning sun gets quite strong in here. I guess when I return I'll know whether the lore is true."

In his current state, Ryder doubted he could withstand any amount of sun for long. He was too weak from blood loss. He bowed his head and closed his eyes.

Rudy laughed loudly and a little wildly. "Such a shame, vampire. I'd hoped you and I could sample her tonight. See how sweet her spirit would taste."

Until now, the human in Ryder had held back any show of emotion. It would only add to Rudy's sick pleasure. But as the man closed the door behind him, sealing Ryder in what he knew would be his tomb, and possibly Diana's, the animal in him howled out his grief, frustration and pain.

The sound echoed against the cinder blocks, a long, eerie wail that rattled the windows and slipped outside into the early morning air.

After hours of being on the job, Diana needed a few solid hours of sleep before heading back. She should have known she wouldn't get them, given how the night with Ryder had ended. As he had before, he came to her, the dream familiar, but as she let herself drift off to meet him, tension crept into her. Tension and fear.

Ryder stood before her, his hand outstretched, spurring her onward. She walked toward him, her shoes sounding loudly against dark cobblestones. The sky had a gray pall to it and the air was cold and damp. She looked past Ryder and noted the golden spire of a building that looked vaguely familiar.

As she took his hand, he brought her close and held her

in his arms, only it wasn't a welcoming embrace. It was as if he was saying goodbye. She pulled away from him, confused and fearful. When she did so, she noted the blood seeping through his clothes and staining their hands.

"Ryder?" she asked, but he closed his eyes and moaned, dropping to his knees.

She knelt down to hold him, her heart pounding loudly as she struggled to stay calm. He opened his eyes. They were the bright, glowing eyes of the demon. His fangs emerged as he reached up and touched her face.

His hand was cold. Too cold. Dread filled her. "Ryder, don't go." His hand dropped and his eyes closed. In her arms, his body was hard and unyielding. She knew then that he was gone.

She awoke with a start. It was close to seven o'clock. She'd barely gotten two hours of rest, if you could call her troubled slumber rest.

Shaken by the emotions that lingered from her dream, Diana knew it was useless to try to get more sleep so she showered and dressed. As she slipped on her suit jacket, the doorbell rang.

She entered the living room to see Melissa Danvers standing there.

"How did you get this address?"

"Ryder didn't come home last night. I was hoping you'd know where he was," Melissa said.

Diana braced her arms across her chest. "Don't know and don't care." Though the concern that lingered from her dream turned into outright fear.

"Hi, I'm Sebastian," her brother, who had followed her to the door, interjected. He held his hand out to Melissa.

Melissa hesitated but took his offering and opted to capitalize on it. "Melissa. Maybe you can help me."

"Sebastian doesn't know a thing about your friend, and I'm sorry I ever did." Diana quickly stepped between the two.

"I need your help to find him, Diana. He can't be out now. You know that."

"What I know is that Ryder jumped to the number-one spot on my suspect list," Diana said.

Melissa shook her head. "You don't mean that. You're just angry at him because he—"

"Deceived me? Betrayed my trust?"

Melissa had the grace to blush, but she still forged ahead in Ryder's defense. "You know he couldn't have killed those women. And you know you can't let your anger jeopardize Ryder's life."

Diana hated that she was right. Despite Ryder's show of the night before, she knew in her heart that he wasn't capable of murder. And his disappearance was probably due to the misunderstanding they'd had last night. If she had a choice, she'd be avoiding the world, as well. "Ryder's a big boy. I'm sure he found somewhere to sleep away the daylight hours."

Sebastian let out a strangled chuckle. "I definitely have stepped into something bizarre. You two are sounding way too weird."

Diana opened the front door. "I think you've overstayed your welcome, Dr. Danvers."

Melissa held her ground. "If he's hurt and can't make it somewhere safe…"

"He'll have a major case of sunburn? Turn into a big pile of dust? Is that what happens?" Her residual anger at Ryder's betrayal drove her to lash out at his friend. Inside, however, she hoped he wasn't in danger.

"He'll die, and I don't think you want that." Melissa laid a hand on Diana's arm. "He can't help being what he is. Please help me find him."

"And just *what* is your friend?" Sebastian asked.

Diana glared at him and held the door open wider. "It's time you got to work, isn't it, Sebastian?"

"Ryder's a vampire," Melissa answered calmly.

Sebastian laughed. "She's a kook, right, Di? One of your strange FBI friends?"

"Sebastian, just go. This doesn't involve you."

"How come you're not answering me, Di? What's going on here?" He headed back into the living room and sat on the sofa, clearly not intending to budge until he had some answers.

Diana looked at Melissa and pointedly inclined her head in the direction of the door. The young woman regally lifted her chin, turned and entered the living room. A moment later, she was seated on the couch by Sebastian's side. "Help me find Ryder."

Diana slammed the door shut and approached the duo, her hands on her hips in an obvious sign of annoyance. "If you're worried that I hurt your friend once he showed me what he was, you're wrong. I wanted to, but he was in one piece when I left him."

"Now tell me something of value."

Sebastian chuckled and muttered beneath his breath, "Ballsy. I like that in a girl."

"Sebastian," Diana warned at the same time that Melissa said, "I'm not a girl. I'm a woman."

Despite her pique, Diana had to admit she admired Melissa's dedication and her ballsyness, as her brother had put it. And deep inside, in the part of her that still cared for Ryder, there was concern for Ryder's safety.

"Did anyone see Ryder leave the club?" she asked finally.

"I called at six when I got worried because the sun was up and Ryder wasn't home—"

"You're not doing drugs, are you, Diana, because this whole vampire thing—"

"Sebastian, it would be best if you went to work," Diana held her hand out in a pointed invitation for him to leave them alone.

"I was worried this whole club thing might drag you—"

"Into nothing I can't handle, *hermanito*. Now, go." But Sebastian didn't budge.

Melissa laid a hand on his thigh and said softly, "Your sister isn't into anything harmful."

Diana let out a harsh laugh. "If you consider a vampire bite not harmful."

Sebastian jumped up, hands in the air to silence both women. "Okay, enough of the comedy routine. This Ryder guy can't be a vampire." He motioned to Melissa. "And you," he continued, pointing a finger at Diana, "did not get bit by a vampire. Vampires do not exist."

"Ryder is a vampire."

"He's been one since the Civil War when he got turned," Melissa added.

"And you're human, I hope?" Sebastian questioned.

"Definitely a mortal," Melissa confirmed, then inclined her head in Diana's direction. "And you… You're the first person that Ryder has loved—"

"He doesn't love me. He couldn't love me and bite me." She almost reached up and rubbed her neck, then pulled her hand away as she realized what she'd done. Shaking her head, she said, "I don't want to be the one he loves."

"And why is that?" Melissa asked.

Diana closed her eyes against the pain. "Because I can't give him the happily ever after that he deserves."

Chapter 24

The security guard told Melissa that Ryder had left close to three, just before Diana and her colleagues had come by to get the surveillance tapes. No one had heard from him since. Diana checked in with David and Peter, neither of whom had more information. They all agreed that she should check out what had happened the night before. She promised to keep them posted if anything came up. In the meantime, Peter and David were headed to the FBI office to once again review the tapes.

Diana parked her car in front of The Lair and turned to look at Melissa and Sebastian in the back seat. "How does he normally go to and from the club?"

"He has a van. Parks it down the block in the loading ramp for another building he owns," Melissa explained.

"Let's go check it out, then."

She followed Melissa to the back of a building about halfway up the block from The Lair. Ryder's van was still parked there, and Melissa turned and gave Diana a worried look. "He never got here."

Diana advanced slowly and immediately noticed the smudge along the driver's window and another on the sideview mirror. A closer inspection of the window made her flinch. There were faint droplets of blood in a splatter pattern.

Turning her attention to the mirror, she noted a thumbprint and what looked like the mark of a palm along its black backing. Ryder must have held himself up, maybe after the first blow, she thought, knowing it would take more than one shot to take him down.

If he'd fallen backward... She inspected the front bumper on the driver's side and found more smudges that confirmed his fall. There was a small patch of blood on the sidewalk. Coldness settled within her as she looked around, spotted another telltale mark a few feet away, and then followed that trail up the steps of the loading dock. On the edge of each step was a stain that might not have caught someone else's attention.

Diana was well aware of what it meant. Ryder had been dragged up the stairs. The blood from his injuries had marked the edges of the steps. She shivered as the images from her dream drifted into her mind. A sick feeling settled in her stomach.

At the top of the platform there were an assortment of garbage cans and a large bin from a commercial laundry company. The laundry bin was empty, but the garbage cans were still full. In the second that followed that observation, the pieces of the puzzle started to fall into place. She turned and called out to Melissa, "Do you know what businesses use this loading dock?"

Melissa started to walk toward her, but Diana waved her back. "I don't want you contaminating the crime scene."

The other woman stopped dead in her tracks and her pale skin blanched. Sebastian quickly offered his support as she swayed slightly. "He'll be fine." He glared at his sister for her bluntness.

Diana didn't wait for Melissa to recover. She needed an immediate answer if she was going to locate Ryder before… She wouldn't think about her dream. She pulled on one of the restaurant doors and found it locked. She quickly went to the next one, yanked and it popped open. She withdrew her badge from her jacket pocket, stuck her head in and called out a warning before stepping inside. "FBI. Anyone here?"

When there was no answer, she entered. It was a storage room lined with shelves that held row upon row of institutional-size cans of food. There was a shuffle from the front of the building and Diana proceeded up the small gap between the shelves until she reached the kitchen. She didn't need to enter to know its specialty was Latino food of some kind. The smells of onions, garlic and citrus were enough proof. "Anyone here?"

A young Latino man popped his head out of the kitchen, a worried look on his face.

"Migra?" he questioned as he saw the badge and seemed ready to bolt.

Diana reassured him in Spanish. "I'm not from Immigration. I'm FBI. All I need is a little information. I won't do anything if you help."

The young man nodded and wiped his hands on the apron tied around his waist. *"Qué quieres?"*

Diana quickly rattled off a question or two, mostly about who cleaned the restaurant's linens and when that company picked up. The ready answers of the young man gave her a good start in tracking down where Ryder might be. She thanked the man and headed back out onto the loading ramp.

Melissa and Sebastian still stood there, waiting. "All of the victims were wrapped in fresh linens and the last one had some kind of sauce in her hair. I think the killer dumps them in that laundry bin, or another like it. Then picks them up, probably while he's making his rounds."

"How does Ryder fit into this?" Melissa asked, and wrung her hands together in worry.

"Ryder thought there was something familiar about the suspect we pointed out in the tapes. Maybe because he had seen him here on the loading docks."

"Do you think Ryder caught him in the act?" Sebastian asked.

Diana shrugged and whipped out her cell phone. "I need to call this in."

When her partner answered, she gave him the information she'd collected. "Call the company and tell them I'm on my way. I'll need access to their employee records and routes. If they give you trouble, call me, get a judge to issue you a warrant and meet me with it."

After David's confirmation, she hung up and faced her two unwanted companions. "You need to go home. I'll call when—"

"No way. If Ryder needs help, I'm the one to do it," Melissa protested.

Diana raised her hands, signaling no, but Melissa didn't stop. "There's medicine in the van, in case of emergencies. We need to take it so that when we find Ryder—"

"Just tell me what to do and go home."

But Sebastian immediately contradicted her. "What if you need to pick him up? There's no way you can swing that."

"And there's no way you can take him to a hospital or another doctor without compromising his secret," Melissa added.

Diana let out a harsh laugh. "Any more than it's been compromised? There're three of us, maybe even the killer by now, who know."

"And as big a circle as that is, we need it not to get bigger." Melissa headed to the van. She pulled keys out of her purse, pushed the remote control button and opened the door. "Come on. Time's a'wasting."

* * *

A warrant wasn't necessary. The manager of the laundry called the owner and within minutes, Diana was looking through their schedules, pinpointing who it was that made the pickup for the restaurant. Gordon Randall. And if he kept to his schedule…

Diana looked up at the manager. "Randall should be back within the hour."

The manager shook his head and held up his hands as if in apology. "Sorry, but Randall is long gone."

"The schedule says—"

"He came in early this morning. Said he had something to do and could he run his route earlier. Wasn't a problem since all the drops were ready."

She returned her attention to the papers. The employee record contained a copy of Randall's commercial driver's license complete with photo. Diana had no problem identifying Randall as the man who had danced with her the other night, despite his being known as Rudy at the club. Still, it was possible that the documents had been doctored or faked, or that he hadn't given the people at The Lair his real name.

With the manager's permission, she quickly made copies and faxed them to David so he could get someone to track down Randall. She also faxed him a copy of Randall's schedule and instructed that David get another team or two of agents to visit the sites at the end of the route and get more information on Randall.

Thanking the manager, she walked out of his office with her copies of the materials and approached Melissa and Sebastian, who waited outside by Ryder's van. As she reached them, she quickly explained what she had planned and immediately encountered objections from her brother.

"Why didn't you put more agents on checking those locations? If we need to find him soon—"

It was Melissa who came to her defense. "She did the

right thing, Sebastian. We don't know what condition Ryder will be in and if someone else finds him…"

"You'd have a big problem on your hands." Sebastian looked up at the bright blue sky and the sun that was heading higher toward its midday peak.

Diana quickly opened the van's doors with the remote. "Come on," she said. "We don't have much time."

"Do you think he's okay?" Melissa asked.

Diana wished she could be optimistic, but she couldn't. "This killer has a lot of rage. It's why he did what he did to the women."

"But Ryder's a guy," Sebastian interjected.

Diana shot a quick glance at Melissa, then said, "The killer may transfer that anger to someone else. Maybe someone he feels is responsible for what the women do."

"Someone like Ryder," Melissa said with concern.

"Maybe. But maybe I'm wrong. Maybe he just grabbed him for now. Either way, we need to get a move on." Diana couldn't fail to notice the fearful glance Melissa and Sebastian exchanged, nor the way he laid a hand on Melissa's shoulder, offering solace.

It was a struggle to draw breath. Each inhalation brought more pain than he had ever imagined.

Ryder barely had the strength to pick up his head, but he struggled to do so, staring at the beams of sunlight reaching into the space through the gaps in the broken windows. The long fingers of the sun had bathed his body, setting his torso ablaze. Slowly stealing the life from him, making his skin and muscles stiff and painful. As the sun inched higher, the rays had moved downward, shifting their attack to his abdomen and then moving ever slower, taking more and more of him away with their touch.

From mid-chest down, his body was stiff, as if in death. There was no way he could free himself now.

Diana, he thought, and groaned, praying she would be

safe. Trusting she had the intelligence and strength to avoid the killer and, maybe, find him. Perhaps he could see her one last time. Tell her how sorry he was for everything that had happened.

His body protested as he feebly pulled at the hook, accomplishing nothing. The bindings were too strong and he was too weak. So weak it was an effort just to hold on to consciousness. He struggled to stay awake, his head hanging down. His eyes trained on the rays of light as they finished sweeping down his body, then thankfully slipped off onto the floor, signaling the arrival of high noon.

Rudy would be back soon, Ryder knew. Back to torment him. Back to kill. Funny thing was, Ryder thought with a dry laugh that racked his body with pain, he almost welcomed Rudy's return.

Chapter 25

The glare of the sun hurt her eyes, and Diana slipped on her sunglasses. She tried not to think about how Ryder must be feeling. She tightened her hands on the steering wheel. Too much time had passed and they were no closer to finding him.

This would be their third stop. It was almost one in the afternoon. The other agents, who had begun at the end of the route, had only a few more stops before they all ran into one another. If they reached that point, it would probably be too late for Ryder.

She was convinced he was somewhere in this area. It would make sense, according to the hypothetical timetable she had mapped out. The first stop was the restaurant and would normally happen at four in the morning.

Rudy, for that was what she preferred to call him until they verified whether or not Randall was an alias, would normally be done with his route by midday. That would leave him plenty of time to return to his hideout and work on his victim. It matched the medical examiner's approximate times of death for the victims—late afternoon to early evening for all of them.

She stopped the van by the back of a small, upscale hotel on the edge of the South Street Seaport. Examining the area around the hotel, she didn't even bother to get out. There wasn't anywhere vacant enough for the killer to store and play with his victims.

"What are you doing?" Melissa asked.

"Thinking." Before either of her two companions could say anything else, she grabbed her cell phone and dialed David.

He answered almost instantly. "Anything?"

Diana sighed and ran a hand through her hair in frustration. "I was hoping you'd have something for me." She searched the area again through the windshield of the van.

"Nothing, except that Randall is an alias. Social security number he gave was a fake. So was the address on all the papers."

"So we're back to Rudy and nothing to go on." She glanced at her companions out of the corner of her eye. Melissa's face showed her concern and Sebastian grabbed her hand to offer comfort.

Diana looked away, controlling her own fear as she grasped at straws. "Did Rudy have any bank accounts with the alias? Make any payments?"

"Still checking on it," David replied.

Diana lost her temper. "Can't you get anyone to check on it faster?" David's tired sigh came across the line. "You're letting the personal get in the way, Di. You know how long this can take."

She bit back her response, for it would only worry her companions more. Taking a deep breath, she finally said, "I know, David. But call me as soon as you have anything. Anything at all."

She turned in the driver's seat and looked at Melissa and

Sebastian. "I need a second," she said, and stepped out of the van.

After pacing along the sidewalk, Diana looked toward the sky. A moment later, she hustled back into the van, started it up and pulled away.

"What's up?" Sebastian asked, leaning forward in his seat.

"Something familiar," she answered, but was unable to explain. It was the edifice from her dreams—the New York Life building with its unique golden top. But had she thought of it only because it was something she saw every day or because it was meant to guide her to Ryder?

She didn't know. "I'm backtracking to the road by the docks. He would have come that way on his route before reaching this stop." She paused at a corner as the light turned red. She looked at him and then Melissa. "Look for a warehouse or building, probably abandoned. Or one with no activity at this hour."

It took a few more turns before they were on the roadway beneath FDR Drive. On one side of the street were assorted docks and buildings, some of them fitting the bill, but Diana suspected the killer would not have crossed the road and lost time.

She drove slowly, ignoring the horns of the annoyed drivers behind her. She examined each building. At this hour of the day most seemed vacant. In the stretch of four or five blocks before the turn for the hotel there were dozens of possible buildings.

Too many possibilities and too little time—unless she called in more troops. But if she did so, she risked exposing Ryder's secret. Could she do that in order to save him?

She didn't know. For now, all she could do was turn off the road and repeat the trip. Maybe she would see something she hadn't the first time.

Moving even slower, she earned more horn blasts. Again, there was nothing, but the turn to the hotel was blocked by traffic. Too impatient to wait, she passed the intersection, hoping to head up a block or two and then cut across. As she did so, she noted a small alley. Barely large enough to let a small truck through. She pulled in and stopped the van. Looking skyward, she saw the top of the New York Life building. Then she knew. Ryder was nearby.

There were two buildings on either side of the road, but only one of them had an entrance into the alley. It was a small two-story warehouse that had seen better days. Most of the windows along the upper floors were broken. The only ones still in place were those along the street level and they were cracked in spots and blackened with grime from the street.

Diana walked down the steps to the metal door that opened into the alley. It was locked. She went back to street level, lay down on her stomach and peered through a broken pane of glass. It was dark inside the space, except for a few weak shafts of light from the windows along the front of the building. The light wasn't enough to let her see anything, but she couldn't walk away without checking it out.

Rising, she brushed off the front of her white shirt, reached into her jacket and withdrew a small locksmith's kit. She wouldn't normally break in without a warrant and risk losing a suspect, but she had enough evidence for probable cause. Or at least, she hoped she would be able to convince a judge of that if it was necessary.

Taking out the lock picks, she worked at the mechanism until the cylinders clicked into place. She shot a glance at Melissa and Sebastian and motioned for them to join her as she opened the door.

They were familiar sounds by now. The grate of metal against metal. The groan as the door opened. The loud metallic clank as it closed again. Footsteps sounded against the cement floor and drew closer. ''Back for more? The hell with you, Rudy.'' He said the words out loud, but they were barely more than a whisper.

He expected Rudy's satisfied laugh and immediate punishment. Instead, startled gasps and the rush of footsteps reached his ears until Diana, Melissa and an unknown man stood before him.

''Oh, no. Ryder,'' Melissa said, and covered her mouth with her hand.

Diana met his gaze for only a second before she ordered the man to help take Ryder down. Melissa undid the ropes around his legs as the man brought over a metal folding chair. Diana climbed up on it and undid the bindings on his arms. Then her arms held him close as she and the man eased Ryder onto the ground.

He sighed, closed his eyes and let himself slip away.

His body was rigid in her arms and surprisingly light-weight.

Melissa took Ryder's pulse and examined him as best she could. ''He's barely alive.''

Diana pulled Ryder closer, cradling his head against her and bending to lay a kiss across his forehead.

''He's cold,'' she said as the temperature of his body registered against her lips.

''We need to get him home, take care of his wounds and let him feed.'' Melissa rushed into action, racing out of the building.

Diana looked up at her brother and he asked softly, ''Do you love him?''

A wave of pain washed over her, and she couldn't answer. All she could do was bow her head, press it against Ryder's and pray. She hadn't prayed in a long time. Not since her dad. She held Ryder the way she had held her dad as his life slipped away. Her hands had been covered with her dad's blood in much the same way that they were now slick with Ryder's. "Sebastian, I can't survive this again."

Sebastian dropped to his knees by her side and placed his hand on her shoulder. "You need to, Diana. Whether he survives or not. You need to stop the animal who did this. You can't let him do it again."

Melissa came back, sparing Diana from answering. The doctor withdrew a bottle and syringe from a medical bag. The needle was long and Melissa squirted out a little of the liquid, then motioned to Diana to ease Ryder away. "I need to give him this shot."

Diana nodded and shifted him so Melissa had access to his neck. She flinched as Melissa drove the needle into his skin and depressed the plunger. Ryder's body immediately began to convulse in her arms.

"Hold him down," Melissa instructed.

Diana tightened her grip, and Sebastian joined her in keeping Ryder fairly immobile until Melissa had delivered all the medication.

"What is it?" she asked as Ryder strained against her hands and his body lost some of its stiffness.

Melissa looked at her and withdrew the needle. "A cocktail my dad mixed. Adrenaline to get things moving and other medicines to counteract the effects of the sun."

Ryder opened his eyes then and tried to talk, but it was clear it taxed his strength to do so.

Diana laid her fingers on his lips. "Shh. You're going to be all right."

There was an almost imperceptible shake of his head in denial and then he drifted off again. She looked at her brother. "Can you carry him to the van?"

Sebastian nodded, eased his arms beneath Ryder and lifted him. With Melissa at his side, they walked to the van. Diana dialed David's number and gave him the address and instructions on having a team in place to catch Rudy when he returned.

"Diana, you're going to have to help me," Melissa said. "Sebastian, you drive."

Sebastian took the keys from his sister and got behind the wheel. Diana rattled off the address of Ryder's apartment building. As Sebastian pulled away from the warehouse, Diana knelt beside Ryder and grimaced as she took in all the wounds he had suffered.

Deep slashes marred his chest and upper arms. A nasty wound marked the lower left side of his abdomen, as if he had been staked. It was more than an inch wide and the blow had been so forceful there was bruising around the area. There were two deep incisions, one along the middle of his chest and another along his midsection. Everywhere there was a wound, streaks of dried blood, the color of dark red rust, painted his body.

Diana reached up and caressed the side of his face. His body was cold, chilled by the sweat still pouring off of him. She slipped off her jacket and balled it into a cushion of sorts to pillow his head. Beneath her hands, his muscles were stiff and unyielding. If not for the occasional shudder from his body and his faint breath, she might have said he was gone already.

She laid her hand on his chest, careful to avoid the worst of the knife wounds. There was barely a hint of a heartbeat. She turned her head and glanced uneasily at Melissa, who was busy preparing another hypodermic. "He's really bad," she said softly.

"It's too much for him—the blood loss and sun. He may be too far gone."

Diana shook her head, unwilling to accept the other woman's words. "We're not going to lose him."

Melissa looked away from Diana. "You love him," she said simply as she tapped the hypo to remove the air bubbles.

Diana tore her gaze away from Melissa and looked back down at Ryder's unnaturally pale face, made even paler in comparison to his dark, sweat-drenched hair. "I... He's my only witness. I can't lose him."

Melissa bent over Ryder as she slipped the hypo into him again. She depressed the plunger on the syringe, slowly feeding the clear liquid into Ryder's body. "One day you'll be able to admit what you feel."

But Diana didn't respond.

Chapter 26

They were jostled around in the bed of the van as Sebastian hit a particularly big pothole.

Ryder moaned and Diana reached out to reposition his head on her folded jacket. She brushed her thumb over his lips and whispered softly, "Ryder, you cannot quit now."

As if he heard her, he moaned again, and beneath her hand, the muscles of his cheek twitched.

"Ryder?"

His eyes popped open and his body began to shake with faint tremors. Diana laid her hands on his shoulders as the contractions increased. It was almost as if he were having a seizure. Diana glared at Melissa. "What's happening?"

"It may be the medicine," she said, her voice filled with doubt, as if she was beginning to question the wisdom of her judgment. "It's never been this bad before." She turned away and rooted around in her medical bag.

The spasms became so powerful that Ryder's body nearly jumped off the floor of the van. Diana straddled his chest, pinning him down to keep him from injuring himself.

She held his head in her hands and his eyes focused on her. His next words, uttered in a pained whisper, tore at her heart. "Let me die."

Diana shook her head and bent to lay her cheek alongside his. "I can't let you go."

Beneath her legs, Ryder's body continued to convulse. As Melissa injected him again, the tremors worsened then gradually slowed. Beneath her cheek, the cold sweat disappeared as his body warmed. Diana sat back up. His eyes were closed. His breathing was a little deeper and more regular. She slipped off of his chest and joined Melissa in binding his wounds. "What now?"

Melissa put pressure bandages on the incisions on his chest and midsection, while Diana packed the deeper puncture wound on his side and taped the packing into place.

"I need to close up the more serious wounds. Then he needs to feed," Melissa said calmly.

Sebastian shot a look back as he rounded a corner. "Feed? What kind of feed?"

"Sebastian, watch the road," Diana said as he hit the curb and barely avoided a pedestrian in the crosswalk.

Sebastian cursed under his breath, muttering about domineering women, and sped up a little. Diana caught a glimpse of a familiar landmark from the view out of the windshield of the van, and she realized they were only blocks from the apartment building. "Does he need to feed now?"

Melissa shook her head. "He's weak but seems to have stabilized a little. But I don't know how long this will last."

"What do you mean?" Diana asked.

Sebastian brought the van to an abrupt halt in the small loading dock of the apartment building and turned to face the two women. "How are we going to get him inside without anyone noticing?"

Melissa reached into a small bag tacked to the side of the van and hauled out a raincoat. "Help me get this on him,'' she said to Diana. Between the two of them, they slipped the garment on Ryder so that his wounds were hidden.

Melissa motioned to the back door of the van. The chrome of a wheelchair caught Diana's eye. ''Go around the back and get that chair ready.''

Sebastian quickly popped open the large back doors of the van. He undid the bungee cords that held the chair in place, unfolded it and placed it on the ground. Then he helped Diana and Melissa in half dragging, half carrying Ryder to the chair. Ryder slipped into a heap in the seat, his body loose, but lacking control since he was still unconscious.

''We'll get him upstairs, Sebastian. Go park the van and come back. Apartment 2401,'' Diana said.

Sebastian nodded, and they wheeled the chair up the loading ramp and to the freight elevator. Melissa pushed the button and within seconds, the elevator opened. They boarded and headed up to the duplex apartment. That was easy. The hard part was getting Ryder into Melissa's bed on the lower floor of the duplex. His body was heavy and cumbersome, even with the two of them working together. It took some time, but they finally managed to get him comfortably settled.

Melissa filled a basin with warm water and brought Diana a towel. ''Get him cleaned up while I get some sutures and bandages ready.''

Diana nodded, then stripped off the raincoat and went to work wiping away the dried blood on his chest and abdomen. She winced as she realized how much blood had soaked into the bandages they had applied in the van. She was nearly done when Melissa returned, holding a tray with various sutures, instruments and bandages.

Melissa's gaze met hers. ''You may want to leave for this.''

Diana had spent too much time running. She stepped away but couldn't leave.

Melissa took a spot on the edge of the bed and laid the tray on the nightstand. She inspected one incision on Ryder's chest and then began to stitch it up. With each pass of the needle, Ryder's body twitched, but he didn't wake.

Diana passed Melissa the items she requested while tending to Ryder's wounds. As Melissa applied disinfectant, Diana was actually relieved to hear Ryder moan. The sound reassured her he was still alive. They were just patching up the stake wound when the doorbell rang.

Diana ran to open the door for Sebastian. As soon as he saw her, he held his arms wide. She took comfort in the tight hug he gave her. "Have faith, Diana."

She let out a harsh little laugh. "Faith? Even if he lives…" She lingered in his embrace for a moment. "I have to go see how he is." As she started to go, he took her hand. "Is there anything I can do?"

Diana gave her cell phone to her brother. "Call David and tell him… He doesn't know about Ryder, so just tell him we're still with Ryder at the doctor's. Ask him where we stand with the stakeout of the warehouse."

"If he asks when you'll be there—"

"Tell him I'll be there as soon as I can." When Diana entered the bedroom, Melissa rose from the bed.

"I'm going to get a bag so he can feed."

Ryder was pale and very still. His chest barely moved as he breathed. Diana reached out and lightly touched him. His skin had grown ice cold again. The cold transferred itself to her and settled within her heart.

Melissa returned and held out the bag of blood to Diana. "I think he might be more willing to take this from you."

She grabbed the blood. It was warm. "Did you just draw this?"

Melissa shook her head. "Just nuked it a little. It would be better if it were fresh. It's more potent when it's fresh."

Diana sat on the edge of the bed and ran her hand along Ryder's shoulder. He roused slightly, glanced at her and the bag she held, and then shook his head.

"No," he whispered. "Let me go."

"Ryder, please." But he answered with a stronger no that seemed to drain him of what little strength he had left. He lapsed into unconsciousness and nothing Diana did seemed to rouse him.

"What do we do now?" she asked Melissa.

"I don't know."

It wasn't enough of an answer for Diana. She grabbed Melissa's arm. "What do you mean, you don't know? You and your family have been with him for—"

"One hundred and thirty-eight years," Melissa finished for her.

"There must be some other way of helping him if he won't feed. You have to know how to help him after all that time."

"My father had journals kept by each and every Danvers. Histories of their lives, Ryder's, and all that they knew."

Diana sensed reluctance in the young doctor's voice. "There must be something there."

"Ryder never wanted me to look at the journals. He felt they were too much for me to handle, at first....." Melissa stopped, clearly uncomfortable.

"So what do we do?"

"I don't know," Melissa answered softly.

Tears came to Diana's eyes, and she fought them back. Taking a deep, shaky breath, she said, "We have to try something."

Melissa laid a hand on Diana's shoulder and gave a squeeze. "I can try, but nothing will help if he's made up his mind—"

"To die? We'll just have to convince him otherwise."

"Not we, Diana. *You.* You are the only one who has the power to convince him."

Diana dropped her gaze to Ryder. He lay nearly motionless on the bed, his skin paler than before. She laid her hand on his chest. A fine sweat was breaking out all over his body once more. She raised her face to look at Melissa. "What do you want me to do?"

"Talk to him. Convince him to feed. And I need you to donate some blood."

Diana nodded. "Take as much as you can."

"Diana," Sebastian interrupted, waving the cell phone in the air as he stood by the door. "David says he needs to talk to you."

She took the phone from her brother. "What's up?"

"We've got the place surrounded. Can you get any more info from Ryder?" David asked.

"Ryder isn't conscious. He's… We don't know if he'll make it," she confessed as she watched Melissa draw the comforter over Ryder.

"I'm sorry. I know that you and he—"

"What do you need, David? I'd like to get back to Ryder."

"We need you here. Soon," he replied in a whisper. "ADIC Hernandez thinks the special agent in charge should be in charge."

"Tell Hernandez to go…" She stopped herself, knowing it would accomplish nothing. "Tell the ADIC I'm with one of the victims and trying to get a death-bed statement. I'll be there as soon as I can."

"Diana—"

She shut off the phone, unwilling to waste another second with her partner, knowing every moment she delayed might be one she missed with Ryder.

Chapter 27

The blood bags lay on the nightstand next to the bed, still warm. Diana sat by Ryder's side as Melissa drew her blood. Ryder's companion was now with Sebastian, getting his donation. After, Melissa planned on giving some herself.

Diana leaned close to Ryder, laid a hand on his chest and spoke softly. There was no response, which meant she had only one choice. She reached for the hypo Melissa had prepared and left behind after instructing her on how to use it. Diana's hand shook as she removed the bandage covering the middle of Ryder's chest and placed the hypo directly above his heart. Melissa had said it was extreme to do it this way, but they had reached the moment for extreme measures.

Feeling for the bottom of his sternum with one hand, Diana shifted the needle and slowly eased it in. She took a deep breath as she depressed the plunger, forcing the drugs into him. As soon as she was done, she quickly removed the needle, knowing he would respond to the medications.

It took only a second for the reaction to begin.

Ryder's eyes popped open and his body gave the first twitch.

She leaned over him and called his name. He focused on her face and whispered, "Don't do this again. Please, don't."

"You need to feed." She grabbed the bag and held it up for him to see.

Ryder shook his head and looked away from it. "No." He grabbed the comforter as his body started to shake more violently.

Diana cupped his cheek and applied gentle pressure until he was facing her. "You need to feed otherwise—"

"I want to die. I want my freedom."

She only shook her head and held the bag up to him again. "I need you to live. Now, drink."

His body went into spasm again and she was forced to straddle him until the seizures passed. Sweat glistened on his face and she wiped it away with her hand and brought the bag to his lips. "Drink."

He pulled away once more.

Frustrated with his resistance, she reached over to the tray holding the remaining bag of blood and the empty hypodermic needle. She grabbed the hypo and dragged the edge of the needle along her wrist until she drew blood. Bright red drops welled along the deep scratch and she brought her wrist to Ryder's lips. His body jumped beneath her.

He tried to pull his head back, but since he was so weak she held him there with little effort. A moment later, his fangs erupted and, as he turned his face, she saw the glow of his animal eyes.

"No," he said. "This is why you don't want me."

She moved her wrist and, with her thumb, traced the edges of his lips and then his fangs. Bending, she brought her lips to his and kept him there when he would have pulled away. She kissed him, her eyes open and locked with his.

When she was done, she whispered against his mouth, "Feed or I'll kick your ass…again." She brought the bag of blood to his mouth once more.

He gave her a weak fangy grin, hesitated for a second, and then sank his teeth through the plastic of the bag.

He closed his eyes as he drained the bag. Once it was done, she quickly replaced it with the second bag, which he sucked down a little more slowly. As he did so, a faint trace of color returned to his face. When he finished with the second bag, he was breathing more deeply, and his gaze filled with both love and anger.

"Why?" he asked, but got no answer to his question as Sebastian came in, holding up her cell phone once more. "It's David. He says it's urgent."

She grabbed the phone and listened as her partner advised that they had the suspect trapped in the warehouse and needed her. "I'll be there in fifteen minutes." She shut off the phone and met Ryder's gaze. "Promise me you'll feed on whatever Melissa brings you."

"Why?" he asked again.

When she eased away and sat on the edge of the bed, he laid his hand on her shoulder. "Tell me why, darlin'."

"I…I need you. I know I shouldn't but…" She shrugged and rose from the bed. "Promise me you'll feed."

"Promise me you'll come back."

Diana knew she'd return, only it might be to say good-bye. Nodding, she whispered, "I'll be back."

That seemed to satisfy him, and she walked into the hall where Melissa and Sebastian waited. She was deeply troubled by Ryder's condition, about her case and her career, and about what she would do once she returned. But all she said to her brother and Melissa was "He fed."

Melissa was clearly wondering about Ryder's reversal. As her gaze locked with Diana's, Melissa seemed to realize that it had cost Diana dearly to achieve Ryder's change of heart.

Melissa hugged her hard. Diana hesitated, but then relented and returned the embrace.

She pulled away from Melissa and stroked her hand over Melissa's blond hair. "I have to go. They've cornered the serial killer in the warehouse." She walked to Sebastian and stopped. "Are *you* going?"

He inclined his head in Melissa's direction. "Do you need my help?"

Melissa glanced through the open door to where Ryder lay in the bed. "Possibly."

Diana detected a hint of challenge in the young doctor's voice. Glancing at Sebastian, she realized something was up between these two. It concerned her that Sebastian had been dragged into this, and now it seemed like he was getting even more involved. She stood there, hoping he would decide to go or that Melissa would send him away. Instead Melissa said, "I could use some support. Just in case. Do you think you can handle it?"

Sebastian's shoulders pulled back. Diana knew that stance well. She was therefore prepared when he said, "You'd be surprised at just how much I can handle."

Diana didn't wait any longer. She brushed a quick kiss on her brother's cheek and headed out.

She arrived at the warehouse just as David and the others were preparing to go in. She grabbed a vest from one of her colleagues and then eased into an FBI windbreaker. "What do we have?"

"He was in there when we got here about an hour ago. The imaging shows he's sitting in the middle of the space. There's some kind of light, powered by either gas or kerosene, judging from the heat it's throwing off."

She nodded and made sure her holster was securely

tucked into the small of her back. "Have you been able to make contact?"

"We've tried on several occasions, but his first response came only about five minutes ago. He said he wanted to talk to 'the slut on the dance floor,'" David explained.

Diana nodded and grabbed the walkie-talkie he held out to her. "You and I go in together." She glanced around at the other agents who were waiting for her instructions and picked out positions for them to take on the roof and along the perimeter of the building.

"Do we know if there are other exits?"

"We've got them all covered and Daly's on the roof with some members of his SWAT team." David pointed out Daly's silhouette on the building across the way.

ADIC Hernandez walked over and inclined his head in greeting. "Glad you could make it, Special Agent in Charge Reyes. How's Latimer?"

"Badly hurt and under a doctor's care. It looks like he may make it," she replied, and reached for the bullhorn sitting on the hood of David's car. "He can confirm who took and tortured him."

"Good. We'll need his testimony."

Diana wasn't about to contradict him in front of everyone. There was no way Ryder could testify. She was afraid of what the killer might reveal once captured, but she would have to cross that bridge when she got to it.

"Let's go." She waited until the other agents were in place before approaching the windows along the street level. She brought the bullhorn to her mouth and said, "Rudy. You wanted me and now I'm here."

She listened carefully. There was a scrape, like that of a metal chair on cement and a shuffling sound. "I've been waiting for you. I wanted to tell you about what I did to your friend," he called out.

Diana tightened her grip on the bullhorn. Anger swept over her at the glee she heard in Rudy's voice. He'd enjoyed hurting Ryder, just as he'd savored what he did to his earlier victims. She wanted him to pay. She reached for her gun and pulled it from the holster even as she responded to him via the bullhorn. "Well, I'm coming in now so you can tell me, Rudy."

She glanced over her shoulder at David and motioned for him to head toward the door. He grabbed the handle, pulled and it opened freely. He held it open with his body, his gun ready.

Diana laid the bullhorn on the ground and entered the space, quickly moving out of the fatal funnel created in the doorway opening. She paused once she was inside and against the wall. It took a moment for her eyes to adjust to the darkness. Rudy stood within a small circle of light thrown off by a gas-powered lantern, right by the beam on which Ryder had been suspended. The wood of the beam was dark in spots, stained with the blood of Rudy's victims. "I'm here, Rudy." She inched closer, her gun trained on him.

"Do you really think you need that—Diana, is it? Your friend Latimer called your name more than once," he said, his hands tucked into the pockets of the nylon jacket he wore.

"It is Diana. Is Rudy your real name?" She pressed forward, with David behind her as backup.

"Yes. Rudolph Alexander Williams Jr. to be precise. But you can call me Rudy," he said nonchalantly, as if either totally unaware or uncaring of the situation.

"Take your hands out of your pockets," David requested.

Rudy laughed and ignored him. "Your friend Latimer was very interesting, but you must know that." He smiled.

She couldn't let him say any more about Ryder. She had no doubt from the tone of his voice that Rudy knew. "Why did you kill the girls?" she asked, trying to redirect his attention.

"Why do you think, Diana? Because it felt good," Rudy replied with relish. "Because they deserved it."

"Like your mother or girlfriend deserved it?" Diana challenged, hoping to elicit a rise and additional information.

Rudy fidgeted his hands in his pockets and Diana tightened her finger on the trigger, ready to pull. Rudy made no other move with his hands. He just smiled at Diana and grew slightly more agitated.

"My mother used to whore with her lovers in front of me. She'd stick me in a closet, but I could see what she was doing through the keyhole."

"It must have been difficult for you. It must have made you feel bad."

"It made me feel dirty to watch her. Hear her sounds." He closed his eyes tightly as if seeing it all over again.

"Did you kill her, too, Rudy?"

His eyes snapped open. "No. I didn't, but I wish I had. Then maybe my dad…" His voice trailed off. He took a step away from them and finally pulled his hands out of his pockets as he approached a table a few feet away. Diana walked toward him, and the glint of the knives and other instruments on the table became clear. He picked up one of the knives.

"Drop it, Rudy. You'll never get to use it."

"Oh, but I did, Diana." He picked it up, anyway, but remained feet away from them. "I used this on all of them, except your friend Latimer. I didn't get to take his heart."

"Why the hearts, Rudy?" David asked from behind Diana.

Rudy laughed harshly. "Their cheating hearts, just like in that old country-western tune, only it isn't something to sing about really, is it?"

"Did your father know about—"

"Oh, he found out and when he did…" Rudy held the

knife in his left hand, turning to face them as he reached for something with his right.

Diana fought to keep an eye on what he was doing, but it was difficult to see in the dim light. As long as he stayed where he was... "What did he do? Was he the one who killed your mother?"

"My father was a gifted surgeon. A respected man with a good family name and wealth. None of that was enough, except maybe to protect him." Rudy continued to hold the knife in the air while slipping his right hand behind his back, hiding whatever he had taken. "Or should I say, protect his reputation," Rudy added, almost as an afterthought.

"He killed her with that knife?"

Rudy glanced at the knife and nodded. "My grandparents were able to cover it up." A sad look came to his face. For a moment, Diana almost felt pity for the young boy who had suffered as he watched his parents' tragedy unfold before his eyes.

"Your father didn't go to jail?"

Again Rudy laughed harshly. "No, he didn't. He exacted his own kind of punishment." Rudy whipped his hand from behind his back and she saw the gun. Only, she didn't shoot to kill and neither did David, for Rudy's intentions were clear. She pulled her trigger, aiming to disarm, but it was too late.

Her shot caught him in the shoulder, but Rudy had finished putting the gun to his temple, and even as his body reeled from the impact of Diana's shot, he pulled the trigger.

Diana watched as a stunned look crossed Rudy's face. He remained upright for what seemed like long seconds before falling to the floor. She holstered her piece, and she and David ran over. David radioed instructions to those outside as she knelt beside Rudy and felt for a pulse.

There was none.

She bowed her head and closed her eyes, glad that it was

over. But Rudy's self-inflicted punishment wasn't enough somehow to make up for the pain of all of the victims. To make up for what he had done to Ryder.

Rising, she glanced at her partner, and as his gaze met hers, she knew he felt the same way.

Chapter 28

It took more than three hours to finish the preliminary work at the crime scene. She still had more to do to close the file for the case, including interviews with Rudy's remaining family. She dreaded the thought of speaking to his grandparents, if they were still alive, because of the suffering it would bring to a family that had already had more than its share of heartache.

With Rudy's body on the way to the morgue for examination and identification, and her team cataloging everything at the scene, she excused herself, explaining to the ADIC, David and Peter Daly that she wanted to check on Ryder before it got too late.

She headed back to Ryder's apartment and Sebastian was still there. He and Melissa were in the kitchen, making fresh cups of coffee. "Don't you think it's time you left, *hermanito?*"

"What if Melissa needs more help?"

She held up her hand because she could see that if she pressed, he would get even more stubborn. "I'm here now.'' She directed her next comment to Melissa. ''How is he?''

Melissa rose and motioned for her to follow. As they walked to the stairs, Diana hesitated. ''You've moved him to his room?''

''It took a little doing, but he was strong enough to walk with Sebastian's help. It seemed best since the windows there are treated and mine aren't.''

Diana told herself she could climb the stairs and face her demons, both literally and figuratively. It was what she had been telling herself for the last hour as she sat in the tail end of rush-hour traffic on FDR Drive. Now she had to put what she had decided into action, but somehow her feet weren't cooperating.

''Having second thoughts?''

Diana chuckled. ''How about third and fourth thoughts, too?''

''You're not sure what you want to do?''

''I'm sure of what I'm going to do.'' The problem was, she wasn't quite sure it was what she really wanted. What she really wanted was impossible and would only lead to even greater heartbreak farther down the road.

The other woman nodded and glanced up the stairs. ''I know I have no right to ask this, but don't hurt him too badly.''

Her words cut Diana to the quick. ''You don't think much of me, do you?''

''Actually, I think a great deal of you. I know you love him. But I also know you realize just how unrealistic anything between the two of you could be.''

''Freeing him up for you, right?'' Diana said in anger, though she knew that wasn't the case.

Melissa looked past Diana and smiled at Sebastian. ''Ryder and I have always been friends. And right now, I think my interests lie elsewhere. Let him down easy is all I ask.''

Taking a bracing breath, Diana convinced her feet to take

the first step and then another and another until she was in the upper hall of Ryder's duplex. The door to his room was open and she saw him lying in bed, his chest bare except for the bandages and the comforter.

He opened his eyes and smiled. ''You came back.''

Diana sat on the edge of the bed. ''I promised you that I would. I keep my promises.''

Ryder laid his hand on her thigh. She took hold of it and held it tightly. He was warm once again and it was clear he was regaining strength. Although he remained pale, there was a faint stain of color in his cheeks. His hand was dry and lacked the sickly cold sweat that had bathed him earlier. Smiling, she reached out and brushed her hand through a wayward lock of hair that had drifted onto his forehead. ''You're feeling better.''

''Give me a little time and I'll be back to normal.'' He grinned, only there was a hint of fang, as if he was unable to control what he was right now.

She hadn't planned on getting into it so soon, but his comment and toothy grin gave her no choice. ''But you're not normal, Ryder. You're not even human.''

''A part of me is, Diana. And that part—''

''Betrayed me. Betrayed my trust. Making love to me—''

''Was something I hadn't dared to dream about because in all the time I've been a vampire, I've never cared for anyone the way I care for you,'' he replied, baring his soul to her in the hopes that she could accept his love.

She shook her head and released his hand. ''A long time ago, after my dad died, I didn't care about what I did. And I drove people away because I couldn't deal with the pain that came from caring.''

Ryder understood what she had suffered. ''You did what you had to do to survive.''

Her gaze locked with his and pain still shimmered there. ''I swore I wouldn't let myself feel again. And then you came along and made me break that promise. Made me scared that if I lost you…''

''I love you, Diana.'' He slowly eased himself up, wanting to be closer. It was painful. He groaned and a light sweat broke out at his slight movement.

She reached out to help him, placing her arm beneath his shoulder so he could raise himself into an upright position. Her actions brought them close, intimately close, and she lingered there for a moment. He ran his thumb over the flush of sudden color on her cheeks and she abruptly pulled away.

''You didn't care enough about me to tell me what you were,'' she said softly, and looked away from him.

''Would you have believed me if I had?''

She stiffened her spine. ''We'll never know.''

''Diana, before you, there wasn't anything sacred in my life. No trust. No honor,'' he confessed, wishing he could convince her that he had done the only thing he could. That he hadn't meant to hurt her.

Diana recalled that there had been a time in her young life when she had felt there was nothing worth keeping her on this earth. It had taken a moment of extreme pain to make her realize how far she had sunk. With his many years of existence, Ryder must have suffered through more than one such time, until, at some point, he'd stopped caring. The man she had first met had been aloof, but slowly he had come to feel something for her. She had no doubt about that now, just as she had no doubt about the fact that she loved him. In a perfect world, that was all that mattered. But in the real world, was it enough?

''I'm not sure I can be what you live for, Ryder, because this thing between the two of us…''

''When I lay dying, you said you needed me. You made me feed for what? To rot away the rest of my existence without you?''

She gripped her hands tightly in her lap, fighting the urge to soothe his hurt. "In the alley, when you told me about yourself… You wanted to drive me away. You knew there couldn't be anything between us."

"I did what I thought I had to, but I was wrong." His answer confirmed what she had come to suspect.

"I couldn't watch you die. I did what I had to, as well," she answered, and rose from the edge of the bed, knowing she had to leave before her determination wavered.

Ryder grabbed her hand and kept her close. "Don't go, darlin'."

"I'm not sure I can stay, Ryder."

"More than a hundred years ago, I was plunged into a world of darkness. Without my choice. Without any hope of escaping until you came along. You know what a world of darkness can be like. You let yourself slip into it when your dad died, and even though you think you escaped it, you never really did."

She pulled her hand away and wrapped her arms around herself. "I did. I made a life for myself and—"

"You weren't living until you met me." He realized he had struck home when she flinched.

"And what if you're right? What do we do about it?" she asked.

He leaned toward her, the movement costing him as pain ripped through the wounded parts of his body. "We live, Diana. Together. We share something so strong and sure that it'll fill every day with its light."

With his words belief flared to life deep inside her. Belief in the possibility of a happiness such as she had never known, not even before her father died.

"It may take a little time for me to stop being angry with you," she confessed.

He laughed harshly and settled back against the pillows. "I have all the time in the world."

Easing onto the edge of the bed, she sat facing him. She cupped his cheek and smiled. "Well, that's good, because I plan on spending a lot of time with you."

Joy mingled with disbelief on his face. "You know it won't be easy—loving me," he replied, almost as if giving her another chance to leave. His concern for her made her earlier decision all the more clear.

"That *is* the easy part, Ryder. After all, the love we have for each other is more than most people ever get to share. As long as we have that love—"

"We won't ever regret it?" he questioned with an arch of his brow.

"I won't ever regret living again. Loving you," she said, leaning forward and bringing her lips close to his. "Do you think you can handle a little of that loving now?"

He cupped the back of her head. "A little."

Their kiss was joyful, filled with so many emotions, chief among them—happiness. It went on and on until they were both breathless. But as they eased from each other, they were both smiling broadly.

"I have to head into the office in a few hours to finish up the case. Do you mind if I stay?" she asked, but even as she said it, she was settling onto the bed beside him.

Ryder wrapped his arm around her and they slipped down until they were lying side by side. She eased her head onto his shoulder and carefully put her arm across his midsection. At his flinch, she would have pulled away, but he laid his arm across hers to keep her there.

"Ryder?"

He glanced down at her and their gazes locked.

"There's no amount of pain that would keep me from you, darlin'."

She slid her leg over his thighs and softly said, "There's nothing that will ever keep me from you, *amor mio*. Nothing."

* * *

Her heart pounded as she ran, her feet sinking into the soft sand beneath her feet. The roar of the ocean filled her ears, but above that loud susurrus was another. She bent at the waist as she drew in a choppy breath and listened.

Ryder was calling to her, wanting her to return to him. As she slowed her rough breathing, his aroma peppered her nose, bringing her body to life. She had no control over it, needing him.

Diana looked around, searching the wide-open space of the beachfront for him, her body glistening with sweat from her run and the heat and humidity of the day. Above her the sun was bright, stinging in its intensity.

She turned slowly and the warm lap of an errant wave swept over her bare feet. She dragged a toe through it, and as she did so, she saw him.

He was standing down the beach, dressed in black. His hand was outstretched, inviting her to join him.

It was a familiar dream, she thought as she woke. One that no longer ended badly.

She shifted and held on to Ryder. It had been more than a week since he had been injured, and he'd been healing, although slowly. That hadn't kept her from his sharing his bed.

He tightened his hold on her. "You okay?"

"Hmm," she murmured, and cuddled closer, dropping a kiss over his heart. "I was just dreaming."

He turned to face her, smiling sleepily. "Was it about me?" He eased his hand to the small of her back and dragged her close against him. His arousal was evident against the naked skin of her belly.

Mindful that he wasn't completely healed, she urged him onto his back, then straddled him. Bending her head, she kissed him hungrily and said, "What do you think?"

But he didn't get a chance to answer as she eased over

him and took him inside her body, much as she had let him slip into her heart.

Ryder groaned and closed his eyes, but she said, "No, Ryder. Open your eyes."

He did, and even through the dark of the night, she let her love drive away the animal within him.

The nightmares of her past had somehow become the dreams of her future. And she knew that as long as Ryder was with her, the light of their love would banish the darkness that had ruled their lives for far too long.

*   *   *   *   *

Home Delivery Exclusive!
Warehouse clearance delivered straight to you!!

If you missed out the first time, don't miss out again! Bestselling author Nora Roberts brings you two compelling stories in *Summer Pleasures* - a direct to you exclusive at 50% off!

Limit of 3 per customer - call to order today!

SPOS04

Summer Pleasures
By Nora Roberts

Was $22.95 ~~$22.95~~   **NOW $11.45***

Price includes GST. Plus Postage and Handling $3.95

Don't miss out - stocks are strictly limited!
Call NOW to order!

Aust: 1300 659 500   **NZ: (09) 837 1553**

Harlequin Mills Boon
Direct to you